Extraordinary acclaim for Kate Atkinson's

WHEN WILL THERE BE GOOD NEWS?

A *New York Times* Notable Book of the Year

"Uncategorizable, unputdownable, Atkinson's books are like Agatha Christie mysteries that have burst at the seams—they're taut and intricate but also messy and funny and full of life."
— Lev Grossman, *Time*

"This smart, surprising, darkly funny novel takes the reader on a wild ride that starts with the gut-wrenching first chapter and doesn't stop until the final page."   — Amy Scribner, *BookPage*

"It's hard to imagine a novel starting in a more gripping or terrifying way. . . . What seems of most interest to Atkinson isn't the solving of crimes, but the solving of the problem of being alive. . . . The mysteries she is most invested in are those of the human heart."   — Elissa Schappell, *New York Times Book Review*

"Atkinson is a pro at twisting several story lines without them seeming either convoluted or contrived. Then, like a cherry on a sundae, palpable suspense and a satisfying ending to top it off. Now that's good news."   — Michele Ross, *Cleveland Plain Dealer*

"How Atkinson fits together seemingly random story lines is one of the pleasures of her work, along with the dark sense of humor that belies a deep compassion for her characters."
— Jennifer Reese, *Entertainment Weekly*

"Quite delicious."   — Sherryl Connelly, *New York Daily News*

"By becoming a crime writer, Kate Atkinson has—in a way that other 'literary' types may wish to note—become a better literary writer than ever: funny, bracingly intelligent, and delightfully prickly. . . . Atkinson is that rarest of beasts, a genuinely surprising novelist. In the best possible way, I have no idea what she might write next. Only that I'll certainly want to read it."

—Patrick Ness, *Guardian*

"A page-turner . . . evocative, smart, literary, and funny."

—Nancy Fontaine, *Library Journal* (starred review)

"Thank God, in these hard times, for a cheerful, ghoulish, gory book like *When Will There Be Good News?* . . . This is a grand mystery."   —Carolyn See, *Washington Post*

"I get a little feisty when people make hard-and-fast divisions between literary fiction and crime fiction; the best crime fiction is as good as anything in literary fiction today. But Atkinson, who won the Whitbread Prize for her first novel, *Behind the Scenes at the Museum,* simply doesn't fit within the crime genre no matter how much I would like to claim her for the team. She toys with coincidence while managing to play by the rules of detective fiction. And in this, her third book about private detective Jackson Brodie, she is clearly more interested in other, newer characters. I fell hard for Reggie, a teenage nanny with an intellectual bent. Working on a translation of the *Iliad,* she stops to consider: 'There were an awful lot of the dead in Homer.' Also in Atkinson, by the way."

—Laura Lippman, *Daily Beast*

"Atkinson has cooked up a medley of crime fiction, mystery, and thriller that left my literary palate intrigued. . . . The novel surges to a finale so clever and shocking that you will surely be amazed."

—Vick Mickunas, *Dayton Daily News*

"A deliciously underhanded, echo-filled novel. . . . It is very much to be hoped that Atkinson keeps this gratifying series going."
— Janet Maslin, *New York Times*

"At the end of *When Will There Be Good News?* the reader is satisfied that the unfolding has been well worth a lost night of sleep."
— Helen Verongos, *St. Louis Post-Dispatch*

"You don't need to have read the earlier two books to appreciate this one, but I can't think of any reason to deny yourself the delights of all three. . . . The novel satisfies the question in its own title. The answer is: Right here and right now."
— Laura Miller, *Salon*

"*When Will There Be Good News?* stands out like a blinding supernova."   — Elisabeth Vincentelli, *Time Out New York*

"It's the characters that make this book. . . . Atkinson is a rule breaker who never forgets what counts."
— Mary Ann Gwinn, *Seattle Times*

"Atkinson shows a remarkable ability to shear through layers of secrets and inhibitions and tease out the baldest of truths about her characters. . . . She takes her metaphorical flashlight and shines it so authoritatively that the dark corners where hidden revelations wish to hide don't stand a chance."   — Sarah Weinman, *Baltimore Sun*

"Good news lies on every page of this meticulously plotted and affecting thriller."   — Connie Ogle, *Miami Herald*

"Atkinson's novels crackle with intelligence and wit and wise meditations on life, death, love, and loss."
— Jean Westmoore, *Buffalo News*

"Atkinson, an exact and funny writer, handles her characters and the odd things that befall them with perfect aplomb. She is so clever and disarming."　　　　—Jack Batten, *Toronto Star*

"So satisfying it'll make you believe the gods had their hands in it."
　　　　—Carole E. Barrowman, *Minneapolis Star-Tribune*

"Atkinson delivers a pitch-perfect thriller that careens to a stunning ending as she pushes together the stories of the three characters as well as pulls them apart."
　　　　—Oline H. Cogdill, *South Florida Sun-Sentinel*

"A lesser author would buckle under so many story lines, but Atkinson juggles them brilliantly."
　　　　—*Publishers Weekly* (starred review)

"Atkinson's detective novels are masterworks of character-driven plots and leisurely observation. But they are primarily triumphs not of storytelling, but of tone: sardonic, faithless, and dark as the inside of a cow. As a reader, you might come for the mystery, but you'll return for the prose."
　　　　—Andrew Pyper, *Toronto Globe and Mail*

"A page-turner with heft and emotional resonance."
　　　　—Jennifer Roolf Laster, *San Antonio Express-News*

"This novel reaches a satisfying conclusion that suggests good news is indeed on the way."
　　　　—Bob Hoover, *Pittsburgh Post-Gazette*

"The most satisfying novel of Atkinson's trilogy. . . . One begs her to reconsider ending the series here. It would be great news, indeed, if she were to pick up the pieces all over again."
　　　　—Stephen Humphries, *Christian Science Monitor*

WHEN WILL THERE BE GOOD NEWS?

A Novel

KATE ATKINSON

BACK BAY BOOKS
LITTLE, BROWN AND COMPANY
New York Boston London

ALSO BY KATE ATKINSON

Behind the Scenes at the Museum
Human Croquet
Emotionally Weird
Not the End of the World
Case Histories
One Good Turn

Back Bay Books / Little, Brown and Company
Hachette Book Group
237 Park Avenue, New York, NY 10017
www.hachettebookgroup.com

First published in hardcover in the United States by Little, Brown and Company, September 2008
First Back Bay paperback edition, January 2010

Originally published in the United Kingdom by Doubleday, August 2008.
Back Bay Books is an imprint of Little, Brown and Company. The Back Bay Books name and logo are trademarks of Hachette Book Group, Inc.

The line from "Cargoes" by John Masefield is reproduced by permission of the Society of Authors as the literary representative of the Estate of John Masefield. The interview with Kate Atkinson that appears in the reading group guide in the back of this book was originally aired on *Book Lust with Nancy Pearl* on the Seattle Channel on December 4, 2006. Copyright © 2006 by the City of Seattle. Reprinted with permission.

Library of Congress Cataloging-in-Publication Data
Atkinson, Kate.
When will there be good news? : a novel / Kate Atkinson.— 1st ed.
p. cm.
ISBN 978-0-316-15485-7 (hc) / 978-0-316-01283-6 (pb)
1. Missing persons—Fiction. 2. Physicians (General practice)—Fiction.
3. Edinburgh (Scotland)—Fiction. I. Title.
PR6051.T56W47 2008
823'.914—dc22   2008014738

10 9 8 7 6 5 4 3

RRD-C

Printed in the United States of America

For Dave and Maureen—
Thanks for many good times.
The best is yet to come.

We never know we go,—when we are going
We jest and shut the door;
Fate following behind us bolts it,
And we accost no more.
— *Emily Dickinson*

I
In the Past

Harvest

The heat rising up from the tarmac seemed to get trapped between the thick hedges that towered above their heads like battlements.

"Oppressive," their mother said. They felt trapped too. "Like the maze at Hampton Court," their mother said. "Remember?"

"Yes," Jessica said.

"No," Joanna said.

"You were just a baby," their mother said to Joanna. "Like Joseph is now." Jessica was eight, Joanna was six.

The little road (they always called it "the lane") snaked one way and then another, so that you couldn't see anything ahead of you. They had to keep the dog on the lead and stay close to the hedges in case a car "came out of nowhere." Jessica was the eldest so she was the one who got to hold the dog's lead all the time. She spent a lot of her time training the dog, "Heel!" and "Sit!" and "Come!" Their mother said she wished Jessica were as obedient as the dog. Jessica was always the one who was in charge. Their mother said to Joanna, "It's all right to have a mind of your own, you know. You should stick up for yourself, think for yourself," but Joanna didn't want to think for herself.

The bus dropped them on the big road and then carried on to somewhere else. It was "a palaver" getting them all off the bus. Their mother held Joseph under one arm like a parcel and with her other hand she struggled to open out his newfangled buggy. Jessica and Joanna shared the job of lifting the shopping off the bus. The dog saw to himself. "No one ever helps," their mother said. "Have you noticed that?" They had.

"Your father's country-fucking-idyll," their mother said as the bus drove away in a blue haze of fumes and heat. "Don't you swear," she added automatically. "I'm the only person allowed to swear."

They didn't have a car anymore. Their father ("the bastard") had driven away in it. Their father wrote books, "novels." He had taken one down from a shelf and shown it to Joanna, pointed out his photograph on the back cover, and said, "That's me," but she wasn't allowed to read it, even though she was already a good reader ("Not yet, one day. I write for grown-ups, I'm afraid," he laughed. "There's stuff in there, well . . .").

Their father was called Howard Mason and their mother's name was Gabrielle. Sometimes people got excited and smiled at their father and said, "Are you *the* Howard Mason?" (Or sometimes, not smiling, "*that* Howard Mason," which was different, although Joanna wasn't sure how.)

Their mother said that their father had uprooted them and planted them "in the middle of nowhere." "Or Devon, as it's commonly known," their father said. He said he needed "space to write" and it would be good for all of them to be "in touch with nature." "No television!" he said as if that was something they would enjoy.

Joanna still missed her school and her friends and *Wonder Woman* and a house on a street that you could walk along to a shop where you could buy *The Beano* and a licorice stick and choose from three different kinds of apples instead of having to walk along a lane and a road and take two buses and then do the same thing all over again in reverse.

The first thing their father did when they moved to Devon was to buy six red hens and a hive full of bees. He spent all autumn digging over the garden at the front of the house so it would be "ready for spring." When it rained the garden turned to mud and the mud was trailed everywhere in the house; they even found it on their bedsheets. When winter came, a fox ate the hens without them ever having laid an egg and the bees all froze to death, which was unheard of, according to their father, who said he was going to put all those things in the book ("the novel") he was writing. "So that's all right, then," their mother said.

Their father wrote at the kitchen table because it was the only room in the house that was even the slightest bit warm, thanks to the huge temperamental Aga that their mother said was "going to be the death of her." "I should be so lucky," their father muttered. (His book wasn't going well.) They were all under his feet, even their mother.

"You smell of soot," their father said to their mother. "And cabbage and milk."

"And you smell of failure," their mother said.

Their mother used to smell of all kinds of interesting things, paint and turpentine and tobacco and the Je Reviens perfume that their father had been buying for her since she was seventeen years old and "a Catholic schoolgirl," and which meant "I will return" and was a message to her. Their mother was "a beauty" according to their father, but their mother said she was "a painter," although she hadn't painted anything since they moved to Devon. "No room for two creative talents in a marriage," she said in that way she had, raising her eyebrows while inhaling smoke from the little brown cigarillos she smoked. She pronounced it *thigariyo,* like a foreigner. When she was a child she had lived in faraway places that she would take them to one day. She was warm-blooded, she said, not like their father, who was a reptile. Their mother was clever and funny and surprising and nothing like their friends' mothers. "Exotic," their father said.

The argument about who smelled of what wasn't over, apparently, because their mother picked up a blue-and-white-striped jug from the dresser and threw it at their father, who was sitting at the table staring at his typewriter as if the words would write themselves if he was patient enough. The jug hit him on the side of the head and he roared with shock and pain. With a speed that Joanna could only admire, Jessica plucked Joseph out of his high chair and said, "Come on," to Joanna, and they went upstairs, where they tickled Joseph on the double bed that Joanna and Jessica shared. There was no heating in the bedroom and the bed was piled high with eiderdowns and old coats that belonged to their mother. Eventually all three of them fell asleep, nestled in the mingled scents of damp and mothballs and Je Reviens.

When Joanna woke up, she found Jessica propped up on pillows, wearing gloves and a pair of earmuffs and one of the coats from the bed, drowning her like a tent. She was reading a book by torchlight.

"Electricity's off," she said without taking her eyes off the book. On the other side of the wall they could hear the horrible animal noises that meant their parents were friends again. Jessica silently offered Joanna the earmuffs so that she didn't have to listen.

When the spring finally came, instead of planting a vegetable garden, their father went back to London and lived with "his other woman"—which was a big surprise to Joanna and Jessica, although not, apparently, to their mother. Their father's other woman was called Martina—*the poet;* their mother spat out the word as if it were a curse. Their mother called the other woman *(the poet)* names that were so bad that when they dared to whisper them *(bitch-cunt-whore-poet)* to each other beneath the bedclothes, they were like poison in the air.

Although now there was only one person in the marriage, their mother still didn't paint.

★   ★   ★

They made their way along the lane in single file, "Indian style," their mother said. The plastic shopping bags hung from the handles of the buggy, and if their mother let go, it tipped backwards onto the ground.

"We must look like refugees," she said. "Yet we are not down-hearted," she added cheerfully. They were going to move back into town at the end of the summer, "in time for school."

"Thank God," Jessica said, in just the same way their mother said it.

Joseph was asleep in the buggy, his mouth open, a faint rattle from his chest because he couldn't shake off a summer cold. He was so hot that their mother stripped him to his nappy and Jessica blew on the thin ribs of his little body to cool him down, until their mother said, "Don't wake him."

There was the tang of manure in the air, and the smell of the musty grass and the cow parsley got inside Joanna's nose and made her sneeze.

"Bad luck," her mother said, "you're the one that got my allergies." Their mother's dark hair and pale skin went to her "beautiful boy," Joseph, her green eyes and her "painter's hands" went to Jessica. Joanna got the allergies. Bad luck. Joseph and their mother shared a birthday too, although Joseph hadn't had any birthdays yet. In another week it would be his first. "That's a special birthday," their mother said. Joanna thought all birthdays were special.

Their mother was wearing Joanna's favorite dress, blue with a pattern of red strawberries. Their mother said it was old and next summer she would cut it up and make something for Joanna out of it if she liked. Joanna could see the muscles on her mother's tanned legs moving as she pushed the buggy up the hill. She was strong. Their father said she was "fierce." Joanna liked that word. Jessica was fierce too. Joseph was nothing yet. He was just a baby, fat and happy. He liked oatmeal and mashed banana and the mobile of little paper birds their mother had made for him that hung above his cot. He liked being tickled by his sisters. He liked his sisters.

Joanna could feel sweat running down her back. Her worn cotton dress was sticking to her skin. The dress was a hand-me-down from Jessica. "Poor but honest," their mother laughed. Her big mouth turned down when she laughed so that she never seemed happy even when she was. Everything Joanna had was handed down from Jessica. It was as if without Jessica there would be no Joanna. Joanna filled the spaces Jessica left behind as she moved on.

Invisible on the other side of the hedge, a cow made a bellowing noise that made her jump. "It's just a cow," her mother said.

"Red Devons," Jessica said, even though she couldn't see them. How did she know? She knew the names of everything, seen and unseen. Joanna wondered if she would ever know all the things that Jessica knew.

After you had walked along the lane for a while, you came to a wooden gate with a stile. They couldn't get the buggy through the stile so they had to open the gate. Jessica let the dog off the lead and he scrambled up and over the gate in the way that Jessica had taught him. The sign on the gate said "Please Close The Gate Behind You." Jessica always ran ahead and undid the clasp, and then they both pushed at the gate and swung on it as it opened. Their mother had to heave and shove at the buggy because all the winter mud had dried into deep, awkward ruts that the wheels got stuck in. They swung on the gate to close it as well. Jessica checked the clasp. Sometimes they hung upside down on the gate and their hair reached the ground like brooms sweeping the dust and their mother said, "Don't do that."

The track bordered a field. "Wheat," Jessica said. The wheat was very high, although not as high as the hedges in the lane. "They'll be harvesting soon," their mother said. "Cutting it down," she added, for Joanna's benefit. "Then we'll sneeze and wheeze, the pair of us." Joanna was already wheezing, she could hear the breath whistling in her chest.

The dog ran into the field and disappeared. A moment later he sprang out of the wheat again. Last week Joanna had followed the dog into the field and got lost, and no one could find her for a long time. She could hear them calling her, moving further and further away. Nobody heard her when she called back. The dog found her.

They stopped halfway along and sat down on the grass at the side of the track, under the shady trees. Their mother took the plastic carrier bags off the buggy handles and from one of the bags brought out some little cartons of orange juice and a box of chocolate finger biscuits. The orange juice was warm and the chocolate biscuits had melted together. They gave some of the biscuits to the dog. Their mother laughed with her downturned mouth and said, "God, what a mess," and looked in the baby-bag and found wipes for their chocolate-covered hands and mouths. When they lived in London they used to have proper picnics, loading up the boot of the car with a big wicker basket that had belonged to their mother's mother, who was rich but dead (which was just as well, apparently, because it meant she didn't have to see her only daughter married to a selfish, fornicating waster). If their grandmother was rich, why didn't they have any money? "I eloped," their mother said. "I ran away to marry your father. It was very romantic. At the time. We had nothing."

"You had the picnic basket," Jessica said, and their mother laughed and said, "You can be very funny, you know," and Jessica said, "I do know."

Joseph woke up, and their mother undid the front of her strawberry-covered dress and fed him. He fell asleep again while he was sucking. "Poor lamb," their mother said. "He can't shake off this cold." She put him back in the buggy and said, "Right. Let's get home. We can get out the garden hose and you can cool off."

★   ★   ★

He seemed to come out of nowhere. They noticed him because the dog growled, making an odd bubbling noise in his throat that Joanna had never heard before.

He walked very fast towards them, growing bigger all the time. He was making a funny huffing, puffing noise. You expected him to walk past and say "Nice afternoon" or "Hello," because people always said that if you passed them in the lane or on the track, but he didn't say anything. Their mother would usually say "Lovely day" or "It's certainly hot, isn't it?" when she passed people, but she didn't say anything to this man. Instead she set off walking fast, pushing hard on the buggy. She left the plastic bags of shopping on the grass, and Joanna was going to pick one up, but their mother said, "Leave it." There was something in her voice, something in her face, that frightened Joanna. Jessica grabbed her by the hand and said, "Hurry up, Joanna," sharply, like a grown-up. Joanna was reminded of the time their mother threw the blue-and-white-striped jug at their father.

Now the man was walking in the same direction as they were, on the other side of their mother. Their mother was moving very fast, saying, "Come on, quickly, keep up," to them. She sounded breathless. Then the dog ran in front of the man and started barking and jumping up as if it were trying to block the man's path. Without any warning he kicked the dog so hard that it sailed into the air and landed in the wheat. They couldn't see it, but they could hear the terrible squealing noise that it was making. Jessica stood in front of the man and screamed something at him, jabbing her finger at him and taking great gulps of air as if she couldn't breathe, and then she ran into the field after the dog.

Everything was bad. There was no question about it.

Joanna was staring at the wheat, trying to see where Jessica and the dog had gone, and it took a moment for her to notice that her mother was fighting the man, punching him with her fists. But the man had a knife, and he kept raising it in the air, so that it shone like silver in the hot afternoon sun. Her mother started to scream. There was blood on her face, on her hands, on her strong legs, on her strawberry dress. Then Joanna realized that her mother wasn't screaming at the man, she was screaming at her.

Their mother was cut down where she stood, the great silver knife carving through her heart as if it were slicing butcher's meat. She was thirty-six years old.

He must have stabbed Jessica too before she ran off, because there was a trail of blood, a path that led them to her, although not at first, because the field of wheat had closed around her like a golden blanket. She was lying with her arms around the body of the dog and their blood had mingled and soaked into the dry earth, feeding the grain, like a sacrifice to the harvest. Joseph died where he was, strapped into the pushchair. Joanna liked to think that he never woke up, but she didn't know.

And Joanna. Joanna obeyed her mother when she screamed at her. "Run, Joanna, run," she said, and Joanna ran into the field and was lost in the wheat.

Later, when it was dark, other dogs came and found her. A stranger lifted her up and carried her away. "Not a scratch on her," she heard a voice say. The stars and the moon were bright in the cold black sky above her head.

Of course, she should have taken Joseph with her, she should have snatched him from the buggy, or run with the buggy (Jessica would have). It didn't matter that Joanna was only six years old, that she would never have managed running with the buggy and that the man would have caught her in seconds, that wasn't the point. It would have been better to have tried to save the baby and been killed than not trying and living. It would have been better to have died with Jessica and her mother rather than being left behind without them. But she never thought about any of that, she just did as she was told.

"Run, Joanna, run," her mother commanded. So she did.

It was funny, but now, thirty years later, the thing that drove her to distraction was that she couldn't remember what the dog was called. And there was no one left to ask.

II
Today

Flesh and Blood

The green ran the whole length of the village and was bisected by a narrow road. The primary school looked over the village green. The green wasn't square, as he'd first imagined, nor did it have a duck pond, which was something else he had imagined. You would think, coming from the same county, he would know this countryside, but it was alien corn. His knowledge of the Yorkshire Dales was secondhand, garnered from TV and films — the occasional glimpse of *Emmerdale,* a semiconscious night on the sofa, watching *Calendar Girls* on cable.

It was quiet today, a Wednesday morning at the beginning of December. A Christmas tree had been erected on the green, but it was still as nature intended, undecorated and unlit.

The last time (the first time) he had come here to scope out the village, it had been a Sunday afternoon, height of the midsummer season, and the place had been humming, tourists picnicking on the grass, small children racing around, old people sitting on benches, everyone eating ice creams. There was a kind of sandpit at one end, where people — natives, not tourists — were playing what he thought might be quoits, throwing big iron rings as heavy as horseshoes. He hadn't realized people still did things like that. It was bizarre. It was medieval. There were still stocks on the green, by the market cross, and—according to a guidebook he had bought—a "bull ring." He'd thought of the Birmingham shopping center of that name until he'd read on and discovered its purpose was bullbaiting. He presumed (he hoped) that the stocks and the bull ring were historic—for the tourists—and not still in use. The village was a place to which people drove in their cars in order to get out and walk. He never did that. If he walked, he started from where he was.

He hid behind a copy of the *Darlington & Stockton Times* and studied the small ads for funeral homes and decorators and used cars. He thought it would be a less conspicuous read than a national newspaper, although he had bought it in Hawes rather than in the village shop, where he might have drawn too much attention to himself. These people had a well-developed radar for the wrong kind of stranger. They probably burned a wicker man every summer.

Last time he'd been driving a flashy car, now he blended in better, driving a mud-spattered Discovery rental and wearing hiking boots and a fleece-lined North Face jacket, with an OS guide in a plastic wallet hanging round his neck that he'd also bought in Hawes. If he could have got hold of one, he would have borrowed a dog, and then he would have looked like a clone of every other visitor. You should be able to rent dogs. Now *there* was a gap in the market.

He had driven the rental from the station. He would have driven all the way (in his flashy car), but when he had got into the driving seat and switched on the engine, he found his car was completely dead. Something mysterious, like electronics, he supposed. Now it was being nursed in a garage in Walthamstow by a Polish guy called Emil who had access (a nice euphemism) to genuine BMW parts at half the price of an official supplier.

He checked his watch, a gold Breitling, an expensive present. Quality time. He liked male paraphernalia—cars, knives, gadgets, watches—but he wasn't sure he would have laid out so much money on a watch. "Don't look a gift horse in the mouth," she said and smiled when she gave it to him.

"Oh, fucking hurry up, would you," he muttered and banged his head off the steering wheel, but gently in case he attracted the attention of a passing local. Despite the disguise, he knew there might be a limit to how long you could hang about in a small place like this without someone beginning to ask questions. He sighed and looked at his watch. He'd give it another ten minutes.

After nine minutes and thirty seconds (he was counting—what else was there to do?—watching the watch), a vanguard of two boys and two girls ran out of the door of the school. They were carrying football nets and in a well-practiced maneuvre erected them on the green. The green seemed to serve as a school playground. He couldn't imagine what it would be like to be educated in a school like this. His primary school had been an underfunded, overpopulated sinkhole where social Darwinism applied at every turn. Survival of the fastest. And that was the good part of his education. His proper education, where he had actually sat in a classroom and learned something, had been provided courtesy of the army.

A stream of children, dressed in PE kit, poured out of the school and spread over the green like a delta. Two teachers followed and started dishing out footballs from a basket. He counted the children as they came out, all twenty-seven of them. The little ones came out last.

Then came what he was waiting for—the playschool kids. They gathered every Wednesday and Friday afternoon in a little extension at the back of the school. Nathan was one of the tiniest, tottering along, holding on to the hand of a much older girl. Nat. Small like a gnat. He was bundled into some kind of all-in-one snowsuit. He had dark eyes and black curls that belonged incontrovertibly to his mother. A little snub nose. It was safe, Nathan's mother wasn't here, she was visiting her sister, who had breast cancer. No one here knew him. Stranger in a strange land. There was no sign of Mr. Arty-Farty. The False Dad.

He got out of the car, stretched his legs, consulted his map. Looked around as if he'd just arrived. He could hear the waterfall. It was out of sight of the village but within hearing of it. Sketched by Turner, according to the guidebook. He meandered across a corner of the green, as if he were going towards one of the many walkers' paths that spidered out of the village. He paused, pretended to consult the map again, ambled nearer to the children.

The bigger kids were warming up, throwing and kicking the ball to one another. Some of the older ones were practicing headers. Nathan was trying to kick a ball to and fro with a girl from the toddler class. He fell over his own feet. Two years and three months old. His face was scrunched up with concentration. Vulnerable. He could have picked him up with one hand, run back to the Discovery, thrown him in the backseat, and driven out of there before anyone had time to do anything. How long would it take for the police to respond? Forever, that was how long.

The ball rolled towards him. He picked it up and grinned at Nathan, said, "Is this your ball, son?" Nathan nodded shyly, and he held out the ball like a lure, drawing the boy towards him. As soon as he was within reach, he gave the ball back with one hand and with the other touched the boy's head, pretending to ruffle his hair. The boy leapt back as if he had been scalded. The girl from the toddler class grabbed the ball and dragged Nathan away by the hand, glaring over her shoulder. Several women — mothers and teachers — turned to look in his direction, but he was studying the map, pretending indifference to anything going on around him.

One of the mothers approached him, a bright, polite smile stuck on her face, and said, "Can I help you?" when what she really meant was "If you're planning on harming one of these children, I will beat you to a pulp with my bare hands."

"Sorry," he said, turning on the charm. He surprised even himself sometimes with the charm. "I'm a bit lost." Women could never believe it when a guy admitted to being lost, they immediately warmed to you. ("Twenty-five million sperm needed to fertilize an egg," his ex-wife used to say, "because only one will stop to ask directions.")

He shrugged helplessly. "I'm looking for the waterfall?"

"It's that way," the woman said, pointing behind him.

"Ah," he said, "I think I've been reading the map back to front. Well, thanks," he added and strode off down the lane towards the waterfall before she could say anything else. He'd have to give it a good ten minutes. It would look too suspicious if he went straight back to the Discovery.

It was pretty at the waterfall. The limestone and the moss. The trees were black and skeletal, and the water, brown and peaty, looked as if it was in spate, but maybe it always looked like that. They called the waterfall a "force" around here, which was a good word for it. An unstoppable force. Water always found a way, it beat everything in the end. Paper, scissors, rock, water. May the force be with you. He checked his expensive watch again. He wished he still smoked. He wouldn't mind a drink. If you didn't smoke and you didn't drink, then standing by a waterfall for ten minutes with nothing to do was something that could really get to you because all you were left with were your thoughts.

He searched in his pocket for the plastic bag he'd brought with him. Carefully, he dropped the hair into it and closed it with a plastic clip and pushed it into the pocket of his jacket. He had been clutching the thin black filament in his hand ever since he'd plucked it from the boy's head. Job done.

Ten minutes up. He walked quickly back to the mud-caked Discovery. If he didn't hit any problems, he'd be in Northallerton in an hour and back on the train to London. He jettisoned the OS map, left it on a bench, an unlooked-for gift for someone who thought walking was the way to go. Then Jackson Brodie climbed back into his vehicle and started the engine. There was only one place he wanted to be. Home. He was out of here.

The Life and Adventures of Reggie Chase, Containing a Faithful Account of the Fortunes, Misfortunes, Uprisings, Downfallings, and Complete Career of the Chase Family

Reggie spooned some kind of vegetable mush into the baby's mouth. It was just as well the baby was strapped into his high chair, because every so often he would suddenly fling out his arms and legs and try to launch himself into the air like a suicidal starfish. "Uncontrollable joy," Dr. Hunter had explained to Reggie. Dr. Hunter laughed. "Food makes him *very* happy." The baby wasn't fussy, the vegetable mush ("sweet potato and avocado") smelled like old socks and looked like dog diarrhea. All the baby's food was organic, cooked from scratch by Dr. Hunter before being mashed up and frozen in little plastic tubs so that all Reggie had to do was defrost it and warm it through in the microwave. The baby was just a year old, and Dr. Hunter still breast-fed him when she came back from work. "So many long-term benefits for his health," she said. "It's what breasts are meant for," she added when Reggie averted her eyes in embarrassment. The baby was called Gabriel. "My angel," Dr. Hunter said.

This was Reggie's sixth month as Dr. Hunter's "mother's help." They had agreed on this old-fashioned term at what passed for a job interview, as neither of them liked the word *nanny.* "Like a goat," Reggie said. "I had a nanny once," Dr. Hunter said. "She was an absolute horror."

Reggie was sixteen and could have passed for twelve. If she forgot her bus pass, she could still get on board for a child's fare. Nobody asked, nobody checked, nobody really took any notice of Reggie at all. Sometimes she wondered if she was invisible. It was very easy to slip between the cracks, especially if you were small.

When her bus pass ran out, Billy offered to make her another one. He had already made her an ID card—"So you can get into pubs," he said, but Reggie never went into pubs. For one thing, she didn't have anyone to go into a pub with, and for another, no one would have believed the fake ID. Just last week, when she was doing the early Sunday morning shift in Mr. Hussain's shop, a woman had told her that she was too young to wear makeup. Reggie would have liked to say, "And you're too old to wear it," but unlike, apparently, everyone else in the world, she kept her opinions to herself.

Reggie spent her life going around saying, "I'm *sixteen,*" to people who didn't believe her. The stupid thing was that inside she was a hundred years old. And anyway, Reggie didn't want to go into a pub; she didn't see the point of alcohol, or drugs. People had little enough control over their lives without losing more. Reggie thought of Mum and the Man-Who-Came-Before-Gary knocking back cheap white wine from Lidl and "getting jiggy," as the Man-Who-Came-Before-Gary liked to call it. Gary had two big advantages over the Man-Who-Came-Before-Him—one, he wasn't married, and two, he didn't leer at Reggie every time he saw her. If Mum hadn't met

Gary, she would at this moment—Reggie checked her watch—be skimming bar codes over scanners and looking forward to her afternoon break *("Tea, Twix, and a fag, lovely")*.

"Do you want a phone?" Billy was always saying to Reggie, taking two or three out of his pocket. "Wadjyerwan—Nokia, Samsung?" There was no point, Billy's phones never worked for more than a week. It seemed safer, in all ways, for a person to stick with her Virgin Pay as You Go. Reggie liked the way Richard Branson had made Virgin into a huge global brand-name, the way the Catholics had done with Jesus's mother. It was good to see the word out there. Reggie would be quite happy to die a virgin. The virgin queen, *Virgo Regina*. A vestal virgin. Ms. MacDonald said that vestal virgins who "lost their sexual innocence" were buried alive. Letting the vestal fires go out was a sign of impurity, which seemed a bit harsh. How neurotic would that make you? Especially in a time before firelighters.

They had done an unseen translation together of some of Pliny's letters. "Pliny the *Younger*," Ms. MacDonald always emphasized, as if it were of crucial importance that you got your Plinys right, when in fact there was probably hardly anyone left on earth who gave a monkey's about which was the elder and which was the younger. Who gave a monkey's about them, period.

Still, it was good to think that Billy was willing to do things for her, even if they were nearly always illegal things. She had accepted the ID card because one day it might come in handy, but she had never taken up the offer of the bus pass. You never knew, it might be the first step on a slippery slope that would eventually lead to something much bigger. Billy had started with pinching sweets from Mr. Hussain's shop, and look at him now, pretty much a career criminal.

Have you had much experience with children, Reggie?" Dr. Hunter had asked at her so-called interview.

"Och, loads. Really. Loads and loads," Reggie replied, smiling and nodding encouragingly at Dr. Hunter, who didn't seem very good at the whole interviewing thing. "Loads, sweartogod."

Reggie wouldn't have employed herself. Sixteen and no experience of children, even though she had great character references from Mr. Hussain and Ms. MacDonald and a letter from Mum's friend Trish saying how good she was with children, based on the fact that in exchange for her tea she had spent a whole year of Monday evenings with Grant, Trish's eldest muppet of a son, trying to coax him through his Maths Standard Grade exam (a hopeless case if ever there was one).

Reggie had never actually had a close encounter with a one-year-old child before, or indeed any small children, but what was there to know? They were small, they were helpless, they were confused, and Reggie could easily identify with all of that. And it wasn't that long since she had been a child herself, although she had an "old soul," a fortune-teller had told her. Body of a child, mind of an old woman. Old before her time. Not that she believed in fortune-tellers. The one who told her about her old soul lived in a new brick house with a view of the Pentlands and was called Sandra. Reggie had encountered her on a hen night for one of Mum's friends who was about to embark on another disastrous marriage, and Reggie had tagged along as usual, like a mascot. That was what happened when you had no friends of your own—your social life consisted of outings to fortune-tellers, bingo halls, Daniel O'Donnell concerts ("Pass the Revels along to Reggie"). No wonder she had an old soul. Even now that Mum was gone, her friends still phoned her up and said, "We're going over to Glasgow for a shopping trip, Reggie, want to come with us?" or "Fancy seeing *Blood Brothers* at the Playhouse?" No and no. Now are our revels ended. Ha.

There had been nothing unearthly about fortune-telling Sandra. A plump legal secretary in her fifties, she wore a rose-pink cardigan

with a shawl collar pinned by a coral cameo brooch. In her bathroom all the toiletries were Crabtree & Evelyn's Gardenia, lined up
a precise inch from the edge of the shelves as if they were still on
display in the shop.

"Your life is about to change," Sandra said to Mum. She wasn't
wrong.

Even now, Reggie thought that she could sometimes catch the
sickly sweet smell of gardenias.

Dr. Hunter was English but had trained to be a doctor in Edinburgh and had never gone back south of the border. She was a GP in
a practice in Liberton and had a morning surgery at half past eight,
so Mr. Hunter did "the early shift" with the baby. Reggie took over
from him at ten o'clock and stayed until Dr. Hunter came home
at two (although it was usually nearer to three—"Part-time but it
feels like full-time," Dr. Hunter sighed) and then Reggie stayed on
until five o'clock, which was the time of the day that she liked best
because then she got to be with Dr. Hunter herself.

The Hunters had a forty-inch HD television on which she
watched *Balamory* DVDs with the baby, although he always fell
asleep as soon as the theme tune began, snuggled into Reggie on
the sofa like a little monkey. She was surprised Dr. Hunter let the
baby watch television, but Dr. Hunter said, "Oh, heavens, why not?
Now and again, what's the harm?" Reggie thought that there was
nothing nicer than having a baby fall asleep on you, except perhaps
a puppy or a kitten. She'd had a puppy once, but her brother threw
it out the window. "I don't think he meant to," Mum said, but it
wasn't exactly the kind of thing you did accidentally, and Mum
knew that. And Reggie knew that Mum knew that. Mum used
to say, "Billy may be trouble, but he's our trouble. Blood's thicker
than water." It was a lot stickier too. The day the puppy went flying
through the window was the second-worst day of Reggie's life so
far. Hearing about Mum was the worst. Obviously.

Dr. and Mr. Hunter lived on the really nice side of Edinburgh, with a view of Blackford Hill, quite a distance in every way from the third-floor shoe box in Gorgie where Reggie lived on her own now that Mum was gone. Two bus journeys away in fact, but Reggie didn't mind. She always sat on the top deck and looked into other people's houses and wondered what it was like to live in them. There was the added bonus now of spotting the first Christmas trees in windows. (Dr. Hunter always said that simple pleasures were the best, and she was right.) She could get quite a lot of schoolwork done as well. She wasn't at school anymore, but she was still following the curriculum. English literature, ancient Greek, ancient history, Latin. Anything that was dead, really. Sometimes she imagined Mum speaking Latin *(Salve, Regina),* which was unlikely, to say the least.

Of course, not having a computer meant that Reggie had to spend a lot of time in the public library and in Internet cafés, but that was okay because a person didn't have to listen to someone saying, "Regina rhymes with vagina," to them in an Internet café, unlike the horrible posh school she went to. Until it breathed its last gasp, Ms. MacDonald used to have an ancient dinosaur of a Hewlett-Packard that she let Reggie use. It had been bought at the beginning of time—Windows 98 and AOL dial-up—and meant that getting on the Internet was a grim exercise in patience.

Reggie herself had briefly been in possession of a MacBook, which Billy had turned up with last Christmas. No way had he actually gone into a shop and bought it, the concept of retail being foreign to Billy. She had made him spend Christmas with her ("our first Christmas without Mum"). She cooked a turkey and everything, even flamed the pudding with brandy, but Billy only made it to the Queen's speech before he had to "go and do something," and Reggie said, "What? What could you possibly need to do on Christmas Day?" and he shrugged and said, "This and that." Reggie spent the rest of the day with Mr. Hussain and his family, who were having a surprisingly Victorian Christmas. A month later Billy came to the flat when Reggie wasn't there and took the MacBook away because he obviously didn't understand the concept of gifts either.

And, let's face it, libraries and Internet cafés were better than Reggie's empty flat. "Ah, a clean, well-lighted place," Ms. Mac-Donald said. Which was a Hemingway story that Ms. MacDonald had made Reggie read ("A seminal text," she buzzed) even though Hemingway wasn't even on the A-level syllabus, so wouldn't she, Reggie protested, be better off reading something that was? "*Mzzz* MacDonald," she always insisted, so that she sounded like an angry wasp (which was a pretty good definition of her character).

Ms. MacDonald was very keen on "reading round the subject" ("Do you want an education or not?"). In fact, most of the time she seemed keener on the reading-round bit than she did on the subject itself. Ms. MacDonald's idea of reading round the subject was more a case of catching a plane and seeing how far you could get away from it. Life was too short, Reggie would have protested, except that probably wasn't a good argument to use with a dying woman. Reggie had chosen *Great Expectations* and *Mrs. Dalloway* as prescribed texts and felt she had quite enough to do with reading round the subject of Dickens and Virginia Woolf (i.e., their entire "oeuvre," as Ms. MacDonald insisted on calling it), including letters, diaries, and biographies, without being distracted onto the side road of Hemingway's stories. But resistance was futile.

Ms. MacDonald had lent Reggie nearly all of Dickens's novels, and the rest she had bought in charity shops. Reggie liked Dickens, his books were full of plucky abandoned orphans struggling to make their way in the world. Reggie knew that journey only too well. She was doing *Twelfth Night* too. Reggie and Viola, orphans of the storm.

Ms. MacDonald used to be a classics teacher, used to be Reggie's classics teacher, in fact, at the horrible posh school she once went to, and was now attempting to guide Reggie through her A levels.

Ms. MacDonald's qualification for tutoring Reggie in English literature was based on the fact that Ms. MacDonald claimed to have read every book that had ever been written. Reggie didn't dispute the claim, the evidence was all over Ms. MacDonald's criminally untidy house. She could have started up a branch library (or a spectacular house fire) with the number of books she had piled around the place. She was also in possession of every single Loeb Classic that had ever been published, red for Latin, green for Greek, hundreds of them crammed into her bookcases. Odes and epodes, eclogues, and epigrams. Everything.

Reggie wondered what would happen to all the lovely Loebs when Ms. MacDonald died. She supposed it wasn't very polite to put in a request for them.

The tutoring wasn't exactly free, because in exchange Reggie was always running errands for Ms. MacDonald, picking up her prescriptions and buying tights from British Home Stores, hand cream from Boots, "and those little pork pies they have in Marks and Spencer." She was very specific about which shops you bought things in. Reggie thought that a person at death's door shouldn't really be too fussy about where her pork pies came from. With a little effort, Ms. MacDonald could probably have got these things herself, as she was still using her car, a blue Saxo that she drove in the way that an excitable and nearsighted chimpanzee might have done, accelerating when she should be braking, braking when she should be accelerating, going slow in the fast lane, fast in the slow lane, like someone on an amusement-arcade simulator rather than a real road.

Reggie didn't go to the horrible posh school anymore, because it made her feel like a mouse in a house of cats. *Extras, vacations, and diet unparalleled.* She had won a scholarship when she was twelve, but it wasn't the kind of school where a person arrived halfway through from another planet with nothing but their brains to recommend them. A person who never seemed to be wearing the right bits of uniform, who never had the proper sports kit (who was rubbish at sports, anyway, right kit or not), who never understood the secret language and hierarchies of the school. Not to mention a person who had an older brother who sometimes hung around the school gates, ogling all the girls with their good haircuts and nice families. Reggie knew that Billy was dealing to some of the boys (nice families, good haircuts, et cetera), boys who, although destined to follow the genetic code spiraled into their veins and become lawyers in the Edinburgh courts, were, nonetheless, scoring recreational drugs off Reggie Chase's runty brother. He was their contemporary in years but in every other way he was different.

You could have bought two really good cars a year for the price of the fees. Her scholarship covered only a quarter of that, the army paid the rest. "Delayed guilt," Mum said. Unfortunately, there was nobody to cover all the extras, those bits of uniform she was always missing, the books, the school trips, the good haircuts. Reggie's father had been a soldier in the Royal Scots, but Reggie never got to know him. Her mother was six months pregnant with Reggie when he was killed during the Gulf War, shot by "friendly fire." Most people were out of the womb before they first encountered irony, Reggie said to Ms. MacDonald.

"Consigned to history," Ms. MacDonald said.

"Well, we all are, Ms. Mac."

Both Mum and Reggie always had jobs on the go. As well as working in the supermarket, Mum did ironing for a couple of B and Bs, and Reggie worked in Mr. Hussain's shop on Sunday mornings. Even before she left school Reggie had always worked, paper routes and Saturday jobs and the like. She squirreled away money in her savings account, budgeting down to the last penny for the rent and bills, her Pay as You Go mobile and her Topshop card. "Your attempts at domestic economy are creditable," Ms. MacDonald said. "A woman should know how to manage money."

Mum was from Blairgowrie, and when she left school, her first job had been in a chicken factory, keeping an eye on a continually moving line of goose-pimpled carcasses as they were dipped in scalding water. This had set a standard for Mum; ever afterwards, whatever she did, she said, "It's not as bad as the chicken factory." Reggie reckoned the chicken factory must have been pretty bad because Mum had had some rubbish jobs in her time. Mum loved meat—bacon sandwiches, mince and tatties, sausage and chips—but Reggie never once saw her eat chicken, even when the Man-Who-Came-Before-Gary used to bring in a KFC bucket, and the Man-Who-Came-Before-Gary could get Mum to do just about anything. But not eat chicken.

Despite the educational aspects—ten top-grade GCSEs—it was really quite a relief when Reggie forged a letter from Mum saying that they were moving to Australia and Reggie wouldn't be coming back to the horrible posh school after the summer vacation.

Mum had been so proud when Reggie got her scholarship place ("A genius for a child! Me!"), but once she was gone, there didn't seem much point, and it was bad enough leaving for school in the morning with no one to say good-bye to her, but coming home to an empty house with no one to say hello was even worse. You would never have thought that two little words could be so important. *Ave atque vale.*

Ms. MacDonald didn't go to the horrible posh school anymore either, because she had a tumor growing like a mushroom in her brain.

Not to be selfish or anything, but Reggie hoped that Ms. MacDonald would manage to guide her through her A levels before the tumor finished eating her brain. *"Our nada who art in nada,"* Ms. MacDonald said. She was really quite bitter. You might expect a person who was dying to be a little bit resentful, but Ms.

MacDonald had always been like that. Illness hadn't made her a nicer person; even now she had religion, she was hardly full of Christian charity. She could be kind in the particulars but not in the general. Mum had been kind to everybody, it was her saving grace, even when she was being stupid—with the Man-Who-Came-Before-Gary, or indeed with Gary himself—she never lost sight of being kind. However, Ms. MacDonald had her saving graces too—she was good to Reggie and she loved her little dog, and those two things went a long way in Reggie's book.

Reggie thought Ms. MacDonald was lucky that she'd had lots of time to adjust to the fact that she was dying. Reggie didn't like the idea that you could be walking along as blithe as could be and the next moment you simply didn't exist. Walk out of a room, step into a taxi. Dive into the cool blue water of a pool and never come back up again. *Nada y pues nada.*

Did you interview a lot of girls for this job?" Reggie asked Dr. Hunter, and she said, "Loads and loads," and Reggie said, "You're a terrible liar, Dr. H.," and Dr. Hunter blushed and laughed and said, "It's true. I know. I can't even play Cheat. I had a good feeling about you, though," she added, and Reggie said, "Well, you should always trust your feelings, Dr. H." Which wasn't something that Reggie actually believed, because her mother had been following her feelings when she went off on holiday with Gary and look what happened there. And Billy's feelings rarely led him to a good place. He might be a runt but he was a vicious runt.

"Call me Jo," Dr. Hunter said.

Dr. Hunter said that she hadn't wanted to go back to work and that if it were up to her she would never leave the house.

Reggie wondered why it wasn't up to her. Well, "Neil's"

business had "hit a sticky patch," Dr. Hunter explained. (He'd been "let down" and "some things had fallen through.") Whenever she talked about Mr. Hunter's business, Dr. Hunter screwed up her eyes as if she were trying to make out the details of something a long way off.

When she was at the surgery, Dr. Hunter phoned home all the time to make sure the baby was okay. Dr. Hunter liked to talk to him, and she had long one-sided conversations while, at his end, the baby tried to eat the phone. Reggie could hear Dr. Hunter saying, "Hello, sweet pea, are you having a lovely day?" and "Mummy will be home soon, be good for Reggie." Or a lot of the time, she recited scraps of poems and nursery rhymes. She seemed to know hundreds, and she was always suddenly coming out with "Diddle, diddle, dumpling, my son John" or "Georgie Porgie pudding and pie." She knew a lot of stuff that was very English and quite foreign to Reggie, who had been brought up on "Katie Bairdie had a coo," and "A fine wee lassie, a bonnie wee lassie was bonny wee Jeannie McCall."

If the baby was asleep when she phoned, Dr. Hunter asked Reggie to put the dog on instead. ("I forgot to mention something," Dr. Hunter said at the end of their "interview," and Reggie thought, Uh-oh, the baby's got two heads, the house is on the edge of a cliff, her husband's a crazy psycho, but Dr. Hunter said, "We have a dog. Do you like dogs?"

"Totally. Love 'em. Really. Sweartogod.")

Although the dog couldn't speak, it seemed to understand the concept of phone conversations ("Hello, puppy, how's my gorgeous girl?") better than the baby did, and it listened alertly to Dr. Hunter's voice while Reggie held the receiver to its ear.

Reggie had been alarmed when she first saw Sadie—a huge German shepherd who looked as if she should be guarding a building site. "Neil was worried about how the dog would react when the baby came along," Dr. Hunter said. "But I would trust her with my life, with the baby's life. I've known Sadie longer than I've known anyone except for Neil. I had a dog when I was a child, but it died, and then my father wouldn't let me get another one. He's dead now too, so it just goes to show."

Reggie wasn't sure what it went to show. "Sorry," Reggie said. "For your loss." Like they said in police dramas on TV. She'd meant for the dead dog but Dr. Hunter took it to mean her father. "Don't be," she said. "He outlived himself a long time ago. Call me Jo." Dr. Hunter had quite a thing about dogs. "Laika," she would say, "the first dog in space. She died of heat and stress after a few hours. She was rescued from an animal center, she must have thought she was going to a home, to a family, and instead they sent her to the loneliest death in the world. How sad."

Dr. Hunter's father continued a half-life in his books — he had been a writer — and Dr. Hunter said he had once been very fashionable ("Famous in his day," she laughed), but his books hadn't "stood the test of time." "This is all that's left of him now," she said, leafing through a musty book titled *The Shopkeeper*. "Nothing of my mother left at all," Dr. Hunter said. "Sometimes I think how nice it would be to have a brush or a comb, an object that she touched every day, that was part of her life. But it's all gone. Don't take anything for granted, Reggie."

"No fear of that, Dr. H."

"Look away and it's gone."

"I know, believe me."

Dr. Hunter had relegated a pile of her father's novels to an unstable heap in the corner of the little windowless boxroom on the top floor. It was a big cupboard really, "not a room at all," Dr. Hunter said, although actually it was bigger than Reggie's bedroom in Gorgie. Dr. Hunter called it "the junk repository," and it was full of all kinds of things that no one knew what to do with — a single ski, a hockey stick, an old duvet, a broken computer printer, a portable television that didn't work (Reggie had tried), and a large number of ornaments that had been Christmas or wedding presents. *"Quelle horreur!"* Dr. Hunter laughed when she occasionally poked her head in there. "Some of this stuff is truly hideous," she said to Reggie. Whether they were hideous or not, she couldn't throw them away because they were gifts, and "gifts had to be honored."

"Except for Trojan horses," Reggie said.

"But, on the other hand, don't look a gift horse in the mouth," Dr. Hunter said.

"Perhaps sometimes you should," Reggie said.

"Timeo Danaos et dona ferentes," Dr. Hunter said.

"Totally."

Not honored forever, Reggie noticed, because every time a plastic charity bag slipped through the letter box, Dr. Hunter filled it with items from the junk repository and put it—rather guiltily—out on the doorstep. "No matter how much I get rid of, there's never any less," she sighed.

"Law of physics," Reggie said.

The rest of the house was very tidy and decorated with tasteful things—rugs and lamps and ornaments. A different class of ornament from Mum's collections of thimbles and miniature teapots that, despite their size, took up valuable space in the Gorgie flat.

The Hunters' house was Victorian, and although it had every modern comfort, it still had all its original fireplaces and doors and cornices, which Dr. Hunter said was a miracle. The front door had colored glass panels, starbursts of red, snowflakes of blue, and rosettes of yellow, that cast prisms of color when the sun shone through. There were even a full set of servants' bells and a back staircase that had allowed the servants to scurry around unseen. "Those were the days," Mr. Hunter said and laughed because he said if he had been alive when the house was built, he would have been making fires and blacking boots, "and you too, probably, Reggie," while "Joanna" would have been "swanning around upstairs like Lady Muck" because her family came from money.

"It's all gone," Dr. Hunter said when Reggie looked at her inquiringly.

"Unfortunately," Mr. Hunter said.

"Bad investments, nursing-home bills, squandered on trifles," Dr. Hunter said, as if the getting and spending of money were meaningless. "My grandfather was rich but profligate, apparently," she said.

"And we are poor but honest," Mr. Hunter said.

"Apparently," Dr. Hunter said.

Actually, Dr. Hunter admitted one day, there had been some money left and she had used it to buy this "very, very expensive house." "An investment," Mr. Hunter said. "A home," Dr. Hunter said.

The kitchen was Reggie's favorite room. You could have fitted the whole of Reggie's Gorgie flat into it and still had room for swinging a few elephants if you were so inclined. Surprisingly, Mr. Hunter liked cooking, and he was always making a mess in the kitchen. "My creative side," he said. "Women cook food because people need to eat," Dr. Hunter said. "Men cook to show off."

There was even a pantry, a small, cold room with a flagged floor and stone shelves and a wooden door that had a pattern of cutout hearts on the panels. Dr. Hunter kept cheese and eggs and bacon in there, as well as all her tinned and dried goods. "I should make jam," she said guiltily in the summer. "A pantry like this begs for homemade jam." Now that it was nearly Christmas she said, "I feel bad that I haven't made mincemeat. Or a Christmas cake. Or a pudding. The pantry is begging for a pudding, wrapped in a cloth and full of silver sixpences and charms." Reggie wondered if Dr. Hunter was thinking about her own Christmases when she was a child, but Dr. Hunter said, "Heavens, no."

Reggie didn't think that the pantry was begging for anything, except possibly a bit of a tidy. Mr. Hunter was always rooting through there, looking for ingredients and spoiling Dr. Hunter's neat ranks of tins and jars.

Dr. Hunter ("Call me Jo"), who didn't believe in religion, who didn't believe in "any kind of transcendence except that of the human spirit," believed most firmly in order and taste. "Morris says that you should have nothing in your house that you don't know to be useful, or believe to be beautiful," she said to Reggie when they were filling a pretty little vase ("Worcester") with flowers from the garden. Reggie thought she meant someone called Maurice, probably a gay friend, until she noticed a biography of William Morris on the bookshelf and thought, Duh, stupid, because of course she knew who he was.

Twice a week a cleaner called Liz came in and moaned about how much work she had to do, but Reggie thought she had it pretty easy because the Hunters had everything under control. They weren't housework Nazis or anything, but they knew the difference between comfort and chaos, unlike Ms. MacDonald, whose entire *house* was a "repository of junk"—bits of old crap everywhere, receipts and pens, locks without keys, keys without locks, clothes piled on top of chests, pillars of old newspapers, half a bicycle in the hallway, which just appeared there one day, not to mention the forest's worth of books. Ms. MacDonald used the imminence of the Rapture and the Second Coming as an excuse ("What's the point?"), but really she was just a slovenly person.

Ms. MacDonald had "got" religion (goodness knows where from) shortly after her tumor was diagnosed. The two things were not unrelated. Reggie thought that if she were being eaten alive by cancer, she might start believing in God because it would be nice to think that someone out there cared, although Ms. MacDonald's God didn't really seem the caring sort; in fact, quite the opposite, indifferent to human suffering and intent on reckless destruction.

Dr. Hunter had a big notice board in the kitchen, full of all kinds of things that gave you an insight into her life, like an athletics certificate that showed she had once been a county sprint champion, another to show that she reached grade 8 in her piano exams, and a photograph ("when I was a student") of her holding aloft a trophy, surrounded by people clapping. "I was an all-rounder," Dr. Hunter laughed, and Reggie said, "You still are, Dr. H."

There were other photographs on the notice board that charted Dr. Hunter's life, some of Sadie over the years, and lots of the baby, of course, as well as one of Dr. and Mr. Hunter together, laughing in the glare of foreign sunshine. The rest of the notice board was a medley of shopping lists and recipes *(Sheila's Chocolate Brownies)* and messages that Dr. Hunter had left to herself—*Remember to tell Reggie that Joe Jingles is canceled on Monday* or *Practice meeting changed to Fri PM*. All the appointment cards were pinned there too, for the dentist, the hairdresser, the optician. Dr. Hunter wore spectacles for driving, which made her look even smarter than she was. Reggie was supposed to wear spectacles, but on her they had the opposite effect, making her look like a complete numpty, so she tended to wear them only when there was no one else around. The baby and Dr. Hunter didn't count, Reggie could be herself with them, right down to the spectacles.

There were a couple of business cards on the notice board as well, stuck up by Mr. Hunter on returning from "working lunches," but really it was Dr. Hunter's notice board.

A woman had come to see Dr. Hunter yesterday afternoon. She rang the doorbell two minutes after Dr. Hunter came home, and Reggie wondered if she had been parked nearby, waiting for Dr. Hunter to arrive.

Reggie, the baby balanced on her hip, led her into the kitchen and went to tell Dr. Hunter, who had gone upstairs to get changed out of the black suit she always wore for work. When Reggie came back downstairs, the woman was examining the notice board in a way that Reggie thought was too presumptuous for a stranger. The woman looked a bit like Dr. Hunter, same dark hair that skimmed her shoulders, same slim build, a bit taller. She was wearing a black suit too. She wasn't the Avon lady, that was for sure. Reggie wondered if she would ever have a life where she got to wear a black suit.

Dr. Hunter came into the kitchen, and the woman took a card from her bag and, showing it to Dr. Hunter, said, "Can I have a word?" and Dr. Hunter said to Reggie, "Can you look after the baby for a few minutes, Reggie?" even though the baby was doing his suicidal starfish thing, his little plump arms held out to Dr. Hunter like he was asking to be rescued from a sinking ship. But Dr. Hunter just smiled at him and led the woman away into the living room and shut the door. Dr. Hunter never ignored the baby, Dr. Hunter never took anyone into the living room — people always sat at the big table in the comfy kitchen — and for a minute Reggie worried that the woman had something to do with Billy. She would be revealed as the sister of Bad-Boy Billy and would be cast out. Reggie had never mentioned to Dr. Hunter that she had a brother. She hadn't lied, she had simply left him out of the story of her life, which was what he did to her, after all.

The dog tried to follow, but Dr. Hunter shut the door in her face without saying anything to her, which was *so* not Dr. Hunter, and an exiled Sadie sat down outside the door and waited patiently. If a dog could frown, she would have frowned.

After the woman left, Dr. Hunter had a funny, tight look on her face, as if she was trying to pretend that everything was normal when it wasn't.

Now there was a new card on the notice board. It was embossed with "Lothian and Borders Police," a phone number, and a name, "Detective Chief Inspector Louise Monroe."

★   ★   ★

Reggie fed the baby a yogurt, not regular yogurt but a special organic baby yogurt, no additives, no sugar, nothing artificial. She finished it off for him when he lost interest in it.

Outside, it was cold and damp, but in the kitchen it felt cozy and safe. There were no Christmas decorations up yet, just the Advent calendar they had bought on the baby's birthday, but Reggie could imagine the scent of pine and clementines and log fires and all the other good smells that she was sure Dr. Hunter would fill the house with any day now. It would be Reggie's first Christmas with Dr. Hunter and the baby, and she wondered if there was any way she could go about suggesting that she should spend Christmas Day itself with them rather than on her own or with the Hussains. Nothing against the Hussains or anything but they weren't her *family*. And Dr. Hunter and the baby were.

Sadie waited patiently at the side of the high chair. Every time the baby dropped any food, she licked it off the floor. Sometimes she managed to catch it in midair. She had a lot of dignity for a dog hustling for scraps. ("She's starting to get old," Dr. Hunter said sadly.)

Reggie gave the baby a finger of whole wheat toast to chew on while she washed his bowls, by hand because she didn't trust the dishwasher with them. The baby's dishes were real china in an old-fashioned pattern. His toys were tasteful wooden ones—nothing garish or noisy—and his clothes were all expensive and new, not handed down or bought in secondhand shops. A lot of them were French. Today he was wearing the cutest-ever navy-blue-and-white-striped all-in-one ("his matelot outfit," Dr. Hunter called it) that reminded Reggie of a Victorian bathing suit. He had a Noah's Ark rug in his room and a night-light in the shape of a big red-and-white-spotted fairy toadstool. His sheets were embroidered with sailboats, and there was a framed sampler above his bed with his date of birth and his name, "Gabriel Joseph Hunter," in pale blue chain stitch.

The baby wasn't afraid of anything except unexpected loud

noises (Reggie wasn't too keen on those either), and he could clap his hands if you said, "Clap your hands," and if you said, "Where's your red ball?" he would crawl to his toy box and find it. He had just yesterday taken his first wobbly but unaided step. ("One small step for mankind, one giant leap for a baby," Dr. Hunter said.) He could say the word *dog* and the word *ball* and *banky*, which was his word for his most precious possession — the little square cut from a blanket that had been bought for him by Mr. Hunter's sister before he was born, a pale green ("moss," Dr. Hunter said) blanket to suit either sex. Dr. Hunter told Reggie that "actually" she had known what sex the baby was, but she hadn't told anyone she knew, not even Mr. Hunter, because she "wanted to keep the baby all to herself for as long as possible." Now the green blanket of which the baby was obsessionally fond had been cut down to make it more manageable. "His Winnicottian transitional object," Dr. Hunter said mysteriously. "Or perhaps it's his talisman."

It had been his first birthday a week ago, and, to celebrate, the three of them (not Mr. Hunter, he was "all tied up," and anyway, "it's not as if he *knows* it's his birthday, Jo") had driven to a hotel near Peebles for afternoon tea, and the waitress had made a big fuss of the baby because he was so gorgeous and so well-behaved. He had a small dish of pink ice cream. "His first ever! Imagine!" Dr. Hunter said. "Imagine eating ice cream for the very first time, Reggie." The baby's eyes almost popped out of his head with surprise when he tasted the pink ice cream.

"Aw, bless," Reggie said.

Reggie and Dr. Hunter ate a whole plate of cakes between them. "I think I have a fat person inside me trying to get out," Reggie said, and Dr. Hunter laughed and then nearly choked on a miniature coffee éclair, which would probably have been okay because Reggie had asked Dr. Hunter to teach her the Heimlich maneuver for exactly this kind of occurrence.

"I'm *very* happy," Dr. Hunter said when she'd recovered, and Reggie said, "Me too." And the nice thing was that they really were, because it was surprising how often people said they were happy when they weren't. Like Mum with the Man-Who-Came-Before-Gary.

That was on the first day of Advent, and Dr. Hunter said that was a nice day to have a birthday on, even though she wasn't religious. They bought the Advent calendar in Peebles. Peebles was full of all the kinds of shops that old people liked. Reggie liked them too, she supposed it was something to do with her old soul.

The Advent calendar had chocolates behind every door, and Dr. Hunter said, "Let's put it up in the kitchen and you can open a door every day and have the chocolate." Which is what Reggie did, what she was doing now, holding the melting Santa-shaped chocolate in her cheek to extend its life while she dipped the baby's Bunnykins dishes in the sink, squirting Ecover washing-up liquid into the hot water. Dr. Hunter didn't use any products that weren't ecological—washing powder, floor soap, everything. "You don't want harmful chemicals around a baby," she said to Reggie. The baby was precious, he was as valuable as the most valuable object. "Well, I had to go to a lot of trouble to get him," Dr. Hunter laughed. "It wasn't easy."

Dr. Hunter had to be careful because she had asthma (*"Physician, heal thyself,"* she said), which she got "from my mother." She was always getting colds as well, which she said was because a doctor's surgery was "the unhealthiest place on earth to work—full of sick people." Sometimes, if Reggie was standing close to Dr. Hunter, she could hear a wheezing in her chest. The breath of life, Dr. Hunter said to Reggie. The baby didn't seem to have inherited any of Dr. Hunter's problems with her lungs. ("Dickens had asthma," Ms. MacDonald said. "I know," Reggie said. "I've read round the subject.")

★　　★　　★

There was no obvious evidence of Mr. Hunter's sticky patch. The Hunters had a lovely house, two cars, and a fridge full of expensive food, and the baby wanted for nothing.

Some mornings when Reggie arrived, Mr. Hunter behaved like a runner in a relay race, handing the baby over to Reggie so quickly that the baby's little mouth and eyes went completely round with astonishment at the speed of the changeover. Then Reggie and Sadie listened to the mesmerizing sound of the huge Range Rover roaring away from the house in a crunch and spit of gravel, as if Mr. Hunter were a getaway driver. "He's like a bear in the morning sometimes," Dr. Hunter laughed. Living with a bear didn't seem to bother her. Water off a duck's back.

Mr. Hunter and Sadie didn't have much of a relationship. The most Mr. Hunter said to her was, "Out of the way, Sadie," or "Get off the couch, Sadie." She was "part of the package," he said to Reggie. "You don't get Jo without Sadie."

"Love me, love my dog," Dr. Hunter said. "A woman's best friend." Timmy, Snowy, Jumble, Lassie, Greyfriars Bobby. Everyone's best friend. Except for poor Laika, the space dog, who was no one's friend.

On other mornings, Mr. Hunter stayed at home and made endless phone calls. Sometimes he went outside so that he could smoke while talking. He wasn't supposed to smoke, in or out of the house, but the phone calls seemed to drive him to it. "Don't tell," he said, winking at Reggie as if Dr. Hunter wouldn't smell the smoke on his clothes or notice the cigarette butts nestling amongst the gravel.

Reggie couldn't help but overhear Mr. Hunter because he always spoke very loudly to the unseen people at the other end of the phone. He was "exploring new avenues," he told them. He had "very interesting prospects on the horizon" and "opportunities opening up." He sounded brash but really he was pleading. "Jesus, Mark, I'm fucking bleeding out here."

Mr. Hunter was handsome, in a rough, slightly battered kind of way, which actually made him more good-looking than if he'd been conventionally attractive. Dr. Hunter had met him when she was a senior registrar "at the old Royal Infirmary," although he wasn't from Edinburgh. He was from Glasgow, "a Weegie," Dr. Hunter laughed, which was generally intended as an insult by people from Edinburgh, but maybe Dr. Hunter didn't know that, being English. He had courted her for a long time before she "caved in" and married him. Mr. Hunter was "something in the leisure industry" but exactly what was unclear to Reggie.

Dr. Hunter and Mr. Hunter seemed to get along pretty well, although Reggie didn't really have anything to compare their relationship to except for Mum and Gary (uninspiring) and Mum and the Man-Who-Came-Before-Gary (horrible). Dr. Hunter laughed at Mr. Hunter's shortcomings and never seemed to get annoyed with him about anything. "Jo's too easygoing for her own good," Mr. Hunter said. Mr. Hunter, for his part, would bang into the house with a bunch of nice flowers or a bottle of wine and say, "Hiya, doll," to Dr. Hunter like a comedy Glaswegian and give her a big kiss, and wink at Reggie and say, "Behind every great woman there's some shite guy, Reggie, don't forget that."

Most of the time Mr. Hunter behaved as if he couldn't see Reggie at all, but then sometimes he would take her by surprise and be really nice to her and tell her to sit down at the kitchen table while he made her a coffee and tried to make rather awkward conversation ("So what's *your* story, Reggie?"), although usually before she could start telling him her (not inconsiderable) "story," his phone would ring and he would leap up and pace around the room while he talked ("Hey, Phil, howy'are doing? I was wondering if we could get together, I've got a proposition I'd like to run by you.").

Mr. Hunter called the baby "the bairn" and tossed him in the air a lot, which made the baby shriek with excitement. Mr. Hunter said he couldn't wait until "the bairn" could talk and run around and go to football matches with him, and Dr. Hunter said, "Time enough for all that. Make the most of every second, they're gone before you know it." If the baby hurt himself, Mr. Hunter picked him up and said, "Come on, wee man, you're fine, it was nothing," in an encouraging but not very sympathetic way, whereas Dr. Hunter hugged him and kissed him and said, "Poor wee scone," which was a phrase she had got from Reggie (who had in turn got it from Mum). When she said Scottish words and phrases, Dr. Hunter said them in a (pretty good) Scottish accent, so it was almost like she was bilingual.

The baby liked Mr. Hunter well enough but he worshipped Dr. Hunter. When she held him in her arms, his eyes never left her face, as if he were absorbing every detail for a test he might have to sit later.

"I'm a goddess to him now," Dr. Hunter said, laughing, "but one day I'll be the annoying old woman who wants to be taken to the supermarket."

"Och, no, Dr. H.," Reggie said. "I think you're always going to be a deity for him."

"Shouldn't you have stayed on at school, Reggie?" Dr. Hunter asked, a little frown worrying her pretty features. Reggie imagined this was how she was with her patients ("You really have to lose some weight, Mrs. MacTavish.").

"Yes, I should have," Reggie said.

Come on, sunshine," Reggie said to the baby, lifting him out of his high chair and planting him on the floor. She had to keep an eye on him all the time because one moment he'd be sitting contentedly trying to work out how to eat his fat little foot and the next he'd be commando-crawling towards the nearest hazard. All he wanted to do was put things in his mouth, and you could be sure if there was an object small enough to choke on, then the baby would make a beeline for it, and Reggie had to be constantly on the lookout for buttons and coins and grapes—of which he was particularly fond. All his grapes had to be cut in half, which was a real chore, but Dr. Hunter had told her about a patient whose baby had died when a grape got stuck in his windpipe and *"no one had been able to help him,"* Dr. Hunter said, as if that were worse than the dying itself. That was when Reggie got Dr. Hunter to teach her not just the Heimlich maneuvre but mouth-to-mouth, how to stop arterial bleeding, and what to do for a burn. And electrocution and accidental poisoning. (And drowning, of course.) "You could go on a first-aid course," Dr. Hunter said, "but they do such an awful lot of unnecessary bandaging. We can do some strapping of wrists and arms, a basic head bandage, but you don't need anything more complicated than that. Really, you just need to know how to save a life." She brought home a CPR dummy from the office so that Reggie could practice resuscitation. "We call him Eliot," Dr. Hunter said, "but no one can remember why."

When Reggie thought about the baby who had choked on a grape, she imagined him stoppered up like the old-fashioned lemonade bottle with a marble in its neck that she had seen in the museum. Reggie liked museums. Clean, well-lighted places.

Mr. Hunter was very easygoing about the baby. He said babies were "virtually indestructible" and that Dr. Hunter worried too much, "but then, you can't expect anything else given her history." Reggie didn't know anything about Dr. Hunter's history (imagined herself saying, "What's *your* story, Dr. H.?" but it didn't sound right). All Reggie really knew was that William Morris sat on the bookshelf in Dr. Hunter's living room, while her own father was officially declared junk and lived in the old curiosity shop on the top floor. Reggie herself thought babies were extremely destructible, and after the grape story she became particularly paranoid about the baby not being able to breathe. But what else could she expect, given her history? ("The breath," Dr. Hunter said, "the breath is everything.")

Sometimes Reggie lay in bed at night and held the breath in her lungs until she thought they would burst so that she could feel what it was like, imagining her mother anchored underwater by her hair like some new, mysterious strain of seaweed.

"How long does it take to die from drowning?" she asked Dr. Hunter.

"Well, there are quite a few variables," Dr. Hunter said, "water temperature and so on, but roughly speaking, five to ten minutes. Not long."

Long enough.

Reggie placed the baby's dishes in the draining rack. The sink was at the window and overlooked a field at the foot of Blackford Hill. Sometimes there were horses in the field, sometimes not. Reggie had no idea where the horses went when they weren't there. Now it was winter, they wore dull green blankets like Barbour jackets.

Sometimes when Dr. Hunter came home early enough, before the winter dark descended, they would take the dog and the baby into the field and the baby would crawl around on the rough grass and Reggie would pursue Sadie round the field because she loved it when you pretended to chase her, and Dr. Hunter would laugh and say to the baby, "Come on, run, run like the wind!" and the baby would just look at her because of course he had no idea what running was. If the horses were in the field they remained aloof, as if they ran, which they must surely do, but in secret.

The horses were big, nervy creatures, and Reggie didn't like the way their lips curled back over their huge yellow teeth; she imagined them mistaking the baby's excited fist for an apple and biting it off his arm.

"Horses worry me as well," Dr. Hunter said. "They always

seem so *sad,* don't you think? Although not as sad as dogs."
Reggie thought dogs were pretty happy creatures, but of course
Dr. Hunter saw the potential for sadness everywhere. "How sad," Dr.
Hunter said when the leaves came off the trees. "How sad," she said
when a song came on the radio (Beth Nielsen Chapman). "How
sad," when Sadie whined quietly at the sight of her getting ready
to leave the house. Even when it had been the baby's birthday and
they had all been so happy eating cake and pink ice cream, afterwards as they drove home, Dr. Hunter said, "His first birthday, how
sad, he'll never be a baby again."

For his birthday, Reggie had given the baby a teddy bear and
a bib embroidered in blue with ducks and the words *Baby's First
Birthday.* First things were nice, last things not so much so.

Often, after one of her moments of sadness, Dr. Hunter would
give her head a little shake, as if she were trying to get rid of something from it, and smile and say, "And yet we are not downhearted,
are we, Reggie?" and Reggie would say, "No, indeed we are not,
Dr. H."

"Call me Jo," Dr. Hunter said to Reggie. "Fiddle-dee-dee, fiddle-
dee-dee, the fly has married the bumblebee," she said to the baby.

Reggie had never told Dr. Hunter about her mother, about
her being dead. The weight of the sadness of it might have been
too much for Dr. Hunter to bear, even without the unnecessary
and tragic manner of Mum's going. And every time she looked at
Reggie, Dr. Hunter would have had the sad expression on her face
and that too would have been unbearable. Instead, Reggie made
up her mother. She was called Jackie and worked on the check-
out at a supermarket in a shopping center that Dr. Hunter never
went to. When she was young she had been a champion highland
dancer (although you would never have guessed that). Her best
friends were called Mary, Trish, and Jean. She was always planning
the next diet, she had long hair (lovely hair, sadly Reggie had not
inherited it) that she said she was going to have to start wearing up

because she was getting too old to wear it down. She was thirty-six this year, the same age as Dr. Hunter. She was sixteen when she got engaged to Reggie's father, seventeen when she had Billy, and a widow at twenty. Reggie supposed it was just as well she had packed everything in early on.

She took a terrible photograph, made worse by the goofy faces she always pulled the moment a camera was pointed in her direction. One of her favorite sayings was "It's a funny old world," said affectionately, as if the world were a mischievous child. She liked reading Danielle Steel and her favorite flower was a daffodil and she made a really good shepherd's pie. Actually all of these things were true. It was just the being alive bit that was made-up.

While Reggie was wiping down the draining board, her eye was caught by something moving at the far end of the field. The sun had hardly popped its head up today and it was hard to distinguish anything more than smudged shapes at that distance. Not a horse, this was not a day for horses, they were living their mysterious lives somewhere else. Whoever or whatever it was seemed to scuttle along the hedge, a blur of something black. Reggie glanced at the dog to see if her canine senses were alerting her to anything, but Sadie was sitting stoically on the floor next to the baby while he tried to stuff her tail in his mouth.

"I don't think so, mister," Reggie said to the baby, gently releasing a fistful of fur and lifting him in her arms. She carried the baby over to the window but there was nothing to be seen out there now. The baby clutched a hank of her hair, he was a terrible hair grabber. "Atavistic instinct, I expect," Dr. Hunter said. "From the days when I would have been swinging through trees and he would have been clutching on to my fur for dear life." The idea of Dr. Hunter, always so neatly groomed in the little black suit she wore for work, as a primitive tree dweller was comical. Reggie had to look up *atavistic*. She still hadn't found an opportunity to use it. She was working her way through the *a*'s, so it fitted in well with the drive to improve her vocabulary.

Lately, Reggie had got into the habit of staying longer and longer at the Hunters' house, while Mr. Hunter seemed to be out of the house more and more. "He's setting something up, a new venture," Dr. Hunter said brightly. Dr. Hunter seemed glad that Reggie was there so much. She would suddenly look out the window and say, "Heavens, Reggie, it's dark, you must be getting home," but then she would say, "I hate this horrid weather so. Shall we have another cup of tea?" Or "Stay and have some supper, Reggie, and then I'll give you a lift home." Reggie hoped that one day soon Dr. Hunter might say, "Why go home, Reggie? Why not move in here?" and then they would be a proper family — Dr. Hunter, Reggie, and the baby and the dog. ("Neil" didn't really figure in Reggie's daydream of family life.)

On one of these evenings, apropos of nothing (*apropos* was another new word), when Dr. Hunter and Reggie were giving the baby a bath, Dr. Hunter turned to Reggie and said, "You know there are no rules," and Reggie said, "Really?" because she could think of a lot of rules, like cutting grapes in half and wearing a cap when you went swimming, not to mention separating all the rubbish for the recycling bins. Unlike with Ms. MacDonald, recycling was something that Dr. Hunter was very keen on. She said, "No, not those kinds of things, I mean the way we live our lives. There isn't a template, a pattern that we're supposed to follow. There's no one watching us to see if we're doing it properly, there is no *properly*, we just make it up as we go along."

Reggie wasn't entirely sure that she knew what Dr. Hunter was talking about. The baby was distracting her, squawking and splashing like a mad sea creature.

"What you have to remember, Reggie, is that the only important thing is love. Do you understand?"

That sounded okay to Reggie, a bit Richard Curtis, but okay.

"Loud and clear, Dr. H.," she said, taking a towel from the radiator, where it had been warming. Dr. Hunter lifted the baby out of the water—he was slipperier than a fish—and Reggie wrapped him in the towel.

"'*Knowing that when light is gone, Love remains for shining*,'" Dr. Hunter said. "Isn't that lovely? Elizabeth Barrett Browning wrote it for her dog."

"Flush," Reggie said. "Virginia Woolf wrote a book about him. I've read around the subject."

"When everything else has gone, love still remains," Dr. Hunter said.

"Totally," Reggie said. But what good did it do you? None at all.

Ad Augusta per Angusta

This would be the scenic route, then. He was taking the long way round. Jackson tipped a metaphorical hat in the direction of the Dixie Chicks.

For reasons best known to itself the GPS stopped working five miles after leaving the village. At some point they had obviously taken a wrong turning, because Jackson found himself on a one-way road that wound its leisurely way up through a deserted dale. There was no signal on his phone, and the radio had given out nothing but crackle and hiss for some time now. The CD player contained one disc accidentally left over from the previous rental and Jackson wondered in what circumstances he would feel so desperate for the sound of another voice that he would listen to Enya's.

He should have brought his iPod, he could have been listening to songs of heartache and redemption and redneck righteousness. And it had obviously been a really bad idea to leave that OS map behind, although he wasn't convinced that the roads around here actually conformed to any map. If it hadn't been for a signpost a mile back reassuring him that they were heading for the right destination, he would have turned round by now. (Although should he put so much faith in signs?)

Bleak in its beauty, the landscape was beginning to bring out the mournful streak in Jackson that he was usually better off keeping at bay. Hello, darkness, my old friend. Life was easier if you were an unimaginative pragmatist, a happy idiot. "Well, you've got the idiot part right," he heard his ex-wife Josie's voice say in his head.

The road stretched tightly over the contours of the land and, apart from its taking the occasional dip, they were climbing the whole time. Although Jackson would have referred to himself in the singular if he had been (God forbid) on foot, when he was in a car, he became a plural pronoun. *They, we, us.* The car and me, a biomechanical fusion of man and vehicle. Pilgrims on God's highway.

They were alone. Not another car in sight. No tractors or Land Rovers, no other drifters on the high plains, no fellow travelers at all. No farmhouses or sheep barns either, only grass and barren limestone and a dead December sky. He was on the road to nowhere.

There were still a lot of hardy sheep wandering around, though, aloof to the dangers posed by a bloody great Discovery bearing down on them. They must surely lamb late up here on these wuthering heights. Jackson wondered if they were already carrying next year's lambs. He had never considered the gestation period of a sheep before, it was surprising what a lonely road drove you to. His daughter had recently announced her conversion to the vegetarian cause. In a word-association test his automatic response to the word *lamb* would be "mint sauce," Marlee's would be "innocent." The slaughter of. She was being brought up as an atheist, but she spoke the language of martyrs. Perhaps Catholicism was genetic, in the blood.

"Becoming a vegetarian seems to be a rite of passage for teenage girls these days," Josie said, during his last visit to Cambridge at the end of the summer. "All her friends have given up meat." No more father-daughter bonding over a burger, then.

"I know, I know, meat is murder," he said, as they sat down at a table in a café of Marlee's choice called something like Seeds or Roots ("Weeds," he called it, to her annoyance.) He had had a hankering for a beef-and-mustard sandwich but settled for a chewy brown roll with an anemic-looking filling that he guessed to be egg but that turned out—horror of horrors—to be "scrambled tofu."

"Yum," he said, and Marlee said, "Don't be so cynical, Daddy. It suits you too much."

When had his daughter started speaking like a woman? A year ago she had skipped along like a three-year-old on the path by the river to Grantchester (where, if his memory served him right, she had eaten a ham salad in the Orchard Tea Room, no guilt at all about ingesting Babe). Now, apparently, that girl had run on ahead out of sight. Turn your back for a minute and they were gone.

When you had children, you measured your years in theirs. Not "I'm forty-nine," but "I have a twelve-year-old child." Josie had another child now, another girl, two years old, the same age as Nathan. Two children united by the common thread of DNA they shared with their half sister, Marlee. Just because Nathan didn't look like him didn't mean he wasn't his son. After all, Marlee didn't look like him either. Julia claimed that Nathan wasn't his child, but when had anyone ever believed anything that his ex-girlfriend said? Julia was born to lie. Plus, she was an actress, of course. So when she looked him earnestly in the eye and said, "Really, Jackson, the baby isn't yours, I'm telling the truth, why would I lie?" his instinct was to say, "Why change the habit of a lifetime now?" Instead of arguing (*"I generally only argue with people I like,"* she had once said to him), she had given him a pitying look.

He wanted a son. He wanted a son so he could teach him all the things he knew, as well as how to learn all the things he didn't know. He couldn't teach his daughter anything, she knew more than he did already. And he wanted a son because he was a man.

Simple as that. He suddenly recalled the surge of emotion he had felt when he touched Nathan's head. That was the kind of thing that made a strong man weak for life.

And anyway, he had said to Josie, since when was twelve a teenager? "*Teen* is the clue — thirteen, fourteen, et cetera. She's only twelve."

"Double figures count," Josie said casually. "They start earlier these says."

"Start what?"

Jackson had passed through his teens without ever being aware of them. He had been a boy at twelve and then he had joined the army at sixteen and become a man. Between the two he had walked in the valley of the shadow of death, with no comfort to hand.

He hoped his daughter would have a sunny passage through those years. He had a crumpled postcard from her in the pocket of his jacket from when she had been on a school trip to Bruges in her half-term. The postcard showed a picturesque view of a canal and some old redbrick houses. Jackson had never felt the need to go to Belgium. He had transferred the card from his old leather jacket to the North Face jacket — his disguise — although from no clear motive, only that a message from his daughter, banal and dutiful though it was ("Dear Dad, Bruges is very interesting, it has a lot of nice buildings. It is raining. Have eaten a lot of chips and chocolate. Missing you! Love you! Marlee xxx"), seemed like something you shouldn't just throw away. Did she really miss him? He suspected her life was too full to notice his absence.

A ragged-looking sheep, long-in-the-tooth mutton, stood four-square in the road ahead, like a gunslinger waiting for high noon. Jackson slowed to a stop and waited it out for a while. The sheep didn't move. He hooted his horn but it didn't even twitch an ear, just continued chewing grass laconically like an old tobacco hand.

He wondered if it was deaf. He got out of the car and looked at it threateningly.

"Are you gonna pull those pistols or whistle 'Dixie'?" he said to it. It looked at him with a flicker of interest and then went back to its incessant chewing.

He tried to shift it bodily. It resisted, leaning its stupid weight against his. Shouldn't it be frightened of him? He would be frightened of him if he were a sheep.

Next he tried moving its hindquarters, to get some grip and torque, but it was impossible, it might as well have been cemented into the road. A headlock also got him nowhere. He was glad there was no one around to witness this absurd wrestling match. He wondered about the ethics of punching it. He backed off a few steps to rethink his tactics.

Finally, he tried pushing its front legs from beneath it, but he ended up losing his balance and found himself sprawled on his back on the road. Across the pale winter sky an even paler cloud floated overhead, as white and soft as a little lamb. From his prone position, Jackson watched its progress from one side of the dale to the other. When the cold had not only seeped into his bones but had begun to freeze the marrow inside them, Jackson sighed, and getting to his feet, he saluted his opponent. "You win," he said to the sheep. He climbed back in the car, turned on the CD player, and put on Enya. When he woke up, there were no sheep anywhere.

He was definitely off the map now. The sky was leaden, threatening snow. Higher and higher, heading for the top and some mysterious summit. The celestial city. It was a gated road and it was laborious having to get out of the car and open and close the gates each time. He supposed it was a way of corralling the sheep. Were there shepherds still? Jackson's idea of a shepherd was a rough-bearded man wearing a homemade sheepskin jerkin, seated on a grassy hillside on a starlit night, a ram's-horn crook in hand as he watched for the wolves creeping on their bellies towards his flock. Jackson surprised himself with how poetically detailed and completely inaccurate his image of a shepherd was. In reality it would be all tractors and hormones and chemical dips. And the wolves were long gone, or, at any rate, the ones in wolves' clothing were. Jackson was a shepherd, he couldn't rest until the flock was accounted for, all gathered safely in. It was his calling and his curse. Protect and serve.

Snow poles at the side of the road measured up to three meters. He cast a wary eye at the sky; he wouldn't like to get stuck in a drift up here, no one would ever find you. He would have to dig in until spring, fleece a couple of sheep for blankets. No one knew he was here, he hadn't told anyone he was leaving London. If he was lost, if something happened to him, there was no one who would know where to come and look. If someone he loved was lost, he would stalk the world forever looking for them, but he wasn't entirely sure that there was anyone who would do the same for him. ("*I love you,*" she said, but he wasn't sure how tenacious an emotion that was for her.)

He passed a fence post that had a bird of prey, a hawk or falcon, perched on top of it like a finial. Jackson was no good at the naming of birds. He knew buzzards, though, there was a pair above him, circling idly in a holding pattern above the moorland, like black paper silhouettes. *When thou from hence away art past, every nighte and alle, to Whinny-muir thou com'st at last; and Christe receive thy saule.* Jesus, where had that come from? School, that was where. Rote learning, still in fashion when Jackson was a boy. The "Lyke Wake Dirge." His first year at secondary school, before his life went off the rails. He suddenly saw himself standing in front of the coal fire in their little house, reciting the poem one evening for a test the next day. His sister, Niamh, listening and correcting as if she were catechizing him. He could smell the coal, feel the heat on his legs, bare in the gray woollen shorts of his uniform. From the kitchen came the scents of the peasant food their mother was cooking for tea. Niamh slapped him on his leg with a ruler when he forgot the words. Looking back, he was astonished at the amount of casual brutality in his family (his sister almost as bad as his brother and father), the punches and slaps, the hair tweaking, ear pulling, Chinese burns—a whole vocabulary of violence. It was the nearest they could get to expressing love for one another. Maybe it was something to do with the bad mix of Scots and Irish genes that their parents had brought to the union. Maybe it was lack of money or the harsh life of a mining community. Or maybe they just liked it. Jackson had never hit a woman or a child, he restricted himself entirely to duffing up his own sex.

If hosen and shoon thou ne'er gav'st nane, every nighte and alle, the whinnes sall prick thee to the bare bane; and Christe receive thy saule.

A whinny was a thorn, he remembered that. Trust his school to set a dirge for its first-year pupils to learn, for God's sake. What did that say about the Yorkshire character? And not just a dirge, but the journey of a corpse. A testing. As you sow, so shall you reap. Do as you would be done by. Give away your shoes in this life and you'll be shod for your hike across the thorny moor in the next life. *This ae nighte, this ae nighte, every nighte and alle, fire and fleet and candlelighte, and Christe receive thy saule.* Jackson shivered and turned the heater up.

It seemed he was not alone on the road to nowhere after all. There was someone else ahead, on foot, walking towards him. The sight was so unexpected that for a moment he wondered if it was a kind of mirage brought on by staring for too long at the road, but no, it wasn't a phantom, it was definitely a human being, a woman, even. He slowed down as he approached her. Not a walker or a tourist, she was dressed in a longish cardigan, blouse and skirt, moccasin-type shoes. Her only concession to the weather was a hand-knitted scarf twined casually round her neck. Fortyish, he guessed, brown-to-gray hair in a bob, something of the librarian about her. Did librarians live up to their cliché? Or were they indulging in uninhibited sex behind every stack and carrel? Jackson had not set foot inside a library for some years now.

The walking woman had no distinguishing marks. No dog either. Her hands were thrust into her cardigan pockets. She wasn't walking, she was *strolling*. From nowhere to nowhere. It felt all wrong. He came to a stop and rolled down the window.

As the woman neared the car she gave him a smile and a nod. "Can I give you a lift?" he asked. (*"Don't ever take lifts from strangers, not even if you're lost in the middle of nowhere, not if they say they know your mother, that they have a puppy in the back, that they're a policeman."*)

The woman laughed in a pleasant way—no fear or suspicion—and shook her head. "You're going the wrong way," she said. Local accent. She gestured with her arm in the direction he had just come from and said, "I've not got far to go."

"It looks like snow," Jackson said. Why wasn't she wearing a coat, did they breed them to be more hardy up here? She contemplated the sky for a moment and then said to him, "Oh, no, I don't think so. Don't worry about it," before giving him a kind of half wave and carrying on with her unseasonable saunter. He could hardly pursue her, either on foot or in the car, she would think he was a psycho. She must be heading for a farmhouse that he had missed. Perhaps it was in a dip, or over the brow of a hill. Or invisible. "As we say in this part of the world," he said to the Discovery, "there's nowt so queer as folk."

The day was dimming down and he wondered how dark it would be when the winter sun finally gave up the struggle. Country dark, he supposed. He switched on his lights.

In his rearview mirror, he watched the woman growing smaller and smaller until she disappeared into the gathering dusk. She never looked back. In her shoes, in her librarian moccasins, he would definitely have looked back.

He was a man on the road, a man trying to get home. It was about the destination, not the journey. Everyone was trying to get home. Everyone, everywhere, all the time.

It was dark now. He drove on, just a poor wayfaring stranger. Was he progressing from this world to that which was to come? "You're going the wrong way," she had said. She had meant he was going the wrong way for her. Hadn't she? Or was there a message in her words? A sign? *Was* he going the wrong way? The wrong way for what? The road had to end up somewhere, even if it was where it began. "Don't," he said out loud to himself. "Don't get into that existential crap." (*Yea, though I walk through the valley of the shadow of death.*)

Just when he had decided that they were lost forever in the Twilight Zone, they drove over the brow of a hill and he saw the glittering lights of vehicles on the A1 down below, the lost highway, a great gray artery of logic, helping to speed cars from one known destination to another. Alleluia.

She Would Get the Flowers Herself

She would drive into town and go to Maxwell's in Castle Street and get the florist to put something together for her, something elegant. Blue, for the living room—a flat-backed basket arrangement for the fireplace—would he have delphiniums? Was it too late for delphiniums? Of course, it didn't matter what the season was, florists didn't get their flowers from gardens, they got them from greenhouses in Holland. And Kenya. They grew flowers in Kenya, where there probably wasn't enough drinking water for the people who lived there, let alone for irrigating flowers, and then they flew the flowers over in planes that dumped tons of carbon dioxide into the atmosphere. It was wrong but she needed flowers.

Could you *need* a flower? When they went shopping for her engagement ring in Alistir Tait's in Rose Street, Patrick said to the jeweler, "This beautiful woman needs a big diamond." It sounded corny in retrospect, but it had been charming at the time. Sort of. Patrick chose an old diamond in a new setting, and Louise wondered what poor bugger had dug that out of the heart of darkness a long time ago. Blood on her hands.

Patrick was an orthopedic surgeon and was used to being in charge. "Orthopedics is just hammers and chisels, really, a superior form of joinery," he joked when he first met her, but he was at the top of his field and could probably have been making a fortune in private practice. Instead he spent his time sticking NHS patients back together with pins. ("That's where a boyhood playing with a Meccano set gets you.")

Louise had never liked doctors, nobody who'd been at university with medical students would ever trust a doctor. (Was Joanna Hunter the exception to the rule?) And how did they choose doctors? They took middle-class kids who were good at science subjects and then spent six years teaching them more science and then they let them loose on *people*. People weren't science, people were a mess. "Well, it's one way of looking at it," Patrick laughed.

They had met over an accident, of course. How else did the police meet people? Two years ago, Louise had been on the M8, driving to Glasgow for a meeting with Strathclyde Police, when she saw the crash happen on the opposite carriageway.

She was first on the scene, arriving before the emergency services, but there was nothing she could do. A sixteen-wheeler had smashed into the back of a little three-door sedan, two baby seats crammed in the back, the mother driving, her teenage sister in the passenger seat. The car had been stationary in a queue at temporary traffic lights at some roadwork. The driver hadn't seen the signs for the roadwork, hadn't seen the queue of traffic, and only caught the briefest glimpse of the little three-door sedan before he rammed into it at sixty miles an hour. The truck driver was texting. A classic. Louise arrested him at the scene. She would have liked to kill him at the scene. Or preferably run him over slowly with his own truck. She was beginning to notice that she was more bloodthirsty than she used to be (and that was saying something).

The car and everyone in it was completely crushed. Because she was the smallest, slimmest person at the scene, Louise ("Can you try, boss?") had squeezed a hand through what had once been a window, trying to search for pulses, trying to count bodies, find some

ID. They hadn't even known there were babies in the back until Louise's fingers had brushed against a tiny limp hand. Grown men wept, including the traffic cop who was the family liaison officer, and good old Louise—hard-boiled in vinegar—put an arm round him and said, "Well, Jesus, we're only human," and volunteered to be the one to tell the next of kin, which was, without doubt, the worst job in the world. She seemed to be more fainthearted than she used to be. Bloodthirsty yet fainthearted.

A week later she had attended the funeral. All four of them at once. It had been unbearable but it had to be borne, because that's what people did, they went on. One foot after another, slogging it out day by day. If her own child died, Louise wouldn't keep on going, she would take herself out, something nice and neat, nothing messy for the emergency services to deal with afterwards.

Archie wanted driving lessons for his seventeenth birthday and Patrick said, "Good idea, Archie. If you pass your test, we'll get you a decent secondhand car." Louise, meanwhile, was trying to think of ways of preventing Archie from ever sitting in the driving seat of a vehicle. She wondered if it was possible to gain access to the DVLA computer and put some kind of stop on his provisional license. She was a chief inspector, it shouldn't be beyond her, being police was just the obverse of being criminal, after all.

The driver of the car in front had been badly injured as well, and it had been Patrick who had spent hours in the operating theater putting the man's leg back together. The truck driver, who didn't even have a bruise, was sentenced to three years in jail and was probably out by now. Louise would have removed his organs without anesthetic and given them to more worthy people. Or so she told Patrick afterwards over a nasty cup of coffee in the hospital staff canteen. "Life's random," he said. "The best you can do is pick up the pieces." He wasn't police but it wasn't like marrying out. He understood.

★　　★　　★

He was Irish, which always helped. A man with an Irish accent could sound wise and poetic and interesting even when he wasn't. But Patrick was all of those things. "Between wives at the moment," he said and she had laughed. She hadn't wanted a diamond, big or otherwise, but she'd ended up with one anyway. "You can cash it in when you divorce me," he said. She liked the way he took over in that authoritative way, didn't stand for any of her shit yet was always amiable about it, as if she were precious and yet flawed and the flaws could be fixed. Of course, he was a surgeon, he thought everything could be fixed. Flaws could never be fixed. She was the golden bowl, sooner or later the crack would show. And who would pick up the pieces then?

For the first time in her life she had relinquished control. And what did that do to you? It sent you completely off balance, that's what it did.

Or a centerpiece for the dining-room table. Something smallish, something red. For the red figure in the carpet. Not roses. Red roses said the wrong thing. Louise wasn't sure what they said, but whatever it was, it was wrong.

"Don't try so hard," Patrick laughed.

But she was no good at this stuff, and if she didn't try she would fail. "I can't do relationships," she said, the first morning they woke up in bed together.

"Can't or won't?" he said.

He had broken her in as if she were a high-strung, untamed horse. (But what if he had just broken her?) One step at a time, softly, softly, until she was caught. The taming of the shrew. Shrews were small, harmless furry things, they didn't deserve their bad reputation.

He knew how to do it. He had been happily married for fifteen years before a carload of teenage joyriders overtaking on a bit of single carriageway on the A9 had smashed head-on into his wife's Polo ten years ago. Whoever invented the wheel had a lot to answer for. Samantha. Patrick and Samantha. He hadn't been able to fix *her,* had he?

She still had enough time, time to buy the flowers, time to shop at Waitrose in Morningside, time to cook dinner. Sea bass on a bed of Puy lentils, twice-baked Roquefort soufflés to start, a lemon tart to finish. Why make it easy when you could make it as difficult for yourself as possible? She was a woman, so, technically speaking, she could do anything. The Roquefort soufflés were a Delia Smith recipe. The rise and fall of the bourgeoisie. Ha, ha. Oh, God. What was happening to her, she was turning into a normal person.

She was buzzing with tiredness, that was what was wrong with her. (Why? Why was she so tired?) In a former life, before her beauty was measured in the size of a diamond, she would have wound down with a (very large) drink, ordered in a pizza, taken out her contacts, put her feet up, and watched some rubbish on television, but now here she was, running around like a blue-arsed fly, worrying about delphiniums and cooking Delia recipes. Was there any way back from here?

"We can cancel," Patrick said on the phone. "It's no big deal, you're tired." No big deal to him, maybe, huge deal to her. Patrick's sister and her husband, up from Bournemouth or Eastbourne, somewhere like that. Irish diaspora. They were everywhere, like the Scots.

"They'll be happy with cheese on toast, or we'll get a take-away," Patrick said. He was so damned relaxed about everything. And what would they think if she didn't make an effort? They had missed the wedding, but then everyone missed the wedding. The sister (Bridget) was obviously already put out by the whole wedding thing. "Just the two of us, in a registry office," Louise said to Patrick, when she finally gave in and said yes.

"What about Archie?" Patrick said.

"Does he have to come?"

"Yes, he's your *son, Louise.*" Actually Archie had behaved well, looking after the ring, cheering in a muffled, self-conscious way when Louise said, "I do." Patrick's own son, Jamie, didn't come to the wedding. He was a postgrad on an archaeology dig in the middle of a godforsaken nowhere. He was one of those outdoor types—skiing, surfing, scuba diving—"a real boy," Patrick said. In contrast to her own boy, her little Pinocchio.

They had brought in two people from the next wedding to be witnesses and gave them each a good bottle of malt as a thank-you. Louise had worn a dress of raw silk, in what the personal shopper in Harvey Nichols had referred to as "oyster," although to Louise it just looked gray. But it was pretty without being fussy and it showed off her good legs. Patrick had arranged flowers or she wouldn't have bothered—an old-fashioned posy of pink roses for her and pink rosebuds for the buttonholes for himself and Archie.

A couple of years ago, not long after she met Patrick and when Archie's behavior was at its most worrying, she had gone for therapy, something she had always sworn she would never do. Never say never. She did it for Archie, thinking that his problems must be a result of hers, that if she could be a better mother, his life would improve. And she did it for Patrick too because he seemed to represent a chance for change, to become like other people.

It was cognitive behavioral stuff that didn't delve too deeply into the murk of her psychopathology, thank God. The basic principle was that she should learn to avoid negative thinking, freeing her to have a more positive attitude to life. The therapist, a hippie-ish, well-intentioned woman called Jenny who looked as if she'd knitted herself, told Louise to visualize a place where she could put all her negative thoughts and Louise had chosen a chest at the bottom of the sea, the kind that was beloved of pirates in storybooks—hooped and banded with metal, padlocked and hasped to keep safe, not treasure, but Louise's unhelpful thoughts.

The more detailed the better, Jenny said, and so Louise added coral and shells to the gritty sand, barnacles clinging to the sides of the chest, curious fishes and sharks nosing it, lobsters and crabs crawling all over it, fronds of seaweed waving in the tidal currents. She became an adept with the locks and the keys, could visit her underwater world at the flick of a mental switch. The problem was that when she had safely locked up all the negative thoughts at the bottom of the sea, there was nothing else left, no positive thoughts at all. "Guess I'm just not a positive person," she said to Jenny. She thought Jenny would protest, pull her to her maternal, knitted bosom and tell her it was just a matter of time (and money) before she was fixed. But Jenny agreed with her and said, "I guess not."

She stopped going to Jenny and not long after she accepted Patrick's proposal.

Archie went to Fettes now. Two years ago, at the age of fourteen, he had been on the edge of something bad. It had only been some petty thieving, some bunking off school, trouble with the police (oh, the irony), but she could tell, because she'd seen it enough times in other teenagers, that if it weren't nipped in the bud, it wouldn't be just a phase, it would be a way of life. He was ready for a change or it wouldn't have worked. She used her mother's life insurance to pay his exorbitant school fees ("So the drunken old cow's good for something at last," Louise said.). The school was the kind of place that Louise had spent her red-flagged life railing against—privilege, the perpetuation of the ruling hegemony, yada, yada, yada. And now she was subscribing to it because the greater good wasn't an argument she was going to deploy when it came to her own flesh and blood. "What about your principles?" someone said to her, and she said, "Archie is my principles."

The gamble had paid off. Two years later and he had gone from Gothic to geek (his true métier all along) in one relatively easy move and now hung about with his geek confrères in the astronomy club, the chess club, the computer club, and God knew what other activities that seemed entirely alien to Louise. Louise had an MA in literature, and she was sure that if she'd had a daughter, they would have had great chats about the Brontës and George Eliot. (While what? They baked cakes and did each other's makeup? Get real, Louise.)

"It's not too late," Patrick said.

"For what?"

"A baby."

A chill went through her. Someone had opened a door into her heart and let in the north wind. Did he want a baby? She couldn't ask him in case he said yes. Was he going to seduce her into it, like he'd seduced her into marriage? She already had a child, a child who was wrapped around her heart, and she couldn't walk on that wild shore again.

All her life she had been fighting. "Time to stop," Patrick said, massaging her shoulders after a particularly grueling day at work. "Lay down your arms and surrender, take things how they come."

"You should have been a Zen master," she said.

"I am."

She hadn't expected ever to hit forty and suddenly find herself in a two-car family, to be living in an expensive flat, to be wearing a rock the size of Gibraltar. Most people would see this as a goal or an improvement but Louise felt as if she might have taken the wrong road without even noticing the turning. Sometimes, in her more paranoid moments, she wondered if Patrick had somehow managed to hypnotize her.

She had changed their insurance policy when they moved, and the woman on the other end of the phone went through all the standard questions — age of the building, how many rooms, is there an alarm system in place — before asking, "Do you keep any jewels, furs, or shotguns on the premises?" and for a moment Louise felt an unexpected thrill at the idea of a life containing those elements. (She'd made a start — she had the jewel.) She had clearly missed her way, parceled everything up nice and neat, settled down, when the real Louise wanted to be out there somewhere, living the outlaw life, wearing jewels and furs, toting a gun. Even the idea of furs didn't worry her that much. She could shoot something and skin it and eat it. Better than the unfeeling distance between the abattoir and the soft, pale packages at the Waitrose meat counter.

"No," she said to the woman at the insurance company, returning to sobriety, "only my engagement ring." Twenty thousand pounds' worth of secondhand bling. Sell it and run, Louise. Run fast. Joanna Hunter had been a runner (was she still?), a university athletics champion. She had run once and it had saved her life, perhaps she had made sure that no one was ever going to catch her. Louise had read the notice board hanging in the Hunters' kitchen, the little everyday trophies and mementoes of a life—postcards, certificates, photographs, messages. Nothing, of course, about the event that must have shaped her entire existence; murder wasn't something you tended to pin up on your kitchen corkboard. Alison Needler, on the other hand, didn't run. She hid.

Louise hardly saw Archie now. He had elected to board during the week because he would rather live in a school than with his mother. On weekends he sought out the same boys he spent all week at school with.

"Stop fretting," Patrick said. "He's sixteen, he's spreading his wings."

Louise thought of Icarus.

"And learning to fly."

Louise thought of the dead bird she had found outside the flat on the weekend. A bad omen. Little cock sparrow shot by a boy with a bow and arrow.

"He has to grow up."

"I don't see why."

"*Louise,*" Patrick said gently, "Archie's happy."

"Happy?" *Happy* wasn't a word she had employed in the context of Archie since he was a little boy. How wonderfully, joyously untrammeled he had been then in his happiness. She thought it was fixed forever, didn't realize that childhood happiness dissolves away, because she herself had never known happiness as a child. If she had realized that Archie wasn't going to be that sunny innocent forever, she would have laid up every moment as treasure. Then she could have it again if she wanted. The north wind howled. She shut the door.

She was on her way back from a meeting with the Amethyst team out at the Gyle. That was how Louise first came across Alison Needler, six months before the murders, when she was seconded for a few months to Amethyst, the Family Protection Unit. David Needler, defying the court injunction against him, had taken up a position on the family lawn in Trinity, where he was threatening to set himself alight with his kids and ex-wife watching from an upstairs window. When Louise arrived, hot on the heels of the Instant Response Vehicle, he was being berated by Alison's sister Debbie, standing on the front doorstep. ("Lippy, our Debs," according to Alison. Well, she paid the price for that, didn't she?) Taunted, perhaps, rather than berated (*"Go on then, you bastard, let's see you torch yourself."*).

In court the next day, David Needler had been cautioned and told to obey the injunction and stay away from his family, which he did, until he came back six months later with a shotgun.

Louise pulled into the car park at Howdenhall. Check in at the station, pick up her own car, back on the road in five minutes. She had plenty of time.

Final report's back from Forensics, boss," her baby DC, Marcus McLellen, said to her, handing her a folder. "As was anticipated, the amusement-arcade fire was definitely willful fire-raising."

Twenty-six years old, Marcus had a BA in media studies from

Stirling (who didn't?) and a head of hair that would have given Shirley Temple a run for her money if he had allowed it to grow instead of sensibly shearing it into astrakhan. He was a rugby player, and Louise had once shivered in freezing-cold stands on a Saturday morning, shouting herself hoarse in support of him (a great outlet for aggression, she discovered), which was something she had never been able to do for weedy, sports-phobic Archie.

Marcus's baptism of fire after coming from uniform had been the Needler case, and he'd handled it even better than she'd expected. He was a sweet boy, downright cherubic, straight as a Roman road, tougher than he looked, and always cheerful. Like Patrick. Where did it come from, this cheerfulness? Did they imbibe it with their mother's milk? (Poor Archie, then.)

She had taken Marcus under her wing, a mother hen. Louise had never felt maternal towards anyone she had worked with before, and it was an unsettling experience. It must be age, she concluded. But *Marcus?* — a strangely Latinate name for someone born in Sighthill. ("Aspirational mother, boss," he said. "Better than Titus. Or Sextus.") He had been razor-keen on the Needler case, but she had taken him off it and put him on something else. "So you can get more experience," she told him but really she just didn't want him to end up as obsessed with Alison Needler as she was. So now he was working on an amusement arcade in Bread Street that had mysteriously gone up in flames a couple of weeks ago.

"Insurance?" Louise speculated. "Or malicious? Or just neds messing about with matches?"

Willful fire-raising, a baroque Scottish term for arson, the chief suspect for which, in Louise's book, was always going to be the owner of the property. Insurance money was just too tempting a prospect when you were needing money. Twenty thousand for a diamond, how much for an amusement arcade? An amusement arcade owned by none other than the lovely Dr. Joanna Hunter's husband, Neil. ("And what does Mr. Hunter do?" she had said conversationally to Joanna Hunter when she visited her yesterday. "Oh, this and that," Joanna Hunter said lightly. "Neil's always looking for the next big opportunity, he's a natural-born entrepreneur.") Just what the lovely Dr. Hunter was doing being married to someone with business interests in the pubic triangle (as it was known) of Bread Street, with its strip joints, dodgy pubs, and show bars, was anyone's guess. Shouldn't she be married to somebody more respectable — an orthopedic surgeon, for example?

According to his wife, Neil Hunter was in "the leisure industry," a term that seemed to cover a lot of possibilities. In his case it seemed to be two or three amusement arcades, a couple of health clubs (not particularly upmarket), and a small fleet of private-hire vehicles (tired-looking four-door sedans masquerading as "executive cars") and a couple of beauticians, one in Leith, one in Sighthill, that looked like health hazards — Louise was pretty sure that Joanna Hunter had never had a facial in one of them, the Sheraton One Spa they weren't.

"Fill me in on our Mr. Hunter."

"Well, when he first came to Edinburgh," Marcus said, "he started with a burger van parked in Bristo Square. That way he caught the students as well as the pubs coming out."

"Burger van. Classy."

"Which burned to the ground in the wee small hours when it was unattended."

"Well, there's a coincidence."

"Moved on to a wine bar, a café, a food-delivery service, anything he could try his hand at, really."

"Any of them catch fire?"

"The café, actually. An electrical fault."

"And the arcade?"

"A lot of petrol splashed around inside," Marcus said. "Not a spur-of-the-moment thing. Door was broken into at the back, all the alarms were on, but by the time the fire brigade arrived at the scene, the place was well alight."

"And the word on the pavement on Mr. Hunter these days?"

"Word is he's clean," Marcus said. "Bit of a rogue, but to all intents and purposes, a legitimate businessman."

"So it's just the people he associates with who are dodgy?"

She had already seen the photos that the Fraud squad had sent over, nice crisp images of Hunter sharing a variety of beverages over the weeks with one Michael Anderson from Glasgow, plus various hangers-on. "His retinue," Marcus said. "Look at these guys, faces only a mother could love." Anderson was suspected of drug dealing in his hometown but was so far up the food chain in his luxury penthouse that Strathclyde Police had found it hard to hang anything on him. "Good lawyers," Marcus said.

"Or bad lawyers, depending on how you look at it."

The Fraud officers thought that Anderson had run out of ways to clean his money in Glasgow and was looking to Edinburgh, to utilize a bit of Neil Hunter's "this and that," as his lovely wife would have it. Dr. Hunter wore the word *wife* so much better than Louise did.

"How did you two meet?" Louise had asked her yesterday, pretending to be the kind of woman who was interested in romantic anecdotes, who listened to Steve Wright's *Sunday Love Songs* while making breakfast in bed for her husband, and not some hard-nosed cow who was probably about to send a report about your husband to the procurator fiscal, who would then probably order his arrest. Joanna Hunter laughed and said, "I treated him in Accident and Emergency, he asked me out to dinner."

"And you *went?*" Louise couldn't quite keep the incredulity out of her voice.

"No, highly unethical." Joanna Hunter laughed again as if the memory were part of some long-treasured amusing story *(How I met your father)*. "He persisted," she said, "and eventually I gave in."

Me too, Louise thought but instead said, "My mother and father met on holiday," and Joanna Hunter said, "Ah, a holiday romance!" and Louise didn't say, Actually, he picked her up in a bar on Gran Canaria and she never could remember his name, which hardly mattered as he wasn't the only contender for the coveted role of totally absent father to Louise.

"Why was Mr. Hunter in A and E?" Louise asked.

"He'd been set upon by some thugs."

Accident-prone, keeping bad company, all the signs there at the beginning. Why on earth would the lovely doctor go out with someone like that?

"I liked his energy," she offered, unprompted. Dogs are energetic, Louise thought and smiled and said, "Yes, that's what my mother said about my father."

She didn't mention the arcade fire to Joanna Hunter, it seemed impolite given the nature of the news she had brought to her doorstep.

"Call me Jo," she said.

There's nothing concrete to link Hunter to any of the Glaswegian guys," Louise said to Marcus. "Maybe Anderson and Hunter were wee pals at primary school."

"Well, word on the pavey also says Hunter's on the edge of going under," Marcus said. "Has been for a while. Going into business with Anderson might be one way of keeping afloat, but then so might the insurance payout from a big fire."

"I'll talk to him," Louise said, picking up the file.

"Boss?"

"What? Not my job, me being such a high big wig? He lives round the corner from me. I'll pop in on my way to work tomorrow morning." She didn't say, *"I'm reading my way through his father-in-law's canon."* Certainly didn't say, *"I'm fascinated by Joanna Hunter, she's the other side of me, the woman I never became— the good survivor, the good wife, the good mother."* "Let's apply to the procurator fiscal for a warrant to get our hands on Hunter's documentation."

"Yes, boss." He looked disappointed at having the case snatched literally from under his nose.

"I'll just talk to him," Louise soothed, "and then you can have him back. I have a bit of a connection, I had to go and see his wife yesterday, that's all."

"His wife?"

"Joanna."

DS Karen Warner came through the open door to Louise's office and dropped a pile of files on her desk. "Yours, I think," she said, resting her weight against the desk. A walking filing cabinet, eight months pregnant with her first baby and still at work. ("Going down fighting, boss.") She was older than Louise (*"Elderly primigravidas*— how disgusting does that sound?"). Motherhood was going to be a shock to her, Louise thought. She was going to hit the wall at sixty miles an hour and wonder what happened.

Karen was still on the Needler team, halved in size now from what it had been six urgent months ago, moved back now from St. Leonard's to Howdenhall and occupying a smaller incident room. Louise's superintendent had suggested it was time for her to "move on a little" from the Needler case, to start taking on other cases. "You're obsessed with Alison Needler," he said.

"Yeah," she agreed cheerfully. "I am. It's my job to be obsessed."

Karen unwrapped a Snickers bar and bit into it, patting her stomach. "License to eat," she said to Louise. "Want a bit?"

"No, thanks."

Louise was starving, but there wasn't anything she fancied. Marriage seemed to have affected her normally good appetite. Patrick seemed to grow healthier on it, while she was fading away. She had flirted briefly with bulimia in her teens, between the self-cutting and an early bout of binge drinking (Bacardi and Coke, the thought of it now made her want to throw up), but all those things felt like an addiction of one kind or another, so she had stopped. Only room for one addict in the family, and her mother had had no intention of giving up her place.

Karen looked at the report on Louise's desk. "Same Hunter?" she said. "Neil Hunter is Joanna Hunter's husband? Wow. There's a coincidence."

"Is Joanna Hunter a name I should know?" Marcus asked Louise.

"The one that got away," Karen said. "Gabrielle Mason, three kids? Thirty years ago?"

Marcus shook his head.

"Sweet. You're so young," Karen said. "A guy killed the mother and two of her kids in a field in Devon, Joanna ran away and hid and was found later unharmed. Joanna Hunter née Mason."

"The man who was convicted of her murder was called Andrew Decker," Louise said. "He was declared fit to plead. If stabbing a mother and her two children is sane, then what's the definition of insane? Makes you wonder, doesn't it? And now he's getting out—is out, in fact—and someone's leaked it. It's going to be all over the news for at least, I dunno, two hours. Feeding the empty maw of the press. I went yesterday to warn her."

Karen crumpled up the Snickers wrapper and threw it in the bin. "And is she still a victim, boss?"

"Good question," Louise said.

Too late now to go to Maxwell's, she could pick up some flowers at Waitrose. She still had enough time. Just. She got into her own car, a silver 3 Series BMW that was a lot more stylish than Patrick's über-sensible Ford Focus. He was straight as a die, right down to the car he drove.

And then her phone rang. For a beat she thought about not answering it. Her instinct, her police sixth sense, told her—yelled loudly at her—that if she answered, there would be no sea bass, no twice-baked soufflés.

She answered on the third ring, "Hello?"

Sanctuary

Sadie's ears pricked up. The dog always heard Dr. Hunter's car long before Reggie did. The dog's excitement was expressed in the merest quiver of her tail but Reggie knew that if she touched her, she would find Sadie's entire body was electric with anticipation. The baby too. When he caught sight of Dr. Hunter coming into the kitchen, Reggie could feel the thrill go through his solid torso as he prepared to catapult himself into the air, his little, fat arms reaching out towards his mother.

"Whoa there, cowboy, steady on," Dr. Hunter laughed, catching him in her arms and giving him a big hug. Dr. Hunter had brought in a blast of icy air with her. She was carrying, as usual, her expensive Mulberry bag *("The Bayswater—isn't it handsome, Reggie?")* that Mr. Hunter had given her for her birthday in September and, draped over her arm, one of her black suits encased in a dry-cleaning bag. She had three identical suits that she rotated—one she wore, one in the wardrobe, one in the dry cleaners.

"Quelle horreur," she said, shivering theatrically. "Talk about the bleak midwinter. It's freezing out there."

"Baltic," Reggie agreed.

"The north wind doth blow and we shall have snow, and what will poor robin do then, poor thing?"

"I expect he'll sit in a barn and keep himself warm, and hide his head under his wing, poor thing, Dr. H."

"Has everything been all right here, Reggie?"

"Totally, Dr. H."

"How's my treasure?" Dr. Hunter asked, nuzzling the baby's neck ("He's edible, don't you think?"), and Reggie felt something seize in her heart, a little convulsion of pain, and she wasn't sure why exactly except that she thought it was sad (very sad, indeed) that no one could remember being a baby. What Reggie wouldn't have given to be a baby, wrapped in Mum's arms again. Or Dr. Hunter's arms, for that matter. Anyone's arms, really. Not Billy's, obviously.

"It's so sad he won't remember this," she said to Dr. Hunter. (Was Dr. Hunter's sadness catching in some way?)

"Sometimes it's good to forget," Dr. Hunter said. " 'As I went to Bonner, I met a pig without a wig, upon my word and honor.' "

Reggie's mother had been a hugger and kisser. Before Gary, and before the Man-Who-Came-Before-Gary, they would sit on the sofa in the evenings, cuddled up, watching television, eating crisps or a takeaway. Reggie liked to put her arm round Mum's waist and feel the comfortable roll of fat that girdled her middle and her squashy tummy. ("My jelly belly," she used to call it.) That was it—Reggie's fondest memories were of watching *ER* and eating a chicken chow mein and feeling her mother's spare tire. It was a bit crap, really, if you thought about it. You would hope two lives entwined would add up to more. Reggie imagined that Dr. Hunter and her son would make amazing memories for themselves, they would canoe down the Amazon and climb up the Alps and go to the opera in Covent Garden and see Shakespeare at Stratford and spend spring in Paris and New Year's in Vienna, and Dr. Hunter wouldn't leave behind an album of photos in which she didn't look anything like herself. It was funny to think of the baby growing up into a boy and then a man. He was just a baby.

"My own little prince," cooed Dr. Hunter to the baby.

"We're all kings and queens, Dr. H.," Reggie said.

Is Neil home yet?"

"Mr. Hunter? No."

"He's babysitting, I hope he hasn't forgotten. I'm going to Jenners with Sheila, it's their Christmas shopping night. You know — free glass of wine, mince pie, people singing carols, all that kind of thing. Why don't you come, Reggie? Oh, no, I forgot, it's Wednesday, isn't it? You have to go to your friend's."

"Ms. MacDonald isn't really my friend," Reggie said. "Perish the thought."

Dr. Hunter, with the baby in her arms, always saw Reggie off on the doorstep and watched her walk down the drive. Dr. Hunter was trying to teach the baby to wave good-bye and moved his arm from side to side as if he were a ventriloquist's dummy, all the time saying (to the baby rather than Reggie), "Bye-bye, Reggie, bye-bye." Sadie, sitting at Dr. Hunter's side, drummed her own farewells with her tail on the tiled floor of the porch.

After her mother died, Reggie had tried hard to remember the last moments they had shared. Between them, with no help from the taxi driver, they had heaved her enormous, ugly suitcase into the cab, a suitcase that was stuffed with cheap, skimpy tops and thin cotton trousers and the embarrassingly revealing swimming costume in a horrible orange Lycra that would turn out to be the last outfit she ever wore, unless you counted the shroud she was buried in (because there was nothing in her wardrobe that seemed suitable for eternity).

Reggie couldn't remember the expression on her mother's face as she left on holiday, although she supposed it must have been hopeful. Nor could she remember the last words Mum spoke, although they must, surely, have included "good-bye." "Back soon" was her usual farewell. *Je reviens.* Reggie saw it as the first half of something that had never been completed. She had expected the second half to conclude with everything happening the same, only in reverse, *vale atque ave.* Mum at the airport, Mum on the plane, Mum landing in Edinburgh, getting in a taxi, arriving at the front door, stepping out of the taxi—browner and probably plumper—and saying, "Hello." But it had never happened. *Back soon,* a promise never fulfilled. Her last words, and they were a lie.

Reggie remembered waving as the taxi pulled away from the curb, but had her mother turned back to wave at her or had she been fussing still with her suitcase? The memory was murky, half made-up, with the missing bits filled in. Really, every time a person said good-bye to another person, they should pay attention, just in case it was the last time. First things were good, last things not so much so.

Dr. Hunter was framed in the porch, like a portrait, the baby reaching for her hair, the dog gazing up at her in devotion. Beneath her suit she was wearing a white T-shirt. She had on her usual low-heeled black pumps and sheer tights and a thin strand of pearls round her neck, with matching pearl studs in her ears. And the baby, Reggie could see him too, in his little matelot suit, his thumb corking his mouth, clutching his scrap of green blanket in the same hand that he was strap-hanging onto Dr. Hunter's hair with.

And then Dr. Hunter turned away and went into the house.

Reggie was standing at the bus stop, reading *Great Expectations,* when she felt a hand grip the back of her neck, and before she could even get a scream going, something jabbed hard into her lower back and a voice in her ear whispered, menacingly, "Don't make a sound, I've got a gun."

"Aye, right," Reggie whispered back. She groped behind her back before finally grabbing onto the "weapon." "A tube of Trebor *mints?*" Reggie said sarcastically. "Ooh, I'm so scared."

"Extra strong," Billy said with a smirky kind of grin.

"Ha-fucking-ha." Reggie never swore in Dr. Hunter's house. Both Reggie and Dr. Hunter (who said she "used to swear like a trooper," something Reggie found difficult to believe) used harmless substitutes, impromptu nonsense — sugar, fizz, winkle, cups and saucers — but the sight of Reggie's brother merited more than a "Jings and help me, Bob." Reggie sighed. If Mum had been able to have any last words for Reggie, she was pretty sure they would have been, "Look after your brother." Reggie could remember when they were both little and Billy was still her hero and defender, someone she looked up to and relied on, someone who looked after *her*. She couldn't betray her memories of Billy, even though Billy himself betrayed them every day.

Billy was nineteen, three years older than Reggie, so although he didn't really remember their father, he did at least have photographs of himself with him to prove that they had both existed on the planet at the same time. In most of those photos Billy was holding something from his toy arsenal — plastic sword, space gun, bow and arrows. When he was older, it was air guns and pocketknives. God knows what he was into now, rocket launchers, probably.

Reggie supposed he got his love of weapons from their father. Mum had some faded photographs of her soldier husband with his comrades in the desert, all of them holding their big rifles. He had smuggled home a "souvenir" when he was on leave, a big, ugly Russian handgun that Mum had kept in a box on the top shelf of her closet in the absurd belief that Billy wouldn't find it. She couldn't think how to get rid of it ("You can hardly put it out with the bins, a bairn might find it."), and she couldn't hand it in to the police either, for such a law-abiding person, Mum had something of an aversion to the police, not just because they were always chapping at the door about Billy but because she was from Blairgowrie, a country girl, and her father had been a bit of a poacher apparently.

It was no coincidence that Billy and the gun left home on the same day. "Makarov," he said proudly, waving it around and scaring the life out of Reggie. "Don't tell Mum."

"Jesus, Billy, we're not living in the Wild West," Reggie said, and he said, "Yes, we are." Really, you wondered why he didn't just join the army himself, then he could get his hands on all the weapons he wanted. Money for something and the guns for free.

Billy in such close proximity to Dr. Hunter's house made her uncomfortable. He had turned up at Ms. MacDonald's house in Musselburgh a couple of times, offering to give her a lift home. (He always had a car. Always a different one.) Ms. MacDonald invited him in but only because she wanted to press religion on him and get him to fix a block in a U-shaped pipe. Billy was *so* not the person to ask to do DIY, even though a lot of its accoutrements (new word) would have appealed to him—hammers, Stanley knives, power drills—but not in a good way. It was funny because in another life, on another path, he would have been talented at that kind of thing. He was really good with his hands when he was still a boy. Before he went all wrong, he would spend forever meticulously gluing bits of scale models together, and his woodwork teacher said he had a future as a joiner if he wanted. That was before he drilled holes in all the workbenches and sawed the teacher's desk in half.

Anyone who could convert Billy these days would have to be a real miracle worker. He had been an embarrassment to Reggie, strutting around Ms. MacDonald's cluttered house, running his fingers over the dusty books as if he were a person who knew something about cleanliness, which he most certainly wasn't. Reggie hadn't liked the sly look on her brother's face, she recognized it all too well. When he was little it meant mischief, now that he was bigger it meant trouble.

Reggie worried that one day Billy would drive by Dr. Hunter's house and offer Reggie a lift home and she would have to introduce him to Dr. Hunter. She could just imagine how his pinched, ferrety features would light up at the sight of all the lovely things in the Hunters' home. Or, even worse, that he would react in the same way to Dr. Hunter herself. Reggie thought she would have to deny him. *("He's not my brother. I don't know who he is.")* "Flesh and blood," she could hear Mum saying. Rotten flesh.

"What are you doing here, Billy?"

"This and that," he shrugged. (That was Billy, this and that, something and nothing.) "It's a free country, isn't it? Last time I checked, I didn't need a passport for southwest Edinburgh."

"I don't trust you, Billy."

"Whatever."

"Quidquid." Ha.

"What?"

When the bus came, Billy made a performance of helping her onto it as if he were a footman helping a princess into a carriage, doffing an imaginary hat and saying, "See ya, wouldn't wanna be ya," before strolling off up the street.

Hark! Hark! The dogs do bark, the beggars are coming to town.

To Brig o' Dread Thou Com'st at Last

Jackson eventually found himself crammed into a late-running and oversubscribed cattle truck of a train that buzzed and hummed with exhaustion. The buffet couldn't make hot drinks, and the heating had failed, so some people looked as if they might soon be dying from hypothermia. Bags and suitcases blocked the aisles, and anyone wanting to move about the carriage had to perform a slow-motion hurdle race. This obstacle course didn't prevent several small children, feral with sugar and boredom, from screaming up and down the aisle. It felt like a train returning from a war, one that had been lost, not won. There were, in fact, a couple of burned-out squaddies in desert camouflage fatigues squatting on their rucksacks between the carriages. That had been Jackson once, in another lifetime.

When Jackson left the army, he swore he would not do what so many had done before and go into security. Half the squaddies who had served under him could be found at the grunt end of the business — in black overcoats, shivering outside the doors of pubs and clubs. So he joined the Cambridgeshire Constabulary, he'd been a Class One Warrant Officer in the military police and it felt like a natural move. When he left the police, he swore he wouldn't do what so many had done before and go into security—Marks & Spencer security guards, Tesco store detectives—half of them were guys he'd served with in the force. He left the police with the rank of detective inspector, which seemed a good basis for setting himself up in a one-man private agency, and he didn't need to swear anything when he gave that up, thanks to an elderly client who left him a legacy in her will.

Now, ironically, if people asked him what he did, he said, "Security," in a cryptic don't-ask-me-anything-else tone of voice that he'd learned in the army and perfected in the police. In Jackson's long experience, *security* covered a multitude of sins, but actually it was pretty straightforward—he had a card in his wallet that said "Jackson Brodie—Security Consultant" (*consultant,* now there was a word that covered an even greater multitude of sins). He didn't need the money, he needed the self-respect. A man couldn't lie idle. Working for Bernie might not be a righteous cause (in his heart Jackson was a crusader, not a pilgrim), but it was better than kicking his heels at home all day long.

And being in security was better than saying, "I live off an old woman's money," because, of course, the money that his client had left him in her will had in no way been deserved and it hung as heavily on him as if he carried it in a sack on his back. He owned a money tree, it seemed; having invested most of the two million, his returns grew incrementally all the time. (It was true what they said, money made money.)

What's more, he'd managed, more or less, to keep to the ethical side of the street. Jackson reckoned there was enough misery in the world without it being funded by him, although he had such a big spread of alternative-energy portfolios that when the oil ran out, he was going to profit from the end of the-world-as-we-know-it. "Like Midas," Julia said. "Everything you touch turns to gold."

In his previous life, when bad luck dogged his heels like a faithful hound and when everything he touched turned to shit, he had barely made the mortgage each month and the occasional lottery ticket was the only investment he made. And you could be sure that if he had put money into stocks and shares (laughably unlikely), the global market would have collapsed the next day. Now he couldn't give the stuff away. Well, no, that wasn't strictly true, but Jackson wasn't quite ready to go all Zen and divest himself of his worldly assets. ("Then quit whining," his ex-wife said.)

Jackson had managed to get an uncomfortable seat at a table for four, near the end of the carriage. Next to him, at the window, was a man in a tired suit, intent on his laptop. Jackson expected the screen to be full of tables and statistics, but instead there were screeds of words. Jackson looked away; numbers were impersonal things to cast an eye over, but another man's words had an intimacy about them. The man's tie was loosened and he gave off a faint smell of beer and perspiration as if he'd been away from home too long. There were two women seated on the other side of the table: one was old and armed with a Catherine Cookson novel; the other, leafing indifferently through a celebrity magazine, was a fortyish blonde, buxom as an overstuffed turkey. She was wearing siren-red lipstick and a top to match that was half a size too tight and that burned like a signal fire in front of Jackson's eyes. Jackson was surprised she didn't have "Up for It" tattooed on her forehead. The old woman looked blue with cold, despite wearing a hat, gloves, and scarf and a heavy winter coat. Jackson was glad of the North Face jacket that he'd donned as part of his disguise and then felt guilty and offered it to the old woman. She smiled and shook her head as if someone long ago had warned her not to speak to strangers on trains.

The suit next to him coughed, an unhealthy, phlegmy noise, and Jackson wondered if he should offer up his jacket to him as well. Strangers on a train. If there was an emergency, would they help one another? (Never overestimate people.) Or would it be every woman for herself? That was the way to survive in a plane or a train, you had to ignore everyone and everything, get out at any cost, gnaw off a limb—someone else's if necessary—climb over seats, climb over people, forget anything your mother ever taught you about manners, because the people who got to the exit were the people who, literally, lived to tell the tale.

The aftermath of a bad train crash was like a battlefield. Jackson knew, he'd attended one at the beginning of his career in the civilian police and it had been worse than anything he'd seen in the army. There'd been a small child trapped in the wreckage. They could hear it calling for its mother, but they couldn't even begin to get to it beneath the tons of train.

After a while the crying stopped, but it continued in Jackson's dreams for months afterwards. The child—a boy—was eventually rescued, but strangely, that didn't mollify the horror of recalling his sobs ("Mummy, Mummy"). Of course, this was not long after Jackson himself had become a parent to Marlee, a condition that had left him torn and raw and completely at odds with his prenatal preoccupations, which had mainly revolved around choosing a pram—with the kind of masculine attention to specs that he would normally have afforded a car (lockable front swivel wheels? adjustable handle height? multiposition seat?). The mechanics of fatherhood turned out to be infinitely more primitive. He fingered the plastic bag in his pocket. A different pregnancy, a different child. His. He remembered the surge of emotion he had felt earlier in the day when he had touched Nathan's small head. Love. Love wasn't sweet and light, it was visceral and overpowering. Love wasn't patient, love wasn't kind. Love was ferocious, love knew how to play dirty.

He hadn't seen Julia in her later stages. Short and sexy, in pregnancy she would be ripely voluptuous, he imagined, although she told him that she had piles and varicose veins and was "almost

spherical." They had maintained a low-grade kind of communica-
tion with each other; he phoned her and she told him to sod off,
but sometimes they spoke as though nothing had ever come between them. Yet still she maintained the baby wasn't his.

He had visited her in the hospital afterwards. Walking into the
six-berth maternity ward, he had taken a blow to the heart when
he caught sight of her with the baby cradled in her arms. She was
propped up on pillows with her wild hair loose about her shoulders, looking for all the world like a madonna—this vision spoiled
only by the interloper, Mr. Arty-Farty photographer, lying next to
her on the bed, gazing adoringly at the baby.

"Well, look at this—the unholy family," Jackson said (because
he couldn't help himself—the story of his life where shooting off
his mouth to his women was concerned).

"Go away, Jackson," Julia said placidly. "You know this isn't a
good idea." Mr. Arty-Farty, a little more proactive, said, "Get out of
here or I'll deck you."

"Fat chance of that, you big pansy," Jackson said (because he
couldn't help himself). The guy was pampered and unfit. Jackson
liked to think that he could have taken him out with one punch.

"The better part of valor is discretion, Jackson," Julia said, a
warning note creeping into her voice. Trust Julia to be *quoting* at
a time like this. She put her little finger in the baby's mouth and
smiled down at him. A world apart. Jackson had never seen her
so happy and he might have turned on his heel and left, out of
deference to Julia's newfound redemption, but Mr. Arty-Farty (his
name was actually Jonathan Carr) said, "There's nothing for you
here, Brodie," as if he owned this nativity scene, and Jackson felt
himself go so beyond reason that he would have beaten the guy
up right there on the floor of the ward, with nursing mothers and
newborn babies for an audience, if Julia's baby (his baby) hadn't
started crying and shamed him into retreat. Jackson had the grace
to be mortified by this memory.

And now the two of them, soft southerners to the core, were living in his homeland, his heartland, while every day he walked a step further away. And Julia living a country life as a country wife beggared belief. He could believe in a billion angels dancing on a pinhead more readily than he could believe in Julia cooking on an Aga. Yes, okay, the Dales weren't part of his heritage of dirt and industrial decay, but they were within the boundaries of God's own county, which was also Jackson's own county, flowing in the stream of his blood, laid down in the limestone of his bones even though neither of his parents was born here. Was it in his son's DNA, carried now in Jackson's pocket? The blueprint of his child. A chain of molecules, a chain of evidence. There would be traces of his sister in that single hair. Niamh, killed so long ago now that she existed more as a story than a person, a tale to be told, *My sister was murdered when she was eighteen.*

He took his BlackBerry out and put it on the table in front of him. He was half expecting a text message. *Arrived safely.* As none came, he texted, *Miss you, Jx.* That passed a minute or two. He left the phone out so that he could see if he received a reply.

The old woman opposite sighed and closed her eyes as if the book she was reading had quite worn her out. The woman in red — neither lady nor librarian but a good old-fashioned tart (rather like Julia) — could have been the same age as his strolling woman. Where was she now? Still walking up hill and down dale? The suit took out a battered-looking packet of cheese and onion crisps from his briefcase and in a rather reluctant act of camaraderie silently offered them around.

The women refused but Jackson took a handful. He was starving, and his chances of getting to the buffet car were minimal, given the crush in the carriages. *If ever thou gavest meat or drink, the fire sall never make thee shrink. If meat or drink thou ne'er gav'st nane, the fire will burn thee to the bare bane.* That damned dirge. Had the suit bought his way into heaven with a packet of cheese and onion crisps? Jackson should have insisted that the old woman take his North Face jacket; otherwise he might find himself shivering his way through the fires of hell.

The crisps tasted unnatural and made him thirsty. There was a throbbing behind his eyes. He wanted to be home.

It was black outside the carriage window, not even a pinprick of light from a house, and rain lashed incessantly on the glass. It was deeply inhospitable out there. Where were they? He guessed somewhere in the no-man's-land between York and Doncaster. Closer to his birthplace. His birthright gone, sold off with the family silver in the eighties by That Woman.

Had they even stopped at York yet? If they had, he hadn't noticed. He had a feeling he might have dozed off for a while.

He found himself thinking about Louise. They hadn't really kept in touch, just the occasional text from her when he suspected she was drunk. There'd never been anything between them, at least nothing that was ever spoken. Their relationship in Edinburgh two years ago could have been described as a professional one if you were playing fast and loose with the dictionary. They had never kissed, never touched, although Jackson was pretty sure she had thought about it. He certainly had. A lot.

Then, a couple of months ago, she announced that she was getting married, an event that seemed so unlikely (if not absurd) that he suspected she was joking. He had thought at one point that he might feature in her future, and the next thing he knew he had been drop-kicked into her past. They were two people who had missed each other, sailed right past in the night and into different harbors. The one that got away. He was sorry. He wished her well. Sort of.

How ironic that both Julia and Louise, the two women he'd felt closest to in his recent past, had both unexpectedly got married, and neither of them to him.

★   ★   ★

They passed through a station at speed, and Jackson struggled and failed to read the name.

"Where was that?" he asked the woman in red.

"I didn't see, sorry." She took out a mirror from her handbag and reapplied her lipstick, stretching her mouth and then baring her teeth to check for any smears. Jackson's suited neighbor tensed briefly and paused in his incessant typing, staring sightlessly at the laptop screen, not daring to look at the woman, but not quite able to keep his eyes away from her either. Some animal instinct briefly flared and flickered inside his suit, but then it must have burned itself out, because he slumped a little and returned to the tap-tap-tapping on his keyboard.

The woman in red ran her tongue over her lips and smiled at Jackson. He wondered if she was going to give him a tangible sign, nod in the direction of the toilets, expecting him to inch his way after her, squeezing past the blank-eyed squaddies to take her, thrusting urgently against the soap-and-grime-smeared little sink, with his hastily dropped trousers in an undignified pool around his ankles. *For I am wanton and lascivious and cannot live without a wife.* A memory of Julia, playing Helen in *Doctor Faustus* in a stripped-down production above a smoky London pub. Jackson wondered what, if anything, would drive him to be tempted to barter his soul to the devil, or indeed anyone. To save a life, he supposed. His child. (His *children*.) Would he follow the woman in red if she gave him the sign? Good question. He had never been what you would call promiscuous (and he had never once been unfaithful, making him almost a saint), but he was a man and he had taken it where he found it. *O, Man, thy name is Folly.*

When he glanced at her reflection in the dark glass of the window, she was innocently reading her trashy rag again. Perhaps she hadn't been giving him the come-on after all, perhaps his imagination was charged by the fetid atmosphere of the carriage. He was relieved he'd been spared the test.

Julia had done it in train toilets with complete strangers, and once on a plane, although admittedly that had been with him, not a stranger (at the time, anyway, different now). Julia gobbled up life because she knew what the alternative was, her catalogue of dead sisters a constant reminder of life's fragility. He was glad she'd had a son, she might worry less for him than she would for a daughter.

And now, Amelia, the only sister she had left, had cancer, her breasts at this very moment being "lopped off," according to Julia. They had spoken, briefly, on the phone, Jackson wanting to be sure that Julia wasn't at home before heading north to see his child. Their child.

"Poor, poor Milly," Julia said, more choked up than usual. Grief always brought on her asthma.

Once, on holiday with Julia in sunnier times, he couldn't re-member where now, Jackson saw a painting by some Italian Re-naissance guy he'd never heard of, showing the martyred St. Agatha holding her severed yet perfect breasts up high, on a plate, as if she were a waitress serving up a pair of blancmanges. No hint of the torture that had preceded this amputation — the sexual assaults, the stretching on the rack, the starvation, the rolling of her body over burning coals. St. Agatha was a saint whom Jackson was acquainted with only too well. After his mother was diagnosed with the breast cancer that would kill her, she had wasted a lot of her time praying to St. Agatha, the patron saint of the disease.

He was shaken out of his thoughts by the old woman suddenly asking him if they had passed the Angel of the North and would she be able to see it in the dark. Jackson wasn't sure what to say to her — how to break the news that she was traveling the wrong way, that this train was bound for London, and she had endured several hours in cramped, unpleasant conditions and was now going to have to turn round and do it all over again. The next stop would probably be Doncaster, maybe Grantham, birthplace of That Woman, the very person who had single-handedly dismantled Britain. ("Oh, for God's sake, Jackson, give it a rest," he heard his ex-wife's voice say in his head.)

"We're not going that way," he said gently to the old woman.

"Of course we are," she said. "Where do you think we're going?"

He slept. When he woke up, the suit was still tap-tapping on his laptop. Jackson checked for text messages but there were none. A station flashed by and the old woman gave him a smug look. "Dunbar," she announced like an old soothsayer.

"Dunbar?" Jackson said.

"The train terminates at Waverley."

She was obviously a little senile, Jackson thought. Unless . . .

The woman in red leaned over the table, displaying her own ample and healthy breasts for his connoisseurship, and said to him, "Do you have the time?"

"The time?" Jackson echoed. (The time for what? A quickie in the train toilet?) She tapped her wrist, in an exaggerated dumb show. "The time, do you know what time it is?"

The *time*. (Idiot.) He looked at his Breitling and was surprised to see it was nearly eight. They should be in London by now. Unless . . . "Ten to eight," he said to the woman in red. "Where is this train going to?"

"Edinburgh," she said, just as a young guy who had been weaving his way unsteadily through the carriage stumbled and pitched towards Jackson, clutching onto his can of lager as if it were going to stop him from falling. Jackson jumped up, not so much to save the guy as to save himself from being showered with lager. "Steady there, sir," he said, instinctively finding his voice of authority, while using his body weight to prop the guy up. He remembered the sheep from this afternoon. The drunk guy was more pliable. He stared blearily at Jackson, confused by the "sir," unsure whether he was under attack or not—probably no one, but the police had previously addressed him in such a polite manner. He started to say something, slurred and incoherent, when the carriage jolted suddenly and he staggered and fell headlong, slipping through Jackson's fumbled attempt to catch him.

There was a certain amount of alarm registered by the carriage's occupants at this unexpected stutter in the train's progress, but it was soon replaced with relief. "What was that?" Jackson heard someone say and another voice laughed, "Wrong kind of leaves on the line probably." It was all very British. The suit seemed the most twitchy. "Everything's going to be fine," Jackson said and immediately thought, Don't tempt fate.

Julia believed in the Fates (let's face it, Julia believed in everything and anything). She believed they had "their eye on you," and if they didn't, then they were certainly looking for you, so it was best not to draw attention to yourself. They had been in the car once, stuck in traffic and running late to catch a ferry, and Jackson said, "It's fine, I'm sure we're going to make it," and Julia had ducked down dramatically in the passenger seat as if she were being shot at and hissed, "*Shush,* they'll hear us."

"Who will hear us?" Jackson puzzled.

"The Fates." Jackson had actually glanced in his rearview mirror as if they might be traveling in the car behind. "Don't tempt them," Julia said. And once on a plane that had been bucking with turbulence, he had held her hand and said, "It won't last long," and had been subjected to the same histrionic performance, as if the Fates were riding on the wing of the 747. "Don't put your head above the parapet," Julia said. Jackson had innocently inquired whether the Fates were the same thing as the Furies, and Julia said darkly, "Don't even go there."

Looking back, he was astonished at how much traveling he had done with Julia—they were always on planes and trains and boats. He'd been hardly anywhere since their breakup, just a few hops across the Channel to his house in the Midi. He had sold the house now, the money should arrive in his account today. He had liked France but it wasn't as if it were home.

Jackson was currently less concerned with the Fates and more concerned by the direction they were traveling. They were going to Edinburgh? He hadn't caught the train *to* King's Cross, he had caught the train *from* King's Cross. The strolling woman had been right. He was going the wrong way.

Satis House

When Reggie arrived at the bleak bungalow in Mussel-burgh, Ms. MacDonald opened the door and said, "Reggie!" as if she were astonished to see her, although their Wednesday routine was invariable. From once being a woman who took pride in the fact that nothing could surprise her, Ms. MacDonald had turned into one who was amazed at the simplest things ("Look at that bird!" "Is that a *plane* overhead?"). Her left eye was bloodshot, as if a red star had exploded in her brain. It made you wonder if it wasn't better just to dive down into the blue and check out early.

No sign of the advent of Christmas in Ms. MacDonald's house, Reggie noticed. She wondered if it was against her religion.

"The meal is on the table," Ms. MacDonald said. Every Wednesday they ate tea together and then Ms. MacDonald drove across to the other side of Musselburgh (God help anyone else on the road) to her "Healing and Prayer" meeting (which, let's face it, wasn't doing much good) while Reggie did homework and kept an eye on Banjo, Ms. MacDonald's little old dog. When Ms. Mac-Donald returned, all prayered-up and full of the spirit, she checked Reggie's homework over tea and biscuits—"a plain digestive" for

Ms. MacDonald and a Tunnock's Caramel Wafer bought specially for Reggie.

Reggie didn't know what kind of a cook Ms. MacDonald was before her brain started to be nibbled at by her crabby tumor, but she was certainly a terrible one now. "Tea" was usually a stodgy macaroni and cheese or a gluey fish pie, after which Ms. MacDonald would heave herself up from the table with an effort and say, "Dessert?" as if she were about to offer chocolate cheesecake or crème brûlée when in fact it was always the same low-fat strawberry yogurt, which Ms. MacDonald watched Reggie eat with a kind of vicarious thrill that was unsettling. Ms. MacDonald didn't eat much anymore, now that she herself was being eaten.

Ms. MacDonald was in her fifties, but she had never been young. When she was a teacher at the school, she looked as if she ironed herself every morning and had never betrayed a trace of irrational behavior (quite the opposite), but now not only had she embraced a crazy religion but she dressed as if she were one step away from being a bag lady, and her house was two steps beyond squalid. She was, she said, preparing for the end of the world. Reggie didn't really see how a person could prepare for an event like that, and anyway, unless the end of the world happened very soon, it seemed unlikely that Ms. MacDonald would be around to see it.

Tonight it was oven-baked spaghetti. Ms. MacDonald had a recipe that made real spaghetti from a packet taste exactly like tinned, which was quite an achievement.

Over the spaghetti, Ms. MacDonald was blathering on about the "Rapture" and whether it would be before or after the "Tribulation," or "the Trib," as she called it with cozy familiarity, as if persecution, suffering, and the end of days were going to be on the same level of inconvenience as a traffic jam.

Religion had introduced Ms. MacDonald, rather late in the day, to a social life, and her church (aka weird religious cult) was keen on potluck suppers and uninspiring barbecues. Reggie had been to an agonizing few and eaten cautiously of the burnt offerings.

Ms. MacDonald belonged to the Church of the Coming Rapture and was herself, she announced smugly, "rapture ready." She was a pretribulationist ("pretribber"), which meant she would be whizzed up to heaven business class, while everyone else, including Reggie, had to suffer a great deal of scourging and affliction ("seventy weeks, actually, Reggie."). So a lot like everyday life, then. There were also posttribulationists, who had to wait until after the scourging but got to bypass heaven and enter the Kingdom of Heaven on earth, "which is the whole point," Ms. MacDonald said. There were also midtribulationists, who, as their name implied, went up in the middle of the whole confusing process. Ms. MacDonald was saved and Reggie wasn't, that was the bottom line. "Yes, I'm afraid you're going to hell, Reggie," Ms. MacDonald said, smiling benignly at her. Still, there was one consolation: Ms. MacDonald wouldn't be there, nagging her about her Virgil translation.

Whenever some horrible tragedy happened, from the big stuff, like planes crashing and bombs exploding, to the smaller stuff, like a boy falling off his bike and drowning in the river or a crib death in the house at the end of the street, it would always be put down to "God's work" by Ms. MacDonald. "Going about His mysterious business," she would say and nod sagely as people ran from disasters on the television news, as if God were running a secretive office dealing in human misery. Only Banjo seemed able to ruffle her feelings. "I hope he goes first," Ms. MacDonald said. It was going to be a race between Ms. MacDonald and her gnarled old misfit of a terrier. It was surprising how much soppy, maternal love Ms. MacDonald lavished on Banjo, but then, Hitler was very fond of his dog. ("Blondi," Dr. Hunter said. "She was called Blondi.")

Ms. MacDonald's dog was on his last legs, literally—sometimes his back legs collapsed under him and he sat in the middle of the floor looking completely bewildered by his sudden immobility. Ms. MacDonald had begun to worry that he might die on his own while she was off doing her Wednesday-evening healing and praying, so now Reggie stayed with him in case he popped his paws. There were worse ways to spend an evening. Ms. MacDonald had a TV that worked, although not the Hunters' extensive cable package, sadly, and Reggie got the run of the bookcases and a hot meal for her pains, plus the entire congregation (of eight) always said a prayer for her, which wasn't a gift horse she was about to look in the mouth. She might not believe in all that stuff, but it was nice to know that someone was thinking about her welfare, even if it was Ms. MacDonald's flock of loony tunes, who all felt sorry for Reggie on account of her orphan status, which was totally fine by Reggie—the more people who felt sorry for her, the better, in her opinion. Not Dr. Hunter, though. She didn't want Dr. Hunter to think of her as anything but heroically, *cheerfully* competent.

When the yogurt was ceremoniously finished, Ms. MacDonald exclaimed, "Goodness, look at the time!" Nowadays she was continually amazed by the time—"It can't be six o'clock!" or "Eight o'clock? It feels more like ten," and "It's not really that time, is it?" Reggie could just see her when all that scourging and affliction started, turning to Reggie in astonishment, saying, "That's never the end of the world!"

Was there a kind of lottery (Reggie imagined a raffle) where God picked out your chosen method of going—"Heart attack for him, cancer for her, let's see, have we had a terrible car crash yet this month?" Not that Reggie believed in God, but it was interesting sometimes to imagine. Did God get out of bed one morning and draw back the curtains (Reggie's imaginary God led a very domesticated life) and think, "A drowning in a hotel swimming pool today, I fancy. We haven't had that one in a while."

The Church of the Coming Rapture was a made-up kind of religion. Really it consisted of a bunch of people who believed unbelievable things. They didn't even have a building but held their services in their members' front rooms on a rotational basis. Reggie had never attended one of these services, but she imagined it was much like one of their potluck suppers, with everyone earnestly debating *dispensationalist* and *futurist* views while they passed round a plate of fig rolls. The only difference would be that Banjo wouldn't be in attendance, slavering and groaning at the sight of the fig rolls. "I was never blessed with children of my own," Ms. MacDonald told Reggie once, "but I have my wee dog. And I have you, of course, Reggie," she added.

"But not for long, Ms. Mac," Reggie said. No, of course she didn't say that. But it was true.

The awful thing was that Ms. MacDonald was the nearest thing that Reggie had to a family. Reggie Chase, orphan of the parish, poor Jenny Wren, Little Reggie, the infant phenomenon.

Reggie did the washing-up and cleaned the worst bits of the kitchen. The sink was disgusting, decaying food in the trap, old tea bags, a filthy cloth. No one seemed to have told Ms. MacDonald that cleanliness was next to Godliness. Reggie poured full-strength bleach into the tea-stained mugs and left them to soak. Ms. MacDonald had mugs that said things like "It's All About Jesus" and "God Is Watching You," which Reggie thought was unlikely, you would think he would have something better to do. Mum had a Charles-and-Diana wedding mug that had survived longer than the marriage itself. Mum had worshipped Princess Di and frequently lamented her passing. "Gone," she would say, shaking her head in disbelief. "Just like that. All that exercise for nothing." Diana-worship was the nearest thing Mum had to a religion. If Reggie had to choose a religion, she would go for Diana too, the real one—Artemis, pale moon goddess of the chase and chastity. Another powerful virgin. Or flashing-eyed Athene, wise and heroic, a warrior virgin.

You would have thought that with her background in the classics, Ms. MacDonald would have chosen from a more interesting pantheon—Zeus throwing bolts of lightning like javelins, or Phoebus Apollo driving his fiery horses across the heavens. Or, given her mushrooming tumor, Hygeia, goddess of health, and Asklepios, god of healing.

Reggie separated the rubbish into the red, blue, and brown bins. Ms. MacDonald didn't recycle anything, she was possibly the least green person on the planet. There was no point in preserving the earth, Ms. MacDonald explained in a kindly tone, because the Last Judgment couldn't occur until every last thing on the planet had been destroyed, every tree, every flower, every river. Every last eagle and owl and panda, the sheep in the fields, the leaves on the trees, the rising of the sun, and the running of the deer. Everything. And Ms. MacDonald was *looking forward* to that. ("It's a funny old world," Mum would have said.)

Reggie was definitely going to start up her own religion, one where things were cared for, not destroyed, one where the dead were reborn—and not in a symbolic way either—without everything else having to die. Then her mother would be back on the sofa watching *Desperate Housewives* and working her way through a packet of tortilla chips. No Gary sitting there pawing her, though, just Mum and Reggie. Together forever.

It had been just Mum and her for so long—well, Billy too, but Billy wasn't the kind of person who sat around and ate and chatted and watched TV (just what he did do was hard to say)—and then the Man-Who-Came-Before-Gary came along, who turned out to be "a total arse," according to Mum (not to mention married), and then the "real deal" came along in the form of Gary, and Mum started saying "my boyfriend this" and "my boyfriend that," and suddenly she was having sex and all her friends wanted to come round and talk about it. Her mother preening and giggling, "Three times in one night!" and her friends shrieking with excitement and spilling their wine.

Unlike the Man-Who-Came-Before-Him, Gary wasn't evil, he was just a big lump who, until he met Mum (after he met Mum as well, actually), spent his time sitting around all day in his greasy denims at the back of the bike shop with a load of Gary clones talking about the Harley-Davidson Sportster 883L he was going to buy when he won the lottery. He courted Mum with cheap hothouse roses from the Shell Shop and boxes of Celebrations, and when Reggie protested at this clichéd attitude to romance, her mother said, "You won't hear me complaining, Reggie," fingering the thin silver chain of the heart-shaped locket he had bought her for her birthday.

Gary was going to take her to Spain for two weeks ("Lloret de Mar—how nice does that sound, Reggie?"). Reggie's mother hadn't been on a "proper grown-up" holiday since she went to Fuerteventura in 1989, so he could have taken her to Butlin's in Skegness and she would have been impressed. Mum had taken Reggie and Billy to Scarborough for a week once, but it was rather spoiled when Billy disappeared from their B and B one night and was brought back by a policeman the next morning after being found wandering along the prom smashed out of his mind on lager. He was twelve at the time.

Reggie received a postcard a week into the fortnight so her mother must have written it not long after she'd arrived. It was a photograph of the hotel, a white concrete building that looked as if it had been constructed out of badly stacked blocks, the rooms all at odd angles to one another. At the rectangular heart of it was the swimming pool, turquoise and empty, bordered by neatly arranged white plastic recliners. There were no people at all in the photograph, so it was probably taken very early in the morning, everything as yet unsullied by wet towels and sunblock and half-eaten plates of chips.

On the back, Mum had written, "Dear Reggie, Hotel very nice and clean, food plentiful, our waiter is called Manuel, like in that John Cleese thingy! Drinking a lot of sangria. Naughty, naughty! Already made friends with a couple called Carl and Sue from Warrington who are a good laugh. Missing you loads. Back soon, love, Mum xxx." Gary had added his name at the bottom in the big round hand of someone still not convinced by the concept of cursive writing. *Sangria* came from the same Latin root as *blood.* Bloodred wine. There was a poem they had done in school about a Scottish king drinking bloodred wine, but Reggie couldn't remember more than that. She wondered if eventually she would forget everything she'd learned. That was death, she supposed. Reggie wondered if her life would get back on track before she died. It seemed unlikely, every day it felt as if she were being left further behind.

Reggie was working on her own translation for Ms. MacDonald of Book Six of the *Iliad,* one of her Greek set texts. She thought she might sneak a peek at the relevant Loeb to check what she had so far ("Nestor then called to the Argives, shouting aloud, 'Brave friends and Greeks, servants of Ares, let no one now stay behind.' "). She wasn't supposed to refer to the Loebs, of course; that was cheating, according to Ms. MacDonald. "Helping," Reggie would have said.

Volume One of the *Iliad* had definitely been there last week, but when she came to look for it now, there was no sign of it. She noticed other gap-tooths in the bookshelf—the second volume of the *Iliad* too, as well as both volumes of the *Odyssey* and the first of the *Aeneid* (one of her Latin set texts). Ms. MacDonald had probably hidden them. She carried on laboriously, " 'Let us kill men.

Afterwards at your leisure you shall strip the bodies of the dead.' "
There were an awful lot of the dead in Homer.

After her mother died, Reggie always kept the postcard from
Spain close, in her bag or at her bedside. She had studied every
detail of it as if it might contain a secret, a hidden clue. Her mother
had died right there in the empty space of turquoise water, and,
although Reggie had seen her in the undertaker's after she was
shipped home, a tiny part of her believed that her mother was still
inhabiting that bright postcard world, and if she scrutinized the
picture long enough, she might catch a glimpse of her.

Mum had woken up before any other guests were about—she
was always an early riser—and, leaving Gary snoring off the previous night's sangria, she had put on her unsuitable swimming costume beneath her pink terry cloth dressing gown and made her
way down to the pool. The pink terry cloth dressing gown had
been dropped where she stood poised at the edge of the deep end.
Mum was never one for neatly folding clothes. Reggie imagined
her raising her arms above her head—she was a good swimmer
and a surprisingly graceful diver—and then plunging into the
cool blue of oblivion, her hair streaming after her like a mermaid.
Vale, Mater.

Afterwards, at the inquest in Spain that neither Billy nor Reggie
attended, the police reported that they had found her cheap silver
Valentine's locket at the bottom of the pool ("Bit of a dodgy clasp,"
Gary admitted guiltily to Reggie) and speculated that it had come
off while she was swimming and that she had dived down to re-
trieve it. No one could know for sure, no one was there to witness
what happened. If only it had been the morning that the postcard
photographer was taking his shots of the hotel. Perched high in
his eyrie, possibly on the roof of the hotel, he would have watched
Mum slicing down through the blue water, contemplated putting

her into a photograph—probably decided against it given the orange Lycra and the pale plumpness of Mum's northern skin—and then alerted someone *("Hola!")* when she didn't come back up again. But that wasn't how it happened. By the time someone noticed that her beautiful long hair was trapped in a drain down in the turquoise depths, it was too late.

It was a waiter who spotted her, setting up tables for breakfast. Reggie wondered if it was the Manuel of the postcard. He had dived in, in his waiter's uniform, tried and failed to pull the English mermaid free. Then he had climbed out of the pool and run to the kitchen, where he grabbed the nearest knife, dashed back to the pool, dived into the water again, and sawed through Mum's hair to finally liberate her from her underwater prison. He attempted to revive her—at the inquest he was commended for his attempts to save the poor unfortunate tourist—but of course to no avail. She was gone. No one was to blame, it had been a tragic accident. Et cetera.

"Which it was, after all, Reg," Gary said. He had attended the inquest and came to see Reggie on his return from Spain, appearing unannounced on the doorstep, a six-pack of Carlsbergs in his hand, "to toast a wonderful woman." He had slept through everything. By the time he was woken, bleary and hungover, by "Carl and Sue from Warrington" hammering on his door, it was all over. He was, he said to Reggie, "all choked up" about what had happened.

"Yeah," Reggie said. "Me too."

The Spanish police returned the heart-shaped locket to Gary, who kept it "as a souvenir." No mention was made at the inquest of what had happened to the thick lock of Mum's hair left down in the pool. Or indeed of the knife that had cut through it. Did it go in the dishwasher, was it back chopping vegetables for a paella by the time the day was out? Reggie would have liked to have Mum's hair as a "souvenir." She would have slept with it beneath her pillow. She would have held on to it the way the baby held on to Dr.

Hunter's hair, like he held on to his green blanket. It would have been Reggie's talisman.

"Aye, it just goes to show," Gary said, turning philosophical after the third Carlsberg. "You never know what's waiting around the corner." Reggie sat out this visit of condolence, the nearest thing her mother would have to a wake. She had been to a wake, with Mum, a proper Irish one held by their neighbors the Caldwells a couple of years ago when old man Caldwell had died. It had been a cheerful affair with a lot of singing, some of it very bad, and endless bottles of Bushmills produced by the many and various mourners, so that Mum had to be carried home by a big Caldwell boy who told everyone next day how Mum had tried to get him to climb into bed with her before she threw up all over him. Still, as Mum said later, it had been a good send-off for the old man.

Gary left after the fourth Carlsberg, and Reggie didn't see him again until a few weeks later, when she ran into him in the supermarket, where he was browsing the tinned soup aisle in the company of a woman with too much henna in her hair. Reggie waited to see if he would recognize her, but he didn't even notice her, his brain already stretched to breaking point from making the choice between Heinz's Big Soup Beef Broth and Batchelor's Cream of Tomato. It was the same supermarket Mum used to work in, and it seemed disrespectful to be in it with another woman. Almost like infidelity.

The postcard had arrived in the letter box at virtually the exact moment (taking into account the time difference between Britain and Spain) that Mum was leaving the planet. Reggie thought about Laika the poor space dog rocketing into the sky and looking down on Earth with eyes as dead as stars. Reggie had thought she might still be up there, but no, Dr. Hunter said, she fell back to earth after a few months and burned up in the atmosphere. Lassie, come home.

★   ★   ★

Usually, round about this time of the evening, Banjo would sit by the back door and start to whine, and Reggie would say to him, "Come on then, poor wee scone, time for your constitutional," and Banjo would waddle unsteadily along the street to his favorite gatepost, where he would awkwardly lift an arthritic leg. He could just about make it to the gatepost but usually had to be carried back. Reggie was always surprised when she lifted him up in her arms at how little he weighed compared with the baby.

Ms. MacDonald lived in a housing estate that almost backed onto the East Coast main line. The whole house shook every time an express train hurtled past. Ms. MacDonald was so used to trains that she didn't even hear the regular earthquakes they caused, at least not if the trains were running to timetable. Occasionally, over tea, Ms. MacDonald would suddenly cock an ear, in much the same way that Banjo used to before he lost his hearing, and say something like, "That can't be the six-twenty Aberdeen to King's Cross, can it?"

Reggie, on the other hand, heard every train. They gave her an odd feeling in the pit of her stomach when she heard them approaching, something fearful and primitive (atavistic!), and she wondered if her Stone Age brain thought the train was a woolly mammoth or a saber-toothed tiger or whatever other creatures sent her ancestors running to the back of the cave, because Dr. Hunter said that "after all," we still had the DNA of Paleolithic hunter-gatherers and as far as she could see, we hadn't evolved biologically and emotionally and we were all still Stone Age people with "a thin veneer of culture and sophistication on top. Strip that off and we're back to basics, Reggie—love, hate, food, survival. Although not necessarily in that order." It was certainly a theory that helped to explain Billy.

Tonight Banjo was lethargic and showed no interest in going out, lying instead in front of the heat of the gas fire. Reggie was grateful, it was a horrible night, gusts of wind repeatedly lifting and dropping the brass knocker on Ms. MacDonald's front door, so that it sounded as if an unseen visitor were desperate to get in. Cathy come home to Wuthering Heights. Mum's ghost looking for Reggie. Back soon. *Je reviens.* Or just nobody and nothing.

Fast falls the eventide; the darkness deepens.

Rapture Ready

Everyone was fastidiously ignoring the drunk guy who was lying completely immobile on the floor, and Jackson felt a twinge of guilt. He had once arrested someone for being drunk and disorderly, and it turned out the man was suffering from a bleed in the brain as a result of a concussion and had nearly died right there in the holding cell. Bearing this in mind, he knelt down to inspect the prostrate form on the carriage floor.

His position gave him a close-up view of the feet of the woman in red, clad in a pair of ferocious spiked heels, shoes that were half fetish, half weapon. A banshee of a woman had once attacked him with the heel of her shoe when he'd been trying to wrangle a hen night that had got out of hand, giving a whole new meaning to the words *killer heels*. The mother of the bride, he seemed to remember, had been the owner of the shoe. He was trying to recall what Cambridge pub that had been in at the same time as he was checking the drunk guy's vital signs (who said men couldn't multitask?), when the train suffered another jolt, and then a rapid series of jolts, each one worse than the one before. The train started to speed up, which really didn't seem like a good thing in the circumstances. There was the smell of burning—rubber and something unpleasantly chemical—accompanied by a high-pitched shrieking noise like metal grating on metal. Jackson could actually feel the train swaying as if it were trying to keep its balance.

Christ, here we go, he thought. Not bound for London, not bound for glory, this train was bound for hell.

People screamed, the woman in red included. Jackson tried to reach out and reassure her (or at least get her to stop screaming), but the carriage started to tip to one side and she slipped out of his sight.

Jackson hoped there were angels in the cab with the driver, he hoped the driver could hardly breathe for the number of wing feathers in the air and that he had Gabriel himself as his wingman. It went without saying that Jackson didn't believe in angels, but in extremis he was always willing to give credence to anything. Indeed, he hoped that well-known hobo, the Angel of the North, had caught a ride at Gateshead and was even now directing his rusty flock in how to ride the rails.

The song "Jesus Take the Wheel" came into his head and he thought he might not go quite *that* far, but he wouldn't mind if the Virgin Mary took her foot off the dead man's handle and slowed them up a bit.

The carriage suddenly righted itself and Jackson had just begun to think that they might be okay when it just as suddenly canted over again, only this time it flipped ninety degrees onto its side. *"The train terminates at Waverley,"* the old woman had said, but she was wrong after all. It terminated here.

You can't fight a train crash. People and luggage were thrown around indiscriminately in a grotesque jumble, lit only by the sparks from metal on metal and the occasional unpleasant light intermittently shed by something electrical that was shorting overhead. Instinctively, Jackson tried to protect the drunk guy by throwing himself on top of him. If he'd had time for a considered decision, this wasn't the person he would have chosen to save (babies, children, women, animals, in that order, was his preferred roster). It made no difference anyway, because he was discovering that a derailing train didn't give you much choice about where you went and what you did. And trying to hang on to something was futile when everything was in cataclysmic, chaotic free fall. The noise was terrifying, unlike anything he'd experienced before (even war), and there seemed to be no end to it, as the train, or at any rate the carriage they were in, kept on traveling on its side. He supposed time had expanded as it did in all accidents, but how long could it carry on for? What if it went on forever? What if this was hell? Was he dead? Did everything hurt this much when you were dead?

Finally it came to a stop. They were in pitch darkness, and for a second, as if time were suspended, there was absolutely no sound. For an eerie moment Jackson wondered if everyone else was dead. Then people started to cry out, groaning and screaming. Perhaps *this* was hell? Darkness, the smell of burning, children crying for their mothers, mothers crying for their children, general lamenting and weeping. In Jackson's book you didn't get much closer to hell than that.

Someone close by whimpered like a dog in pain. A woman, it sounded like the woman in red, kept saying the word *no* over and over again. A mobile phone rang, the ringtone incongruously the theme from *The High Chaparral*. A man's voice murmured, "Help me, please someone help me." Jackson, the sheepdog, always had a Pavlovian response to a plea for help, but he couldn't work out which direction the words had come from—there was no up or down, no backwards or forwards anymore. He could feel something warm and wet that he thought might be blood, but he had no idea if it was his own or someone else's. He was surrounded by dark shapes and objects that might have been bags or bodies, it was impossible to tell. He could feel broken glass everywhere around him, and when he gingerly made a move, he heard a soft cry of pain. "Sorry," Jackson murmured.

He tried to work out the orientation of the carriage. He was pretty sure they hadn't rolled completely over, so there should be windows where the roof had been. The smell of burning was growing stronger all the time, there was no emergency lighting but there was a dull glow in the distance that didn't augur well, and there was the foul smell of an electrical fire. The train needed evacuating in double-quick time.

He decided to maneuvre over to where he thought the roof was (a trail of *sorry's*), thinking it might be easier to get some purchase there if he was going to climb up toward the window.

"Help me," the voice said again and Jackson realized it was coming from beneath him, from someone he was actually crawling over. Jesus. *Climb over seats, climb over people, forget anything your mother ever taught you about manners,* but it didn't work like that, not in reality. (In the other time dimension that he was occupying, where life was continuing as normal and he wasn't expecting to die at any moment, he wanted to sit down and write a note to posterity, to Marlee, that said, *You'll want to stop and help other people. Don't!*)

Jackson shifted his weight as much as he could. "All right, mate," he said, one injured soldier to another, "we'll get you out of here." Leave no man behind. He explored warily, got his arms around the guy's chest as if he were saving him from drowning, pulling him to shore. Heaving and dragging him over to where he thought the roof was. If he'd been thinking logically he might have considered the risk of spinal injury from hauling someone like a sack of coals, but there was no logic in this mayhem. One at a time, he thought. I'll get them out one at a time.

And then suddenly, with no warning, the two of them were falling through nothingness. Jackson clung on to the man as they performed their odd waltz into the abyss, Butch and Sundance going over the cliff. A bit of Jackson's brain was going *What the fuck?* while another bit was wondering where they were going to land. There was another more paranoid part of his brain that was worrying that they were never going to land at all. *Why this is hell, nor am I out of it.* (And he slagged off Julia for quoting at inappropriate times.)

Then it was over. They landed with a sickening thud, parachutists without a parachute, and rolled down a steep incline before coming finally to a stop. He banged his head hard when they landed and felt sick with the pain of it. He lay on his back for a second, trying to breathe, sometimes breathing was all you could manage. Sometimes breathing was enough. He remembered lying on the road after his showdown with the sheep this afternoon (really only this afternoon?), looking at the pale sky. There were days that really surprised you with the way they turned out.

The rain falling on his face revived him a little, and he managed to struggle to a sitting position. He was shivering with cold, with the onset of shock. There were lights somewhere, and he realized that they weren't in the middle of nowhere after all. There were houses, strung out along the track, and now there were voices as the first people arrived at the scene, civilians, not professionals; he could hear their confusion as they encountered a whole new definition for *nightmare.*

Jackson understood what had happened now. He had been trying to find the roof of the carriage but there had been no roof to find — it had peeled back like the top of a sardine can, and Jackson and his accidental new companion had plunged straight out of the train and down an embankment and now they were lying in a kind of gully. The man he had fallen with (*"Help me"*) lay without moving, facedown in the mud a few feet away. Jackson dragged himself over to him. He didn't have the strength to roll him over; he seemed to have hurt his arm when he fell, and the best he could do was to turn the man's head to the side to stop him from suffocating in the mud. He thought of his grandfather's brother going over the top at the Somme, drowning in the mud at Paschendale.

A light appeared at the top of the embankment, a torch, providing enough faint light for Jackson to see his companion's face. For some reason he had presumed it was either the young drunk guy or the tired suit and he was surprised to see that it was one of the squaddies. He looked pretty much dead. Survive a war where death stalks you at every moment and then find yourself picked off on the East Coast main line.

Jackson had thought the torch signaled rescue, but the light disappeared as quickly as it had appeared and Jackson shouted "Hey," his voice coming out as a reedy croak. He started trying to clamber up the embankment. He had to get more people out of the train. People who were still alive, preferably. He got about halfway up and had to stop, as weak as a kitten. There was something wrong, he'd been injured in some way but he wasn't sure how. It dawned on him suddenly, unexpectedly, that it was bad. Combat injury. He needed medevacing out of the field. He slipped back down the embankment.

He could feel the lifeblood ebbing away. On a couple of previous occasions when Jackson had found himself facing the possibility of death, he had clung on to life because he considered himself too young to die. Now it struck him that that wasn't really the case anymore, he felt plenty old enough to die.

I cut mine arm, and with my proper blood, assure my soul to be great Lucifer's. He was going to quote himself to death if he wasn't careful. Jesus, his arm really was bleeding, pumping the stuff out like there was no tomorrow. There wasn't going to be a tomorrow, was there? He had finally run out of road. You're a long way from home now, Jackson, he thought.

He closed his eyes, if he could sleep for a minute, he might be able to make it back up to the top. A nagging little voice in his head was trying to remind him that if he went to sleep now, it would be the big one, the last one. He debated this idea briefly and decided he didn't mind if he never woke up again. He was surprised, he had expected to fight at the end but it was actually a relief to close his eyes. He was so tired. His thoughts ran briefly to the woman walking in the dale. He had feared for her safety, when it was himself he should have been worried for.

So this was how the world ended. *This ae nighte, this ae nighte, every nighte and alle, fire and fleet and candle-lighte, and Christ receive thy saule.* Or the devil. He supposed he would find out soon enough. He struggled to eradicate the enigmatic walking woman from his mind and put in its place a picture of Marlee's face (*Missing you! Love you!*). He wanted her face to be the last thing he saw before he went into the black tunnel.

The Discreet Charm of the Bourgeoisie

She should have got the flowers, she should have gone to Waitrose, but here she was, parked outside Alison Needler's house in Livingston. The curtains were drawn, the porch light off. No sign of life within or without now, everything calmed down again. When she heard Alison's hysterical voice on the phone, Louise had expected the worst—he was back. But he wasn't, it turned out to be a false alarm, not David Needler come back to finish off his family but some innocent bystander in a baseball cap walking his dog. Not that innocent actually, as the dog in question was a Japanese Tosa, according to one of the Livingston uniforms who had turned up in response to Alison Needler slamming her hand on her panic button.

The innocent bystander was arrested and taken down to the station to be charged under the Dangerous Dogs Act, and the dog was carted off by a cautious vet. The squad car was already there when Louise turned up, so all in all they had provided quite a circus outside Alison Needler's so-called safe house. Why not just put a big flashing neon sign on the roof saying, "If you're looking for Alison Needler, David, she's right here."

It wasn't the first false alarm, and Alison's nerves were tuned as tight as piano wires twenty-four hours a day. Her life was a train wreck. Louise would like to introduce Alison Needler to Joanna Hunter. Alison would see that it was possible to survive with grace, that there could be life after death. But, of course, the big difference was that Andrew Decker had been caught, whereas David Needler — dead or alive — was still out there somewhere. If they could find him, if they could put him away for the rest of his life, then perhaps Alison Needler could start to live again. (But what did *life* mean? In Andrew Decker's case, thirty years, plenty of life left for him to live.)

"I have to tell you that Andrew Decker has been released from prison." Louise had never seen anyone go so pale so quickly and remain upright, but give Joanna Hunter her due, she'd held it together. Of course she must have known that he was coming up for release, that he'd already been out on conditional release, being prepared for his newfound freedom, because after thirty years inside, the world was going to come as a shock to him.

"He's living with his mother in Doncaster."

"She must be old. He was an only child, wasn't he?" Joanna Hunter said. "How sad for her."

"He's a Category A prisoner," Louise said. "MAPPA will monitor his release. Keep an eye on him, make sure he is where he says he is."

"MAPPA?"

"Multi Agency Public Protection Arrangements, bit of a mouthful, eh?"

"You don't need to apologize to me, the medical profession loves its acronyms too. I'm surprised you're telling me," Joanna Hunter said. "I would have thought after all this time . . ."

"Well, that's not all, I'm afraid." Louise Monroe, always the purveyor of bad news, like some dark messenger angel. "The press have got hold of his release, I think they're going to make a thing of it."

" 'Beastly Butcher Goes Free'—that kind of thing?"

"Exactly that kind of thing, I'm afraid," Louise said. "And, of course, it's not just Decker they'll be after. They'll be wanting to know what happened to you."

"The survivor," Joanna Hunter said. " 'Little Girl Lost.' That's what I was in the evening papers. By the morning I was 'Little Girl Found.' "

"Did you keep all that stuff, newspaper clippings, articles?"

Joanna Hunter laughed drily. "I was six years old. I didn't get to keep anything."

Really it was the job of a family liaison officer, but the call happened to have gotten passed on to her and she realized that Joanna Hunter lived just around the corner from her, a handful of streets away in their unrelentingly middle-class ghetto, where there were no council houses, no pubs, no nightlife of any kind, not much life in the day either, given the huge proportion of retired and elderly. The streets were dead after eight o'clock at night, and there was fat equity as far as the eye could see. Welcome to the dream. Louise felt vaguely as if she'd joined the other side without ever having been on a side to begin with. "Rejoice in good fortune," Patrick said, more fortune cookie than Zen.

"Just to give you a heads-up," the guy on the phone from MAPPA had said. "A recently released prisoner knew Decker was getting out and sold his story to the tabloids for twenty pieces of silver. It'll be a storm in a teacup, but she should know in case they find her. They'll come looking, they're better at finding people than we are."

Louise had been vaguely aware of the Mason case, not in detail, not the way Karen seemed to be, but as one of a catalogue—guys who attacked women and children. They were different from guys who attacked women on their own, different too from the ex-partners who jumped off cliffs and balconies with their kids, who ran exhaust pipes into their cars with the kids in the back, who suffocated them in their beds, who ran after them to the furthest corners of the house with knives and hammers and clotheslines, all on the basis that if they couldn't have their kids, then nobody was going to have them, and particularly not their kids' mothers.

Those were the ones who turned up uninvited at their daughter's Unicorn Magic–themed birthday party and shot their mother-in-law in the head while she was dishing up Jell-O and ice cream in the kitchen and then hunted down their sister-in-law like a deer and shot her in the head too — in front of ten screaming seven-year-old girls, one of whom was their own daughter. Three Needler children altogether, Simone, Charlotte, and Cameron. Ten, seven, and five. The birthday girl, Charlotte, pistol-whipped by their father when she tried to come between him and her aunt Debbie. ("Always a brave wee girl, our Charlie," Alison said.) Debbie must have understood the moment the first shot rang out in the kitchen, because she had herded the children into the conservatory at the back of the house, and when David Needler raised his gun at her, she was trying to shield them with her body, all ten of them. Right up to the last she was yelling at him, telling him what a bastard he was. Give a medal to Aunt Debbie.

Alison herself had been upstairs with Cameron, who was throwing up in the toilet after too much sugar and excitement, when her ex rampaged through the houseful of women and girls. Alison's mother was dead on the kitchen floor, her sister, Debbie, lay dying in the conservatory, her bloody head being mopped by her own ten-year-old daughter with handfuls of Unicorn Magic napkins. David Needler tried to carry off Simone, and a neighbor, one of the party mothers, fought him off. On a day when she thought the most testing thing she was going to have to do was survive two hours of hysterical seven-year-olds, she ended up battling for her life after David Needler shot her point-blank in the chest. She lost the fight. Three lives, three deaths, the same tally as Andrew Decker.

David Needler ran, no child as a trophy. At the first shot, Alison Needler had snatched up Cameron and hid with him in the wardrobe in her bedroom.

Andrew Decker didn't destroy his own family, he destroyed someone else's. He destroyed Howard Mason's. Men like Decker were inadequates, they were loners, maybe they just couldn't stand to see people enjoying the lives they never had. A mother and her children, wasn't that the bond at the heart of everything?

Hide or run? Louise hoped she would stand and fight. If you were on your own, you could fight, if you were on your own, you could run. You couldn't do either when you were with children. You could try. Gabrielle Mason had tried, her hands and arms were covered in defensive wounds where she had tried to stave off Andrew Decker's knife. She had fought to the death protecting her young. Give a medal to Gabrielle Mason.

Louise had been there, been there with Archie when he was little, at the empty play parks and deserted duck ponds, suddenly aware of the nutter's sloping walk, his shifting gaze. Don't make eye contact. Walk past briskly, don't draw attention to yourself. Somewhere, in some Utopian nowhere, women walked without fear. Louise would sure like to see that place.

Give medals to all the women.

There had been flowers in a blue-and-white jug on a side table in the Hunters' living room. No, not flowers, not cheap, thoughtless, hothouse flowers grown in Kenya, but leggy, twiggy things from the Hunters' own garden—"winter honeysuckle and Christmas box," Joanna Hunter had said. "They both have a lovely scent. It's so nice to have flowers in winter." Louise feigned interest. She suspected that she was genetically incapable of growing things, that nurturing wasn't in her mitochondrial DNA. Samantha and Patrick had "shared the gardening" in their old house. Now Louise and Patrick's small, new garden was all turfed lawn, trimmed with a few tedious perennials and shrubs. Louise wasn't really sure what a shrub was, the only time she had actually been in their garden was when they had a last-chance housewarming barbecue in Indian summer for the great and good of the neighborhood, including two senior policemen, a sheriff, and a crime writer. That was Edinburgh for you.

The first Mrs. de Winter, Samantha, had been the green-thumbed type. "Sweet peas, tomatoes, hanging baskets, she loved the garden," Patrick said. She could identify a shrub at a hundred paces, presumably. The Good Wife.

"Lovely," Louise said to Joanna Hunter, breathing in the scent of the winter honeysuckle. She wasn't lying, it *was* lovely. Joanna Hunter was lovely, her house was lovely, her baby was lovely. Everything about her life was just lovely. Apart from the whole family-massacred-in-childhood thing.

"You can't get over something like that," Louise had said to Patrick in bed last night.

"No, but you can try," he said.

"Who made you the voice of wisdom?" Louise said, but only in her head, because the love of a good man wasn't something to be thrown away like a piece of paper. Even Louise wasn't so blunt-headed that she couldn't see that.

Joanna Hunter had gone upstairs and come back with a photograph, black-and-white in a plain frame. She passed it silently to Louise. A woman and three children — Gabrielle, Jessica, Joanna, Joseph. It was an arty kind of photograph ("My father took it"), a close-up, their faces crowded together, Jessica smiling self-consciously, Joanna grinning happily, the baby just a baby. Gabrielle was beautiful, no arguing with that. She wasn't smiling.

"I don't keep it out," Joanna Hunter said. "I couldn't bear to look at them every day. I take it out now and then. Put it away again."

Howard Mason had married several times after his wife was murdered. How had the subsequent wives felt about their dead predecessor? The first wife. Gabrielle, beautiful, talented, a mother of three, and murdered into the bargain—that was an impossible act to follow. The second wife, Martina, killed herself; the third—the Chinese one (as everyone referred to her)—was divorced by Howard Mason; the fourth had some kind of horrible accident, fell downstairs or set herself on fire, Louise couldn't remember. There was a fifth one somewhere—Latin America, who outlived him. Louise wouldn't be surprised if there was a beheading in there somewhere. You would certainly have thought twice before saying "I do" to Howard Mason. "My Last Duchess"—the Browning poem—came unexpectedly into her mind. The thought brought a chill with it.

As time had gone by, Howard Mason had become more famous for his dead wives than for any literary talent that he possessed. Louise had never read any of his novels, he was before her time. After her meeting yesterday with Joanna Hunter, she had looked his books up on Amazon, but he seemed to be out of print. You might have thought that after the murders, a certain notoriety would have boosted his sales, but instead he became a kind of pariah. He might be dead and out of fashion as well as print, but he continued to live on, on the Internet, the ghost in the machine.

As chance would have it, on her way home Louise had stopped off at the Oxfam Bookshop on Morningside Road and found a secondhand copy of Howard Mason's first, most famous novel, *The Shopkeeper,* and had read most of it in bed last night.

"Could he write?" Patrick asked. He was reading some kind of abstruse medical journal. (Should she take more interest in his profession? He was always interested in hers.)

"Yeah, he can write, but it's of its time. It must have felt very cutting-edge way back when, but it's all very, I don't know, *northern*."

" 'Eeh ba gum'?"

"More like *Saturday Night and Sunday Morning.*"

Howard Mason was a northern grammar-school boy with an Oxford scholarship who wrote as if he'd read too much D. H. Lawrence as a teenager. *The Shopkeeper,* written after he graduated, was an "acid critique" (according to the *Dictionary of Literary Biography*) of his dull parents and his provincial background, an autobiographical source that he always freely admitted to. To Louise, it read like a rather spiteful revenge text. There was a thin line between fact and fiction in Howard Mason's life.

The Shopkeeper was written when Howard Mason was still green, before his life became Grand Guignol, before he fathered three children, before he married Gabrielle Ascher, handsome, clever, and rich, with a comfortable home and happy disposition, the last three attributes lost the minute she signed the marriage register in Gretna Green at the age of seventeen. Was Howard Mason such a terrible choice that the parents felt they had to disinherit her? What happened after she died, did Joanna Mason become a rich little orphan? Questions, questions. Joanna Hunter had got under Louise's skin. She had stood on the edge of the unknowable, she had been to a place that no one would choose to go to, and she had come back. It gave her a mysterious power that Louise envied.

Andrew Decker had, surprise, surprise, been a model prisoner. Helped to run the library, worked in the Braille shop, converting books to Braille, refurbished wheelchairs, all very worthy. Sometimes Louise hankered after the days when prisoners were made to walk endlessly on treadmills or turn crank handles. Pedophiles, murderers, rapists, should they really be making books? If it were up to Louise, she would put the lot of them down, though obviously this was not the kind of opinion she voiced at divisional meetings.

("Have you always been a fascist?" Patrick laughed. "Pretty much," she replied.)

Andrew Decker had done his A levels, got an Open University degree in philosophy (of course), showed no sign of wishing harm to anyone. Right. And thirty years ago he'd slaughtered a family when, according to his workmates, he'd been "an ordinary guy." Yeah, Louise thought, you had to watch out for the ordinary ones. David Needler was ordinary. Decker was only fifty, he might have another good twenty years left in him of being ordinary. Still, look on the bright side — he had a degree in philosophy.

"At least he served the full sentence," Joanna Hunter said. "That's something, I suppose." But it wasn't really, and they both knew it.

"I might go away," Joanna Hunter said. "Escape, for a bit, just until the fuss dies down."

"Good idea."

In Livingston, Alison Needler was under siege, staying inside her house all day, growing pale, venturing out only to walk the children to school. She wouldn't drive them because she was convinced that David Needler would rig a device to the car and blow them all up. David Needler had been a quantity surveyor and had no apparent knowledge of explosives, but Louise supposed that once paranoia had got lodged in your brain, it was pretty hard to shift. On the other hand, of course, who would have expected David Needler to have a gun, or to know how to shoot it?

Louise didn't know what Alison did all day, all her shopping was done on the Internet and she said she was "too wound up" to pound the carpet to an exercise video or sit peacefully and quilt a patchwork (two amongst several suggestions from a social worker). Whenever Louise went inside the house, it was immaculate, so she guessed Alison did a lot of cleaning. The TV was usually on and there was no sign of any books; she said she used to enjoy reading but now she couldn't concentrate. Louise remembered the Needlers' house in Trinity, it had been a good one, semi-detached sandstone, big garden back and front, the front one just right for a man to immolate himself in.

Alison Needler had two locks on every window, three each on the back and front doors, plus dead bolts. She had a security system with bells and whistles, she had a panic button, a mobile dedicated to an emergency number, and her kids had personal alarms hanging round their necks when they weren't locked in school.

She'd been moved to a safe house but Alison would never be safe. If Louise were Alison Needler, she would get a big dog. A really, really big dog. If she were Alison Needler, she would change her name, dye her hair, move far away, to the Highlands, to England, France, the North Pole. She wouldn't be in a safe house in Livingston, waiting for the big bad wolf to come and blow it all away.

Louise thought that perhaps she should station a car outside the house for the duration of the festive season. If David Needler was ever going to come back, then Christmas seemed a likely time, season of goodwill and all that. Louise hoped he would, she would have liked to get an Incident Response Vehicle over here, rouse the Gold Commander from his Christmas merrymaking to give the order to shoot the bastard dead.

Louise's phone rang. Patrick. He would be wondering where she was. She wondered herself. Louise checked her watch. Christ, six o'clock. So much for twice-baked soufflés, it was going to have to be an omelette for the in-laws.

"Louise?"

"Yes." To her own ears she sounded efficient, maybe just this side of snappy. What she should be saying is "I'm incredibly sorry, I'm letting you down," et cetera, but the give-and-take, the push and pull, the compromise and negotiation of a partnership just didn't seem to be in her. It felt like she'd been doing it all her life with Archie, she couldn't start again with a grown man. Patrick genuinely didn't seem to mind, but you could bet your bottom dollar that he would one day.

She should have got the flowers. They would have made it look as if she cared. She *did* care. Possibly not quite enough.

"I'm on my way home," she said. "Sorry."

"Aren't you off duty now?" he said mildly.

"Something came up."

"Where are you? You're in Livingston, aren't you? You're sitting in your car outside that woman's house, aren't you? You're obsessed, sweetheart."

"No, I'm not." She was, but hey. "And her name's Alison, not 'that woman.' "

"Sorry. He's long gone, you know. Needler's not coming back."

"Yes he is. Want to take a bet?"

"I'm not a betting man."

"You're Irish, of course you are. Anyway, I'll be home soon. Sorry," she added again for good measure. They seemed to spend a lot of time apologizing to each other. Maybe that was a good thing, showed they had manners.

Alison Needler's curtain opened a few inches and her face appeared, pale and disembodied, cigarette smoke curling around her head like an aura. She didn't used to smoke around the kids, once she never smoked at all, once she'd had a normal kind of life, part-time admin assistant at Napier, three kids, husband, nice house in Trinity, not this tired gray pebble-dash with rubbish in the neighboring garden. Not really normal at all, of course, it just looked normal. Ordinary. The curtain closed and Alison disappeared.

Louise cared, about Alison Needler, about Joanna Hunter. Jackson Brodie had cared about missing girls, he wanted them all found. Louise didn't want them to get lost in the first place. There were a lot of ways of getting lost, not all of them involved being missing. Not all of them involved hiding. Sometimes women got lost right there in plain sight. Alison Needler, making accommodations, disappearing inside her own marriage, a little more every day. Jackson's sister stepping off a bus and stepping out of her life one evening in the rain. Gabrielle Mason gone forever on a sunny afternoon.

At the thought of Jackson Brodie, her heart gave a guilty little twitch. Bad Wife.

There was no longer a regular police presence at the Needler house. Only Louise driving out there, keeping her vigils at random times of day and night until the section of the M8 between Edinburgh and Livingston was a groove in her brain. There was something meditative about watching over Alison. One day David Needler was going to come back. And when he did, Louise was going to get him.

She started the engine and Alison Needler reappeared at the window. Louise raised her hand, but Alison didn't acknowledge the farewell.

Patrick had ordered a "banquet for four" from a local Chinese restaurant. They'd eaten from there a few times and Louise had thought the food was okay, but beneath the long, rather bulbous nose of Patrick's elder sister, Bridget, the contents of the sticky foil containers looked less enticing.

Louise had been so starving on the drive home that she had almost given in to her Scottish genes and stopped to pick up a fish supper, but as soon as she crossed the threshold of their house ("their house," not "her home"), she had somehow lost her appetite.

"Sorry. I was hindered," she said to her new in-laws when she came in the door.

All Louise wanted to do was strip and stand under a hot shower, but they were already seated at the table, waiting for her. She felt like a recalcitrant teenager dragging herself in late. She imagined this was how it was for Archie. She felt a tug deep inside somewhere. She wanted her son here, she wanted to put her arms round him and hold him. Not as he was now, but as he was in the past. Her little boy.

Patrick poured a glass of red wine and passed it to her. *The king sits in Dunfermline toun, drinking the blude-red wine.* Red wine didn't go with Chinese food, would she look boorish if she went to the kitchen and got a beer from the fridge? (*Yes* was obviously the answer to that.) Patrick filled his own glass and clinked it against hers. "Welcome home," he said, smiling at her.

She could see the bottom of her wineglass already.

Bridget picked at a dish of sweet-and-sour chicken with her chopsticks and took a tentative bite. The food looked even less tempting now that Patrick had decanted it into the Wedgwood china dishes that were part of his wedding service. His first wedding service, from his marriage to Samantha. The first Mrs. de Winter, his Last Duchess.

Bridget must have eaten off the Wedgwood dozens of times before. Nice home-cooked food slaved over by Samantha because she cared about making Patrick happy. ("It wasn't like that at all," Patrick said. "Sam was an anesthetist. She worked almost as much as I did.")

What was she doing? She was living with a dead woman's things. Not in a dead woman's house, she wasn't that crazy. Patrick was still living in "the family home" when they met, a really lovely house in Dick Place, the kind of house that Louise used to fantasize about living in when she was growing up in a top-floor two-room tenement in Fountainbridge with her mother. Nonetheless, Patrick didn't hesitate to sell the Dick Place house—for an unbelievable sum of money—and they bought a swanky new duplex flat near the Astley Ainsley Hospital. It had looked vile on the outside—wood trim and metal balconies—but on the inside it had a kind of bland corporate luxury that Louise found strangely appealing. It started out as sterile as an operating theater, but they soon filled it with all the stuff from Patrick's old house and it lost its neutrality. The first Mrs. de Winter lingered on in her belongings. Patrick had offered to change everything, "right down to the last teaspoon," and Louise had said, "Don't be silly," even though that was exactly what she had wanted him to do but without her having to ask for it. Marry at leisure, repent in haste.

Patrick and Samantha had nice things: the Wedgwood, the canteen of silver cutlery, the damask tablecloths, the napkin rings, the crystal glasses. Wedding-present stuff, the goods and chattels of a traditional marriage. Louise's possessions looked like a refugee's beside his, a refugee who spent a lot of time in IKEA. When she had first opened the linen chest (a linen chest—who had a linen chest? Patrick and Samantha, that was who), she had felt alarmed at the neatly starched and ironed contents that looked as if they hadn't been given an airing since Samantha last sat in the driving seat of her car.

Louise remembered a ballad or poem set in some long-ago time when a wedding had taken place in a great house and all the guests had played hide-and-seek as part of the celebrations (imagine that now). The new bride had hidden in a huge chest in a remote part of the house where no one had thought to look for her. The lid of the chest had a hidden spring and could be opened only from the outside, and she suffocated inside it before she'd even had her wedding night. Years later they found her skeleton, dressed in all her wedding finery. Buried alive—but then some relationships were like that too. Who knew, perhaps the poor bride had been better off dead. Alison Needler said her ex-husband would have kept her "in a locked box if he could have." "The Mistletoe Bride," that was what it was called. If you waited long enough, your memory always caught up with you. One day it wouldn't.

"Sweetheart?" Patrick was standing over her, smiling. He had opened another bottle of the wine and went round the table like a waiter, refilling the crystal glasses. He gave her shoulder a little squeeze and she returned his smile. He was far too good for her. Too nice. It made her want to behave badly, to see how far she could push him, to smash the niceness. A bit of a problem with intimacy perhaps, Louise?

"Well, cheers again," Patrick said when he sat down. They all chinked their glasses and the crystal rang out like a bell. Calling her home. Not this home, some other home she hadn't discovered yet.

"Cheers," Tim said, and Louise said, "*Slainte,*" just to remind them that they were in her country now.

She ran her finger round the rim of the crystal. Samantha's crystal.

"Louise?"

"Mmm?"

"I was just saying to Patrick," Bridget said, "that you must come and visit us in the summer."

"That would be great, I've never been to Eastbourne. Are you near the beach?"

"Wimborne actually. It's not on the coast," Bridget said. Inside Bridget's smug and well-upholstered middle-class body, there might be a perfectly decent human being. Or not.

Louise knocked back the rest of the wine in her glass and searched for her own inner adult. Found her. Lost her again.

★ ★ ★

There's ice cream in the freezer," Patrick said. "Cherry Garcia," he said to Bridget. "Is that okay with you?"

"What does that *mean?*" she said querulously. "I've never understood."

"The Grateful Dead," Patrick said. "Never your kind of music, Bridie. As I seem to remember, you were more of a Partridge Family fan."

"And you weren't?" Louise said to him. "You don't seem like you were ever a Deadhead to me."

"Sometimes I wonder who you think you married," he said. What did *that* mean? He stood up and began to clear the plates. The food, cold and congealed, looked disgusting now.

"I'll get the ice cream," Louise said, jumping up so quickly that she nearly knocked Tim's glass over. She managed to catch it just in time.

"Good save," he murmured. He was so *English*. A different class of person from Louise. Louise had a knee-jerk reaction to the accent of a dominant culture. It was funny how sometimes you could realize you were all alone in a roomful of people. Well, four people, one of whom was you. Stranger in a strange land, a Ruth amongst an alien middle-class corn.

Instead of going straight to the kitchen, she ran up the stairs to her bedroom (*their* bedroom) and took her ring out of the safe. The safe had been a proviso of the insurance company because of the value of the diamond. When she changed her insurance, the new insurance company insisted that Louise install a monitored security system and a safe, "For the ring, Mrs. Brennan," the girl on the other end of the phone said. Louise had never been called *Mrs.* in her life and couldn't believe the amount of bile that shot into her system at the word, and not just at that word, but to add insult to injury, the girl had called her by Patrick's surname as if she were chattel. She was baffled by women who changed their names when they got married—your name was the closest thing to your self. Sometimes your name was all you had. Joanna Hunter changed her name when she married, but then you would, wouldn't you? But at least she could cling to the epithet of *Doctor* to give her an identity. If Louise were in Joanna Hunter's shoes, she would have changed her name long before marriage. She wouldn't have wanted to be known forever as that little girl lost in the bloody field of wheat. Louise might not have had an idyllic childhood but it had been a whole lot better than Joanna Hunter's.

"That would be Detective Chief Inspector Monroe," she said coldly to the girl from the insurance company. "Not Mrs. Brennan."

Louise only found out afterwards that Patrick had bought the diamond ring with some of the money invested from Samantha's life insurance. Truly a blood diamond, after all.

She didn't often wear the big diamond, just occasionally if they were going out somewhere. He made her go out places, theater, restaurants, opera, concerts, dinner parties — even, God help her, to charity fund-raisers where the rich and richer hobnobbed at two thousand a table. Kilts and ceilidhs, Louise's idea of hell. Still, it made her realize how narrow she had let her life become, it had been just Archie, work, and her cat, although not necessarily in that order. And now her cat was dead and Archie had spread his wings. "Live your life, Louise," Patrick said, "don't endure it."

She didn't wear her wedding ring either. Patrick wore his. He never mentioned her unworn wedding ring or the diamond in the safe. Lying in bed at night Louise could see the rings glinting in the dark, even when the safe was shut. Band of gold. Band around the heart. Heart of darkness. Darkness evermore.

There had been another man once. The kind of man she could have imagined standing shoulder to shoulder with, a comrade in arms, but they had been as chaste as protagonists in an Austen novel. All sense and no sensibility, no persuasion at all. She had kept vaguely in touch with Jackson, but it had been going nowhere because it had nowhere to go. He'd had a pregnant girl-friend and neither of them had talked about the consequences of that in their occasional drunken, late-night texts. Then the pregnant girlfriend dumped him and told him it wasn't his baby and they hadn't talked about the consequences of that either. Perhaps it was only Louise who had been drunk. She wasn't a drinker, not really ("Only days with a *y* in them"), she would never go down the same path as her mother, but sometimes, before she met Patrick, she had found herself looking forward to pouring the first drink of the evening in a way that went beyond pleasant anticipation. Now her drinking followed Patrick's civilized regime, a glass or two of a good red with a meal. Just as well, she made a maudlin drunk.

Patrick believed in the health-giving properties of red wine. He had embraced the Red Wine Diet, buying cases of some French wine that was going to make him live forever. He went for a swim five mornings a week, played golf twice a week, had a positive attitude every day of the week. It was like living with an alien pretending to be human. He was solicitous about her health too ("Ever thought of doing yoga? Tai chi? Something meditative?"). He didn't want to be widowed a second time. A surgeon seeing off two wives in a row, it wouldn't look good.

She slipped the ring on her finger. Let Bridget see that her price might not be above rubies, but she was worth a three-and-a-half-carat piece of ice. She added her wedding ring, and her finger felt suddenly weighed down. The rings were tight. For a second she thought they had shrunk, until she realized that it was more likely that her finger had grown bigger.

Catching sight of herself in the mirror, she felt shocked — her skin was alabaster and her eyes were huge and black, as if she'd been taking belladonna. At her temple a large vein throbbed like a worm buried beneath her skin. She looked like someone who had been in a terrible accident.

She had heard the phone ringing insistently downstairs, and by the time she came reluctantly down, Patrick was in the hallway, pulling on his Berghaus and making eagerly for the door. "There's been a train crash," he said to her. "A bad one. All hands on deck tonight," he added cheerfully. "Coming?"

Funny Old World

Reggie Chase, as small as a mouse, as quiet as a house with no one home. She was absentmindedly scratching the top of Banjo's head. Homer was open on her lap, but she was watching *Coronation Street*. She had almost finished an old box of violet creams that she'd rummaged out of the back of one of Ms. MacDonald's kitchen cupboards (any port in a storm). She checked the clock. Ms. MacDonald would be home soon.

She could hear a train approaching, the noise muted at first by the wind and then growing louder and louder. Not the usual train noise, but a great rumbling wave of sound that seemed to be rolling towards the house. Reggie leapt instinctively to her feet, she had the feeling that the train was actually going to come *through* the house. Then another higher-pitched sound, as if a giant hand were clawing a giant blackboard with giant fingernails, and finally a tremendous bang, like an explosive clap of thunder. The apocalypse had come to town.

And then . . . nothing. The gas fire hissed, Banjo snored and grunted, the rain continued to throw itself against the living-room window. The *Coronation Street* theme music started up for the credits. Reggie, book in hand, a half-eaten violet cream in her mouth, was still standing in the middle of the floor, poised for flight. For a moment it was as if nothing had happened.

Then she heard voices and doors banging as people from the neighboring houses ran into the street. Reggie opened the front door and stuck her head out into the wind and rain. "A train's crashed," a man said to her. "Right out back." Reggie picked up the phone in the hall and dialed 999. Dr. Hunter had told her that in an emergency everyone presumed that someone else would call. Reggie wasn't going to be that person who presumed.

"Back soon," she said to Banjo, pulling on her jacket. She picked up the big torch that Ms. MacDonald kept by the fuse box at the front door, put the house keys in her pocket, pulled the door shut behind her, and ran out into the rain. The world wasn't going to end this night. Not if Reggie had anything to do with it.

What larks, Reggie!

The Celestial City

The tunnel was white, not black. Not so much a tunnel as a corridor. It was very brightly lit. And there were seats, white molded plastic benches that seemed to be part of the wall. He was sitting on one as if he were waiting for something. It reminded him of a scene from a science-fiction film. Jackson expected that at any minute his sister or his brother would appear and invite him to follow them into the light. He knew it was altered temporal-lobe function or oxygen deprivation to his brain as his body shut down. Or even an excess of ketamine — he'd read somewhere about that, *National Geographic* probably. Still, it was a surprise when it happened to you. You would think it would feel like a cliché or a dream, but it didn't. He was at ease, in a way that he didn't ever remember feeling when he was alive. It no longer mattered that he wasn't in control. He wondered what was going to happen next.

On cue, his sister suddenly appeared, sitting next to him on the bench. She touched the back of his hand and smiled at him. Neither of them spoke, there was nothing to say and everything to say at the same time. Words would never have been able to convey what he was feeling, even if he had been able to speak, which he wasn't.

He was experiencing euphoria. It had never happened to him before, even at the happiest times in his life—when he was in love, when Marlee was born—any possibility of clear, uncut joy had been fogged by the anxiety. He had never floated free of the world's cares before. He hoped it was going to go on forever.

His sister moved her face close to his and he thought she was going to kiss him on the lips but instead she breathed into his mouth. His sister's signature scent was violets—she wore April Violet cologne and her favorite chocolates were violet creams, even the sight of which made Jackson feel sick when he was a boy—so he wasn't surprised that her breath tasted of violets. He felt as if he had inhaled the Holy Ghost. But then he felt himself being pulled out of the tunnel, away from Niamh, and he had to fight to resist. She stood up and started to walk away. He exhaled the Holy Ghost and shut his mouth so it couldn't get back in. He stood up and followed his sister.

Some slippage, some interruption in the space-time continuum. Something had punched him in the chest, incredibly hard. He wasn't in the white corridor. He was in the Land of Pain. And then, just as suddenly, he was back in the white corridor, his sister walking ahead, looking over her shoulder, beckoning to him. He wanted to tell her that it was okay, he was coming, but he still couldn't speak. More than anything in the world, he wanted to follow his sister. Wherever it was, it was going to be the best thing that had ever happened to him.

Something jackhammered him in the chest again. He felt suddenly furious. Who was doing this, who was trying to stop him from going with his sister?

III
Tomorrow

The Dogs They Left Behind

What did he mean, she'd gone away? Gone away? Gone away where? And why? *"To see an elderly aunt who's been taken ill,"* he'd said. She'd never mentioned having an aunt, let alone one who might get ill.

"She's only just been taken ill," Mr. Hunter said impatiently, as if Reggie were a nuisance, as if it were *she* who had phoned *him* at half past six in the morning, waking in a fumbling daze of sleep, unable to understand why Mr. Hunter was on the other end of the phone, saying, "You don't need to come in today." For a moment Reggie thought it must be something to do with the train crash, and then—worse—that something had happened to Dr. Hunter or the baby—or, worst of all, that Dr. Hunter and the baby had been *involved* in the train crash in some way. But no, he had phoned at an unearthly hour to tell her about a sick aunt.

"What aunt?" Reggie puzzled. "She's never mentioned an aunt."

"Well, I don't expect Jo tells you everything," Mr. Hunter said.

"So everything's definitely okay with Dr. Hunter and the baby?" Reggie said. "They're not ill or anything?"

"Of course not," Mr. Hunter said. "Why should they be?"

"When did Dr. Hunter leave?"

"She drove down last night."

"Down?"

"To Yorkshire."

"Where in Yorkshire?"

"Hawes, since you must know every detail."

"Whores?"

"H-a-w-e-s. Can we stop this catechism now? Tell you what, take a wee holiday, Reggie. Jo will be back in a few days. She'll phone you then."

Why hadn't Dr. Hunter phoned *her,* that was the question. Dr. Hunter always had her mobile with her, she called it her "lifeline." She used it for everything—the house phone "belonged to Neil," she always said. But then perhaps she had been driving, in too much of a hurry to get to this mysterious aunt to stop and call Reggie. But Dr. Hunter wasn't the kind of person not to *call* you. It made Reggie feel dismissed, a bit like a servant. When had she left? "Last night," Mr. Hunter said.

It would have been darkest dark when she drove away. Reggie imagined Dr. Hunter plowing through the night, through the rain, the baby asleep in the car seat in the back, or awake and noisily distracting Dr. Hunter from the road ahead while she scrabbled in the baby-bag for a mini-oatcake to keep him quiet while the Tweenies' *Greatest Hits* (the baby's favorite) added further to the potential accident scenario. It was funny that Dr. Hunter had driven down to Yorkshire at the same time the train hurtled away from it into disaster, into Reggie's life.

Reggie had an aunt in Australia—her mother's sister, Linda. "Never close, Linda and me," Reggie's mother used to say. When Mum died, Reggie had to endure an awkward phone call with Linda. "Never close, your mum and me," Linda echoed. "But I'm sorry for your loss," as if it wasn't her loss at all but Reggie's alone to bear. Before the phone call, Reggie had wondered if Linda would invite her to come over to Australia to live or at least to stay for a holiday *("Oh, you poor thing, come here and let me look after you"),* but clearly this thought had never even entered Linda's mind ("Well, take care of yourself then, Regina.").

The day suddenly stretched emptily ahead. "It'll be nice for you to have some time off," Mr. Hunter said, but it wasn't nice at all. Reggie didn't *want* time off. She wanted to see Dr. Hunter and the baby, she wanted to tell Dr. Hunter about what had happened last night—the train crash, Ms. MacDonald, the man. Especially the man, because, if you thought about it, the fact that the man was alive (if he *was* still alive) was all down not to Reggie but to Dr. Hunter.

All night—or what little was left of it by the time she got to bed—Reggie had tossed restlessly in the unfamiliar surroundings of Ms. MacDonald's back bedroom, going over the events of the last hours and bursting with excitement at the idea of telling them to Dr. Hunter. Well, perhaps *excitement* was the wrong word, terrible things had happened on that railway track, but Reggie had been involved in them, a witness and a participant. People she knew had died. People she didn't know had died. *Drama*—that was a better word. And she needed to tell someone about the drama. More specifically, she needed to tell Dr. Hunter about it because Dr. Hunter was the only person she knew who was interested in her life now that Mum had gone.

Dr. Hunter would have led her into the kitchen, where she would have switched on the coffee machine and made Reggie sit down at the nice big wooden table, and when, but only when *("Strict house rules, Reggie"),* they had mugs of coffee and a plate of chocolate biscuits in front of them, Dr. Hunter, face bright with anticipation, would have said, "Right, Reggie, come on, then, tell me all about it," and Reggie would have taken a deep breath and said, "You know the train crash last night? I was there."

And now because of some *aunt,* an aunt who lived in *H-a-w-e-s,* Reggie had no one to tell. Although, of course, Dr. Hunter would have been at work by the time Reggie arrived and there would only have been Mr. Hunter *("What's your story, Reggie?"),* who was an unsatisfactory audience at the best of times.

Reggie went downstairs to Ms. MacDonald's kitchen, flicked on the kettle, and spooned instant coffee into an "I Believe in Angels" mug. While she waited for the kettle to boil, she bundled her disgusting clothes from last night into the washing machine, after which she found half a stale sliced white loaf in the bread bin, made a Jenga tower of toast and jam from it, and turned on the television in time to catch the seven-o'clock headlines on GMTV.

"Fifteen people dead, four critical, many severely injured," the news reader said with her best serious face on. She handed over to a reporter who was "live at the scene." The man, who was in a trench coat and was clutching a microphone, was trying to look as if he wasn't freezing cold, as if he hadn't raced through the night like a ghoul to get to Scotland, high on adrenaline at the idea of a disaster. "As dawn begins to break here, you can see that behind me there is a scene of utter devastation," he intoned solemnly. Across the bottom of the screen it said "Musselburgh Train Crash."

In the arc-lit background, people in fluorescent yellow jackets moved around in the wreckage. "The first of the heavy-lifting gear is beginning to arrive," the reporter said, "as the investigation into the causes of this tragic accident begin." The noises of engines revving and machinery clanking were the same sounds that Reggie could hear from Ms. MacDonald's living room. If she had stood on tiptoe at the bedroom window, she probably could have seen the reporter.

After Mum died, a journalist had come round to the flat. She had been a lot more dowdy and a lot less perky than any of the reporters that you saw on TV. She had brought a photographer with her, "Dave," the woman said, indicating a man lurking in the stairwell as if waiting for a cue to come up onstage. He gave Reggie a sheepish little wave. Even he, battle-hardened veteran of a hundred local tragedies of one kind or another, could understand why a girl who had just lost her mother might not want to be photographed at eight in the morning with her eyes red-raw from weeping. "Fuck off," Reggie said and shut the front door in the reporter's face. Mum would have been horrified at her language. She was pretty horrified herself.

The reporter wrote the piece anyway. "Local woman in holiday swimming-pool tragedy. Daughter too upset to comment."

Banjo, lying on the sofa next to her like a deflated cushion, whimpered in his sleep, his paws moving as if he were chasing dream rabbits. He hadn't wanted to wake up last night, hadn't shown any interest in anything, so Reggie had put him on the sofa, covered him up with a blanket, and—because she could hardly leave him all alone—had herself slept in Ms. MacDonald's inhospitable guest room between brushed nylon sheets, beneath a thin, slightly damp eiderdown.

At home, Reggie now slept in Mum's double bed, pillowed and downy, made up with the pink broderie-anglaise sheets Mum had liked best, and exorcized of all trace of Gary's sweaty, hairy biker's body. Before Spain, Reggie had lain in bed on the other side of the wall, three pillows over her head, trying not to hear the (barely) muffled laughs and creaks coming from Mum's room. It had been incredibly embarrassing. No mother should subject her teenage daughter to that.

It was nice when she was lying in Mum's bed in the dark to have the comfort of a street lamp outside, like a big orange night-light. It was only the bed that Reggie had taken over the occupation of, on account of her own bedroom being a window-less storeroom. The rest of the room was still Mum's, her clothes in the wardrobe, her cosmetics on the dressing table, her slippers beneath the bed, waiting patiently for her feet. *Miracle* by Danielle Steel was still on the bedside table, the corner of page 251 turned down where Mum had left off to go to Spain. Reggie couldn't move it from its final resting place. Mum hadn't taken any books with her on holiday. "I don't suppose I'll have time for reading," she giggled.

Mary, Trish, and Jean had given up trying to persuade Reggie to give Mum's stuff to charity — they had offered to box everything up and "get rid of it" — but Reggie went into charity shops herself and imagined herself raking through the secondhand paperbacks and bits of old-lady china and finding one of Mum's skirts or a pair of her shoes. Even worse — a complete stranger pawing Mum's stuff. *"We go and leave nothing behind,"* Dr. Hunter said, but that wasn't true. Mum had left a lot.

Banjo suddenly made an odd grunting noise that Reggie had never heard before. The phone number for the vet, written in black felt tip, was taped to the wall beside the phone. Reggie hoped she wouldn't be the one who would have to call it. She stroked the dog's head absentmindedly while she finished her toast. She was still ravenous, as if she'd skipped several meals. It felt like a whole lifetime since she had sat at the dining-room table with Ms. Mac-Donald, eating her "speciality" spaghetti. Reggie's stomach did a funny flip at the thought of Ms. MacDonald. She was never going to sit at that table again, never eat spaghetti, never eat anything at all. She had had her last supper.

The man live at the scene was still speaking. "Reports vary as to what actually happened here last night and the police have so far neither confirmed nor denied that at the time of the accident, there was a vehicle on the track a few hundred yards from here." A picture flashed on the screen of a bridge over the railway line. A car had obviously driven off the road and knocked down the wall of the bridge and fallen onto the track below.

The reporter didn't add that the vehicle was a blue Citroën Saxo or that it contained Ms. MacDonald, very dead at the scene. These facts hadn't been made public yet. Only Reggie knew because the police had come to Ms. MacDonald's house last night, after Reggie had got back from the train crash, and asked her lots of questions about "the occupant of the house"—where was she, and what time was Reggie expecting her back? There were two uniformed policemen, one florid and middle-aged ("Sergeant Bob Wiseman"), the other Asian, small and handsome and young and apparently nameless.

For some reason they had their wires crossed and thought Reggie was Ms. MacDonald's daughter. ("Has your mother left you alone in the house?") The handsome young Asian PC made her a cup of tea and handed it to her nervously, as if he weren't sure what she would do with it. She was starving then as well and had thought about the Tunnock's Caramel Wafer that she should have been eating with Ms. MacDonald at that moment. She supposed it wasn't appropriate to suggest biscuits when the older policeman had just said to her, "I'm really sorry but I'm afraid we think your mother may be dead."

For a moment Reggie was confused, Mum had been dead for over a year, so it seemed a little late to be telling her about it now. Her brain was fudge. She had come in from the train crash, soaked to the skin and covered in mud and filth and blood. The man's blood. She had stripped and endured an eternity beneath Ms. MacDonald's lukewarm shower before putting on her lavender fleece dressing gown, which smelled slightly unpleasant and had stains where Ms. MacDonald's nighttime Horlicks had dribbled down the front. There had still been sirens wailing outside and the sound of helicopters put-puttering in the sky.

They had taken the man away in a helicopter. Reggie had

watched it lift off from a field on the other side of the track. "You did well," the paramedic said to her. "You gave him a chance."

She's not my mother," Reggie said to the older policeman.

"Where *is* your mother, then?" he asked, looking concerned.

"I'm *sixteen,*" Reggie said. "I'm not a child, I just look young for my age. I can't help it." Both policemen studied her doubtfully, even the handsome Asian one, who looked like a sixth-former.

"I can show you my ID, if you want. And my mother's dead already," Reggie said. "Everybody's dead."

"Not everybody," the Asian guy said, as if he were correcting misinformation rather than being kind. Reggie frowned at him. She wished she wasn't wearing Ms. MacDonald's grotty dressing gown. She didn't want him to think she dressed like that out of choice.

"We're not releasing these details to the press yet," the middle-aged policeman said. He looked familiar; Reggie had a feeling he had once come to the flat looking for Billy.

"Right," Reggie said, trying to concentrate on what he was saying. She was so tired, down to the bone.

"We're not quite sure what happened," he said. "We think Mrs. MacDonald must have driven off the road and fallen down onto the track somehow. You don't know if she had been feeling at all depressed lately?"

"*Mzzz* MacDonald," Reggie corrected him on Ms. MacDonald's behalf. "You think she *killed* herself?" Reggie was prepared to give this idea consideration—Ms. MacDonald was dying, after all, and might have decided to go quickly rather than slowly—until she remembered Banjo. She would never leave the dog on his own. If Ms. MacDonald were going to commit suicide by driving off a bridge and landing in front of an express train, she would have taken Banjo with her, sitting up in the front of the Saxo like a mascot.

"Nah," Reggie said, "Ms. MacDonald was just a rubbish driver." She didn't add that Ms. MacDonald was rapture ready, that she embraced the end of all things and was expecting to live eternally in a place that when she described it sounded a bit like Scarborough.

Reggie imagined Ms. MacDonald nodding serenely at the 125 express train that was charging towards her, saying, "That'll be God's will, then." Or was she astonished, did she consult her watch to check if the train was on time, did she say, "Not already, surely?" One second there, the next gone. It was a funny old world.

Of course, alternatively, she might have been out of her mind with panic when she realized she was stuck with the instrument of her death bearing down on her at over a hundred miles an hour, too confused in the moment to do anything as sensible as get out of the car and run for her life. But Reggie would rather not think about that scenario.

"Plus she had a brain tumor," she added, trying not to catch the eye of the Asian policeman in case she embarrassed herself by blushing. "I mean it might just have, I dunno, exploded."

"We need someone to identify her," Sergeant Wiseman said. "Do you think you can do it?"

"Now?"

"Tomorrow will do."

And now it was tomorrow.

"We will bring you more news as we have it," the news reader said, staring seriously at the camera. The program cut to his co-presenter, whose smile was only slightly tempered by the proximity of disaster. "Now," she said, "we're delighted to welcome to the studio the newest resident of Albert Square, already making waves in *EastEnders* with her—." Reggie switched the television off.

She noticed how still the air in the house was, as if someone had breathed out and not breathed in again. Reggie looked closely at

Banjo. His eyes were rheumy slits, and his tongue was lolling out of the side of his mouth. No movement in his ancient little lungs. Dead. Here one second, gone the next. The breath was the thing. It was everything. Breathing was the difference between alive and dead. She had breathed life into a man, should she try and do the same with a dog? But no, really, if he were a person, he would have "Do Not Resuscitate" written on a piece of paper inside the tiny barrel that hung from his collar. Some people left early (a lot of people closely related to Reggie), but some people (and dogs) went when they were supposed to.

A great bubble of something like laughter but that she knew was grief rose up in Reggie's chest. She'd had the same reaction when she was told about Mum's death—in a phone call from Sue (minus Carl) from Warrington because Gary was "too choked" to talk. "Sorry, love," Sue said, in a voice husky from fags. She sounded like she meant it, sounded like she cared more about Mum after a couple of days' acquaintance than Mum's sister, Linda, did after a whole childhood together.

Reggie wished she had a sister, someone else who had known and loved Mum so that she wasn't all alone keeping her memory alive. There were Mary, Trish, and Jean, but in the last year they had moved on, making Mum into a sad memory, no longer a real person. Billy was no good, Billy only cared about Billy. When Reggie died, that would be the end of Mum. And when Reggie died, that would be the end of Reggie, of course. Reggie wanted a dozen kids so that when she was gone they could all get together and talk about her *("Do you remember when . . . ?"),* and not one of them would feel they'd been left alone in the world.

Reggie had asked Dr. Hunter if she wanted more children, a brother or a sister for the baby, and she'd made a funny face and said, *"Another* baby?" as if that were an outlandish idea. And Reggie could see her point. This baby was everything, he was emperor of the world, he *was* the world.

Reggie visited Mum's grave every week and talked to her, and then on the way home from this pilgrimage, she stopped in at the Catholic church and lit a candle for her. Reggie didn't believe in any of that hocus-pocus, but she believed in keeping the dead alive. There would be more candles to light now.

She knew it was wrong, but Reggie felt more affected by the dog's death than she did by his owner's. Reggie stroked Banjo's ears and closed his dim eyes. The dead guy, the soldier, last night had his eyes half open, but Reggie hadn't closed them. There'd been no time for such niceties. The Asian policeman was wrong, everybody *was* dead. It was like being cursed. It was like being in some horror movie. *Carrie*. All those people on the train, perhaps they should be on her conscience as well. "Troubled teen or angel of death?" she said to the dead dog. "You have to wonder." Was the man dead too? Perhaps instead of saving him she had killed him, simply by being near him. Not the breath of life but the kiss of death.

He was the second man she'd come across after half sliding, half falling down the muddy embankment. The first one was the soldier. Reggie shone her torch on him and moved on. She expected there would be plenty of time later to think about how he looked dead. The torch beam was thin and wavery. *Thigh high, not eye high.* Mum had once worked as an usher at the Dominion but was sacked after two weeks for eating ice creams without paying for them.

The second man had a pulse, pretty weak, but a pulse was a pulse. His arm was a mess, he was bleeding from an artery, and, in the absence of anything else, Reggie took off her jacket, rolled up a sleeve, and used it as a pad to press on the bleeding arm the way that Dr. Hunter had shown her. Reggie tried calling out for help, but everyone was down in a dip where no one could see or hear them. The first sirens had begun to wail in the distance.

She checked the pulse in the man's neck again and this time couldn't find one. Her fingers were slippery with his blood. Perhaps she was mistaken? She felt herself beginning to panic. She thought about Eliot, the CPR dummy that Dr. Hunter had brought home. Eliot wasn't anything like the man whose life was suddenly and unexpectedly in her hands. She couldn't work out how to breathe into his mouth—let alone do the heart compressions—without taking the pressure off his bleeding artery. It was like a nightmare game of Twister. She thought of the Spanish waiter trying to breathe life into her mother's lungs. Had he felt this same sense of desperation? What if he had kept on going a little longer, what if her mother hadn't been dead but in a watery suspension, waiting to be restored to life? The thought galvanized Reggie and she transferred her knee onto the improvised pressure pad and then stretched over the man's body like a large awkward spider. She could manage it if she really tried.

"Just hang on," she said to the man. "Please. For my sake if not for yours." She breathed in as deeply as she could and put her mouth over his. He tasted of cheese and onion crisps.

Reggie took the bus home from Ms. MacDonald's house. Before leaving she had wrapped Banjo's body in an old cardigan of Ms. MacDonald's and dug a hole for him in one of the flower beds. A little parcel of bones. It had been like the Somme in Ms. MacDonald's back garden, and it had been a horrible task dropping the small body into the unfriendly, muddy hole. *Nada y pues nada,* as Hemingway and Ms. MacDonald would have said. First things were good, last things not so much so. As Reggie would have said.

It had rained when they buried Mum as well, dropped her into her own muddy hole. There were quite a few mourners at the graveside—Billy, Gary, Sue and Carl from Warrington, which was nice of them, considering they hardly knew Mum—a couple of Gary's biker mates, some neighbors, Mary, Trish, and Jean, of course, quite a lot of coworkers from the supermarket, the manager himself in black tie and black suit, even though the month before he'd threatened Mum with her cards for "persistently poor timekeeping." Even the Man-Who-Came-Before-Gary turned up, lurking in the cemetery's hinterland. Billy made an obscene gesture at him, which caused the vicar to stumble over his intonement.

"Not a bad turnout," Carl said as if he were some kind of professional funeral inspector.

"Poor Jackie," Sue said.

In the church beforehand they had sung "Abide with Me," a hymn chosen by Reggie on the grounds that Mum always cried when she heard it because they had sung it at her own mother's funeral. Reggie had arranged the service with the help of Mary, Trish, and Jean. Mum wasn't a churchgoer, so it was hard to know what she would have liked. "Aye, hatched, matched, and dispatched within a church, like most of us," Trish said as if she were saying something wise. "There must be *something,* when you think about it," Jean said. Reggie didn't see why there had to be anything. "We're all alone," Dr. Hunter once said to her. "All alone and cast adrift in the vast infinity of space" (was she thinking about Laika?), and Reggie said, "But we have one another, Dr. H.," and Dr. Hunter said, "Yes we do, Reggie. We have one another."

Quite a few people on the bus had given Reggie funny looks because of the way she was dressed, and a couple of girls on the top deck, no more than twelve, all fruity lip gloss and incredibly tedious secrets, openly sniggered at the clothes she was wearing. Reggie felt like saying, You try going through the wardrobe of a middle-aged, born-again ex-teacher to find something you could wear in public without attracting scorn. Lacking any other option, Reggie had chosen the most nondescript of Ms. MacDonald's garments she could find—a viscose cream sweater, a nylon maroon anorak, and pair of polyester black slacks rolled over a hundred times at the waist and held up with a belt. As far as Reggie could tell, Ms. MacDonald didn't own (*hadn't* owned) a single garment that wasn't made from synthetic fibers. It was only when she put on Ms. MacDonald's clothes that Reggie realized just how big and tall she had been before she shrank inside her clothes so that they had draped themselves on her body as if she were no more than a coat hanger.

"That's a big-boned woman," Mum said after she met Ms. Mac-Donald for the first time at a parents' evening. Reggie thought of Mum, awkward and ill at ease at the horrible posh school, Ms. MacDonald rattling on about Aeschylus as if Mum had the foggiest. Now they were both dead (not to mention Aeschylus). Everyone *was* dead.

Reggie didn't put on Ms. MacDonald's underwear; the big pants and stretched gray bras were a step too far. Her own clothes were still drying on a rack in Ms. MacDonald's bathroom, except for her jacket, which was so saturated with the man's blood that it was past the point of rescue. "Out, damned spot," she said to the wheelie-bin as she threw the jacket into it. They had done *Macbeth* for standard grade. *Who would have thought the old man to have had so much blood in him?* He wasn't that old. Old enough to be her father. His name was Jackson Brodie. She'd had his blood on her hands, warm blood in the cold night. She had been washed in his blood.

As he was being loaded onto the stretcher, she had plunged her hand into his jacket pocket, hoping to find some form of identity, and had pulled out a postcard with a picture of Bruges on the front, and on the back his address and a message: *Dear Dad, Bruges is very interesting, it has a lot of nice buildings. It is raining. Have eaten a lot of chips and chocolate. Missing you! Love you! Marlee xxx.*

The postcard was still in her bag, muddy and bloody and wrinkled up. She had two postcards now, their bright messages touched with death. She supposed she should hand the man's in to someone. She would like to give it back to the man himself. If he was still alive. The air-ambulance doctor told her they were taking him to the Royal Infirmary, but when she had phoned this morning, they had no record of a Jackson Brodie. Reggie wondered if that meant he had died.

Adam Lay Ybounden

Not dead then, not yet. Not exactly alive, though. In some mysterious place in between.

He'd always imagined it, if he'd imagined it at all, as something like the Hilton at Heathrow Airport—a beige, bland limbo where everyone was in transit. If he had paid more attention during his Catholic childhood, he might have remembered Purgatory's purifying flames. They now consumed him continually, a fire with no end as if he were some kind of everlasting fuel. Nor could he recollect any teaching that had ever referred to the continuous radio static in the head and the sensation of giant millipedes crawling all over his skin and the other, even more unpleasant feeling, that large *clackety-clack* cockroaches were grazing on his brains. He wondered what other surprises God's halfway house was going to present.

It wasn't fair, he thought peevishly. *"Who said life was fair?"* his father had said to him a hundred times. He had said the same himself to his own daughter. *("It's not fair, Daddy.")* Parents were miserable buggers. It *should* be fair. It should be paradise.

Death, Jackson noticed, had made him crabbed. He shouldn't be here, he should be with Niamh—wherever that was—the idyllic place where all the dead girls walked, risen up and honored. Fuck. His head really hurt. Not fair.

People came to visit him occasionally. His mother, his father, his brother. They were all dead, so Jackson knew he must be too. They were vague round the edges, and if he tried to look at them for too long, they started to wobble and fade. He supposed he was vague round the edges too.

The catalogue of the dead seemed full of random choices. His old geography teacher, an antagonistic, apoplectic sort who had a fatal stroke in the staff room. Jackson's first-ever girlfriend, a nice, straightforward girl called Angela who died of an aneurysm in her husband's arms on her thirtieth birthday. Mrs. Patterson, an old neighbor who used to sit drinking tea and gossiping with his mother when Jackson was small. Jackson hadn't thought about her in decades, would have been hard put to name her if she hadn't turned up at his bedside, smelling of camphor and carrying an old leatherette shopping bag. Julia's sister, Amelia, came once (as recalcitrant as ever) to sit at his bedside. He wondered if her presence meant that she had died on the operating table. The woman in red from the train appeared one afternoon, distinctly less vivacious than the last time he saw her. The dead were legion. He wished they would stop coming to see him.

It was exhausting being dead. He had more of a social life than when he was alive. It wasn't as if they had any conversations, the most he had got out of them was a vague mumbling, although Amelia had, to his bafflement, suddenly shouted, "Stuffing!" to him, and a middle-aged woman he had never seen before bent down to whisper in his ear to ask if he had seen her dog. His brother never visited, and his sister never came back. She was the only person he really wanted to see.

He was woken by a small terrier barking at the foot of the bed. He knew he wasn't really awake, not by any previous definition of the word. The voice of Mr. Spock (or Leonard Nimoy, depending on how you looked at it) murmured in his ear, "It's life, Jackson, but not as we know it."

He'd had enough. He was getting out of this madhouse, even if it killed him. He opened his eyes.

"You're back with us, then?" a woman's voice said. Someone loomed in and out of his vision. Fuzzy round the edges.

"Fuzzy," he said. Maybe he said it only in his head. He was in hospital. The fuzzy person was a nurse. He was alive. Apparently.

"Hello, soldier," the nurse said.

Outlaw

What were they doing up at this unearthly hour? All four of them back at the dining-room table, breakfasting together this time. Patrick had made French toast, served it with crème fraîche and out-of-season raspberries, the Wedgwood plates snowy with icing sugar as if they were in a restaurant. The raspberries had been flown all the way from Mexico.

Bridget and Tim had slept undisturbed, but Louise had been up for hours at the train-crash site. She felt drained of her lifeblood, but Patrick, who had operated throughout the night as one accident victim after another was wheeled into theater, was his usual chipper self. Mr. Fix-It.

Louise poured a cup of coffee and contemplated the red raspberries on the white plate, drops of blood in the snow. A fairy tale. She felt sick with tiredness. She was trapped in a nightmare, it was like that Buñuel film where they all sit down to eat but never get any food, only in this case she was constantly being faced with food she couldn't stomach.

Bridget had once been a fashion buyer for a department-store chain, although you would never have guessed it to look at her. She was wearing an aggressive three-piece outfit that was probably very expensive but had the kind of pattern you would get if you cut up the flags of several obscure countries and then gave them to a blind pigeon to stick back together again.

Tim had been the head honcho in a big accountancy company and had taken "the luxury of early retirement." "I'm a golf widow," Bridget said with an expression of mock bereavement. Bridget didn't say what she did with her time now and Louise didn't ask because she suspected that the answer would irritate her. Patrick was good Irish, Bridget was bad Irish.

"Mexican raspberries," Louise said. "How absurd is that? Talk about leaving a carbon footprint."

"Oh, too early in the day, Louise," Tim said, holding a hand to his forehead effetely. "Let's leave the food miles off the breakfast table."

"Where else do they belong?" Louise said. Guess who was the bolshy kid in *this* family?

"Louise didn't have a rebellious phase when she was a teenager," Patrick said. "She's making up for it now, apparently." He laughed and Louise gave him a long look. Was he patronizing her? Of course it was true, she hadn't had a mutinous youth because it was hard to kick against the pricks when your own mother was coming in late (if at all) and puking her guts up like the best of badly behaved teenagers. Louise had been a grown-up for longer than most people her age. *"Making up for it now."* Apparently. She'd never had a father to speak of—one night on Gran Canaria hardly counted—and she wondered if that was Patrick's appeal—had she subconsciously seen him as the father figure she had never had, was that how he had got past her defenses and under her duvet? What did that make her—a complex Electra?

"I don't think it's rebellious to want to talk about the politics of consumption," she said to Tim. "Do you?"

While he was searching for an answer, she turned to Patrick and said, "French toast. Or eggy bread, as we in the lower classes used to call it." Why didn't she just poke him with a fork?

"My father worked for Dublin Corporation all his life," Patrick said genially. "I hardly think that qualified us for belonging to the upper echelons of society." He was an Irishman, his weapons were words, whereas Louise was by her nature a street fighter, and for a brief but satisfying moment she thought about throwing his precious French toast at his head. Patrick smiled at her. Positively beamish. She smiled back. Marriage—tough love.

"Oh, I don't know about that, Paddy," Bridget—the other half of "us"—piped up. "It wasn't as if Dada was a *dustman,* he was a surveyor. The Brennans were never what you would call lower class."

"Huzzah for the bourgeoisie," Louise said. "Oops, did I say that out loud? I didn't mean to."

"Louise," Patrick said gently, laying a hand on her arm.

"Louise what?" she said, shaking his arm off.

"There goes the diet," Bridget said, gamely ignoring everyone and forking up her food. Louise wanted to say, *"Looks to me like it went a long time ago,"* but managed to zip her lips.

"Eat something, Louise," Patrick coaxed. There he went again, Dada knows best. Love is patient, love is kind, she reminded herself. But should she really be taking marital advice from a misogynist first-century Roman? "French bread, eggy toast, whatever you want to call it," he said, "you should eat."

"Shame about last night," Bridget said.

"That the train crash wrecked dinner?" Louise said. "Yeah, big shame."

"Thank goodness we decided to come up by car," Tim said. Louise wondered about pouring coffee on his balding head.

"I am aware it was a terrible disaster," Bridget said primly. "Poor Paddy was operating all night." Louise didn't count, of course. Patrick was a saint. He *saved* people, according to Bridget. "He saves their hips, usually," Louise said, and Patrick barked a laugh.

Nice and clean in an operating theater, only a bit of blood, patients quiet and well-behaved. Not down-and-dirty on a rail track, soaked with rain, finding severed limbs and listening to people crying out, or worse, not crying out at all. She had held a man's hand while a doctor amputated his leg at the scene. She was still wearing her diamond ring, its facets glinting in the emergency arc lights. She hadn't needed to go, but she was police, that's what you did.

"Are the transport police handling the investigation?" Tim asked, all pomp and no circumstance, as if he knew something about accident procedure.

"They're providing the deputy SIO," Louise said without elaboration.

"Senior Investigating Officer," Patrick said helpfully when Tim looked blank. Or blanker than usual.

"But isn't there a—what's it called—Rail Accident Investigation Bureau now?"

"Branch." Louise sighed. "It's called the Rail Accident Investigation Branch. The transport police aren't big enough in Scotland to handle this investigation."

"And sudden loss of life immediately involves the procurator fiscal," Patrick said.

"But why—?"

Christ on a bike. How boring could you get?

Louise didn't care what kind of shit was thrown her way, it had to be better than the company of Bridget and Tim. Patrick was taking them to St. Andrews today.

"I hope neither of you is thinking of playing golf?" Bridget asked fretfully.

"Oh, you never know, we might get a round in," Patrick laughed. He was relentlessly good-humored with his sister, downright twinkly, in fact. It seemed to mollify her quite successfully, and Louise wondered if she could manage twinkly. It felt like a stretch.

Patrick touched the back of Louise's hand with the back of his fingertips, gently, as if she were sick, possibly terminal. "We were thinking of driving up to Glamis tomorrow. We'd like it if you came with us. *I'd* like it," he added softly. "I know you're not working tomorrow."

"Actually something came up. And I am. Working."

Drive carefully," Louise said as she finally escaped the breakfast table.

"I always drive carefully."

"Other people don't."

She could have walked round to the Hunters' but she didn't, she drove.

If you had a good arm you could probably have stood on the roof of their block of flats and thrown a rock that would have landed in the Hunters' driveway. Tuesday Joanna Hunter, today Neil Hunter. Two completely different visits with two completely different goals, but it seemed a very strange coincidence that she should need to drop in on both husband and wife in the space of three days. *A coincidence is just an explanation waiting to happen,* Jackson Brodie had said to her once, but no matter how you looked at it, there was no relation between Andrew Decker's release and Neil Hunter's present troubles. And just because Jackson Brodie said something didn't make it true. He was hardly the oracle of crime solving.

★   ★   ★

The Hunters' house was dead-eyed and quiet. Louise parked next to Mr. Hunter's showy beast of a black-badged Range Rover, a bigger threat to the planet than Mexican raspberries.

Louise rang the front door bell, and when Neil Hunter answered, she showed him her warrant card and with her best rise-and-shine smile said, "Good morning, Mr. Hunter."

Neil Hunter looked rough, although still on the good side of haggard. Louise could see why someone like Joanna Hunter would be attracted to him. He was everything she wasn't.

He was wearing Levi's and an old Red Sox T-shirt, a wolf in wolf's clothing. She could smell last night's whisky still breathing out from his pores. He looked rumpled enough in both face and clothes to have just got out of bed except that Louise could smell coffee and see that there were plastic files and papers scattered across the kitchen table as if he had been up all night doing his accounts. Perhaps he'd been working out if the insurance payout from the arcade fire would cover his taxes.

The table was a big old-fashioned thing that you half expected to see a Victorian cook kneading dough on. Bridget and Tim's wedding present to them, hauled out of the boot of the car yesterday, had been a bread maker. "A good one," Bridget said, "not one of the cheap ones." Louise wondered how long she would have to wait before she could drop it into a charity shop. There were not many things in life that Louise was sure of, but she would bet the house on the fact that she was going to go to her grave without ever having made a loaf of bread.

Neil Hunter glanced at the warrant card and said, "Detective Chief Inspector," with a sardonic lift of the eyebrow, as if there were something amusing about her rank. His voice was a gravelly Glaswegian that sounded as if he'd breakfasted on cigarettes. Twenty years ago she too would have found his moodiness attractive. Now she just wanted to punch him. But then, she seemed to want to punch everyone at the moment.

"Mind if I come in for a minute?" she said, no slippage in her jaunty persona. She was over the threshold before he could protest. Police weren't like vampires, they didn't wait to be invited in.

"I'd like to have a word, about the arcade fire."

"The fire investigation report's come back?" he said. He looked relieved, as if he'd expected her to tell him something else.

"Yes. I'm afraid the fire was started deliberately." He didn't exactly throw up his hands in shock and horror. Resignation, if anything. Or maybe indifference. The house was surprisingly quiet. No sign of Dr. Hunter or her baby. Or the girl. The one good thing about the train crash, if you could say that, which you couldn't really, was that it had got in the way of any lurid stories about Andrew Decker's release or the current whereabouts of Joanna Mason. The dog pattered into the kitchen, sniffed her shoes, and then flopped down on the floor.

"Do you mind if I ask where Dr. Hunter is?" Louise asked Neil Hunter.

"Do you mind if I ask why?" The question seemed to fluster him. He hadn't looked nervous when she talked about the fire, but he looked downright jittery at the mention of his wife. Interesting. With an impatient sigh he said, "She's gone down to Yorkshire, an aunt of hers was taken ill. What's Jo got to do with any of this?"

"Nothing. I was here Tuesday, didn't she tell you? I came to tell her about Andrew Decker's release."

"*That,*" he said with a grimace. "He's out?"

"Yes, *that,* I'm afraid. She didn't tell you?" Wasn't that what marriage was for? The sharing of your deepest, darkest secrets? Perhaps she had more in common with Joanna Hunter than she had first thought. "The news of his release has been leaked to the press. I wanted to warn Dr. Hunter that the past was about to be dredged up again. She really didn't say anything?"

"She was in a hurry to get away. Happy coincidence, I suppose—if she's in Yorkshire, she might be able to avoid all the fuss."

"I don't think Yorkshire's a no-go area for the press," Louise said. "But I suppose it might throw them off the scent." Unless they came looking for the aunt, of course. "An aunt by marriage or by blood?" she asked. "On the mother's side or the father's?"

"Is that relevant in some way?"

Louise shrugged. "Just curious."

"Her father's sister, Agnes Barker. Happy?"

"Cheers," Louise said. She grinned at him. He had *liar* written all the way through him, like a stick of rock. "She did say something about escaping for a bit."

Neil Hunter seemed suddenly tired and he gestured to her to take a seat at the table and said, "Coffee?," pouring beans into a hopper in an expensive espresso machine that did the whole process, from grinding the beans to steaming the milk, and looked as if it would grow the beans as well if you asked it nicely. The smell was too good to resist, Louise would sooner give up an arm than coffee in the morning. That was an unfortunate thought. She had a flashback to last night, picking up an arm from the track and searching desperately for the owner. A small arm.

"Where in Yorkshire?"

"Hawes," Neil Hunter said.

"Whores?"

"*H-a-w-e-s.* In the Dales."

Joanna hadn't mentioned an aunt when Louise met her a couple of days ago (although why should she?). Perhaps he was right, the aunt's illness had happened serendipitously, at just the right time for her *escape*. A very handy aunt.

★　　★　　★

So . . . ," Louise said brightly, "can you think of anyone who might have wanted to burn down your property, someone with a grudge against you, perhaps?"

"Plenty people I've pissed off in my time," Neil Hunter said.

"Perhaps you could draw up a list for us?"

"You're joking?"

"No. We're also going to need all your accounts, business and personal. And your insurance policies as well."

"You think I burned it down for the insurance money," he said wearily, a statement rather than a question.

"Did you?"

"Do you think I'd tell you if I had?"

"Someone will be back later this morning with a warrant for your documentation," Louise said. "It's not going to be a problem for you, is it? The documentation?" She liked it when guys like Neil Hunter got touchy with her because at the end of the day she was police and they weren't. Hearts, clubs, diamonds, spades, warrant. Trumps.

"No," he said. "Nae problem, doll." Ironically self-referential Glaswegians, what were they like?

The phone rang and Neil Hunter stared at it as if he'd never seen one before.

"Problem, doll?" Louise said.

He snatched up the phone just as it went to the answer machine and said, "Do you mind if I take this?" and without waiting for her to answer left the room with the phone. Before he closed the door, she caught a glimpse of the living room across the hall. She could see the winter honeysuckle and Christmas box still in the blue-and-white jug. From here they looked dead.

She took her coffee over to Joanna Hunter's notice board and studied it. She had looked at it the last time she was here and afterwards had driven out to Office World at Hermiston Gate and bought one for their own kitchen, but she had been unable to think of anything that she wanted to put on it.

On Joanna Hunter's notice board, there were lots of pictures of the baby and the dog but only one of Neil Hunter, taken with Joanna Hunter on holiday. They both looked much younger and more carefree than they did now. There was one of Joanna Hunter (Mason then) in her teens, in athletics gear, breasting a finishing tape, and one of her taking part in the London marathon, looking in better shape than Louise could ever hope to be in those circumstances. There was also a photograph of Joanna Hunter, the Edinburgh medical student, holding aloft a trophy with a triumphant grin, surrounded by others in the same rig-out. They were all wearing team sweatshirts with the initials "EURC," familiar letters but Louise couldn't think what they stood for. Edinburgh University something. Louise had done her English degree at Edinburgh, four years ahead of Joanna Hunter. Class of '89. A lifetime ago. Several lifetimes.

The notice board seemed a very public way of recording your life. Perhaps it was her way of countering the hundreds of images of her and her family that had, for a brief period, flooded the media. This is my life, it said, this is me. No longer a victim. Was her heart, her secret self, kept upstairs, shut away in a drawer? Three children and a mother in black-and-white.

Of course. "EURC." Edinburgh University Rifle Club. When she was at university, Louise had gone on a date (a refined term for what happened) with a guy who had been in the EURC. Who would have guessed that Joanna Hunter had once been the Annie Oakley of medical students? She could run, she could shoot. She was all ready for the next time.

★   ★   ★

When Neil Hunter came back into the kitchen, he looked rattled. His skin had acquired a sickly sheen and Louise wondered if he was an alcoholic.

"Another coffee?" he offered with a resigned expression on his face, but then, with a sudden, unexpected attempt at bonhomie, he said, "Or do you fancy a wee dram?" That was Weegies for you, morose one minute, too friendly the next. The cheerfulness was clearly false, he looked pale to the point of passing out. You had to wonder how a phone call could have that effect on someone.

"It's half past nine in the morning," Louise said when Neil Hunter produced two glasses and a bottle of Laphroaig from a cupboard.

"There you go, then, it's almost the night before," he said, pouring himself a generous two fingers of whisky. He held the bottle and looked at her inquiringly. "Come on, join a lonely guy in the hair of a dog."

The Famous Reggie

On her way up to the flat, Reggie stopped off at Mr. Hussain's on the corner of her street. Everyone called it "the Paki shop," racism so casual it sounded like affection. Mr. Hussain would patiently explain to anyone who would listen (which wasn't many) that he was actually a Bangladeshi. "A country in turmoil," he once said gloomily to Reggie.

"This one too," Reggie said.

Reggie thought about the handsome young Asian policeman and wondered if he was Bangladeshi too. He had beautiful skin, completely unblemished, like a child's, like Dr. Hunter's baby. Dr. Hunter should have taken Reggie with her. She could have looked after the baby while Dr. Hunter looked after the so-called aunt.

"What's her name?" she had asked Mr. Hunter.

"What's whose name?" Mr. Hunter said testily.

"The aunt's name," Reggie said.

There was a beat of hesitation before Mr. Hunter said, "Agnes."

"Auntie Agnes?"

"Yes."

"Or Aunt Agnes?"

"Does it matter?" Mr. Hunter said.

"It might matter to the aunt."

Reggie bought a local newspaper and a Mars bar. Mr. Hussain tapped the front cover of the newspaper as he rang up the price on the till. "Terrible," he said.

The *Evening News* was making the most of the train crash. "CARNAGE!," the headline screamed above a full-color picture of a train carriage that was almost broken in two. Carnage from the Latin *caro, carnis,* meaning "flesh." Same root as *carnival*. "The taking away of the flesh." You couldn't really get two more different words than *carnival* and *carnage*. Everywhere — well, perhaps not everywhere, not in Bangladesh, for example, but certainly in an awful lot of places — they had some kind of carnival before Lent, but in Britain all you got were pancakes. Last Shrove Tuesday had been during the dark days between Mum's death and starting to work for Dr. Hunter. Reggie had still made pancakes, though, sat in front of *Rebus* on her own, and ate them all. Then was sick.

The photograph on the front page of the newspaper didn't convey anything about what it had been like last night, in the dark, in the rain. Or what it was like to have your hands sticky with someone else's blood or to feel that one man's life could seem like the whole world on a person's small shoulders.

"Terrible," Reggie agreed with Mr. Hussain.

When the paramedics finally came to relieve Reggie of her burden, one of them put a mask on the man and bagged him while the other one ripped open his shirt and slapped paddles onto his chest. The man jerked and twitched back into life. It was so like an episode of *ER* that it didn't feel real.

"Well done," one of the paramedics said to her.

"Will he be okay?"

"You gave him a chance," he said, and then they took him away and put him in a helicopter. And that was that. Reggie had lost him.

Reggie sighed and picked up her paper and Mars bar. "Well, must get on, things to do, Mr. H."

"Haven't you forgotten something?" he asked. Mr. Hussain always gave Reggie tic tacs for free. She wasn't particularly fond of tic tacs, but gift horses, et cetera. He rattled a box of tic tacs in the air before gently underarm-bowling them to her.

"Thanks," Reggie said, catching them in one hand.

"We make a good team," Mr. Hussain said.

"Totally."

Last week Mr. Hussain had shown her a copy of the Edinburgh property press that said the area was up-and-coming. "Hot spot," he said gloomily. Reggie's block of flats showed no sign of either up or coming. The close always smelled unpleasant, and Reggie was the only one who ever cleaned the stair. The tenement was in a cul-de-sac at the bottom of which brooded an abandoned bonded warehouse, its black-barred windows as grim as anything in Dickens.

Mr. Hussain said there was a rumor that Tesco's was going to knock down the bonded warehouse and build a new Tesco Metro, but Reggie and Mr. Hussain agreed that they would believe it when they saw it, and Mr. Hussain wasn't going to start worrying about the competition yet.

The door to Reggie's flat was not beautiful. Dr. Hunter said that the most beautiful doors in the world were in Florence, on "the Battistero," which was Italian for baptistry. Dr. Hunter had spent six months in Rome on a school exchange when she was sixteen ("Ah, *bella Roma*") and had visited "everywhere," Verona, Firenze, Bologna, Milano. Dr. Hunter pronounced Italian words properly, whether it was "Leonardo da Vinci" or "pizza napolitana" (Dr. Hunter had taken Reggie out for tea on her birthday, Reggie had chosen to go to the Pizza Express in Stockbridge). Reggie couldn't think of anything better than living in Florence for six months. Or Paris, Venice, Vienna, Granada. St. Petersburg. Anywhere.

There was some random spray-painting on Reggie's front door, nothing artistic, just a boy going up and down the stair one night leaving behind him a wobbly snail-trail of red paint. The front door also had scratch marks on it, as if a giant cat had tried to claw its way in (Reggie had no idea how that had happened), and also marks that looked as if someone had tried to chop their way in one night with an axe (they had, looking for Billy, naturally). None of these things was new. What was new was a note, stuck on the door with chewing gum, that read, "Reggie Chase—you cant hide from us." No apostrophe. She took some time reading this message and then took some time wondering why her front door wasn't locked. Perhaps the giant cat had come back. The door swung open as soon as she touched it.

Had careless, infuriating Billy been here? He lived in a flat in the Inch but he often used her Gorgie address to confuse people and came by occasionally to see if he had any interesting mail. Sometimes he gave Reggie cash but she didn't like to ask where he had got it from. One thing was sure, he wouldn't have earned it, by any definition of the word. She always put the money in her savings account and hoped that by sitting there quietly it would clean itself up and somehow rid itself of the taint of Billy.

Reggie stood on the threshold of the living room and stared. It took her brain a while to process what her eyes were looking at. The room was completely trashed. The drawers from the sideboard were pulled out and emptied on the floor, the leather sofa had been slashed, all Mum's favorite ornaments thrown around and broken, thimbles and miniature teapots scattered all over the carpet. All of Reggie's essays and notes had been emptied out of their folders and box files and her books were piled in a huge heap in the middle of the living-room carpet like a bonfire waiting to be lit. There was a funny smell, like cat pee, coming from the pile.

In Mum's bedroom, drawers were upended, and Mum's clothes, strewn around on the floor, had had a knife or a pair of scissors taken to them. Something that looked like chocolate was smeared on the pink broderie-anglaise sheets. Reggie was pretty sure it wasn't chocolate. It certainly didn't smell like chocolate.

Reggie still kept her clothes in her old bedroom, and it was the same story there, all her stuff tossed on the floor. There was a smell of something nasty in here too, and Reggie couldn't bring herself to look too closely at her clothes.

In the kitchen everything had been pulled out of the cabinets, the fridge gaped open, food scattered everywhere. Cutlery was flung around, plates and cups smashed. Milk had been poured on the floor, a bottle of tomato sauce had been thrown against the wall and had left a great arterial spray of red.

In the shower room, which was just a hall closet that had been tiled and plumbed, the walls had been spray-painted rather ineptly with the words, "Your dead." Reggie felt bile rising up, making her nauseous. *You cant hide from us.* Who was *us?* Who were these people who didn't know how to use an apostrophe? They must be looking for Billy. Billy knew a lot of ungrammatical people.

She gave a little cry, a small wounded animal. This was her home, this was Mum's home, and it was wrecked. Desecrated. It wasn't as if it was much to begin with, but it was all Reggie had.

Then a hand gave her a hefty shove and she went sprawling into the shower, pulling down the curtain as she flailed. An unfortunate few frames of *Psycho* played in her mind. She banged her forehead when she fell and she wanted to cry.

Two men. Youngish, thuggish. One ginger-haired, one a bleached blond, his face pitted with old acne scars like orange peel. She hadn't seen either of them before. The blond one was holding a saw-toothed knife that looked as if it could slice open a shark. Reggie could see a scrap of Mum's pink broderie-anglaise downie cover attached to one of the teeth. Her insides melted. She was worried she would wet herself, or worse. *"I'm not a child,"* she'd said to the policemen last night, but it wasn't true.

She thought of her mother laid out on the side of the pool in her unflattering orange Lycra bathing suit. Reggie didn't want to be found dead, sprawled in an undignified heap in the shower in Ms. MacDonald's horrible clothes. She didn't even have any underwear on. She could feel the pulse beating uncomfortably hard in her neck. Were they going to kill her? Rape her? Both? Worse? She could think of worse, it involved the knife and time. She had to do something, say something. Dr. Hunter had once told her that it was important that you talk to an attacker, get him to see you as a person, not just an object. Reggie's mouth was dry, as if she'd been eating sandpaper, and forming words was a real effort. She wanted to say, "Don't kill me, I haven't lived yet," but instead she whispered, "Billy's not here. I haven't seen him for ages. Honestly."

The men exchanged a puzzled look. Ginger said, "Who's Billy? We're looking for a guy called Reggie."

"Never heard of him. Sweartogod."

Unbelievably, the men made to leave. "We'll be back," the blond one said. Then the other, carroty one said, "Got a present for you," and pulled a book from his pocket — unmistakably a Loeb Classic — and tossed it to her like a grenade. She didn't even attempt to catch it, imagined it exploding in her hands, didn't believe it could contain only something as harmless as words. She heard Ms. MacDonald's voice in her head saying, "Words are the most powerful weapons we have." Hardly. Words couldn't save you from a huge express train bearing down on you at full speed. *(Help!)* Couldn't save you from neds bearing gifts. *(No thanks.)*

"*Hasta la vista,* baby," Ginger said, and they both left. They were idiots. Idiots with Loeb Classics.

She picked up the Loeb, a green one, that had flopped open facedown on the shower floor, like a grounded bird. The first volume of the *Iliad.* How was that a message? She picked the book up and read the faded pencil inscription on the flyleaf: *Moira MacDonald, Girton College, 1971.* Funny to think of Ms. MacDonald being young. Funny to think of her being dead. Even funnier to think of one of her missing Loebs being in the hands of Billy's enemies.

Trojan horses had surprising insides and so did Ms. MacDonald's *Iliad.* When Reggie opened the pages, she found it had been the subject of razor-sharp surgery, its heart cut out in a neat square. A casket for something. A casket and a grave. A perfect hiding place. For what?

Reggie thought they had gone, but then the blond one suddenly stuck his head back round the door. Reggie screamed.

"Forgot to say," he said, laughing at the horror on her face. "Don't go to the police about this wee visit or, guess what?" He made the shape of a gun with his finger and thumb and pointed it at her. Then he left again.

Reggie surprised herself by suddenly vomiting up all her toast into the toilet. It took her a while to stop shivering, she felt as if she were coming down with flu, but she supposed it was just horror.

She stumbled down the tenement stairs, drenched in cold sweat and her heart hammering. She barged back into Mr. Hussain's shop. "All right?" Mr. Hussain asked, and she mumbled, "No, half left," which was a poor joke of Billy's when he was small. He wasn't funny, even then. Should she tell Mr. Hussain? What would happen? He would make her a cup of sugary tea in the back of the shop and then he would phone the police and then the men would come back and shoot her with an imaginary gun? Kill her with words? They looked exactly like the types who had real guns. They looked exactly like Billy.

"Got to dash, Mr. H. I'm gonna miss my bus."

If only she had Sadie with her, Reggie thought as she walked as fast as she could to the bus stop. People thought twice about messing with you if you had a big dog by your side. "It's like the parting of the Red Sea when you're out with Sadie," Dr. Hunter said once, fondling the big dog's ears. "I always feel safe with her." Did Dr. Hunter need to feel safe? Why? Something to do with her *history?*

Had they really been looking for her? Made a mistake about her gender *("a guy called Reggie")*? Why? She had done nothing apart from being Billy's sister. Maybe that was enough. She tried phoning her brother and got a "the person you are trying to reach is not available" message. She dialed Dr. Hunter's number, but it rang and rang without answer. *("Your dead.")* Without the apostrophe it implied something else, the dead that belonged to Reggie. There were enough of them.

The thing was, when Mr. Hunter was speaking to her on the phone, Reggie had heard Sadie bark in the background. When she wasn't at work, Dr. Hunter took Sadie with her everywhere, so why would she leave her behind?

"Her aunt's allergic."

"Aunt Agnes?"

"Yes."

"Can't Dr. Hunter give her something for it? Antihistamine or something? Why isn't she answering her phone, Mr. Hunter?"

"Leave Jo alone, Reggie. This is a bad time for her. It's enough the past coming back to haunt her without you hounding her. Okay?"

"But—"

"You know what, Reggie?" Mr. Hunter said.

"What?"

"Just leave it. I've got a lot on my mind right now."

"Me too, Mr. H. Me too."

Missing in Action

A long time ago, a long, long time ago, when the world was much younger and so was Jackson, he had his blood group tattooed on his chest, just above his heart. A soldier's trick so that when you are shot or blown up, the medics can treat you as quickly as possible. Other guys he was in the army with had extended their skin-ink collections, adding on women and bulldogs and Union Jacks and, yes, indeed, the word *Mother*, but Jackson had never been a fan of the tattooist's art, had even promised his daughter a thousand pounds in cash if she made it to twenty-one without feeling the need to decorate her skin with a butterfly or a dolphin or the Chinese character for happiness. Jackson himself had stuck with the one practical, lowercase message—"blood type A positive," until now no more than a faded-blue souvenir of another life. "A positive"—a nice common kind of blood shared by roughly 35 percent of the population. Plenty of donors. And he'd needed them apparently, every precious ounce of red blood having been replaced courtesy of a band of blood brothers and sisters who had stopped him from being erased from his own life.

"We thought we'd got the artery, but you just kept pumping

it out. It took a couple of goes," a cheerful doctor told him. "Dr. Bruce, call me Mike," he said, sitting on the end of Jackson's bed and grinning at him as if they'd just met in a bar. Call-Me-Mike was too young to be a doctor. Jackson wondered if the nurses knew that a boy from the local primary school was loose on the wards.

"Just humor him," the fuzzy—now less fuzzy—nurse murmured in Jackson's ear. "He thinks he's a grown-up."

"Thank you," Jackson said to him.

"No worries, mate."

An Australian schoolboy.

The junior registrar, "Dr. Samms, call me Charlie," looked like Harry Potter. Jackson didn't really want to be treated by a doctor who looked like Harry Potter, but he wasn't in a position to argue. "You seem to have taken a bit of a dunt to the head," Wizard Boy said. "Ever had one before?"

"Maybe," Jackson said.

"Not a good idea," Wizard Boy said as if being banged on the head were something you volunteered for.

"Fuzzy," Jackson said. It was definitely his favorite word. When his daughter was first learning to talk, her first word was *cat*. She used it for everything—ducks, milk, buggy—anything of interest in her life, everything was *cat*. A one-word world. It made life much simpler, he must phone her and tell her. As soon as he could remember her name. Or, come to that, his own name.

He slept, and when he woke again, there was another nurse by the side of the bed.

"Who am I?" he asked. He sounded like an amateur philosopher, but it wasn't a metaphysical question. Really, who *was* he?

"Your name's Andrew Decker," she said.

"Really?" Jackson said. The name rang a tiny, tiny bell somewhere in the dark pit of his abandoned memories, yet he didn't have any relationship with it at all. He didn't *feel* like an Andrew

Decker, but then, he didn't really feel like anyone. "How do you know?"

"Your wallet was in your jacket pocket," the nurse said. "It had a driving license with your name and address on it. The police are trying to contact someone at the address."

His ulnar artery had been partially severed, leading to "profuse and rapid bleeding," the Potter look-alike said. His blood pressure had dropped and he had gone into shock. His brain had been starved of blood. "Fatigue, shortness of breath, chills?" Australian Mike, the flying doctor, said. He looked as if he took more drugs than his patients. "Nausea, confusion, disorientation, hallucinations? Yeah?"

"I was in a white corridor."

"Bit of a cliché," Wizard Boy said.

"Don't knock it till you've tried it," Jackson said.

"You might never remember the accident," the flying doctor said. "It was probably never transferred into your long-term memory. But you'll remember just about everything else. After all, you already know you have a daughter."

Someone had given him first aid, had saved his life at the scene. One more person he would never be able to thank.

A policewoman came and sat by the side of his bed and waited patiently for him to focus on her. Someone had visited the address on his driving license and the people who lived there had never heard of an "Andrew Decker." It was an old driving license, not a photo card, perhaps he had failed to renew it when he changed his address?

Jackson looked at her blankly. "No idea."

"Well, early days," she said cheerfully. "Someone's bound to come forward and claim you."

It was strange to be surrounded by the aftermath of a disaster that you had no memory of. He could remember nothing about the train crash, could remember nothing about anything. He was a blank sheet of paper, a clock without hands. Now he wished that he hadn't been so sparse with the information that he'd been branded with. Alongside his blood group he should have added his name, rank, and serial number.

"I had my cat chipped," a nurse said to him. "It gives me peace of mind."

I died," he said to a new doctor.

"Briefly," she said dismissively, as if you had to be dead a lot longer to impress her. Dr. Foster, a woman, who didn't seem to want to be on first-name terms.

"But technically . . . ," he said, too weak to pursue the argument.

She sighed as if patients were always bickering about their dead or alive status. "Yes. Technically dead," she conceded. "Very briefly."

He'd already been here in another lifetime. How many weeks? "Eighteen hours, actually," the new doctor said. He'd been to hell and back (or possibly heaven and back), and it had taken less than a day. Quite impressive. When would they let him go home?

"How about when you know where you live?" Dr. Foster offered.

"Fair enough," Jackson said.

He slept. That's what he did. He was the sleeper. He slept for years. When he woke up, they told him about the train crash again. A nurse showed him the front page of a newspaper. "CAR-NAGE!" it said. He couldn't remember what the word meant. Nothing to do with cars, he supposed. He liked cars. He was a man called Andrew Decker who liked cars but who had been traveling on a train, destination unknown. No ticket, no phone, no signs of a life. No one who had noticed that he'd gone and not come back.

Now how long had he been here?

"Twenty hours," Dr. Foster said.

Reggie Chase, Girl Detective

I thought I could take the dog for a walk."

"The dog?"

"Sadie."

Mr. Hunter sounded hoarse. He hadn't shaved and looked tired. *("He's like a bear in the morning.")* He smelled of the cigarettes that he was supposed to have given up "ages ago." The kitchen was already a mess. It seemed he was going to keep her hovering on the doorstep rather than invite her in. Reggie caught sight of a half-empty bottle of whisky on the counter. "Bachelor's rules apply," he said. He gave a little laugh, "When the cat's away, the dog will play." Two empty mugs sat on the big kitchen table, one of them had a smear of lipstick on the rim, pale coral, not Dr. Hunter's color. Did that come under Mr. Hunter's bachelor's rules too?

"Seeing as Dr. Hunter usually takes Sadie for her walk," Reggie said, "I thought I could do it for you while she's visiting her aunt. Aunt Agnes."

Mr. Hunter rubbed the stubble on his face as if he were having trouble remembering who Reggie was. Sadie had no such problem, appearing at Mr. Hunter's side, wagging her tail at the sight of Reggie, although in a more subdued way than usual.

"Have you spoken to Dr. Hunter since she left last night?"

"Yes, of course I have."

"How did you speak to her?"

"How?" Mr. Hunter frowned. "On the phone, of course."

"Her phone?"

"Yes. Her phone."

"Only I've been phoning Dr. Hunter, *on her phone,* and get no answer."

"I expect she's very busy."

"With the aunt?"

"Yes, the aunt."

"Aunt *Agnes?* In *Hawes?*"

"Yes and yes. I have spoken to her, Reggie. She's fine. She doesn't want to be bothered."

"Bothered?"

"What did you do to your head?" Mr. Hunter asked, changing the subject. "You look worse than I feel." Reggie gingerly felt the bruise on her forehead where she had hit it in the shower.

"Wasn't looking where I was going," she said.

Sadie whined impatiently. She had heard the word *walk* several sentences ago and still nothing had happened.

"You probably don't have time to take Sadie out," Reggie said. "You having a lot of things to do and everything." Mr. Hunter looked down at the dog as if it were going to answer for him and then shrugged and said, "Aye, right, fine, okay, then." Which seemed like a lot of words for yes, even for a Weegie.

"Can I have a phone number for Dr. Hunter's aunt?"

"No."

"Why not?" Reggie asked.

"Because her aunt needs peace and quiet."

"Can I leave my bag?"

"Bag?" Mr. Hunter echoed as if he couldn't see the enormous Topshop bag that Reggie had lugged all the way over there. She had taken the bus to the town center and bled her Topshop account. She had fled the flat in Gorgie with what she stood up in (Ms. MacDonald's clothes, unfortunately), and she wasn't going back for any of her stuff that was lying in a dodgy-smelling heap in her room. In fact, she wasn't going back to that flat for anything. She just wished that her books and A-level course work had been left undefiled.

In Topshop, Reggie had bought two pairs of jeans, two T-shirts, two sweaters, six pairs of underpants and socks, two bras, a pair of trainers, two pairs of pajamas, a coat, a scarf, a hat, and a pair of gloves. ("Never knowingly underdressed," Dr. Hunter used to laugh when she saw Reggie piling on her layers of winter clothes to go home.) Reggie had never bought so many clothes at one time, apart from when she and Mum had tried to comply with the gargantuan school-uniform list at the horrible posh school. Being in Topshop had been like buying a layette or a trousseau, both pleasingly old-fashioned words for starting a new life. Not much chance of that.

She put on a whole set of new clothes in the Topshop changing room and threw Ms. MacDonald's clothes into a Dumpster on the street. It felt like a cruel act. Ms. MacDonald herself was lying quietly in cold storage, as unwanted as her clothes.

Reggie had caught a bus from town to the hospital and presented herself at reception (she asked again about "Jackson Brodie," but there was still no record of him), where a very nice Polish girl ("from Gdansk") collected her and led her to a room so that she could look at Ms. MacDonald through glass. A room with a view. It was like looking at a tableau or being presented with a small, intimate piece of theater. Ms. MacDonald's face was uncovered and Reggie said, "Yes, that's her." Her face was bruised and swollen but she didn't look as bad as Reggie had expected. She didn't like to think what condition the rest of her was in. It seemed unlikely that she was all in one piece.

Reggie supposed that both her old teacher and her blue Saxo would be the subject of a lot of forensic tests. Last night, Sergeant Wiseman had made a note of Reggie's mobile phone number and said that someone would contact her when "the body" was released. Reggie wanted to say that it was nothing to do with her, but it would have sounded churlish given the circumstances — carnage et cetera. And anyway, she was only sixteen. She might be technically an adult, but really she was just a child. You couldn't make people who were almost children be responsible for dead bodies. Could you?

This was the third dead body Reggie had seen in her life. Ms. MacDonald, Mum, and the soldier last night. Four if you counted Banjo. It seemed a lot for a person of so few years.

She'd identified a dead body, had her flat vandalized, and been threatened by violent idiots, and it wasn't even lunchtime. Reggie hoped the rest of the day would be more uneventful.

No," Mr. Hunter said.

"No what?"

"No, you can't leave your bag, I have to go out."

"I have a key."

"Of course you do." Mr. Hunter gave a long-suffering sigh as if he were conceding a drawn-out argument. "Okay. Give me the bag, I'll get the dog-lead." He took the Topshop bag from Reggie and dropped it unceremoniously on the floor by the sink and then unhooked the dog's lead from behind the door and handed it over. An eager Sadie bounded past him as if set free from prison.

"Oh, and Mr. H.," Reggie said boldly (poking the bear), "it's Thursday. Dr. Hunter pays me on a Thursday."

"Does she, now?" Mr. Hunter said. He smiled at her, one of his nice smiles that recognized you as a special person, and took his wallet from the back pocket of his jeans and pinched out a small sheaf of notes without counting them. "Don't spend it all at once," he laughed, as if he were handing over pocket money rather than payment for a job well done. "Leave some clothes in the shops, okay?"

"Very funny, Mr. H. Thanks." No point in telling him that she'd been on her shopping spree because two jokers had wrecked her house and her clothes. The Hunters didn't live in that kind of world. Reggie didn't want to live in that kind of world either.

When Mr. Hunter had gone back in the house and shut the door, Reggie counted the money. It was half of what Dr. Hunter gave her.

Sadie had a basket of toys in the garage, balls, rubber bones and rings and an old teddy bear, and Reggie said, "Let's get a ball for you, Sadie," and Sadie gave a little *woof* of excitement at the word *ball*.

The garage used to be kept locked but then the key had got lost and no one had got round to cutting a new one. Dr. Hunter said that the worst thing that could happen was that her car might get stolen and it was insured, so what did it matter? Mr. Hunter said that was a cavalier attitude and Dr. Hunter said, "Well, you get one cut, then," which was probably the nearest thing to an argument between them that Reggie had ever witnessed. Mr. Hunter didn't know about the spare car key that she kept on a shelf in the garage, behind a tin of paint (Clouded Pearl, the color that the hall had been decorated in), because then he would "go ballistic," according to Dr. Hunter.

The garage was small because the house was built in the days when most people didn't own one car, let alone two, and the garage had been squashed into a small space next to the house as an afterthought, separated from the house by a narrow passage. Mr. Hunter's big Range Rover couldn't even get into the garage, and so it remained the snug home of Dr. Hunter's Toyota Prius. Reggie squeezed past the car to reach the basket and pick out Sadie's favorite, an old red rubber ball so chewed that it had lost almost all of its bounce.

"Come on, then, old girl," Reggie said to Sadie as she shut the garage door. It was what Dr. Hunter always said to the dog when they set off for a walk. It felt odd to be in charge of Sadie. No Dr. Hunter, no Mr. Hunter, no baby. Reggie realized she'd never been entirely alone with the dog before. They went through the gap in the hedge that let them directly into the field that today was home to three horses, all standing around rather listlessly as if they were waiting for something to happen. Reggie threw the ball and then raced round the field with the dog because that was what she liked best.

Here was the thing. Dr. Hunter had traveled to Hawes last night. *"She drove down last night,"* Mr. Hunter said on the phone this morning. So why was her car in the garage?

When they got back from their walk, the house was locked and there was no sign of Mr. Hunter. A note placed prominently on the kitchen table said, "Dear Reggie—actually I forgot—Jo suggested that maybe you would like to take our mutual friend to your place and look after her until she gets back. You'll probably have more time at the moment than I will, anyway. Thanks, Neil." It took Reggie a moment to realize that the note referred to the dog. Mr. Hunter seemed a different person on paper, he certainly used a lot more words. There was no mention of money for dog food, Reggie noticed.

The thing was. When she brought the dog back from her run in the field, Reggie had gone upstairs to Dr. Hunter's bedroom—Mr.

Hunter's too, of course—not for any reason, just to be there, to look, to feel closer to Dr. Hunter. She shouldn't have, she knew, but she wasn't doing any harm. Dr. Hunter wouldn't have minded, although you could be pretty sure that Mr. Hunter would.

The bed hadn't been made—Mr. Hunter's "bachelor's rules." Otherwise it was pretty tidy, although not as tidy as when Dr. Hunter was home. Sadie circled the room, sniffing everything like a tracker dog—the sheets, the carpet, the dry-cleaning bag that Dr. Hunter brought home with her yesterday lying over the back of a chair. Reggie took the newly cleaned suit out of its plastic shroud and hung it up in the closet next to one of Dr. Hunter's other suits. The closet was a big, walk-in affair, Dr. Hunter had one side, Mr. Hunter the other. All the clothes on Dr. Hunter's side smelled faintly of the perfume that she always wore. The plain blue bottle stood on the chest of drawers next to Dr. Hunter's old-fashioned silver-backed hairbrush, her spare inhaler, and a photograph of the baby taken when he was just a few days old and looking as if he were still waiting to be inflated. Reggie dabbed some of the perfume on the insides of her wrists. Je Reviens. A promise. Or a threat. *Hasta la vista,* baby. Back soon.

Where was the third suit? The one already in the wardrobe still had the dry cleaner's little pink tag attached to its collar with a small safety pin, so the suit that was missing must be the one that Dr. Hunter was wearing yesterday. There was no sign of it anywhere. Had she driven all the way down to Yorkshire to see the mysterious sick aunt without getting changed? That seemed completely out of character for Dr. Hunter, who always got changed the minute she got home from work, kicking off her shoes, hanging up her suit, and throwing on something casual, jeans usually. "There, I'm me again," she sometimes said, as if the suit were a disguise.

On the carpet, in front of the chest of drawers, were Dr. Hunter's low-heeled black pumps, one upright, one fallen over, looking as if Dr. Hunter had just stepped out of them. Sadie sniffed anxiously at each of the shoes as though she were about to be sent off to follow a scent trail. Next to the shoes were Dr. Hunter's discarded tights in a wrinkled heap on the floor, pale and empty, like an abandoned snake skin.

Looking at the contents of the closet gave Reggie a funny feeling, a bit like when she looked at Mum's clothes hanging in the wardrobe or Ms. MacDonald's clothes in the Dumpster. It seemed to have the same effect on Sadie, who lay down on the floor next to the shoes and gave a mournful whine. Reggie wanted to hear Dr. Hunter's voice, hear her say, "I'll be back soon, Reggie, don't worry." Reggie was sure that Dr. Hunter wouldn't feel "bothered" if she phoned her. She dialed Dr. Hunter's mobile number again but just as the number began to ring, she heard the sound of a car approaching. Sadie pricked up her ears and stood to attention. A glance out the window confirmed it was the Range Rover. "Sugar," Reggie said to the dog.

For a mad moment she thought about diving into the bedroom closet, but when people did that in horror films, it never turned out well. They were either found and murdered or they witnessed something horrible from behind the slatted doors of their hiding place.

The thing was, when she dialed Dr. Hunter's phone *("my life-line")* she had heard the unmistakable sound of its ringtone—Bach's "Crab Canon" ("so called," Dr. Hunter explained, "because the second voice plays exactly the same notes as the first, only backwards," which Reggie didn't entirely understand, but she smiled and nodded and said, "Right, I get it."). The phone was ringing from somewhere downstairs. Reggie was halfway down the staircase on a hunt for the phone—the Bach sounded as if it were coming from the kitchen—when Mr. Hunter burst through the front door at his usual velocity and was brought up short at the sight of her.

"*Still* here, Reggie?"

"Just been to the loo," Reggie said, feigning nonchalance. The phone had stopped ringing a beat after Mr. Hunter entered the house.

"Don't you have a home to go to?" Mr. Hunter said.

"Yep, sure do," she said, marching past him and out the front door. Sadie raced past her, hoovering up familiar smells in the border at the side of the drive. When Reggie reached the gate, she whistled to Sadie, who came trotting up, tail whirling round, the way it did when she was excited at retrieving treasure. She was carrying something in her mouth, and when she reached Reggie, she placed her find at her feet and sat obediently, waiting to be praised.

Reggie's heart nearly stopped when she saw what Sadie had dropped on the ground.

The baby's comforter, his square of moss-green blanket. It looked as if it had been trampled in the mud, and when Reggie picked it up and examined it, she could see a stain on it, a stain that wasn't tomato sauce or red wine, a stain that was blood. Reggie knew blood now. She had seen more in the last twenty-four hours than she had seen in a previous lifetime.

Dr. Hunter's surgery was in Liberton, and Reggie started walking because she wasn't sure how Sadie, who had never been on a bus, would fare with all those trampling feet and shoving bodies. Reggie never fared well herself. She ate her Mars bar and would have given a heel of it to Sadie but Dr. Hunter said chocolate was bad for dogs. She would have to buy dog treats, nothing with sugar, Dr. Hunter didn't like Sadie to have sugar (*"Got to look after the old girl's teeth."*). Reggie had bought a couple of tins of dog food from the Avenue Stores on Blackford Avenue, and they were weighing her bag down. She had to keep swapping it with the Topshop bag on her other shoulder. She felt extremely burdened. Mum used to carry loads of heavy bags around with her—they'd never been able to afford a car—she used to say her genes had been spliced with those of a donkey. No, she didn't say that, Mum wouldn't have used the word *spliced*, she might not even have used *genes*. What had she said? She was fading, retreating into a darkness where Reggie couldn't follow. "Bred from a donkey"—that was it. Wasn't it? *The darkness deepens.*

Eventually Reggie felt too tired to walk any farther and caught a bus the rest of the way. Sadie did pretty well for a first-time bus user.

The surgery was a big, modern, single-story building with no obvious place to leave a dog, so Reggie said "Sit" and "Stay" to Sadie in her most authoritative voice, the one she used on the baby ("No!") when he was making an accelerated move on a deathly grape or coin. When Sadie was a puppy, Dr. Hunter had taken her to obedience classes, from which Sadie had graduated top of her class. ("Dog school," Dr. Hunter called it. Which was a lovely idea.) She even had a red rosette, tattered now with age, to prove it, which Dr. Hunter kept pinned to the cork notice board in the kitchen. She was pretty smart for a dog, she could do all the usual sit-and-stay stuff as well as walk tightly to heel like a dog at Crufts. "My Best in Show," Dr. Hunter said fondly. Sadie had what Dr. Hunter called her "party pieces" as well, she could roll over, and play dead, and shake your hand—her big paw softer and heavier in your hand than you expected.

Sadie hunkered down obligingly on the ground outside the big glass doors to the surgery, and Reggie went inside and found the reception desk, where a woman was having a silent stand-off with her computer. Without even glancing in Reggie's direction, she put her hand up and made a kind of halt sign to her. Reggie wondered if she was going to say "Sit" and "Stay." Eventually the receptionist tore her eyes away from the screen and, giving Reg-

gie a starchy look, said, "Yes?" It pained Reggie to think that Dr.
Hunter worked in a place that contained such unfriendly people.

"I know Dr. Hunter's away," Reggie said. "I just wondered when
she would be back?"

"I'm afraid I can't tell you that."

"Because it's confidential information?"

"Because I don't know. Are you looking for an appointment
with her?"

"No."

"Because I can make one with another doctor."

"No, no, thank you. You don't know why she's gone away, do
you?" Reggie asked hopefully.

"No, I can't tell you that."

"Because it's confidential information?"

"Yes."

"Just one last thing," Reggie said. "Did she phone in herself, or
was it Mr. Hunter?"

"Who *are* you?"

Little Miss Nobody. Sister of the lesser Billy. Orphan of the
storm. Little Polly Flinders sitting amongst the cinders. Reggie
didn't say any of that, of course, she just said, "Well, see ya," and
hoped she wouldn't.

On the way out of the surgery, passing a seemingly endless display
of posters urging her to brush her teeth twice a day and eat five
pieces of fruit and watch out for chlamydia, Reggie bumped into
one of the midwives attached to the practice. Dr. Hunter's friend
Sheila.

One afternoon in late summer Dr. Hunter came home with her
and said, "Sheila, this is the famous Reggie, she's my life-support
system," then Sheila and Dr. Hunter sat in the garden with the baby
crawling around on the grass ("I can't believe how he's grown,

Jo!") and drank Pimm's, even though Dr. Hunter said, "God, Sheila, I'm breastfeeding, this is shameful," but they were laughing about it and Sheila said, "It's fine, Jo. Trust me, I'm a midwife," and they laughed even more.

They invited Reggie to join them but Reggie thought someone should keep a sober eye on things in case they became drunk in charge of a baby, but, of course, Dr. Hunter wasn't like that, and she made one drink last until the afternoon had begun to lengthen into twilight, when Mr. Hunter arrived home and said, "Still here, Reggie?"

Both women had looked disconcerted at the sight of Mr. Hunter, striding across the lawn with a can of beer in his hand like someone who'd crash-landed from another world, but then he said, "Can anyone join this session, then?" and Dr. Hunter said, "You've come late to the party, we're as tight as ticks here," which wasn't true, and Mr. Hunter said, "Aye, a right pair of jakies," and they all three laughed and Reggie went out and scooped the baby up from the lawn and put him to bed with a bottle — Dr. Hunter kept a stash of expressed milk in the freezer. Reggie had once seen Mr. Hunter take out the bottle of Stoli he kept in the freezer and frown at the sight of the little containers of frozen breast milk. "The difference between men and women," he laughed when he saw Reggie watching. "By the contents of their freezer shall you know them."

It's Reggie, isn't it?" Sheila said. She pointed at her chest and said, "I'm Sheila, Jo's friend. Sheila Hayes."

"Yes, I know, I remember. Hi."

"How are you? Are you looking for Jo? I don't think she's in today, I haven't seen her, anyway."

"She's gone away to see a sick aunt in Yorkshire."

"Really? She never said anything. That would explain it. We

were supposed to be going to Jenners last night, for their Christmas shopping evening, and she didn't turn up, and that's just not Jo."

"And when you tried to phone her—no answer?" Reggie hazarded.

"Yes, strange, isn't it? Her phone's her—"

"Lifeline?" Reggie supplied.

"Still," Sheila said, "an illness in the family, that explains it. An aunt?"

"Yes."

"She's never mentioned an aunt. Is everything okay with you, Reggie?"

"Totally. Thank you."

Lucy Locket lost her pocket, Kitty Fisher found it. From the pocket of her new jacket, Reggie took out the scrap of green blanket that Sadie had retrieved from Dr. Hunter's front garden. A pocket was where prostitutes kept their money, Dr. Hunter said. (*"Nursery rhymes are never what they seem."*) That could be said about a lot of things, in Reggie's opinion. When Sadie laid the baby's muddy bit of blanket at her feet, she had been horrified. It belonged with the baby. The baby belonged with Dr. Hunter. The dog belonged with Dr. Hunter. Reggie belonged with Dr. Hunter. It was all wrong. The whole world was wrong. Hard times.

Pilgrim's Progress

He was dreaming. He was walking along a desolate country road, following a woman. It was the strolling woman from the Dales. Still strolling. He shouted to her, "Hey!" and she turned round to look at him. She had no face, just a blank oval like a plate where her features should have been. She was terrifying. He woke up.

"Nice cup of tea?" a nurse said to him. A nurse (with a face) was putting a cup and saucer on a bed-tray in front of him. And he remembered everything. Not the train crash, not being on the train at all, the last thing he remembered was finding the lost highway, waiting on the access road to the A1, looking for a gap in the traffic.

But he knew who he was, his name, his history, everything.

"My name's Jackson Brodie," he said to the nurse. "I remember now."

"Jackson Brodie? You're sure?"

"Sure."

Where am I?" Jackson asked a nurse.

"In the Royal Infirmary in Edinburgh," she said.

"Edinburgh? Edinburgh, Scotland?" Listen to him, he sounded like an American tourist.

"Yes, Edinburgh, Scotland," she affirmed.

What on earth was he doing in Edinburgh? The scene of some of his greatest defeats in life and love. Why was he in Edinburgh? "I was on my way to London," he said.

"You must have gone the wrong way," she laughed. "Bad luck."

He might not know where he had come from, but he knew where he was going. He was going home.

Edinburgh. Louise was in Edinburgh. A sudden spasm of panic gripped Jackson. No one had looked for him. Did that mean he had not been alone on the train, that perhaps Tessa had joined him at Northallerton and he couldn't remember? And now she was lying in the hospital somewhere? Or worse?

Jackson sat bolt upright and grabbed the nurse's arm.

"My wife," he said. "Where's my wife?"

"An Elderly Aunt"

Louise had not joined Neil Hunter in his breakfast whisky, even though, more than most, she appreciated the medicinal taste of a Laphroaig. She could drink most guys under the table if she had to (sometimes you had to), but she had her rules. She never drank and drove anymore, and she never drank on duty—she would have been mortified if anyone at work had smelled whisky on her breath. Only alcoholics smelled of alcohol at nine in the morning. (Her mother. Always.) Instead she picked up a double espresso from a street stall and returned to her office, where she sat in solitary confinement and reviewed, for the hundredth time, all the reported sightings of David Needler.

The heat had gone out of the case. Louise could feel it growing colder by the day, feel it slipping away. It had been big news for a while and now it was almost as if it had never happened, and it was beginning to feel that it might turn into a never-ending limbo for everyone concerned, one of those cases that detectives brood over for decades. Louise took this extremely negative thought and held it under the waves until it went limp and then forced open her rusted sea chest on the seabed and threw it in.

There had been no sightings of David Needler at all until they got the case onto *Crimewatch,* after which they had been deluged by callers claiming to have seen him everywhere from Bangor to Bognor, but not one of them had checked out. The man had disappeared off the radar. He hadn't used a credit card, hadn't used his passport. His car was found parked near Flamborough Head, but Louise thought that was the work of someone who believed they were cleverer than the police. She was surprised he hadn't painted "CLUE" on the side of the car in big black letters. She was disinclined to think that he had killed himself, he wasn't the type, his sense of self-importance was too great.

"Hitler killed himself," Karen Warner said. "He was what you might call self-important." She was standing in front of Louise's desk, eating a prawn sandwich from Marks & Spencer that was making Louise feel nauseous.

"Napoleon didn't," Louise said. "Stalin didn't, Pol Pot, Idi Amin, Genghis Khan, Alexander, Caesar. Let's face it, Hitler was the exception to the rule."

"My, you're in a mood," Karen said.

"No, I'm not."

"Yes, you are." Karen's stomach was huge. Louise didn't remember being that big with Archie, he had been tiny, almost premature. Louise blamed herself, she had smoked through the first three months because she had no idea she was pregnant. Louise was sure that buried deep inside her, lurking in the murky labyrinth of her heart, there was an incredibly well-behaved person wondering when she would ever be let out. Patrick probably wondered the same thing. Patient Patrick, waiting for her to come good. Long wait, baby.

Karen was right, she was especially cranky today. All the coffee had taken the edge off for a while, but now she could feel a headache rolling in like haar up the Forth.

"Just came to report back on the woman who said she saw David Needler sitting on the harbor wall in Arbroath—'eating a fish supper,' she said."

"And?"

"Tayside police seem doubtful," she said through a mouthful of food. "No one else remembered him, and when she looked at the photograph again, she wasn't so sure."

"He's gone underground," Louise said. "He's not the kind to be hanging out eating chips in Arbroath." David Needler was the clever, cunning sort, plus he was English, so he had probably run for the border. And he still had lots of blokey mates down south who might have helped him — they all denied it blind, of course, but a few of them were flush with money, so it wouldn't have been impossible for him to get abroad. But Louise thought he was still in the UK somewhere, the ordinary guy living next door to someone. Maybe he was already courting another woman.

She picked up the file photograph of him and studied the bland face that gazed back at her. Alison Needler hadn't been able to find a photograph taken of him on his own in the last few years (photographs were memories, perhaps no one had wanted to remember him), so they had lifted this image and blown it up. The original photograph was of the whole family, taken at Disneyland Paris — three children and a wife gathered round, grinning as if they were in some kind of happiness competition. ("It was a terrible day," Alison said grimly. "He was in one of his moods.") Louise thought of Joanna Hunter's black-and-white photograph of thirty years ago, people held in a moment that could never come again.

Marcus entered her office, waving a piece of paper like a little flag. He caught sight of the photograph and said, "News of Lord Lucan?"

Everyone remembered Lord Lucan's name, but hardly anyone remembered Sandra Rivett, the nanny he clubbed to death. The wrong person in the wrong place at the wrong time. Like Gabrielle Mason and her children, also mostly forgotten by the collective memory. Who could name one of the Yorkshire Ripper's victims? Or the Wests'? The forgotten dead. Victims faded, murderers lived on in the memory, only the police kept the eternal flame alight, passing it on as the years went by.

"What was the nanny that he killed called?" Louise asked Marcus. Here beginneth the catechism.

"Don't know," Marcus admitted.

"Sandra Rivett," Karen said.

"She has the memory of an elephant," Louise said to Marcus.

"Gestating an elephant as well," Karen said. "Can't wait to get the little fucker out."

"You have to stop swearing once you have a baby," Louise said.

"Did you?"

"No."

"You're supposed to be a role model for me."

"Am I? You're in trouble, then."

"Boss?" Marcus said, handing her the piece of paper he'd been holding on to. "Our Mr. Hunter's been unlucky lately. It turns out that a couple of weeks before the fire, the manager of the Bread Street arcade was attacked when he was cashing out and one of the windows in another amusement arcade was smashed last Saturday night. Plus, one of his drivers was dragged from his cab outside the Foot of the Walk and beaten up, and another car had its windows smashed when it was picking up a passenger in Livingston—"

"Livingston?" Louise said sharply.

"It's okay, boss—nothing to do with our lady."

Louise didn't know when or why Marcus had started referring to Alison Needler as *our lady*, but it always threw Louise. Our Lady of Livingston. Our Lady of the Sorrows.

Louise could see Karen's belly clearly through her thin jersey maternity top. Her belly button pushing out like a doorbell asking to be rung. The belly was pulsing as her baby moved around, like something from *Alien*. Louise remembered that odd fluttery feeling of having a freewheeling baby inside you, independent and dependent at the same time, an eternal maternal dialectic. A foot, a little foot, a tiny, tiny little foot, pushed against the thin drum skin of flesh and jersey. It didn't help Louise's queasiness.

"So?" Louise said. "The man has bad karma, or someone's trying to tell him something? He's all yours, by the way, he's giving nothing away, but he looks like a very worried man to me."

DI Sandy Mathieson, a man who had risen above his abilities as far as Louise was concerned, put his head round the door. If there was a collective noun for police like Sandy it would definitely be *plod*.

"MAPPA have been on the phone, about Decker."

"What about him?"

"He's disappeared."

A black crow flapping across the sun, a dark place, a bad feeling in Louise's own belly. A real, physical feeling, probably brought on by the tub of egg mayonnaise that Karen Warner had just produced and was digging into with a teaspoon. The woman couldn't go five minutes without eating something. Something disgusting usually.

"Patrol car in Doncaster did a routine check on him this morning just to see he was where he was supposed to be."

"And he wasn't?"

"Mother said he went out at teatime on Wednesday and never came back."

"He knew the press had got wind of him," Louise said. "He was probably just trying to escape." That word again. What had Joanna Hunter said, *"I think I'll go away, escape for a bit?"* Were they both running from the same thing? Two people who would never be free of each other. Joanna Hunter and Andrew Decker would belong to each other forevermore, their histories twisted and fused together.

"Well, at least the train crash stopped it making the papers for a day or two," Sandy said.

"Every disaster has a silver lining, eh, Sandy?" Karen said. "It won't be long before the press hounds are baying at their heels again. A train crash only gets headlines for what—three days tops?

Anyway, he's in England, isn't he? He's not our problem. MAPPA's e-mailed a photo," she added, placing a picture on the desk in front of Louise.

Decker looked like a completely different person from the teenager who had stared out of the papers thirty years ago (Louise had Googled up his ghost). He *was* a different person, of course. There was a whole wasted lifetime between the two images.

On her way back from a Tasking and Coordinating Group meeting at St. Leonard's, Louise realized she was famished and pulled into Cameron Toll car park and bought an enormous bar of chocolate in Sainsbury's. She never ate chocolate, but she ate the whole bar as soon as she was in the car, and when she got to the station, she had to throw the chocolate straight back up again in the toilet. Served her right for trying to put herself into a diabetic coma.

She was coming out of the toilet when her phone rang. "Reggie Chase," the voice said. The name was familiar, but Louise couldn't place her. The girl was going a mile a minute and Louise couldn't keep up with her. The gist of it was that "something" had "happened to Dr. Hunter."

"*Joanna* Hunter?" Louise said. *My lady,* she thought, another one. Louise's ladies. Reggie Chase, the wee girl who had opened Joanna Hunter's door to her on Tuesday. "What do you mean something's happened to her?"

Wee girl and a big dog, it turned out. Dr. Hunter's dog. It wagged its tail at the sight of her and Louise felt flattered, absurdly. Perhaps a dog would fill the space between her and Patrick that he wanted a baby to occupy. Was there a space between them? Was that a good thing? Or a bad thing?

She had driven back into town to meet the girl. They left the dog on the backseat of Louise's car while they went and had a coffee in a Starbucks on George Street. Louise hated Starbucks. Drinking the Yankee dollar. "Someone has to make money for the evil capitalists," she said to the girl, buying her a latte and a chocolate muffin. "Some days it's you and me. This is one of those days."

The girl said, "Och, we do a lot of things that we shouldn't do."

The girl had a nasty-looking bruise on her forehead that she made some excuse for, but to Louise it looked like she'd been hit by someone. Reggie Chase. Joanna Hunter's nanny, like Sandra Rivett — no, not nanny, *mother's help*. Mother's little helper. Louise had taken Valium after Archie's birth, "Numb the shock a bit," her GP said. The guy had been a pusher, handing out tranquilizers like they were sweeties. Louise couldn't imagine Joanna Hunter doing that. Louise wasn't breastfeeding when she took drugs, her milk had never come in properly and ran out after a week. ("Stress," the GP said indifferently.) Archie seemed to find a bottle more emotionally comforting than his mother's breast.

She stopped taking the Valium after a week, it made her into such a dull-witted person that she was afraid she would drop the baby or lose it or forget she'd ever had it to begin with.

Was Reggie old enough to look after another woman's child when she was almost a child herself? She was the same age as Archie. She tried to imagine putting Archie in charge of a small baby, but the thought made her shudder.

"Look, look what Sadie found in Dr. Hunter's garden," the girl said, thrusting a manky piece of green cotton into Louise's hand.

"Sadie?"

"Dr. Hunter's dog."

"What *is* this?" Louise asked doubtfully, holding the scrap of green between thumb and forefinger.

"It's the baby's bit of blanket, his comforter," Reggie said. "He won't go anywhere without it. Dr. Hunter would never have left it behind. I found it in the garden. *Why* was it in the garden? It was already dark when I left, and he had it in his hand then, and look at it, that stain there, that's *blood*."

"Not necessarily."

Archie had something similar, a bit of egg yolk–yellow plush that had started life as a duck hand puppet before the stitching gave way and the duck was decapitated. He couldn't go to sleep at night without it, she could see him now, clutching it fiercely in his hand as if his life depended on it. Only in sleep did his fingers uncurl. He was the deepest sleeper. Louise would creep into his room in the middle of the night to cut toenails, remove splinters, swab cuts and grazes, all the little acts of everyday child maintenance that would cause him to scream the house down in daylight hours. He would rather have been separated from Louise than from that bit of yellow material.

She handed it back to the girl, saying, "Things get lost." Accidents happen. Milk gets spilled. Platitudes rain.

"Mr. Hunter said Dr. Hunter drove down," Reggie said, "but her car was in the garage. There was nothing wrong with it when she drove home in it yesterday. She's gone away, but she never told me she was going, which isn't like her *at all,* and Mr. Hunter says she's visiting a sick aunt, but she's never mentioned the *existence* of an aunt to me. I spoke to her friend Sheila at work, and she was supposed to have gone to Jenners Christmas shopping yesterday evening, but she didn't tell her she couldn't make it—which is *so* not Dr. Hunter, believe me—and her phone is in the house somewhere because I heard it ringing, I definitely heard it ringing, Bach's 'Crab Canon'—she wouldn't forget her phone, it's her *lifeline*—she isn't forgetful, Dr. Hunter never forgets anything, and her suit is missing, she wouldn't drive all that way in her suit, and—"

"Take a breath," Louise advised.

"She's disappeared," the girl said. "I think someone's *taken* her."

"No one's taken her."

"Or Mr. Hunter has done something to her."

"Done something?"

The girl dropped her voice to a whisper. *"Murdered."*

Louise sighed inwardly. The girl was one of those. An over-excited imagination, could get stuck on an idea and be carried away by it. She was a romantic, quite possibly a fantasist. Catherine Morland in *Northanger Abbey.* Reggie Chase was a girl who would find something of interest wherever she went. Training to be a heroine, that was what Catherine Morland had spent her first sixteen years doing, and she wouldn't be surprised if Reggie Chase had done the same.

"It happens that I was at Dr. Hunter's house earlier today," Louise said. "I was seeing Mr. Hunter about something quite unrelated."

"That's a funny coincidence."

"And that's all it is," Louise said sharply. "A coincidence. Mr. Hunter told me that his wife had gone away, to stay with an aunt who isn't well."

"Yes, I know, I *said* that, that's what he told *me,* but I don't believe it."

"The aunt isn't a matter of faith, she's not Father Christmas, she's a *relative.* She's not part of some grand conspiracy to hide Dr. Hunter."

"No one's seen Dr. Hunter. No one's spoken to her."

"Mr. Hunter has."

"He *says.*"

Louise sighed heavily. "Look—Reggie—why don't I give you a ride home?"

"You should get the phone number for the aunt of Dr. Hunter's, make sure she's okay. Maybe you could send someone to the aunt's house in Yorkshire, someone local. Hawes, *H-a-w-e-s.* Mr. Hunter won't give me an address or a phone number, but he'd have to give it to you."

"Enough." Louise held up a hand like a traffic cop. "Leave it alone. Nothing has happened to Dr. Hunter. Come on, my car's not far away."

"Find out if the aunt exists. Get hold of Dr. Hunter's mobile, it's in the house, then you can see if the aunt *really* phoned her."

"Car. Now. Home."

She said she had saved the life of a man at the train crash. More fantasy, obviously. Louise should have sent a uniform to talk to her. If it had been about anyone else, she would have done, it was just that she had claimed Joanna Hunter and now she couldn't let her go. *Her lady.*

"I might go away. Escape for a bit." Her husband's finances were in meltdown, he was walking on the dark side with some questionable people, the marriage was probably falling apart, and Andrew Decker was back on the streets. Who wouldn't disappear? Was the marriage falling apart, or was she just projecting her own feelings onto Joanna Hunter?

Joanna Hunter had never told Reggie about what had happened to her when she was a child. In fact, she hadn't told anyone as far as Louise could see, apart from her husband, and Louise wasn't about to break that confidence. It was Joanna Hunter's decision to keep her secrets, not Louise's to reveal them. "I don't want Reggie to know something like that," Joanna Hunter said. "It would upset her. People look at you differently when they know you've been involved in something terrible. It's the thing about you that they find most interesting." But it *was* the thing that was most interesting. Survivors of disasters were always interesting. They were witnesses to the unthinkable. Like Alison Needler and her children.

"A burden you have to carry through the rest of your life," Joanna Hunter said. "It doesn't get better, it doesn't go away, you just have to take it with you to the end." Louise thought of Jackson, his sister had been murdered a long time ago, and now he was the only one left who had known her. No such problem with Saman-tha. If her husband and her son didn't remember her, her things did. She lived on, forgotten but not gone, the spirit of Patrick's wife embalmed forever in her napkins and vases and good silver fish knives. Samantha was the real wife, Louise was the pale impostor.

Of course she didn't need to drive all the way out to Musselburgh and back in rush-hour traffic.

"It's out of your way," Reggie said.

It was, but she didn't care. Not out of any real consideration for the girl, it was just a time spinner, an avoidance of the inevitable return home. She'd been on the move all day, her own personal hejira, and the idea of coming to a stop was unsettling. Unable to stay put, she had spent half the day in her car going places and the other half making up places to go to. (*"Sorry I'm going to be late, something came up."* Who had insisted that Bridget and Tim stay five whole days? Louise, that was who.)

"What's Dr. Hunter like?" she asked Reggie Chase on the drive to Musselburgh, and the girl said, "Well . . ." It seemed Joanna Hunter liked Chopin and Beth Nielsen Chapman and Emily Dickinson and Henry James and had a remarkable tolerance for the Tweenies. She could play the piano — "really well," accord-ing to Reggie — and agreed with William Morris that you should have nothing in your house that you didn't know to be useful or believe to be beautiful. She loved coffee in the morning and tea in the afternoon and had a surprisingly sweet tooth and said that it was a medical fact that you had a separate "pudding stomach," which was why when you'd eaten a big meal you could always "find room for dessert." She didn't believe in God, her favorite book was *Little Women* because it was about "girls and women dis-covering their strengths," and her favorite film was *La Règle du Jeu,* which she had lent Reggie a copy of and which Reggie liked a lot, although not as much as *The Railway Children,* which was *her* favorite film. If Dr. Hunter had to rescue three things from a burning building, they would be the baby and the dog but Reggie hadn't been sure what the third thing would be—Louise suggested Mr. Hunter but Reggie said she thought he would probably manage to rescue himself. Of course, if Reggie was in the building, then Dr. Hunter would rescue *her,* Reggie said.

And she loved the baby. Gabriel—of course, Gabriel, Gabrielle. The baby was named for Joanna Hunter's dead mother. Louise hadn't made the connection, probably because neither Joanna Hunter nor Reggie Chase had called him by his name. He was "the baby" to both of them. The only baby, the light of the world.

"Chase and Hunter"—what was that about? It sounded like a bad seventies sitcom about amateur detectives. Or "Hunter and Chase," upmarket country estate agents. Reggie. Regina. You didn't meet many girls called Regina.

"I found this in the man's pocket," the girl said, shyly handing over a filthy postcard.

"What man?" Louise asked, taking the postcard reluctantly between her thumb and forefinger. Like the baby's blanket, the postcard was a biohazard of mud and blood and looked as if it had been trampled by a herd of horses.

"The man whose *life* I saved."

Oh, that man, Louise thought. That imaginary man. The postcard was a picture of somewhere European. Louise struggled to make it out beneath the muck.

"Bruges," the girl said. "In Belgium. His name and address is on the other side. I didn't imagine him."

"I didn't say you did." She turned the postcard over and read the message. Read the name and address.

"Jackson Brodie," the girl said hopefully. "I don't know if he's alive or dead, though. Maybe you could have a wee look for him?"

Louise handed the postcard back and said, "I'm very busy at the moment."

She didn't come off the A1 onto the bypass. Instead of taking the road home, she turned at Newcraighall and headed to the hospital, as obedient as a dog to a shepherd calling her home.

Nada y Pues Nada

No way was she going back to Gorgie, so it was just as well she had the keys to Ms. MacDonald's house. And on the plus side, Musselburgh was currently the focus of national media attention. Reggie couldn't imagine that the would-be terminators would go looking for "a guy called Reggie" in Ms. MacDonald's dull street, especially when it was still crawling with police. The more time that had passed since this morning, the more unlikely it seemed that the idiots, rechristened "Ginger" and "Blondie" in her mind now, were actually looking for her. They were looking for Billy. She should just have given them his address in the Inch, he'd obviously given *her* address to them. She should return the favor.

"This is where you live?" Inspector Monroe said, peering through the windscreen at Ms. MacDonald's house.

"Yes," Reggie said. "My mother's not here at the moment." One lie, one truth. They canceled each other out and left the world unchanged. It seemed so much simpler not to go into any kind of detail whatsoever.

Inspector Monroe had at least listened to her, even if she clearly didn't believe her, but if Reggie had added, "And in an entirely unrelated incident, two men trashed my flat and threatened to kill me this morning, and oh, yeah, they gave me a copy of the *Iliad,* at that point Inspector Monroe would probably have made a swift exit from Starbucks. She didn't really look like a policewoman, beneath her winter coat she was dressed in jeans and a soft sweater, the same off-duty clothes as Dr. Hunter. Her hair was scraped back into a ponytail that it wasn't quite long enough for, and she had to keep tucking a wayward strand behind her ear. "I'm still growing it," she said. "I had it cut really short, but it didn't suit me." Mum used to say that women had drastic haircuts at the end of unsuccessful relationships. Mum's friends were always appearing with shorn heads, but Reggie's mother knew her hair was an asset to be valued. She was so besotted with Gary, though, that she might have cut her hair if he had asked her to. She would have done just about anything to keep Gary, although a lot of his attraction was simply that he wasn't the Man-Who-Came-Before-Him. Imagine if he'd said to Mum, "I'd love to see you with short hair, Jackie." It was difficult to put words into Gary's mouth, he was so tongue-tied. ("You're very articulate, Reggie," Dr. Hunter had said to her once, which she had taken as a great compliment. "Oh, she's a talker, our Reggie," Mum used to say.) And then Mum might have gone to her hairdresser (Philip—"camp but married," according to Mum) and said, "Cut it all off, Philip, it's time for a change," and Philip would have given her a nice short bob, just below her ears or, even safer, an urchin cut like Kylie after the cancer and—*ta-daa*—Mum would at this moment be stirring a pan of mince in the kitchen in Gorgie and looking forward to *EastEnders.*

Reggie wondered if Inspector Monroe had ever suffered a broken heart. She didn't look the type somehow.

Sadie had been a bit of a problem, but in the end Inspector Monroe had put her in the backseat of her car (along with the burdensome Topshop bag), from where the dog had watched them walk away along George Street with such intensity that she might have been trying to burn them onto her retinas. Inspector Monroe didn't seem like a pet sort of person, but then she said, "I had a cat," as if it had meant something.

Reggie was grateful for the muffin, she was ravenous—apart from Mr. Hussain's tic tacs and the Mars bar (hardly a balanced diet), she hadn't eaten all day, the morning's toast having been ejected before it was digested. She wanted to concentrate on eating the muffin, so she got the words out quickly—the car, the phone, the piece of moss-green blanket, the shoes, the suit, the whole unlikely not-being-thereness of Dr. Hunter, as if aliens had descended and whisked her away. She made a point of not mentioning alien abduction to Inspector Monroe.

When Reggie reached the end of her story, Inspector Monroe yawned and said, "Excuse *me*. I'm very tired, I was up all night."

"At the train crash?" Reggie guessed.

"Yes."

"Me too," Reggie said.

"Really?" Inspector Monroe gave her a doubtful look as if she were considering putting her in the fantasizing psycho box after all.

"I gave a man CPR," Reggie said, climbing deeper into the box. "I tried to save his life." The lid of the box banged shut.

This was the first time she had mentioned the man to anyone. She had carried him around all day like a secret, and it felt good to get it out of her head and into the world, even though, once spoken, the idea seemed unlikely. The events of last night already seemed more unreal by the hour; then she remembered looking at the body of Ms. MacDonald this morning and the events of last night seemed less unreal.

"Oh?" Inspector Monroe said. Reggie might as well have played the alien abduction card, because Inspector Monroe couldn't have looked more skeptical if she'd tried.

"How did you get that bruise?" she had said, peering closely at Reggie's forehead.

Reggie tugged her fringe down and said, "It's nothing, I wasn't looking where I was going."

"Sure that's all it was?"

She looked concerned. Reggie knew what she was thinking, domestic violence, et cetera. She wasn't thinking, slipped and fell in a shower when threatened by two idiots.

"Sweartogod," Reggie said.

She could have told Inspector Monroe about Ginger and Blondie but it wasn't going to help find Dr. Hunter (and fantasizing psycho, et cetera). And anyway, perhaps their threats were real *("Don't go to the police about this wee visit or, guess what?")*. What if they were watching her? What if they had seen her in Starbucks drinking coffee with a detective chief inspector, not even a humble uniformed constable. They would never believe it wasn't about them. It was only when Reggie said, "Just here, please," at Ms. MacDonald's front door that Inspector Monroe said, "Oh, I see, it *was* right on your doorstep," as if she finally might believe that Reggie was not lying about the train crash.

"Well, nearly," Reggie said.

"Right, then," Inspector Monroe said, "best be getting off, things to do, you know."

"Tell me about it," Reggie said.

She waved good-bye to Inspector Monroe, who was frowning, not waving, when she drove away.

Reggie pushed the reluctant sash of the bedroom window as far up as it would go to welcome in some fresh air. There were men working under arc lights on the track, accompanied by the constant clatter and whine of the heavy machinery. A huge crane was lifting a carriage from the track. The carriage swung in the air like a toy. A massive bone-white moon was rising in the sky, shining indifferently on the unnatural scene below.

It was too noisy to sleep in the neglected back bedroom, even with the window closed, and there was no way that Reggie would contemplate sleeping in Ms. MacDonald's own bedroom at the front, awash with the stale scents of dirty laundry and half-used medicines.

She caught sight of herself in the mirror on the dressing table. The bruise on her forehead was turning black.

Sadie had spent the last hour tracking the ghostly scent of Banjo around the house but now was flopped miserably in the living room. Reggie supposed that when someone went away, it must seem to their pets that they'd simply disappeared off the face of the earth. Here one minute, gone the next. Dr. Hunter said Sadie was lucky because she didn't know that she was going to die one day, but Reggie said she wanted to know when she was going to die because then she could avoid it. No one could avoid death, of course, but you could avoid a *premature* death at the hands of *idiots*. ("Not always," Dr. Hunter said.)

After foraging in Ms. MacDonald's bare cupboards Reggie came up with half a packet of stale Ritz Crackers but struck gold when she discovered the Cash 'n' Carry–sized stash of Tunnock's Caramel Wafers that Ms. MacDonald kept for her supper. She shared the Ritz Crackers with Sadie and ate a caramel wafer.

Would Chief Inspector Monroe really look for Dr. Hunter? It seemed doubtful somehow. Why had she come to Dr. Hunter's house on Tuesday? "Oh, something and nothing," she said. "To do with a patient." She was a good liar, but then, so was Reggie. It took one to know one.

Something and nothing. This and that. Here and there. People certainly were very evasive around Reggie.

Reggie decided to sleep on the sofa. Sadie jumped into an armchair and turned round and round until she was satisfied with it and then settled down with a huge sigh as if she were getting rid of the day from her body. The sofa Reggie was sleeping on still bore the faint imprint of Banjo's body, but there was a kind of comfort in that. It had been an unbelievably difficult day. Hard times, indeed.

Sometime in the night, Sadie left the chair and joined Reggie on the sofa. Reggie supposed she needed comfort too. She put her arm round the dog and listened to the strong heartbeat in her big chest. The dog didn't smell of anything much but dog. It had never occurred to Reggie before, but usually Sadie smelled of Dr. Hunter's perfume. Dr. Hunter must spend quite a lot of time hugging Sadie for that to happen. If Dr. Hunter were okay she would have phoned, if not to speak to Reggie, then to Sadie (*"Hello, puppy, how's my gorgeous girl?"*).

Where was Dr. Hunter? *Elle revient*. What if she didn't?

Why had Dr. Hunter stepped out of her shoes and walked out of her life? There were so many questions and no answers. Someone had to hunt for Dr. Hunter. Ha.

Ad Lucem

Jackson felt a pang of something very like loneliness. He wanted someone he knew to know he was here. Josie, for example. (Any wife in a storm.) No, not Josie *("Now what have you done, Jackson?").* Julia, perhaps. She would be sympathetic *("Oh, sweetie"),* but probably not in a way that would make him feel better.

"What time is it?"

"Six o'clock," Nurse Fuzzy said. ("My name's actually Marian.")

"In the morning?"

"No."

"In the evening?"

"Yes."

He had to check, just in case there was another time of day where six o'clock could park. Everything else had been turned upside down, why not time itself? "Can I have the phone?"

"No. You will rest if it kills you," the nurse said. She was Irish. That figured, she sounded like his mother. "If it's your wife you're worried about, then I'm sure we'll manage to get in touch with her tomorrow. There's always a lot of confusion in the wake of an accident, so there is."

"I know. I used to be a policeman," Jackson said.

"Did you now? Then you'll do what you're told and go back to sleep."

He wondered when the gratitude would kick in. The "I almost died but I've been given a second chance" thing. Wasn't that what you were supposed to feel after a near-death experience? A sudden falling-away of fear, a resolution to make the most of every day from now on. A new Jackson to step out of the hull of the old one and be reborn into the rest of his life. He didn't feel any of that. He felt sore and tired.

"Are you going to stand there and glare at me until I fall asleep?"

"Yes," Nurse Fuzzy said. Nurse *Marian* Fuzzy.

He was woken by something brushing his cheek, a butterfly wing, or a kiss. More likely a kiss than a butterfly wing.

"Hello, stranger," a familiar voice said.

"Fuzzy," he mumbled.

He opened his eyes and she was there. Of course. He had a moment of supernatural clarity. He was with the wrong woman. He had been going the wrong way. This was the right way. The right woman.

"Hello, you," he said. He had been mute for decades and now suddenly he'd been given a voice. "I was thinking about you," Jackson said. "I just didn't know it."

Her eyes were black pools of exhaustion. She was prettier than he remembered. She put a finger on his lips and said, "Shh. You had me at *fuzzy*." She laughed. He wasn't sure he'd ever seen her laugh before.

Everything suddenly shifted into place.

"I love you," he said.

Fiat Lux

Thank God there was no one sitting at the dining-room table when she came in. There was a note from Patrick instead, propped up against an arrangement of hothouse lilies that hadn't been there this morning. She hated lilies. She was sure their perfume had been specially bred to disguise the smell of rotting flesh, that was why they always pitched up at funerals. *Eating at Lazio's beforehand,* Patrick's note said. *Come and join us if you get in on time.* "Beforehand"—before what?

The idea of more eating and drinking with Bridget and Tim was enough to make Louise vomit. And anyway she had eaten already. She had gone from the hospital to a drive-thru McDonald's and picked up Happy Meals for the Needlers. The kids didn't get to go to burger joints anymore, too public. They had eaten round the TV, watching the DVD of *Shrek the Third.* Louise had picked at some fries. She hadn't been able to eat meat in days, couldn't stomach the idea of putting dead flesh inside her live flesh.

"Happy Meal," Alison said with her thin-lipped smile, not a smile at all. "Not had many of them."

★   ★   ★

Don't you have a home to go to?" Alison said halfway through the movie.

"Well . . . ," Louise said. Which she could see wasn't really the right answer.

She realized that she had left Decker's driving license at the hospital. She had meant to bring it away with her. It had felt like evidence, but she couldn't think of what exactly.

Of course she had forgotten the license, she had forgotten everything. She had forgotten herself for a moment.

She had flashed her warrant card and got onto the wards. Access all areas. They would have to tear that warrant card out of her hands when she left the police force. Then she had walked through wards full of train crash survivors until she found him.

He wasn't dead, although he looked all broken up. An Australian doctor she spoke to said it wasn't as bad as it seemed. Louise stroked the back of his hand, there was a black bruise where the IV went in. The doctor said he had been "out for the count" (a medical term, apparently) but was okay now.

She stayed and watched over him for a while.

When she stood up to leave, she had bent down and kissed him on the cheek and he opened his eyes as if he'd been waiting for her. "Hello, stranger," she said and he said, "I love you," and she felt completely disorientated, as if she had been burled around in an eightsome reel and then let go and flung across the dance floor. She was trying to compose the right response to this declaration of his feelings when the Irish nurse swooped back in and said, "He won't stop asking for his wife, you wouldn't have any idea how to get hold of her, would you, Chief Inspector?" and the spell was broken.

When Reggie had showed her the postcard of Bruges and said, "I don't know whether he's alive or dead," her heart had done the kind of flip-flop of fear with which it would have greeted bad news about Archie. And right in that microsecond of the misbeat, the thought had come to her that she wouldn't have reacted that way if it had been Patrick. She had made a terrible mistake, hadn't she? She had married the wrong man. No, no, she had married the right man, it was just that she was the wrong woman.

"We've only just identified him," the nurse said. "We thought he was called Andrew Decker."

"*Who?*"

She found Sandy Mathieson covering the night shift. "Swapped so I could go to the wee one's football."

"Decker's driving license turned up at the scene of the train crash. So presumably he's in the area, I don't see how else it could have got there. Get someone to put out an All Ports Alert for him."

"Of all the gin joints in all the towns, et cetera, seems too much of a coincidence," Sandy said. "You think he was coming to find Joanna Hunter? Finish the job he started thirty years ago? Surely that only happens in TV crime shows, not real life?"

"Well, if he did, he's out of luck," Louise said. "She's down in England. I think. I hope." Because if she wasn't, then, where was she? "*Taken,*" the girl said. What if the girl was right? What if something had happened to Joanna Hunter? Something bad. Again. No, the girl's paranoia had got under her skin. Joanna Hunter was with her elderly, sick aunt. End of story.

"McLellen left stuff for you on your desk," Sandy said. "Copies of documentation from what's-his-name."

"Neil Hunter?"

"Think so."

★   ★   ★

She checked her phone messages after she'd read the note. "On our way to the theater now," Patrick's recorded voice informed her. So that was the "beforehand." She was sure her husband's affable Irish tones would be very soothing if you were about to be cut open by him on the operating table. *My husband.* The words were stones in her mouth, a noun and an adjective that belonged to someone else, not Louise. She was continually astonished at the ease with which Patrick said *my wife.* He'd had years of practice, of course. How did the other wife feel? The one shut in a wooden box beneath the earth in the Grange Cemetery. Fifteen years on she'd be a skeleton. Her car crash had been on Christmas Eve, the Mistletoe Bride.

He's been asking for his wife. Not only had Jackson managed to get his identity muddled with a psycho killer, the bastard had got married as well.

"We'll have a drink in the bar first," Patrick's message continued. "If you haven't turned up by the time we go in, I'll leave your ticket at the box office. See you soon, don't work too hard, love you." The theater? No one had mentioned the theater. Had they? Perhaps they had discussed it this morning at breakfast after she turned off her brain when Tim was giving out his tips on how to graft roses (*"Make use of the whole blade of the knife, a poor cut always results in a poor graft."*).

She checked her watch, nine thirty. Far too late for the theater now. Anyway, he didn't say which theater — the Lyceum? The King's? Obviously she was supposed to know. She checked the second message, sent on the heels of the first, "Afterwards we're going to Bennet's Bar, join us there if you can." Beforehand, afterwards, he sure was eager for her to join him. Bennet's Bar probably meant they had gone to the King's. She could make it if she tried.

She didn't. Instead, she opened a bottle of Bordeaux that was sitting on the kitchen counter and carried it through to the living room, where she poured it into one of Patrick and Samantha's crystal goblets, put her feet up on the sofa, and caught a rerun of an old *CSI* on Living TV. She could feel the day beginning to seep out of her bones. It was like being single again. It felt good.

In *CSI,* Stokes was in the process of being buried alive. Louise retrieved the remains of the ice cream from the freezer and dug into the tub. She didn't even like ice cream, but at least it didn't count as it was going into her pudding stomach (thank you, Dr. Hunter). Red wine and Cherry Garcia, a reckless combination if ever there was one. Louise could feel the hangover starting already.

Grissom was holding up his badge and shouting, "Las Vegas Crime Lab!," at someone. All that had been on her desk were copies of insurance policies, no accounts, nothing to do with Neil Hunter's business at all. She liked the way Grissom walked, like a bear with a nappy on. "Let's look at the facts," Louise said to him. "Neil Hunter has insurance policies, not just on his businesses but on his wife as well, worth a cool half million." (Not bad, all Patrick had got was a chip of glittering carbon to pay for another wife.) Half a million would go a long way to cushioning Neil Hunter's problems. They already suspected him of destroying a property for money, what if he was capable of disposing of his wife for the same reason? But he'd need a body to trade for the policy, wouldn't he? And a body was what there most certainly wasn't. Because Joanna Hunter *was with a sick aunt,* she reminded herself. Nothing suspicious at all except for Neil Hunter's jangled nerves and a willfully imaginative girl.

The last time she saw Joanna Hunter, Reggie said, she was wearing a black suit and a white T-shirt and black pumps, the uniform, in varying degrees of chic, of the professional woman the world over. Louise's own outfit. Sisters under the suit. Joanna Hunter was still wearing her suit, Reggie said. Why wouldn't she have changed? How much of a medical emergency could an old aunt be having that you wouldn't throw on something casual to drive in? She came home from work, she saw Reggie off on the doorstep, then she went upstairs and got as far as taking off her shoes and tights—and then what?

The suspect that Grissom was talking to suddenly blew himself up.

CSI was a two-parter and ended on a cliff-hanger, Stokes still buried alive and running out of air. Louise poured herself another glass of wine that was the color of old blood.

She was woken a couple of hours later when the theatergoers returned. They spilled noisily into the living room and Louise closed her eyes again and feigned sleep.

"She's asleep," Patrick said, without lowering his voice.

Louise heard the crystal glass chink against the empty bottle of Bordeaux as he picked them both up from the carpet. She wondered if he would kiss her, or cover her with a blanket, or perhaps wake her up and encourage her up to bed, but all she heard was the door closing and Bridget's heavy tread on the stair.

Of course, the right response was "I love you too," and it was only by the merest whisker that she had escaped saying it to Jackson.

Grave Danger

And then nothing. Time that was lost forever in some terrible dark chasm of the brain that Joanna never wanted to descend into again. She presumed that the missing time had been more than filled by tens, if not hundreds, of people with jobs to do — people asking her to describe events, showing her photographs, making drawings. Question after question, gently and relentlessly probing an open wound.

The first thing she remembered afterwards was waking up one morning, alone in a strange bed, in a strange room, and being convinced that everyone else in the world was dead. The light coming through the curtains was unusual, bright and alien, and it was only when Martina entered the bedroom and pulled the curtains open and said, "Hello, darling, look, it's snowed. Isn't it lovely?" that Joanna understood that everyone was alive except for the people she cared about the most. And it was winter. *The bleak midwinter.*

"Why don't you come downstairs and have some breakfast with me?" Martina said, smiling encouragingly at her. "Some oatmeal? Or some eggs? You like eggs, darling." And so Joanna climbed obediently out of bed and allowed the rest of her life to begin.

Martina was brought up in Surrey, but her mother was Swedish, from a small town near the Finnish border, and Martina carried a northern gloom in her blood. She fought it as best she could, but whereas Joanna's mother's downturned smile had signaled happiness, Martina's cheerful upturned one often meant the opposite. Martina the poet. *(Bitch-cunt-whore-poet.)* Martina with her straight fair hair and broad features, her burden of penitence. Martina who longed for a child of her own and who was persuaded into two terminations by the great Howard Mason. "My Scandinavian muse," he called her, but not in a way that was kind.

Nothing left of Martina now. Her one Faber volume of poems, *Blood Sacrifice,* long forgotten. (*The ghosts at the table, their pale faces lighting our feast / We will not be put out, they say. No, not ever.*) It was only a long time afterwards that Joanna realized that the poems were about her lost family. For years, she had owned a dog-eared copy, but it disappeared at some point, the way things do. Written on water. Martina had lain down with two bottles, one of sleeping tablets and one of brandy. *My bottle of salvation.* That was Sir Walter Ralegh, wasn't it? "The Passionate Pilgrim." *Give me my scallop-shell of quiet, my something something something.* Martina had given her poetry, but poetry had failed them all in the end. *Sing, sing, what shall I sing? The cat's run off with the pudding string.*

They had caught the man during the month that followed the murders. He was young, not yet twenty, and his name was Andrew Decker and he was an apprentice draftsman. Martina called him "the bad man," and when Joanna had one of her sudden hysterical fits, she would hold her and murmur into her hair,

"The bad man is locked away forever, darling." Not forever, it turned out, just thirty years.

Decker came to trial the following spring and pleaded guilty. "At least she'll be spared the trial," her father said to Martina. Joanna was always "she" to her father, not said in a malicious way, he just seemed to find the naming of her difficult. She had been his least favorite of the three of them, and now she was the only one and she still wasn't the favorite.

Decker was given a life sentence and ordered to serve the whole of it. He was considered fit to plead, as if there were nothing insane about slaughtering three complete strangers for no apparent reason. Nothing the least deranged about felling a mother and her two children in cold blood. When asked in court why he had done it, he shrugged and said he didn't know "what had come over him." Joanna's father had been there to bear witness to this brief and unsatisfying conclusion.

Looking back now, Joanna could see that she had not been spared a trial but cheated of her day in court. Even now she imagined herself standing in the witness box, in her best red-velvet dress, the one with the white lace Peter Pan collar that was a hand-me-down from Jessica, and pointing dramatically at Andrew Decker and saying, in her high, innocent child's voice, "That's him! That's the man!"

And now he was out. Out and free. "I have to tell you that Andrew Decker was released last week," Louise Monroe said.

Andrew Decker was fifty years old and he was free. Joseph would have been thirty-one, Jessica would have been thirty-eight, their mother sixty-four. *When I'm sixty-four.* Never. Nevermore, nevermore.

Sometimes she felt like a spy, a sleeper who had been left in a foreign country and forgotten about. Had forgotten about herself. She had a pain in her chest, an ache, sharp and sore. Her heart was thudding. Knock, knock, knocking. *Rapping, rapping at my chamber door—*

The baby woke with a squawk and she held him tightly to her chest and shushed him, cradling the back of his head with her hand. There were no limits to what you would do to protect your child. But what if you couldn't protect him, no matter how much you tried?

He was free. Something ticked over, a click in time, like a secret signal, a cue, implanted in her mind long ago. The bad men were all out, roaming the streets. *Darkness now forevermore.*

Run, Joanna, run.

IV
And Tomorrow

Jackson Risen

When he woke up, there was an unpalatable-looking break-fast sitting on his bed-table. He had dreamt about Louise, at least it seemed like a dream. Had she been here? Someone had been here, a visitor, but he didn't know who it was. It wasn't the girl, the girl was there every time he opened his eyes, sitting at the side of his bed, watching him.

In the dream he had opened his heart and let Louise in. The dream had unsettled him. Tessa hadn't existed in the dream world, as if she had never entered his life. The train crash had caused a rift in his world, an earthquake crack that seemed to have put an impossible distance between him and the life he shared with Tessa. New wife, new life. He had proposed to her the day after Louise texted him to tell him she was getting married, it had never struck him at the time that the two things might have been related. But then he'd never been much good at figuring out the anatomy of his behavior. (Women, on the other hand, seemed to find him transparent.)

He wondered if Tessa was trying to get in touch? Was she worried? She wasn't a worrier. Jackson was.

Of course Tessa hadn't got on the train at Northallerton. She was in America, in Washington, at some kind of conference. "Back on Monday," she had said as she was getting ready to leave. "I'll be there to pick you up," he said. He could see the two of them early on Wednesday morning—or whenever it had been, he had no relationship with time anymore—standing in the cupboard she called a kitchen in their little Covent Garden flat (her flat, which he had moved into). She was drinking tea, he was drinking coffee. He'd recently bought an espresso machine, a big, shiny red monster that looked as if it should be powering a small factory during the industrial revolution. Coffee was the one thing Tessa wasn't good at. "I live in Covent Garden, for heaven's sake," she laughed. "I can't throw a stone without hitting someone trying to sell me a cup of coffee."

The coffee machine took up half of the kitchen. "Sorry," Jackson said after he'd installed it. "I didn't realize it was so big." Although what he really meant was that he hadn't realized the kitchen was so small. They had been talking about moving somewhere larger, somewhere less urban, and had been looking in the Chilterns. Hard though it was for Jackson to believe it of himself, he was nonetheless planning on becoming a Home Counties commuter. That was what the love of a good woman did for you, it turned you inside out and into another self you barely recognized, as if all along you'd been reversible and just never knew it. The Chilterns were lovely, even the iron in Jackson's hard northern soul softened a little at the sight of so much rolling green ease. "E. M. Forster country," Tessa said. She was incredibly well-read, the proof of an expensive, wide-ranging education ("St. Paul's Girls' School, then Keble College"). Jackson wondered if it was too late now for him to start reading novels.

A policewoman, not fuzzy at all. "Do you have a phone number for your wife?" She smiled sympathetically at him. "Can you remember?"

"No," he said. The answer in his head was longer and involved not calling Tessa and worrying her, not making her come back early from the States when there was no need because he wasn't dead any longer, but the best he could manage was the no.

That didn't mean he didn't want her here. He tried to conjure up her face, but the best he could manage was a vague Tessa-shaped blur. He tried to fix on the last time he saw her, in the kitchen, where she had drained her cup, rinsed it, and put it on the draining board (she was very tidy, she never left things undone). Her hair had been pinned up, no makeup, no jewelry except for a watch ("traveling mode"), and she was wearing black trousers and a beige sweater. The sweater felt incredibly soft when he held her in his arms. He could recall the sweater better than he could recall Tessa.

Then she kissed him and said, "I should get to the airport. You'd better miss me." He'd wanted to give her a lift to Heathrow but she'd said, "Don't be silly, I'll jump on the Tube to Paddington and catch the Heathrow Express." He didn't like her taking the Tube, he didn't like anyone taking the Tube anymore. Fires and accidents and suicide bombers and police marksmen and nutters who could send you falling under a train with just a quick prod in the back—the Underground was a fertile place for disaster. He didn't used to think like that, he had a couple of wars and a lifetime of appalling events beneath his belt, but somewhere along the lonesome highway he'd passed the tipping point—more years behind him than in front of him—and had suddenly begun to fear the random horror of the world. The train crash was the ultimate confirmation.

"I'm sure it'll come to you soon," the policewoman said. "It's probably best for your recovery if you don't worry."

"I used to be a policeman," Jackson said. Every time he hit the dead end of the existential labyrinth, he seemed to find it necessary to assert this. His identity might have been called into question, but of this one fact he was sure.

It seemed unlikely that news of the train crash would reach Tessa

in Washington, something pretty big had to happen in Europe before it percolated through the American consciousness. At worst,
she would have tried to text him and wondered why he hadn't
replied, but she wouldn't immediately jump to the conclusion that
he had got himself into trouble, unlike his first wife, Josie. His *first*
wife, how strange that sounded, especially as when she was married
to him she used to think it was amusing to introduce herself that
way: *Hello, I'm Jackson's first wife.*

Of course, Tessa had had no idea that he was on that train, had
no idea that he was out of London, because he'd never mentioned
it to her, never said, "Actually, once you're on your way to the
airport, I'm going north to see my son." And the reason he hadn't
said that was because he'd never told her about Nathan. So quite a
lot of sins of omission going on, and in such a new marriage, when
there should have been no secrets. And, of course, even if she *had*
known he was on the King's Cross train, it wouldn't have mattered,
because he wasn't. *"You're going the wrong way."* His head hurt. Too
much thinking makes Jackson a dull boy.

They had hardly been apart since they met. She went to work
every day, of course, but they often met up at the British Museum
during her lunch hour. Sometimes after they had eaten, they wandered around the building, Tessa talking to him about some of the
exhibits. She was a curator, "Assyrian mainly," she said when they
first met. "Well, it's all Greek to me," Jackson joked weakly. *The Assyrian came down like a wolf on the fold.* Even her guided tours of the
Assyrian bit didn't enlighten him much. He was sure there was a
better word than *bit. Department,* was that the word? "The Assyrian
Department"— that didn't sound right, it sounded like a bureau-
cratic niche in the underworld.

Despite some carefully worded explanations from Tessa, he still
wasn't entirely sure that he understood the where/what/when of

Assyria. He thought it might have something to do with Babylon. *By the waters of Babylon we sat down and there we wept when we remembered Zion.* Not a Boney M song but Psalm 137. *We remembered Zion, we remembered our songs, for we could not sing here.* The song of the exile. Wasn't everyone an exile? In their hearts? Was he being mawkish? Probably.

New information was hard to retain, because of the amount of useless old information littering his brain. It was strange that the one thing he seemed to remember from school was poetry, probably the subject he had paid least attention to at the time. *Dirty British coaster with a salt-caked smoke stack.*

He kept a photograph of her in his wallet, alongside one of Marlee, but the wallet was still missing. He could home in on a feature, the long-lashed brown eyes, the nice straightness of her nose, a neat ear, but nothing fitted together into a proper portrait. She was Picasso rather than Vermeer. He should have studied Tessa more, taken more photographs, but she was chronically camera shy; as soon as she spotted a lens, she would mask her face with her hand and, laughing, say, "No, don't! I look terrible." She never looked terrible, even first thing in the morning when she had just woken up she seemed flawless. It was difficult to believe that out of all the men on the planet she had chosen him. ("Very difficult," Josie agreed.)

The objective, more world-weary part of Jackson knew that he was foxed by love, that he was still in the heady spring days of the relationship, when everything in the garden was rosy and blooming. *My love is like a bloodred rose.* No, not blood. Red. *Red, red rose.* "Your salad days," Julia said. "Green in judgment." "And what does this paragon amongst women see in you exactly?" Josie asked. "Apart from the money, of course."

"*How* old is she?" Julia asked, a histrionic look of horror on her face.

"Thirty-four," Jackson said reasonably.

"That's cradle-snatching, Jackson," Josie said.

"Bollocks," Jackson said.

"You know that being in love is a form of madness, don't you?" Amelia said. ("Then it must be a folie à deux," Tessa laughed when he told her.) Amelia had (dreadful to recall) once been in love with Jackson. He must phone Julia, find out how Amelia's operation had gone. Was she dead? Julia would be inconsolable. There was a phone by the side of his bed, but he needed a credit card to operate it and the credit card was in his wallet. If he had Andrew Decker's wallet, did Andrew Decker have his? Andrew Decker's wallet was almost bare, the old driving license, a ten-pound note. Traveling light. Was he in the hospital somewhere?

The photograph in his wallet was the only one he had of Tessa, taken on Jackson's camera by one of their impromptu witnesses after their hasty wedding, and even on that auspicious occasion she had tried to turn away from the camera. Now he didn't even have that. No wallet, no BlackBerry, no money, no clothes. Born naked, reborn naked.

"We hardly know each other," she said when he proposed.

"Well, that's what marriage is for," Jackson said, although his experience of marriage tended to indicate the opposite—the longer he and Josie were married, the less they seemed to understand each other.

Tessa didn't change her name to his, she had never "seen herself" as Mrs. Brodie, she said. Josie hadn't changed her name either when she married him. The last "Mrs. Brodie" that Jackson knew was his mother. Jackson's sister, an old-fashioned girl in every sense, used to tell him that she couldn't wait to be married and ditch her maiden name and "become Mrs. Somebody Else." That's what she was—a maiden, a virgin, "saving herself for Mr. Right." There were always boys after her but she still hadn't found anyone steady when she was raped and murdered. She had a bottom drawer, a little chest in her room that was neatly layered with tea towels and embroidered tray cloths and a stainless-steel cutlery set that she was adding to, one item a month. All for the life to come that never came. All these things seemed so far away now, not just Niamh herself but all the girls who saved embroidered tray cloths and stainless-steel cutlery sets. Where were they now?

Most people carried a couple of photo albums with them through their lives, but he had never come across a single photograph in Tessa's Covent Garden flat. Her parents were dead, killed in a car crash, but there was no sign they had ever existed. There was nothing from her childhood, no souvenirs of the past at all. "I live in the past in my job," she said. "I like to keep my life in the present. And Ruskin says that every increased possession loads us with weariness, and he's right."

There was something spartan in Tessa's makeup that was appealing, especially after Julia, a woman who inclined to the rococo, a subject on which she had once given him an entertaining lecture that had somehow involved sex (typical Julia). Julia was much more educated than she allowed you to believe. Tessa would have been bemused by Julia if she had known her. As it was, she was indifferent, "your ex," no interest, no jealousy (but what if she had known about the baby?). There was something refreshingly neutral about Tessa. He would never have thought he would find *neutral* an attractive adjective for a woman. Just goes to show.

They had known each other for four months, they had been married for two. He had been engaged to Josie for over two years before they married, so he had no personal evidence that a long courtship was the foundation of a long marriage. ("Oh, I think we were married long enough," Josie said.) Nonetheless, the sudden impulsive marriage to Tessa had been completely out of character for him. "No, it wasn't," Josie said, "you've always been the most uxorious of men." "No, it wasn't," Julia said, "you were desperate to marry me, and think how disastrous *that* would have been." *For I am wanton and lascivious and cannot live without a wife.* He was neither wanton nor lascivious (or he liked to think he wasn't), but being married had always seemed an ideal state to him. The Garden of Eden, the paradise lost.

"You're not actually very good at being married," Josie said. "You just *think* you are." "You're a lone wolf, Jackson," Julia said. "You just can't admit it." Josie and Julia lived uncomfortably in his brain, conflated into the voice of his conscience, the twin recording angels of his behavior. "Marry in haste," Josie's voice said. "Repent at leisure," Julia's concluded.

"What day is it?" he asked the policewoman.

"Friday."

Tessa flew back into Heathrow first thing on Monday. He would be home by then, if not before. He would be there to meet her off the plane, as promised. It was good for a man to have a goal, it was good for a man to know where he was going. Jackson was going home.

They had met at a party. Jackson never went to parties. It was the slimmest of chances, a confluence of the planets, a ripple in time.

He had bumped into his old commanding officer in the military police, in Regent Street of all places—again, not an *endroit* where Jackson was usually to be found. The Fates had clocked him crossing Regent Street, but for once in a good way.

His old boss was a rather roguish guy called Bernie, whom Jackson hadn't seen for over twenty years. They had never had much in common apart from the job, but they had got on well and Jackson was surprised by his own pleasure at this unexpected encounter, so when Bernie said, "Look, I've got a few folk coming round next week to the flat for a drink, as casual as it gets, why not join us?" he had been tempted before eventually demurring, at which point he had found himself at the end of a charm offensive from Bernie that finally proved irresistible—or rather, it had become easier to say yes than to keep on saying no. In retrospect, he realized it wasn't so much pleasure at seeing Bernie as it was at unexpectedly getting a reminder of a life that was now lost, two old soldiers reminiscing about the past.

He had been surprised by two things. The first was Bernie's flat in Battersea, which was plushly decorated and full of things—furniture, ornaments, paintings—that even Jackson could recognize as "good." Bernie had mentioned something about being "in security" (what else?) when they met, but Jackson had never suspected that security could be so well remunerated. Jackson didn't mention his own good fortune.

The second surprise was the guests Bernie had assembled. "A few folk round for a drink" had transformed into what Jackson overheard a guest refer to as "one of Bernie's famous soirées." Jackson was pretty sure he'd never been to a "soirée" before.

The flat was peopled by well-dressed London types—men in hip spectacles and women in ugly and extraordinarily uncomfortable-looking shoes. Jackson was innately suspicious of well-dressed men—real men (i.e., men from the north) didn't have the time or the inclination to shop for designer clothes, and he believed that no woman should wear a pair of shoes that she couldn't, if necessary, run away in. (Although a couple of years ago he had observed a girl simply throwing her shoes away in order to run, but she had been Russian and crazy, albeit worryingly attractive. He still thought about her.) None of the women at Bernie's "soirée" looked as if they would be prepared to toss away their Manolos and Jimmy Choos to make a quick getaway. Yes, he knew the names of designer shoemakers, and no, that wasn't the kind of stuff real men from the north should know, but he had been stuck in Toulouse airport with Marlee last summer and had been tutored relentlessly by her from the pages of *Heat* and *OK!*.

★   ★   ★

Bernie greeted him effusively at the door of the flat and led him into the already slightly overheated crowd. How Bernie knew these people was puzzling. None of them seemed like the natural social circle of a fifty-year-old ex-RMP guy.

"Cocktail?" Bernie offered, and Jackson said, "It's against my religion, got any beer?" and Bernie laughed and, punching him on the arm, said, "Same old Jackson." Jackson didn't think he *was* the same old Jackson, he had shed several skins since last seeing Bernie (and acquired a few new ones), but he didn't say so.

Jackson was no good at parties. He couldn't do small talk. *Hi, my name's Jackson Brodie, I used to be a policeman.* Maybe it *was* something to do with the lives he had led, first a soldier and then a policeman—neither profession exactly fostered idle chat. At first sight the people at Bernie's party (sorry, *soirée*) seemed strangely vacuous, as if they'd been hired for the night to play at being festive. Jackson found himself skulking around the fringes of the gathering like a latecomer to the water hole, wondering how long he had to continue to endure the evening before he could make his gruff excuses and leave.

At which point, Tessa pitched up at his elbow and murmured into his ear, "Isn't this ghastly?" Jackson was pleased to note that not only was she wearing a simple linen dress, made all the more attractive in contrast to the odd garb sported by some of the other women, but also low-heeled sandals that she could easily have run away in. She didn't choose to run but stayed close to his side. "You seem like a safe harbor," she said.

After five minutes of conversation made awkward by the volume of noise in the room, he had said boldly to her, "Fancy getting out of here?" and she said, "I can't think of anything I'd like better," and they'd gone to a pub over the river in Chelsea, not really Jackson's kind of place but nonetheless a thousand times better than Bernie's. They had talked until closing time over a civilized bottle of cabernet sauvignon before he walked her all the long way home to her flat ("smaller than a postage stamp") in Covent Garden. On the final stretch he took her hand (*"Shy boys get nothing"*—the words of his long-dead Lothario of a brother came unexpectedly into his head), and when they reached her door, he had planted a firm but decorous kiss on her cheek and was rewarded by her saying, "Shall we do this again? How about tomorrow?"

He couldn't have designed a better woman. She was cheerful, optimistic, and sweet. She was funny, even comical sometimes, and much smarter than he was but, unlike the previous women in his life, didn't find it necessary to remind him of this fact at every turn. She was graceful ("a lot of ballet when I was young") and athletic ("tennis, ditto"), and liked animals and children but not to the point of being oversentimental. She had a job she loved but that she was never overwhelmed by. She was fifteen years younger than he was ("Lucky dog," Bernie said later when he "caught up" with Jackson) and hadn't yet lost the glow of youthful enthusiasm, seemed, in fact, as if she might never lose it. She had long light-brown hair cut in a heavy-fringed style that made her look like an actress or a model from the sixties (Jackson's preferred look in a woman). She was someone who didn't need looking after but who nonetheless was properly grateful when he did look after her. She could drive and cook and even sew, knew how to do simple DIY, was surprisingly frugal but also knew how to be generous (witness the Breitling watch—her wedding present to him), and was the mistress of at least two sexual positions that Jackson had never tried before (hadn't even known existed, actually, but he kept that to himself). She was, in short, how God intended women to be.

How come she knew a guy like Bernie? "Friend of a friend of a friend," she said vaguely. "I don't usually go to parties. I end up standing in a corner like a standard lamp. I'm not much good at small talk. I was taught by nuns until I was eleven—you learn silence early on." Jackson's sister, Niamh, had been a convent girl. When she was thirteen she announced she wanted to become a nun. Their mother, despite being a devout Irish Catholic, was terrified. She had been looking forward to a future where a married Niamh popped in and out of her house, trailing babies in her wake. To everyone's relief, Niamh's enthusiasm for becoming a bride of Christ proved to be short-lived. Jackson was only six at the time, but even then he knew that nuns spent their lives imprisoned away from their families and he couldn't bear the idea that Niamh, so full of life, could be shut away from him forever.

And then, of course, she was.

He could feel his headaches breeding, stacking themselves one upon the other.

When he woke again, the girl was sitting there, blinking at him like a baby owl. She was speaking nonsense. "Dr. Foster went to Gloucester, all in a shower of rain."

Jackson could hear children's voices out in the larger ward, singing Christmas carols, quite badly. He noticed for the first time some halfhearted gaudy decorations hanging in his room. He had forgotten all about Christmas. He wondered if the girl was something to do with the carol concert. She looked about the same age as Marlee and was gazing at him intently as if she were expecting him to do something extraordinary.

"They said you were a soldier," she said.

"A long time ago."

"The nurse said. That's how they knew your blood group."

"Yeah." His voice was still croaky. He was a weak version of himself, a flawed clone, everything working but nothing quite right.

"My dad was a soldier."

He struggled into a sitting position, and she helped him with the pillows. "Yeah? What regiment?" he asked, unexpectedly entering into his conversational comfort zone.

"Royal Scots," the girl said.

"Were you here yesterday?" he said. "The day before today," he clarified. He was pleased to see that he was getting the hang of time again. Yesterday, today, tomorrow, that was how it went, one day after the next. *Tomorrow and tomorrow and tomorrow.* Julia had done *Macbeth* at Birmingham Rep, a crazed, blood-boltered Lady Macbeth. "Acting with her hair again," Amelia snorted in the seat next to him. Jackson thought she was good, better than he'd expected anyway.

"No," she said. "I've only just found you."

He wondered if she was one of those volunteers, like prison visitors, who come and see people who don't have anyone else. (Because apparently he didn't.) Perhaps the army had sent her, like a care package.

"You would have bled to death," she said. She seemed very interested in his blood. His veins ran with the blood of strangers, he wondered if that had any implications for him. Had he lost his immunity to measles? Had he acquired a predisposition to something else? (Something that ran in the blood.) Was he carrying the DNA of strangers? There were a lot of unanswered questions surrounding his transfusion. Was this girl one of his donors? Too young, surely.

"Exsanguinated," she said, pronouncing it carefully.

"Right."

"Exsanguinated," she said again. "*Sangria* comes from the same root, the Latin for blood. Bloodred wine. Wine-dark sea."

"Do I know you?" Jackson said. It suddenly struck him that she might be a fellow survivor of the train crash. She had a nasty bruise on her forehead.

"Not really," she said. Not a very helpful answer. "Are you going to eat that toast?" she asked, eyeing the unappetizing food still in front of him.

"Knock yourself out," Jackson said, pushing the bed-tray towards her. "Have we met?" he pursued.

"In a way," she said, her mouth full of toast.

His headache, blissfully absent when he woke, was beginning to throb again.

"You don't remember me, do you?" she said.

"Sorry, no. There's a lot of things I don't remember at the moment. Are you going to tell me or do I have to guess? I really don't think I have the energy to guess."

"You wouldn't be able to. It would take you forever." She looked pleased with herself at this idea. She took a little dramatic pause from eating toast and said, "I saved your life."

"I saved your life." What did that mean? He didn't understand. "How?"

"CPR, artery compression. At the train crash. At the side of the track."

"You saved my life," he repeated.

"Yes."

At last he understood. "You're the person who saved my life."

"Yes." She giggled at his slowness. He found himself grinning, in fact, he couldn't stop grinning. He felt oddly grateful that his life had been saved by a giggling child and not some burly paramedic.

"They did their bit, as well," she said. "But it was me that kept you alive in the beginning."

She had breathed life into him, literally. His breath was hers. *Then the Lord God formed man of dust from the ground, and breathed into his nostrils the breath of life; and man became a living being.* More rote learning from some murky place in his spiritual past.

What on earth could he say to her? It took a while, but Jackson got there eventually.

"Thank you," he said. He was still grinning.

"How about the Corn Flakes? You gonna eat them?"

★ ★ ★

So, technically speaking, you belong to me."

"I'm sorry?" Her name was Reggie. A man's name.

"You're in my *thrall*." She seemed delighted by the word *thrall*. "You can only be released by *reciprocation*."

"Reciprocation?"

"If you save *my* life." She smiled at him and her small features were illuminated. "Plus, I'm responsible for you now until you do."

"Do what?"

"Save my life. It's a Native American belief. I read about it in a book."

"Books aren't all they're cracked up to be," Jackson said. "How *old* are you?"

"Older than I look. Believe me."

What did she mean he "belonged" to her? Perhaps he had mortgaged his soul after all, not to the devil but to this funny little Scottish girl.

Dr. Foster put her head round the door of the ward and, frowning at the girl, said, "Don't tire him out with talking. Five more minutes," she added, holding up her hand in an emphatic gesture as if they needed to count her fingers to know what five was.

"Do you understand?" she said pointedly to Reggie.

"Totally," the girl said. To Jackson, she said, "I have to go anyway, I have a dog waiting outside for me. I'll be back."

Jackson realized he was feeling much better. He had been saved. He had been saved for the future. His own.

When you had a future, a couple of nurses could gang up on you and remove your catheter without any anesthetic, or even any warning, and then force you out of bed, and make you hobble in your flimsy, open-backed hospital gown to the bathroom, where they encourage you to "try and pee" on your own. Jackson had never previously appreciated that such a basic bodily function could be both so painful and so gratifying at the same time. I piss, therefore I am.

He would look at everything differently from now on. The reborn bit had finally kicked in. He was a new Jackson. Alleluia.

Dr. Foster Went to Gloucester

All in a shower of rain. He stepped in a puddle right up to his middle and never went that way again.' I bet people quote that to her all the time."

"Who?"

"Dr. Foster."

"I bet they don't," Jackson Brodie said.

She had finally found him and now she was keeping a faithful vigil by his bedside, Greyfriars Reggie.

Like Chief Inspector Monroe before her, Dr. Foster didn't really seem to believe Reggie when she said that she had saved Jackson Brodie's life. "Really?" Dr. Foster said sarcastically. "I thought we did that in the hospital." She had seemed harassed by Reggie's questions about Jackson Brodie's condition. "Who are you?" Dr. Foster asked bluntly. "Are you a relative? I can only talk about his medical condition to close relatives."

Good question. Who was she? She was the Famous Reggie, she was Regina Chase, Girl Detective, she was Virgo Regina, the storm-tossed queen of the plucky abandoned orphans. "I'm his daughter, Marlee," Reggie said.

Dr. Foster frowned at her. Dr. Foster frowned every time she spoke, and quite often when she didn't speak. She should think about the wrinkles she was going to have in a few years' time. Mum was always worried about wrinkles. For a while she had gone to bed at night with her jaw strapped up in crepe bandages, so that she looked like an accident victim.

"You're the first thing he remembered," Dr. Foster said.

"That's nice."

"Don't stay for long, he needs to rest."

You would think they would ask for ID, for proof of who you said you were. You could be anybody. You could be Billy. Just as well she was only Reggie.

He was on his own in a little room off a bigger ward. When she was looking for him, she was worried that when she found him she wouldn't recognize him, but she did. He looked more gaunt but less dead. An uneaten breakfast lay on a table across the bed. It seemed an awful waste of food to someone who had breakfasted on a Tunnock's Caramel Wafer two mornings in a row. This morning, groggy with sleep, Reggie took some time to understand that she had slept again on Ms. MacDonald's uncomfortable sofa and that the noise that had woken her was the racket of the heavy recovery machinery gearing up for work on the track. She wondered if she would ever wake up again to her own alarm in her own bed. In her own good time.

The mug she drank her instant coffee from carried a message that was too complicated for this time of the morning. "Bill of sale! Eternal life paid in full in the blood of Jesus Christ." Then she had phoned the hospital and—abracadabra—they had found him.

He was asleep, and a nurse came to check his drip and said loudly to him, "You've got a visitor. You've not been forgotten about after all. He's still a little dozy from the accident," she said to Reggie. "He'll wake up in a bit."

Reggie sat patiently on a chair by his bedside and watched him sleep. She had nothing else to do, after all. He was old enough to be her father. "Dad," she tried experimentally, but it didn't wake him. She'd never said that word to anyone. It felt like a word in a foreign language. *Pater.*

He was a detective. ("Used to be," he muttered.) He used to be a soldier too. What did he do now?

"This and that." Something and nothing.

She peeled off a ten-pound note from the tight wad that cheap-skate Mr. Hunter gave her yesterday. She put it on his locker. "In case you need stuff," she said, "you know, chocolate or news-papers."

"I'll pay you back," he said.

Reggie wondered how he intended to do that. He didn't have any money, he was penniless. He had no wallet, no credit cards, no phone, nothing to his name at all. He only just had his own name. ("Yes, we had some trouble identifying your father," Dr. Foster said.) No wonder the hospital had no record of him when she first phoned, they thought he was someone else altogether. Like Reggie, he'd been stripped of everything. At least now Reggie had a bagful of Topshop clothes. And a dog.

"I thought you must have died," she said to him.

"So did I," he said.

While she was in the hospital, Reggie left the dog lying placidly on the grass verge, near the taxi stand. She had written on a piece of paper *"This dog is not a stray, her owner is visiting in the hospital"* and stuck it inside Sadie's collar in case someone decided to call the SSPCA. Everywhere you went there were "No Dogs Allowed" signs. What was a person supposed to do? It would be good if she could get hold of a guide-dog harness and put it on Sadie. Then she'd be able to take her anywhere. And, as a plus point, people would be sorry for the poor little blind girl and be especially nice to her.

"Good dog," Reggie said to Sadie when she left her, and the dog responded with a soft whine, which Reggie guessed meant "Don't forget to come back." Dog language was pretty easy to interpret compared with human language. (Something and nothing, this and that, here and there.)

As far as she could tell, Jackson Brodie seemed an okay sort of person. It would be a shame if it turned out that she had saved the life of an evil human being when she could have saved someone who was developing the cure for cancer or who was the only support of a large, needy family, perhaps with a small crippled child in tow.

Jackson Brodie had a wife and child, so they would be grateful to her. Was Jackson Brodie's wife also Marlee's mother? It was funny how you could sound like a different person depending on who you were attached to. Jackie's daughter. Billy's sister. Dr. Hunter's mother's help.

Jackson Brodie said that he didn't want to alarm his wife with news of the accident, which was very altruistic of him. Word of the day. From the Latin, *alteri huic,* "to this other." His wife ("Tessa") was "attending a conference in Washington." How sophisticated that sounded. She was probably wearing a black suit. Reggie thought of Dr. Hunter's two black suits hanging patiently in the closet, waiting for her to come back and fill them. Where was she?

★   ★   ★

The automatic front doors of the hospital hissed open and Reggie stepped outside, pausing for a moment to make sure that there were no meds armed with Loebs waiting for her. She still hadn't been able to get hold of Billy, she'd never known a person so good at not being found. Although Dr. Hunter seemed to be trying to give him a run for his money.

Sadie spotted Reggie as soon as she came out of the hospital. She stood to attention, her ears pricked up, the way she did when she was on guard duty. Reggie felt a surge of something very like happiness. It felt good to have someone (if a dog was someone) who was pleased to see her. The dog wagged her tail. If Reggie had had a tail she would have wagged it too.

Been visiting a friend?" an old lady in the queue for the 24 outside the hospital asked her.

"Yes," Reggie said. He wasn't really her friend, of course, but he would be. One day. He belonged to her now.

"I'll be back," she'd said to Jackson Brodie. "I really will," she'd added. Reggie was never going to be a person who didn't come back.

She had forgotten to bring a book with her but found the mutilated *Iliad* in her bag and read around the cavern at its heart. The beginning of Book Six was intact and she checked her translation. *Nestor shouted aloud, and called to the Argives: My friends, Danaan warriors, attendants of Ares, let no man now stay back.* Pretty close.

Her bus journey was fatefully interrupted by a call from Sergeant Wiseman, telling her that Ms. MacDonald was still "unavailable." "Toxicology tests and so on," he said vaguely.

"So when do you think she can be buried?" Reggie asked.

Reggie wondered if Ms. MacDonald (*her dead*) would want to

be buried. Worm food or ash? *She is dead; and all which die, to their first elements resolve.* They had done that at school. They had done Donne. Ha.

There was a horrible emptiness inside Reggie, as if someone had scooped out vital organs. The world was falling away. She began to feel panicky, the way she felt when she was first told that Mum was dead. Where was Dr. Hunter? Where was Dr. Hunter? Where *was* she?

He was a detective. Used to be. Detectives knew how to find people. People who were missing.

A Good Man Is Hard to Find

Bnt easy to lose.

She couldn't breathe. A heavy weight was pressing on her chest and suffocating her, a great stone crushing her, martyring her lungs. Louise woke up with a start, gasping for air. Jesus, what was that about?

It felt unnaturally early, sparrowfart time of day by the feel and sound of it. She fumbled for her spectacles. Yes indeed, the digital numbers on the bedside clock glowed a Halloween green and confirmed that it was all the fives, five fifty-five.

Her head was throbbing and her stomach was roiling, the wine from last night still working its way slowly through her blood. Red wine was never a good idea, it dragged out the maudlin Scot from the dark tartan-lined pit inside her, where it lived. Whisky soothed the embittered monster that lived in there, red wine boiled its blood.

She was still surprised to wake up every morning next to a man. This man. He was a neat sleeper, curled in a fetal position all night, far over on his side of their new emperor-sized bed. Patrick understood, without her having to explain, that she needed a lot of space for her restless sleep.

He had been amused that the brooding presence of Bridget in the bedroom down the hall had made sex a complete nonstarter as far as Louise was concerned. Presumably he had done it with Samantha within earshot of his sister. Louise imagined Samantha was probably docile in extremis. Patrick certainly was, giving out nothing much more than a discreet but complimentary kind of moan. Louise was a bit of a howler.

Sex between them was good, but it didn't tear up the carpet, it wasn't *ravenous*. Not fornication but lovemaking. Louise had always considered that *lovemaking* was a euphemistic word for something that was an animal instinct, but this was clearly not a belief shared by Patrick. The marriage bed was holy, he said, and this from a godless man, although a godless Irishman, which was almost a contradiction in terms.

At first she'd thought there was a considerable charm in their civilized coupling, she'd stewed in enough sweaty, feral encounters in her time, but now she was beginning to wonder. If she ever kissed Jackson, it would be the end of decency and good manners. A pair of tigers roaring in the night. Not yesterday in the hospital, that had been a chaste kiss for an invalid. If they ever kissed properly, they would exchange breath, they would exchange souls. Never think about one man in another man's bed, especially if the man in the bed is your husband. Height of bad manners, Louise. Bad wife. Very bad wife.

She watched the clock tick over to five fifty-six and slipped quietly out of bed. Patrick didn't normally wake until seven, but Bridget and Tim were early birds and Louise didn't think she could face polite conversation with either of them at this hour of the morning. Or, God forbid, another breakfast *en famille*. Still, she was determined that for the rest of their visit she would bite her tongue, bite it off if necessary, and be as polite as Mrs. Polite Well-Mannered. The bitch was muzzled.

She put in her contacts and peered at herself in the mirror of the en suite. She still looked exhausted—she *was* exhausted—but at the same time, she felt overwhelming relief at the idea that she had to go to work today and not play at being a hostess.

The memory hit her of Jackson lying in the hospital bed, beaten up and mauled, down and out for the count. He was the kind who always got back up, but, of course, one day he wouldn't. Why was he always in the wrong place at the wrong time? She could imagine him saying, *"Maybe it was the right place at the right time."* He was *the* most annoying person, even in her imagination.

He had looked so vulnerable lying there in that hospital bed. *The king sits in Dunfermline toun, drinking the blude-red wine.*

The Fisher King, sick and emasculated, the land wasting around him. Did you have to bring the king back to life to restore the land or did you have to sacrifice him? She couldn't remember. *Blood Sacrifice,* that was the title of Martina Appleby's anthology of poems. She wrote under her maiden name, not the ill-fated "Mason." Louise had Googled her and come up with a brief paragraph. Howard Mason had called her "my muse." For a while anyway. In a barely disguised roman à clef, she became Ingegerd, "the gloomy Scandinavian millstone around his neck, pulling him under the water." Not a great one for inventive metaphor, our Howard. Now Martina was out of print. They were all out of print. Every single one of them. Except Joanna.

She tiptoed around the house, thought about making coffee, decided against it as being too noisy.

Hobbled by her hangover, Louise didn't quite make the great escape. Just as she was buttoning up her coat, good old Bridget wafted downstairs—in an inflammatory orange–colored satin dressing gown—and said, "Off to work already?" and Louise said, "No rest for the wicked, or the police."

"Don't worry, I'll look after Patrick," Bridget said, and

Louise — in-law to outlaw at the flick of a switch — growled, "I'm not worried, he's fifty-two years old, he can look after himself." The bitch was out.

The flats shared an underground garage, and as Louise was emerging, she almost ran over the postman, bringing a Special Delivery, another volume of Howard Mason's oeuvre that she'd found on the Net. She signed for it, stuck it in the glove compartment, and drove away.

This time she didn't go in the fancy front door but took the path that went along the side of the house and led to the back door. It took her past the garage, through the window of which she could see Dr. Hunter's virtuous Prius, just as Reggie had said. Louise had parked on the main road on Tuesday, waiting for Joanna Hunter to come in from work. She had watched her car turn into the driveway, watched her coming home, and wondered what it must be like to be the one that got away. ("Guilty," Joanna Hunter said. "Every day I feel guilty.")

Me again," Louise said cheerfully when Neil Hunter opened the door. He seemed more disheveled in every way than yesterday.

"Do you know what time it is?"

Louise looked at her watch and said, "Ten to seven," like a helpful Girl Guide. Early morning — best time for rousing drug dealers, terrorists, and the innocent husbands of caring GPs. Louise never even made it to being a Guider, she was kicked out of the Brownies at age seven. It was funny because she thought of herself as a good team player, although sometimes she suspected that no one else on her team did. ("Not a team player, a team *leader,* boss," Karen Warner said diplomatically.)

"I said I'd be back," she said, the queen of reason, to Neil Hunter.

"So you did." He rubbed the stubble on his chin and stared at her absently for a moment. He didn't look in good fettle. Perhaps he was one of those men who needed a wife to keep his life ticking along (quite a lot of those about).

"I suppose you want to come in?" he said. He squashed himself against the doorpost and she had to squeeze past him. Just a little bit too close to Louise's perimeter fence. He smelled of drink and cigarettes and looked as if he'd been up all night, which was not as unattractive as it should have been. You wouldn't kick him out of your bed. If you weren't married, that is, and he weren't married, and there weren't an outside chance that he'd somehow done away with his wife. Crazy talk, Louise.

"I noticed Dr. Hunter's car is in the garage," Louise said.

"It's dead, must be the electronics. I'm taking it in tomorrow to be fixed. Jo hired a car to go down to Yorkshire."

"I've called Dr. Hunter a couple of times but haven't been able to get an answer," Louise said. She hadn't, but hey. "She does have her phone with her, doesn't she?"

"Yes, of course."

"Perhaps you could give me her aunt's phone number and address."

"Her aunt?"

"Mmm."

He put his fingers to his temple and thought for a few seconds before saying, "I think it's in the study," and reluctantly leaving the room, as if setting off on a particularly challenging quest.

When he'd disappeared into the innards of the house, a phone, a mobile, started to ring. It was somewhere close by but the sound

was muffled as if the phone were buried. Louise traced the ringing to the drawer in the big kitchen table. When she pulled the
drawer open, music suddenly escaped into the air. It sounded
vaguely like Bach, but it was too obscure for Louise to identify.
Thanks to Patrick, she recognized a lot now but could name only
a few obvious pieces—Beethoven's Fifth, bits of *Swan Lake, Car-
mina Burana*—"classic lite," according to Patrick. He was a serious
opera fan as well, he particularly liked the ones that Louise didn't.
She was "a populist," he laughed, because she liked only the big
heartbreak arias. She had a Maria Callas CD, a "Best of" compilation, in the car that she played a lot, although she wasn't sure it was
necessarily a healthy choice of in-car entertainment.

Her instinct was to answer the ringing phone but she could
see there was something intrusive if not unethical about that. She
answered it anyway.

"Jo?" a male voice, a voice that you could hear the crack and the
strain in, even in the one syllable.

"No," Louise said. A perfect little two-footed rhyme *No Jo*, which
was the truth. Louise realized she had been looking forward to seeing Joanna Hunter, and denying the fact to herself. Joanna Hunter
was the reason she had come here this morning, not Neil Hunter.

Whoever it was rang off immediately. If this was Joanna Hunter's
phone, why was it in a drawer? And who was calling her—a wrong
number? A lover? A crazy patient?

She replaced the phone and closed the drawer. It was down to its
last squeak of battery. Neil Hunter must have been able to hear it
ringing for the last couple of days. Why hadn't he just turned it off?
Perhaps he wanted to know who was phoning his wife. He came
back in the room, and Louise said, "I'd like to see Dr. Hunter's
phone if you don't mind."

"Her phone?

"Her phone," Louise said firmly. "We're having a problem locat-
ing Andrew Decker. I need to find out if he's phoned Dr. Hunter

in the past few days." She was improvising. Making it up as she went along, wasn't that what everyone did? No?

"Why would Andrew Decker do that?" Neil Hunter said. "Surely Jo's the last person he would contact?"

"Or the first. Just want to make sure," Louise said. She smiled encouragingly at Neil Hunter and held out her hand. "The phone?"

"She took it with her, I told you that."

"Only there's never an answer from Dr. Hunter's mobile when I call it," Louise said innocently (or as innocently as she could muster). She dialed a number on her own phone and held it aloft demonstrating her inability to reach Joanna Hunter. A few seconds later, the tinny, muffled Bach started up. Neil Hunter stared at the wooden table as if it had just kicked up its legs and danced the can-can. Louise opened the drawer and took out the phone.

"Fancy that. Jo left it behind, can you believe?" he said. He wasn't as good at mugging innocence as Louise. "Honest to God, my wife can be so forgetful sometimes." (What had the girl said? *"Dr. Hunter never forgets anything."*)

"You haven't spoken to her, then?"

"Who?"

"Your wife, Mr. Hunter."

"Of course I have, I told you I had. I must have phoned her on the aunt's number." He handed over a piece of paper with an address and phone number on it. The aunt.

"When?" Louise asked.

"Yesterday."

"Do you mind if I take her mobile?"

"Take her mobile?"

"Yes," she said. "Take her mobile."

She was parked outside Alison Needler's house, drinking a take-away coffee.

Agnes Barker. The elderly aunt, like a character in a farce, not a real person at all (*Enter stage left, An Elderly Aunt*). The aunt was seventy, not that old, not these days. Old age receded the closer you got to it. Live fast, die young, Louise used to joke, but it was hard to move fast when you were hampered by linen chests and silver napkin rings, not to mention having voluntarily shackled yourself to one man for the rest of your life. Was that what they meant by wedlock? One good man, she reminded herself.

Trawling the Net, Louise had come up with some scant details about Agnes Barker — born Agnes Mary Mason in 1936, went to RADA, trod the boards in rep for a few years, married an Oliver Barker, a radio producer with the BBC, in 1965. Lived in Ealing, no children. Retired to Hawes in 1990, husband died ten years ago.

There had been a sister called Margot in *The Shopkeeper* — an uppity, snobbish girl — Agnes's fictional alter ego, presumably. Louise was beginning to feel she could go on *Mastermind* and answer questions on "The Life and Works of Howard Mason."

Arty sister of an arty brother. In *The Shopkeeper*, Margot was still at school but had "foolishly unrealistic" dreams of fame and success.

There wasn't a reason in the world to doubt either the existence of the aunt or the aunt's veracity. Except that when she examined Joanna Hunter's phone, as she was doing now, and checked it against the number that Neil Hunter had reluctantly given her for the aunt, there were no calls to or from Agnes Barker, no calls from Hawes at all. Perhaps Joanna Hunter and her husband were using the aunt as some kind of cover, to give Joanna Hunter some space. For her *escape*. Long odds.

Joanna Hunter had made six calls on Wednesday and received five. On Thursday she had received — or at least the phone had received — several calls. She fished out Reggie Chase's number, and, not surprisingly, most of them were from her. Any further investigation of Joanna Hunter's phone proved impossible as the battery, on its last gasp, finally gave up on life.

She phoned Agnes Barker's home number and a politely robotic voice informed her that this number was no longer in use. She phoned the station, got hold of the handiest DC, and asked him to find out when the number was disconnected. He came back in a snappy ten minutes and said, "Last week, boss." Disconnected and out of print. The Masons were like an illusion, all smoke and mirrors.

Louise flicked through the new Howard Mason novel, *The Way Home,* written a couple of years after his marriage to Gabrielle. The wife in the novel was called Francesca and had some kind of exotic parentage and a cosmopolitan upbringing, a world away from the novel's protagonist, Stephen, brought up in a claustrophobic West Yorkshire mill town — all dirty canals and soot-blackened skylines. (Louise wondered what Jackson would make of Howard's book.)

Stephen, having escaped his inheritance of northern misery, was now living a gypsy life with his new schoolgirl wife — he had eloped with her — amongst the bohemian enclaves of Europe. There seemed to be an incredible amount of sex in the novel, on every other page Stephen and Francesca were going at it like rabbits, sucking and bucking and arching. Louise supposed it was all that fucking that had made Howard Mason fashionable in — she checked the publication date — 1960. Louise yawned. It was amazing how tedious reading about sex could be at this time of the day, any time of the day, in fact.

The Needlers' front door opened and Alison poked her head out and checked the coast was clear before reappearing with the kids a couple of minutes later. She marshaled them down the street to school as if they were an unruly pack of dogs but in reality they were as docile as zombies. Between the four of them, the Needlers were on a pharmacopoeia of downers and uppers. Louise started up the BMW's engine and drove slowly behind them, peeling away once they were through the school gates. Alison Needler acknowledged Louise's presence with an almost imperceptible nod of her head.

It was still dark, they were hurtling towards the winter solstice and it was going to be one of those days when the sun never got out of bed. Louise checked her watch, the surgery where Joanna Hunter worked would be in full swing by the time she got back to Edinburgh. She started the engine and set off again. Louise wondered how many miles she'd have on the BMW's clock when she finally felt she could stop moving.

No word from Dr. Hunter at the surgery, no word since first thing Thursday morning, when the practice had been apprised of her sudden leave of absence. Louise finally managed to track down the receptionist who had taken the call and phoned her from the car, parked outside the surgery. It was the receptionist's day off and she sounded as if she was already out Christmas shopping. "I'm in the Gyle," she said, her voice raised against a Slade track. The woman sounded understandably harassed, Louise would have been harassed if she had been Christmas shopping in the Gyle. What was she going to buy Patrick for Christmas? Archie was easy, he wanted cash ("Lots, please"), but Patrick would expect something personal, something with meaning. Louise was no good with presents, she didn't know how either to receive or to give. And not just presents.

"No," the receptionist said, after a moment's hesitation. "Not Dr. Hunter, it was her husband who phoned. He said there'd been a family emergency."

"You're sure it was her husband?"

"Well, he said he was. He was Glaswegian," she added as if that clinched it. "She's gone to look after a sick aunt."

"Yeah," Louise said. "I heard that."

Sheila Hayes was running a prenatal clinic at the end of the corridor. It unnerved Louise to be amongst so much fecundity, it was bad enough working around Karen, but in the prenatal clinic, the air in the waiting room was saturated with hormones as a roomful of fertility goddesses the size of buses leafed through old, dog-eared copies of *OK!* and shifted their uncomfortable bulk around on the hard chairs.

Louise showed her warrant card to the receptionist and said, "Sheila Hayes?" and the receptionist pointed at a door and said, "She has a lady in with her." More ladies. Ladies of the lake, the lamp, the night. Louise waited until a woman lumbered out, already trammeled by two small infants, and slipped into the midwife's room.

Sheila Hayes smiled a welcome at her and glancing down at her notes said, "Mrs. Carter? I don't think we've met before."

"Not Mrs. Carter," Louise said, showing her warrant card, "Chief Inspector Louise Monroe." Sheila Hayes's professional smile faded. "It's a question about Dr. Hunter."

"Something's happened to her?"

"No. I'm conducting a routine investigation into her husband's affairs—"

"Neil?"

"Yes, Neil. I'd rather you didn't say anything about this to anyone."

"Of course not."

Louise supposed it would be all round the surgery before she was even out of the door. The receptionist was already agog at the sight of her warrant card. "I'm trying to locate Dr. Hunter. She didn't tell you she was going away?"

"No," Sheila Hayes said. "She's gone to stay with an aunt apparently, according to Reggie—Reggie's the girl who helps to look after the baby. Jo was supposed to meet me on Wednesday night but she didn't turn up, didn't answer her phone when I called to find out what happened. It's very out of character for her, but I suppose it's something to do with the story in the newspaper?"

"What story?"

Which do you prefer," Karen Warner said, " 'Mason Murderer Missing' or 'Beast of Bodmin Moor.' It wasn't Bodmin Moor."

"Scottish paper," Louise said, "bound to be hazy on English geography."

" 'After serving a full thirty-year life sentence for the brutal slaying,' blah, blah, blah. 'Face of a killer.' This photo's over thirty years old. 'Joanna Mason, changed her name, believed to be working as a GP in Scotland,' diddum, diddum . . . They haven't found her yet, then. Close on her heels, though."

"I kind of wish they would," Louise said. "Find her."

"Do you?"

A DC called Abbie Nash popped her head round the door and said, "Boss? You wanted me?"

"Yes, phone round the rental companies to check whether a Joanna Hunter rented a car on Wednesday. And Abbie," Louise said, handing her Joanna Hunter's phone, "can you get someone else to run all the numbers on this mobile, also Joanna Hunter's."

"Right away, boss." Abbie was a short, stocky young woman who looked as if she would hold her own in a fight. She was more imaginative than her badly cut hair suggested. "Sandy Mathieson says she's the Mason massacre survivor," she said. "I Googled her when he told me about her. Rumor is she's lost again."

Louise wondered how many people had to die before murder became massacre. More than three, surely?

"Crisp?" Karen offered, rattling an open packet at them both. "Roast beef flavor." Abbie Nash took a handful, but Louise waved the crisps away, even the smell made her nauseous. This must be how people became vegetarians.

"I just want to know where she is and if she's okay," Louise said. "And I want to make sure that Andrew Decker's nowhere near her."

What had Reggie said? *"Has anyone actually spoken to her?"* No, apparently not. "Trouble is, she's a missing person that no one's reported missing." Louise sighed. "I think it's a case of *cherchez la tante.*"

The thing was, as Reggie Chase would have said, Neil Hunter's reaction to the perplexing presence of his wife's phone in the house was worthy of Ingrid Bergman in *Gaslight* but wasn't nearly as hammy as his response to the sound of the Prius's engine purring happily when Louise started it. "Miracle recovery?" she said innocently to Neil Hunter.

He tried to laugh it off. "Do I need a lawyer?" he joked.

"I don't know. Do you?" she said.

Abide with Me

She was nine when Martina died. She came home from school—there was no sign of her father—and found two men carrying a sheet-draped body downstairs on a stretcher. Joanna wasn't sure who it was until she ran upstairs to Martina's room and saw the tumbled sheets, the empty bottles lying on the floor, and smelled something sickly in the air that hinted at disaster.

The note that Martina had left was written on a flowery card, part of a stationery set that had been Joanna's Christmas present to her. It was on the dining-room mantelpiece and had been overlooked by the police. It contained nothing memorable, no poetry, just a sleepy scrawl that said "Too much" and something in Swedish that would forever remain untranslated for Joanna.

She had gone looking for her father, found him in his study, where he had worked his way down to the bottom of a bottle of whisky. She stood in the doorway and held up the card. "Martina left you a note," she said, and he said, "I know," and threw the bottle of whisky at her.

★   ★   ★

So then it was just Joanna and her father for a while. At first, when she had gone to live with him, after everyone she loved had died, he had employed a nanny, a dried-up stick of a witch in severe clothes who believed that the best way for Joanna to get over her tragedy was to behave as if it had never happened.

It was a long time before Joanna was able to go to school. Her legs would collapse under her every time she got near the school gates, and the psychiatrist that her father employed (a tweedy man who smelled of cigarettes and with whom she shared long, awkward silences) suggested she be schooled at home for a while, and so the nanny did double duty as a governess and gave Joanna lessons every day, terrible, tedious hours of arithmetic and English. If she did anything wrong, if she smudged her exercise books or didn't pay attention, she was smacked across the back of her hand with a ruler. When one day Martina caught the nanny midwhack, she grabbed the ruler and hit her across the face with it.

There was a terrible fuss, the nanny talked about getting the police involved, but Howard must have got rid of her somehow. He was good at getting rid of women. All Joanna remembered was Martina turning to her after the woman had left in a taxi, saying, "No more nannies, darling. I'll look after you from now on. I promise." *"Don't make promises you can't keep,"* their mother used to say, and she was right. She didn't used to say it to her children, she said it mainly to their father, Howard Mason, the Great Pretender.

The woman who came after the poet (who, in truth, came before the poet, which was one of the reasons Martina lay down with her bottles of salvation) was Chinese, some kind of artist from Hong Kong, who assured Howard that Joanna would be happier not at the local school, where she had finally settled, but at a boarding school buried deep in the folds of the Cotswolds, and so Joanna was duly packed off until she was eighteen, coming home only for holidays.

Her father spent years in exile in Los Angeles, trying to make a new career, and she spent the school holidays with Aunt Agnes and Uncle Oliver, dreadful people who were terrified of children and treated her as if she were a dangerous wild animal to be harried and contained at every turn. Now their contact was limited to the exchange of Christmas cards. Joanna could never forgive her aunt for not wrapping her in love, the way she would have done in her place.

It was only because she saw an obituary in the newspaper that she knew her own father was dead. His fifth, forgetful wife had omitted to tell her and had him cremated and scattered before Joanna even knew he'd finally gone. He was living in Rio when he died, like a criminal or a Nazi. The fifth wife was Brazilian, and Howard might have neglected to tell her that he had a daughter.

She could have sunk, but school made up for the Masons' short-comings. By sheer chance Howard put her into a boarding school that fostered her and cared for her, and in return she proved buoy-ant, embracing school life with the order of its days and the com-fort of its rules.

By the time Joanna left school for university, Howard had worked his way through another wife and a couple of mistresses, but he never had any more children. "I had my children," he would drunk-enly declare in company, like a grandstanding tragic actor. "They are not replaceable."

"You still have Joanna," someone would remind him, and he would say, "Yes, of course. Thank God, I still have Joanna."

There were ten in the bed," she sang quietly to the baby, even though he was asleep. "And the little one said, 'Roll over, roll over.' " He had fallen asleep easily on the lumpy mattress they were sharing but woke as usual at four in the morning for a feed. The time of night when people died and were born, when the body offered least resistance to the coming and going of the soul. Joanna didn't believe in God, how could she, but she believed in the existence of the soul, believed indeed in the transference of the soul, and although she wouldn't have stood up at a scientific conference and declared it, she also believed that she carried the souls of her dead family inside her and one day the baby would do the same for her. Just because you were a rational and skeptical atheist didn't mean that you didn't have to get through every day the best way you could. There were no rules.

The best days of her life had been when she was pregnant and the baby was still safe inside her. Once you were out in the world, then the rain fell on your face and the wind lifted your hair and the sun beat down on you and the path stretched ahead of you and evil walked on it.

It was black night outside, a winter-white moon rising. The baby was the same age as Joseph was when he died. His foot stopped short when he was so young that it was impossible to imagine what kind of a man Joseph would have become if he had lived. Jessica was easier, her character already fixed at the age of eight. Loyal, resourceful, confident, annoying. Clever, too clever sometimes. *"Too clever for her own good,"* their father said, but their mother said, *"That's impossible. Especially for a girl."* Did they really say those things? Was she just making it up to fill in the gaps, the same way that she imagined (ludicrously, a daydream shared with no one) a Jessica living in the present, a parallel universe in the Cotswolds, in an old house with wisteria strung out along the front wall. Four children, a government adviser on Third World policies. Argumentative. Brave. Reliable. And her mother, living somewhere dazzling with sunshine, painting like a crazy woman, the eccentric English artist.

All made up, of course. She couldn't really remember any of them, but that didn't stop them from still possessing a reality that was stronger than anything alive, apart from the baby, of course.

They were the touchstone to which everything else must look and the exemplar compared to which everything else failed. Except for the baby.

She was bereft, her whole life an act of bereavement, longing for something that she could no longer remember. Sometimes in the night, in dreams, she heard their old dog barking and it brought back a memory of grief so raw that it led her to wonder about killing the baby, and then herself, both of them slipping away on something as peaceful as poppies so that nothing hideous could ever happen to him. A contingency plan for when you were cornered, for when you couldn't run. A famine or a nuclear war. The volcano erupting, the comet dropping to earth. If she was in a concentration camp. Or kidnapped by evil psychopaths. If there were no needles, if there was nothing, she would hold her hand over the baby's face and then she would hang herself. You could always find a way to hang yourself. Sometimes it took a lot of self-discipline. *Elsie Marley's grown so fine, she won't get up to feed the swine.*

If she could, she would run, she would run with the baby, she would run like the wind, until she was safe. She heard footsteps coming up the stairs and held the baby closer. The bad man was coming.

Reggie Chase, Warrior Virgin

She had phoned Chief Inspector Monroe three times so far and got no answer. When she phoned Dr. Hunter's phone, it no longer rang, now a recorded voice on the other end informed Reggie that the number she was trying to reach was currently unavailable. Perhaps it had run out of battery, it must be ailing by now, if not dead. The slender thread that still connected Reggie to Dr. Hunter was broken. Dr. Hunter's *lifeline*. Reggie's too.

If Reggie could get her hands on Dr. Hunter's phone, then the so-called aunt would be in her Contacts list. She could phone the aunt and ask to speak to Dr. Hunter. And then Dr. Hunter would answer and Reggie would say—very casual—"Oh, hi, I just wanted to ask when you'd be back. Everything's fine here. Sadie sends her love." And Dr. Hunter would say, *"Thanks so much for phoning, Reggie. We're both missing you."* And then all would be right with the world.

All she had to do was go into the house and find the phone. And if Mr. Hunter came back, she could always say that she'd left something behind, a book, a brush, a key. It wouldn't be like she was breaking in, technically speaking, you couldn't break in if you had a key, could you? She had to know that Dr. Hunter was all right.

She got off the bus on Blackford Avenue and bought a packet of crisps in the Avenue Stores before setting out to walk the rest of the way to Dr. Hunter's house. The crisps were cheese and onion flavor, and as soon as she tasted them, she had to put them away in her bag because they reminded her too much of the night of the train crash, breathing into Jackson Brodie's airless lungs, willing him into life.

There was no Range Rover, which meant that Mr. Hunter wasn't at home, as the two of them didn't go anywhere without each other. Reggie crouched down in the bushes and watched to make doubly sure that there was no sign of life in the house. Maybe she should have brought Billy along; for once his talents as a natural-born sneak would have come in useful. Billy wasn't answering his phone either. What was the point of phones if no one ever answered them?

Sadie gave a whine of homesickness at the sight of the house and Reggie stroked her ears comfortingly and said, "I know, old girl. I know," the way Dr. Hunter would have done.

Searching for the Hunters' door keys, Reggie's fingers touched the bit of grubby blanket that was nestled in her pocket. A little green flag of distress left for her to interpret, a clue to be tracked, a trail of bread crumbs to follow. How sad the baby must be to lose his talisman. How sad she was to lose the baby.

"Right," she whispered to Sadie, and the dog looked at her inquiringly. "Let's do it."

First the mortise, then the Yale, so far so good. In the hallway she paused for a second to check the coast was clear while Sadie raced up the stairs looking for Dr. Hunter, although it was quite plain to Reggie that neither Dr. Hunter nor the baby was here. The house was empty of breath, as quiet as the grave. Dead air. Even the clocks had stopped, with no one here who cared to wind them. The absence of Dr. Hunter from her own house weighed heavily on Reggie's heart.

The kitchen was messier now, although there was no sign of Mr. Hunter's having cooked anything. There were the remains of a pizza and a lot of dirty glasses that he hadn't bothered to put in the dishwasher. The fridge was still full of the same food that had been in there on Wednesday. The bananas in the fruit bowl were black now, and the apples were beginning to shrivel. There was a large cobweb slung across one corner of the ceiling. It was as if time were accelerating in Dr. Hunter's absence. How long before the house reverted to some kind of primal state? Before it disappeared altogether and was replaced by field and forest.

Reggie searched everywhere in the kitchen for the phone — the drawer in the table, all the cupboards, the fridge, the oven — but there was no sign of it anywhere. She was wondering where else to look when she heard the Range Rover approaching, with its usual brutal pace and dramatic finish. It was followed by another equally aggressive-sounding car.

Car doors slammed and heavy telltale footsteps crunched on the gravel path at the side of the house — they were coming to the back door, to the kitchen. Reggie sprinted up the back stairs, like a scullery maid caught with her hand in the biscuit tin, and ran into Dr. Hunter's bedroom, where she found her companion in crime asleep on the bed. Sadie woke when Reggie entered the room and gave a little bark of excitement. Reggie jumped on the bed and clamped her hand over the dog's muzzle. A person could die from a heart attack under this kind of stress.

She could hear voices down below, in the hallway now. Mr. Hunter and two other men, their voices raised. She couldn't make out the conversation, but it was moving nearer. They weren't in the hallway anymore, they were coming up the stairs. A person was definitely going to die of a heart attack in these circumstances. Reggie grabbed hold of Sadie's collar and tugged at it. "Come on," she whispered desperately, "we've got to hide." There was, of course, only one place to hide in the bedroom, the louvered closet, the last refuge of the slasher's innocent victim in horror films. Reggie stepped quickly into Dr. Hunter's side, pulling a reluctant Sadie in with her.

There wasn't enough room to breathe, it was horrible, it was like going into Narnia, except there was no other world beyond, just Dr. Hunter's clothes, pressed up against Reggie's face, all smelling of Dr. Hunter's perfume. Reggie's heart wasn't even in her chest anymore, it was too big and too loud to fit anymore, it was filling the whole of the bedroom. *Boom, boom, boom.*

The men were having a conversation with Mr. Hunter on the landing outside the open bedroom door. Through the slats in the closet door Reggie could see the back of one of them. He was big, bigger than Mr. Hunter, and was wearing a leather jacket. She could see the thick trunk of his bull neck and his bald head. There was a big, shiny gold watch on his wrist and he tapped the dial ostentatiously and said to Mr. Hunter, "Time's running out, Neil." Another Glaswegian by the sound of him.

They must be able to hear her heart from where they were standing, a great big drum of sound banging away in the closet, *boom, boom, boom.* Any moment one of them would yank the doors open to find the source of the noise. Reggie stretched out her fingers and felt the soft fur on top of Sadie's head for comfort.

"I'm doing my fucking best," Mr. Hunter said, and the man with the gold wristwatch said, "You know the score, Hunter. You and yours. Think about it. Sweet little wife, pretty little baby. Do you want to see them again? Because it's your call. What do you want me to tell Anderson?"

Sadie gave a low growl, upset by the proximity of so much nasty human testosterone. Reggie crouched lower and put her arms round her in an effort to keep her quiet. "Right!" Mr. Hunter shouted, and suddenly he was in the bedroom, halfway across the floor to the closet. Reggie thought her heart was going to explode all over the bedroom and they would find it, like a burst balloon, on the floor of the closet. He opened the door on his own side, pulling on it aggressively, so that Reggie could feel the whole closet shake. He threw things around, looking for something and must have found it, because he left and the men followed him downstairs. Reggie laid her face against Sadie's big body and listened to the dog's heartbeat, solid and regular, unlike her own fluttery organ. The back door slammed and first one and then the other car started its engine and both drove away. Reggie rushed to the window in time to see Mr. Hunter's Range Rover following a monstrous black Nissan. She repeated the license number over and over again until she could grab a notebook and pen from her bag and write it down.

The air in the house felt polluted by the conversation she had just heard. On the one hand it was very bad—the man with the gold wristwatch seemed to have kidnapped Dr. Hunter and the baby—but on the other, good hand, they weren't dead. Yet.

Climbing cautiously out of the closet, Reggie almost tripped on something on the floor inside it—Dr. Hunter's expensive Mulberry handbag. (*"The Bayswater—isn't it handsome, Reggie?"*) Reggie snatched it up and said to Sadie, "Come on, we have to go."

R eggie caught a relay of buses. While still inoculated against fear by her experience in Dr. Hunter's house, she was going to go back to her flat in Gorgie. Her phone was about to run out of battery, and if nothing else she could salvage her phone charger.

She sat on the top deck, holding Dr. Hunter's black Bayswater on her lap, investigating the contents. Technically theft of course, but Reggie didn't feel that the normal rules applied anymore. *"Sweet little wife, pretty little baby. Do you want to see them again?"* Every time she thought of those words her insides hollowed out. They had been kidnapped, that was what had happened to them. They were being held to ransom by gold-watch-wearing Glaswegians. Why? Where? (And what did the aunt have to do with it?)

The innards of the handbag seemed complete—a hairbrush, a packet of mints, a small packet of tissues, a packet of baby wipes, a copy of *That's Not My Teddy,* a small torch, a granola bar, a Ventolin inhaler, a packet of birth control pills, a Chanel powder compact, Dr. Hunter's driving spectacles, and her purse and—fat to bursting— her Filofax.

Now surely Inspector Monroe would believe her? Dr. Hunter wouldn't go away without her driving spectacles, her purse, or her inhaler (the spare one was still on the dressing table). No aunt could be so sick that you left everything behind. The only thing missing was her phone, but that didn't matter anymore because in- side the Filofax was an address for an Agnes Barker in Hawes. The mysterious Aunt Agnes, found at last.

Reggie got off the bus and turned the corner of the street to find that the all-too-familiar calling cards of catastrophe were waiting for her—three fire engines, an ambulance, two police cars, some kind of incident van, and a knot of bystanders—all muddled up in the street outside her flat. Reggie's heart sank, it seemed inevitable that they would be there for her.

All the glass in the windows of her flat was broken, and black streaks of soot marked where flames had shot out from the liv- ing room. A horrible smell still lingered in the air. A thick hose like a boa constrictor snaked into the close. The paramedics were leaning nonchalantly against the bonnet of their ambulance rather than trying to revive her charred neighbors, so hopefully Reggie wasn't going to have the deaths of everyone in the building on her conscience as well. Reggie's life was like the Ilian plain, littered with the dead.

"What happened?" she asked a young boy who was gazing in awe at the aftermath of disaster.

"Fire," he said.

"Duh. But what *happened?*"

Another boy leaned into the conversation and said excitedly, "Someone poured petrol through the letter box."

"Of which flat?" Please don't say number eight, she thought.

"Number eight."

Reggie thought of the books piled on the living-room floor like a bonfire waiting to be lit. All her schoolwork, Danielle Steel, Mum's miniature teapots. Virgil, Tacitus, good old Pliny (Young and Old), all the Penguin Classics she'd rescued from charity shops. Photographs.

"Oh," Reggie said. A little sound. A little round sound. Weightless as a wren. A breath. "Was anyone hurt?"

"Nah," the first boy said, looking disappointed.

"Reggie!" Mr. Hussain said, appearing suddenly from out of the crowd. "Are you all right?"

A piece of charred paper floated slowly down from the sky like a soiled snowflake. Mr. Hussain picked it up and read out loud, "He felt the heart still fluttering beneath the bark."

"Sounds like Ovid," Reggie said.

"I was worried you were in there," Mr. Hussain said. "Come into the shop, I'll make you a cup of tea."

"No, really, I'm okay. Thanks anyway, Mr. Hussain."

"Sure?"

"Sweartogod."

A fireman who looked as if he was in charge came out of the building and said to a policeman, "All clear in there." Firemen began to coil up the fat hosepipe from out of the close. Reggie saw the good-looking Asian policeman, who gave a twitch of recognition at the sight of her, as if he knew her but couldn't place her. She turned away before he remembered who she was.

She turned up her collar and hunched herself into her jacket and walked away briskly, Sadie at her heels. She had no idea where she was going, she was just walking, away from the flat, away from Gorgie. It took her a moment to realize that she was being followed by a white van, which was curb-crawling along behind her in a really creepy way. She picked up the pace, so did the van. She started running, Sadie lolloping along excitedly as if it were a game. The van accelerated too and cut her off at the next crossroad. Blondie and Ginger climbed out. They both walked with a bow-legged swagger, like apes.

They stood intimidatingly close to her, she could smell Ginger's breath, meaty, like a dog's. Close up, Blondie's skin was even worse, pitted and pocked like a barren moon.

"Are you Reggie Chase's sister, Billy?" Blondie demanded.

"*Whose* sister?" Reggie asked, frowning innocently. As if she didn't know, as if she weren't poor Reggie Chase, sister of the Artful Dodger. (As if she weren't all the poor unwanted girls, the Florences, the Esthers, the Cecilia Jupes.)

"That wee shite Reggie Chase's sister," Ginger said impatiently. Sadie growled at his tone of voice and the two men seemed to notice the dog for the first time, which was pretty slow of them considering how big she was, but then, they didn't look like they'd been at the front of the queue when brains were being handed out.

Ginger took a step back.

"She's a trained attack dog," Reggie said hopefully. Sadie growled again.

Blondie took a step back.

"Give your brother a message," Ginger said. "Tell the wee cunt that if he doesn't come up with the goods, if he doesn't give back what isn't his then—" He made a slashing motion across his throat. The pair of them really did like miming weapons.

Sadie started to bark in a way that even Reggie found quite alarming and both Blondie and Ginger retreated into the van. Ginger rolled down the passenger window and said, "Give him this," and threw something at her. Another Loeb, a red one this time, the *Aeneid,* Volume One. It flew through the air, its pages fluttering, and hit Reggie square on her cheekbone before dropping and spread-eagling on its spine on the pavement.

She picked it up. Same neat hole cut into its center. She ran a finger around the sides of the little paper coffin. Was someone hiding secrets inside Ms. MacDonald's Loeb Classics? All of them? Or only the ones that she needed for her A level? The cutout hole was the work of someone who was good with his hands. Someone who might have had a future as a joiner but instead became a street dealer hanging around on corners, pale and shifty. He was higher up the pyramid now, but Billy was someone with no sense of loyalty. Someone who would take from the hand that fed him, and hide what he took in secret little boxes.

Reggie didn't mean to cry, but she was so tired and so small and her face hurt where the book had hit it and the world was so full of big men telling people they were dead. *"Sweet little wife, pretty little baby."*

Where did a person go when they had no one to turn to and nowhere left to run?

Jackson Leaves the Building

There were some metal staples in his forehead that gave him a passing resemblance to Frankenstein's monster. His bandaged left arm was strapped to his chest in a sling that kept his hand pledged on his heart all the time, which was one way of making sure that you were alive. He had a recurrent vision of the artery inside his arm rupturing and spilling his blood again. But he was no longer fettered to a hospital bed. He was free. A little groggy, very sore — some of his bruises could have won competitions — but basically on the road to being a fully functioning human again.

He had to get out. Jackson hated hospitals. He had spent more time in them than most people. He had watched his mother take an eternity to die in one, and as a police constable he had spent nearly every Saturday night taking statements in Accident and Emergency. Birth, death (the one as traumatic as the other), injury, disease — hospitals weren't healthy places to hang around in. Too many sick people. Jackson wasn't sick, he was repaired, and he wanted to go home, or at least to the place he called home now, which was the tiny but exquisite flat in Covent Garden containing the priceless jewel that was his wife, or would contain her when she stepped off the plane at Heathrow on Monday morning. Not his real home; his real home, the one he never named anymore, was the dark and sooty chamber in his heart that contained his sister and his brother and, because it was an accommodating kind of space, the entire filthy history of the industrial revolution. It was amazing how much dark matter you could crush inside the black hole of the heart.

Whenever Jackson started to get fanciful, he knew it must be time to go. "I'm better now," he said to Dr. Foster.

"They all say that."

"No, really. I am."

"The clue is in the word *patient*."

"I don't need to be in hospital."

"Yesterday you were going on about how you died and today you're ready to walk? Roll away the stone? Just like that?"

"Yes."

"No."

I'm okay to leave now," Jackson said to the boy-wizard doctor.

"Really?"

"Yes, really."

"No, no, no, you missed the sarcastic inflection. Listen again—*Really?*"

Pumped-up little Potter pillock.

I'm A-OK," Jackson said to Australian Mike. "I need to get out of this place, it's doing my head in."

"No worries," the Flying Doctor said.

"Does that mean I can go?"

"Knock yourself out, mate. Discharge yourself. What's stopping you?"

"I haven't got any money. Or a driving license." (The latter seemed more important than the former.)

"Bummer."

"I haven't even got any clothes."

They're your size," Reggie said, indicating a large Topman bag at her feet. "I went to Topman because I've got a store card. It might not really be your style. I bought you one of everything." She looked embarrassed. "And three pairs of underpants." She looked even more embarrassed. "Boxers. I took the size from your old clothes, the nurse gave them to me. They were ruined, they had to cut them off you, and anyway they were covered in blood. I've got them in a black plastic bag, you probably want to throw them away."

"Why did they give you my clothes?" Jackson puzzled when she paused for breath.

"I said I was your daughter."

"My daughter?"

"Sorry."

"And you're doing this because you're responsible for me?"

"Well, actually . . . ," Reggie said, "it's more of a two-way thing."

"I knew there had to be a catch," Jackson said. There was always a catch. Since Adam turned to Eve (or more likely the other way round) and said, "Oh, by the way, I wondered if . . ."

She had another fresh bruise, on her cheek this time. What did she do when she wasn't visiting him? Karate?

"You used to be a private detective. Right?" she said.

"Amongst other things."

"So you used to find people?"

"Sometimes. I also lost people."

"I want to hire you."

"No."

"Please."

"No. I don't do that anymore."

"I really need your help, Mr. Brodie."

No, Jackson thought, don't ask for my help. People who asked for his help always led him down paths he didn't want to tread. Paths that led to the town called Trouble.

"And so does Dr. Hunter," she went on relentlessly. "And so does her *baby*."

"You're changing the rules as you go along," Jackson said. "First it was 'you save me, I save you.' Now I have to save complete strangers?"

"They're not strangers to me. I think they've been kidnapped."

"*Kidnapped?*" Now she was getting really extreme.

He knew what she was going to say. Don't say it. Don't say the magic words.

"They need your help."

"No. Absolutely not."

We should start with the aunt."

"What aunt?"

V
And Tomorrow

The Prodigal Wife

According to her Sat Nav it was a hundred and sixty-one miles to Hawes and should take them three hours and twenty-three minutes, "So let's see," Louise said combatively as she started up the engine. Marcus, riding shotgun, gave her a salute and said, "Chocks away." An innocent. He was handsome, polished, and new, like something just out of a chrysalis. Archie would never look like that at Marcus's age. Technically, she was old enough to be Marcus's mother. If she'd been a careless schoolgirl.

She hadn't been careless, she was on the Pill by the age of fourteen. Throughout her teens she had sex with older men, she hadn't realized at the time how pervy they must have been. Then she was flattered by their attentions, now she'd have them all arrested.

With Patrick, in their courting period, when they were exchanging all those little intimacies of a life—favorite films and books, pets you'd had ("Paddy" and "Bridie," needless to say, had been the keepers of a childhood menagerie of hamsters, guinea pigs, dogs, cats, tortoises, and rabbits), where you'd been on holiday (pretty much nowhere in Louise's case), how you lost your virginity and who with—he told her that he met Samantha during Freshers' week at Trinity College, "And that was it." "But before that?" she said, and he shrugged and said, "Just a couple of local girls at home. Nice girls." Three. Three sexual partners until he was widowed (all nice). There'd been girlfriends after Samantha but nothing serious, nothing indecorous. "And you?" he asked. He had no idea how sexually incontinent Louise had been in her life and she wasn't about to enlighten him. "Oh," she said, blowing air out of her mouth. "A handful of guys — if that — pretty long-term relationships, really. Lost my virginity at eighteen to a boy I'd been going out with for a couple of years." Liar, liar, pants on fire. Louise was ever a good deceiver, she often thought that in another life she would have made an excellent con woman. Who knows, maybe even in this life, it wasn't over yet, after all.

She should have told the truth. She should have told the truth about everything. She should have said, "I have no idea how to love another human being unless it's by tearing them to pieces and eating them."

A bit of fresh country air to blow away the cobwebs," she said to Marcus. "Just what the doctor ordered."

Or, on the other hand, not. "Late again?" Patrick said when she phoned to tell him about their "wee jaunt" (as Marcus insisted on calling it). "Couldn't you get the local police to pay this aunt a visit?" he said. "It seems a long way to go just to check this thing out. It's not as if it's a case, it's not official, is it? Nothing's *happened*."

"I don't tell you how to do surgery, Patrick," she snapped, "so I would really appreciate it if you didn't instruct me in police procedure. Okay?" He had taken her on, thinking she would improve, get better under his patient care, he must be disappointed in her by now. The rose with the worm, the bowl with the crack. Nothing the doctor can do here.

"You're pissed off with me," she continued, "because I got drunk on my own last night instead of coming to the 'theater,' aren't you?" She put a camp emphasis on *theater* as if it were something boring and middle class, as if she were Archie at his adolescent worst.

"I'm not accusing you of being drunk," Patrick said placidly, not rising to the argument. "You're doing that yourself." Louise wondered about killing him. Simpler than divorce and it would give her a whole new set of problems to be challenged with instead of the tediously familiar old ones. She wondered if there was a part of Howard Mason that had been relieved when his family was conveniently erased. Just Joanna left, a permanent marker. Much better for him if she'd been wiped out as well.

"Don't get so het up," Patrick said. "That Scottish chip on your shoulder is getting in the way."

"In the way of what?"

"Your better self. You're your own worst enemy, you know."

She bit down on the snarl that was her instinctive response and muttered, "Yeah, well, I've got a lot on my mind. Sorry," she added. "Sorry."

"Me too," Patrick said and Louise wondered if she should read more into that statement.

They had crossed the border. Over the Tweed and under the wire. Frontier country.

"English rules apply now," she said to Marcus.

"Wild aunt chase," he said happily. "Shall we have some music on, boss?" He inspected the Maria Callas compilation in the CD player and said doubtfully, "Jings and help me Bob, boss. Not really road-trip music, is it? I've got a couple of discs with me." He raked around in the rucksack he always had with him and retrieved a CD-carrying case and unzipped it. "Be prepared," he said. Yes, of course, he would have been a Boy Scout. The sort of boy who relished being able to tie knots and light a fire with a couple of sticks. The kind of boy any mother would like to have. And she would bet her bottom dollar that he had joined the police because he wanted to help, to "make a difference."

"Why did you join the police, Marcus?"

"Oh, you know, usual reasons. Wanted to try and make a difference, I suppose, help people. What about you, boss?"

"So I could hit people with a big stick."

He laughed, an uncomplicated sound that wasn't freighted with years of cynicism. Louise tried to guess what kind of music he thought suitable for a "road trip." He was too young for Springsteen, too old for the Tweenies, the baby's preferred drive-time sound track. (Funny how she too now automatically thought of Joanna Hunter's baby as simply *the baby*.) Marcus was twenty-six, so he still probably liked the same stuff as Archie — Snow Patrol, Kaiser Chiefs, Arctic Monkeys — but no, the BMW's music system was being polluted by James Blunt, prince of easy listening. She leaned over and with one hand grabbed the CD case and emptied it onto Marcus's lap, disgorging Corinne Bailey Rae, Norah Jones, Jack Johnson, Katie Melua. "Jesus, Marcus," she said. "You're too young to die yet."

"Boss?"

She swapped places with him at Washington services. In the shop two Red Tops carried the story about Decker being missing. "Freed Killer Flees." Assonance *and* alliteration, you had to hand it to these guys.

"You kind of have to feel sorry for the guy," Marcus said. "After all, he's paid his dues et cetera, but he's still being punished."

"What are you, Mother Teresa?"

"No, but he was brought to justice, he paid, should he pay forever?"

"Yes. Forever," Louise said. "And then some. Don't worry," she added, "when you're my age, you'll be hard and unfeeling too."

"Expect I will, boss."

Never driven a Beemer before," he said, getting into the driving seat and adjusting it. "Cool. Why aren't we taking a police car?"

"Because we're not on police business. Not strictly speaking. It's your day off, it's my day off. We're going for a drive."

"Quite a long one."

"Just be careful with the car, Scout."

"Yes, boss. Off we go. To infinity and beyond!"

He was a good driver, good enough—almost—for her to relax. Almost. So, elderly aunt, here we come, ready or not, Louise thought. The impostor aunt. The farce had grown more farcical. Except it wasn't funny, but then farces rarely were in Louise's opinion, she was drawn more to revenge tragedies. Patrick, surprisingly (or perhaps not), liked Restoration comedy. And Wagner. Should you marry a man who liked Wagner?

The first time a teenage Howard Mason went to a concert was to a performance of Handel's *Messiah* given by the Bradford Choral Society and he had wept during the Hallelujah Chorus. Or was she getting him mixed up with one of his alter egos, his fictional doppelgängers?

The book he was writing in Devon, in the winter before the murders took place, was called *The Brass Band Plays On,* and the protagonist was a struggling playwright (northern, naturally) who was hobbled by domesticity in the form of two small daughters and a wife who had made him move to the country. There was no second, fictional self for the baby, Joseph; Howard Mason's baby son seemed to have escaped being pinned to the page.

After the murders Howard stopped writing his way through his life and moved to Los Angeles, where he worked on a handful of screenplays for unsuccessful movies. (Where was Joanna during this time?) When his screenwriting career went nowhere, Howard had hung out around a swimming pool in Laurel Canyon, producing a pedestrian collection of stories centered on a Brit writer working in Hollywood. Fitzgerald it wasn't. What Howard Mason never wrote (what he never even talked about) was a novel about a man whose family was murdered while he was off dallying with his Swedish mistress. He missed an opportunity there, it would probably have been a best seller.

She had collected three phone messages from Reggie already today. They were all agitated, one of them was a car license plate number (*"a black Nissan Pathfinder,"* the girl was a better witness than most) and she caught the name "Anderson" in the middle of one particularly breathless communiqué. She felt a stab of guilt. Reggie's fantasies were all proving to be grounded in reality, but kidnap—really? (*"Kidnapped! Dr. Hunter's been kidnapped."*) Crazy, crazy talk.

The third message was an itemization of the contents of Joanna Hunter's handbag, which Reggie had found in her bedroom— *"Her driving specs, how can she have driven without them? Her inhaler. Her purse!"* Louise's headache bloomed, and she imagined her brain looked like an atomic explosion, the mushroom growing larger, pressing against the hard plates of her skull. She closed her eyes and pushed her fists into her eye sockets. She had an awful feeling that Reggie Chase might be right, something bad had happened to Joanna Hunter.

"Get someone to run a license number," she said to Marcus.

"Why exactly are we worried about this aunt, boss?" Marcus asked.

"I'm not worried about the aunt," Louise sighed. "I'm worried about Joanna Hunter. There are some, I don't know, anomalies."

"And so the two of us are driving a hundred and sixty miles to knock on a door," Marcus puzzled. "Couldn't the local police do that?"

"Yes, they could," she said patiently (so much more patiently than with Patrick). "But we're doing it instead."

"And do you think it has anything to do with Decker possibly being up in the Edinburgh area? Or is it the dodgy husband? Like a buried-beneath-the-patio scenario?"

"Or kidnap," Louise said. There, she'd uttered the word she'd been avoiding.

"Kidnap?"

"Well, there is no evidence that Joanna Hunter is alive and well and free, is there?" Louise said.

" 'Proof of life,' that's what they call it in kidnap cases, isn't it?"

"I think that might be what they call it in the movies. I don't know, I really don't. I'm probably just being stupid, okay. I just want to be sure. I would have said she's not the kind of person who runs away and hides. But that's exactly what she did once."

"Not criticizing, boss. Just asking."

Louise couldn't remember when she had last admitted stupidity to anyone.

Marcus got a call back about Reggie's Nissan. "Registered to a company in Glasgow, some kind of chauffeur company, weddings and the like, although it's hard to visualize the blushing bride climbing out of a Pathfinder."

"All roads lead to Glasgow," Louise said.

"Who was the guy who wasn't Decker, boss? In the hospital?"

"Nobody. He was nobody. Ordinary guy."

Discharged himself? How? Why?" When she had returned to the hospital and seen the bed stripped and the occupant missing, she had immediately thought that he must be lying in the morgue somewhere, but, "Discharged? Are you sure?"

"Against medical advice," a nurse at the ward station said disapprovingly.

"His daughter was here," the Irish nurse said. "He went with her."

"His daughter?" Louise couldn't remember the name of Jackson's daughter even though they had once in the past traded parental guidance notes, but she was what — eleven, twelve? Louise couldn't remember. "On her own?" she asked.

The nurse shrugged as if it was a matter of indifference to her.

He had gone. Without even saying good-bye. The bastard.

It took less time than you would think to arrive in the middle of nowhere. They made it in just under three hours. "So there," she said to the Sat Nav.

"Break out the biscuits," Marcus said.

Turn left at Scotch Corner and within minutes you were in a different world. A green kind of world. Not as green as water-sodden Ireland, where they had gone on honeymoon. Louise had fancied Kerala but somehow they had ended up in Donegal. "You can go to India on your next honeymoon," Patrick said. How they laughed. Ha, ha, ha.

He talked about "going back to Ireland someday." He meant when he retired, and no matter how hard she tried, Louise couldn't figure herself into this vision of the future.

Hawes was a small market town with a big cheese thing going on that she didn't understand until Marcus said, "Wensleydale, boss. You know"— he made a ridiculous rubber face, baring all his teeth in a grin and said, "Cheeese, Gromit, *cheeese*. Wallace and Gromit are, like, local heroes."

"Uh-huh," Louise said. Don't come between a boy and his cartoon heroes. Archie was fanatical about some American horror comic series. My two boys, Louise thought—light and dark, cherub and demon.

It was the kind of place that had everything an elderly aunt might want, big enough to have shops and doctors and dentists, a nice house with a view, "Hillview Cottage," in fact, which did indeed have a view of a hill but was more of a fifties-style bungalow than a quaint roses-round-the-door kind of dwelling. It was on the outskirts of Hawes, taking in town and country. *"The best of both worlds,"* she imagined Oliver Barker saying to his wife when they retired here. Louise wondered if she should be worried that the entire Mason clan, both real and unreal, had taken up residence in her brain.

Louise was an urbanite, she preferred the gut-thrilling sound of an emergency siren slicing through the night to the noise of country birds at dawn. Pub brawls, rackety roadworks, mugged tourists, the badlands on a Saturday night—they all made sense, they were part of the huge, dirty, torn social fabric. There was a war raging out there in the city and she was part of the fight, but the countryside unsettled her because she didn't know who the enemy was. She had always preferred *North and South* to *Wuthering Heights.* All that demented running around the moors, identifying yourself with the scenery, not a good role model for a woman.

If she was forced at gunpoint to choose where she would prefer to bury herself—Ireland or Hawes—Louise supposed she would go for Hawes. The last time she had talked properly to Jackson, rather than watching him asleep in a hospital bed, he had owned a place in France. That sounded a lot better than either Yorkshire or Ireland to Louise but she suspected that it was the Jackson rather than the France part of the equation that was attractive, as, presumably, rural France had more than its fair share of twittering birds and mind-numbing tranquillity. She had never been to France, never been anywhere, really. Certainly never been to Kerala. Patrick had suggested next April in Paris, "a long weekend," and she had shied away because secretly she was saving Paris for Jackson, which was clearly ridiculous. She was standing in his home county now, but the Dales were not the grim and grime that formed his essence. She should stop thinking about him. This kind of obsession was exactly how you ended up plucking feathers from pillows on your deathbed.

Marcus parked the car a couple of doors down from Hillview. No cars outside, no cars in the drive. No sign of life. No proof of it at all.

"You can have the honors," Louise said to Marcus when they got out of the car and he stepped forward and knocked smartly on the door.

"Very professionally done," Louise said. "You should be a policeman."

A big, deeply unattractive man in a white wife-beater vest opened the door and stared unwelcomingly at them. She could hear a racing commentary blaring from a television somewhere in the background. He had a can of lager in one hand and a cigarette in the other. He was a formidable cliché, Louise felt like congratulating him on his near-iconic status.

"Good afternoon," Marcus said pleasantly. "I wonder if you could help us?" He sounded like an evangelist doorstep-selling Good News and Bibles.

"Unlikely," the missing link said. Louise couldn't tell if he was being insolent or just being English. Both, probably. Her warrant card itched in her bag, but they were in mufti, not here on official business.

"I'm looking for a Mrs. Agnes Barker?" Marcus persisted pleasantly.

"Who?" The man frowned at Marcus as if he'd started speaking in tongues.

"Agnes Barker," he repeated slowly. "This is the address we have for her."

"Well, you're wrong."

Louise couldn't help herself. She pulled her warrant card out and thrust it in his ugly face and said, "Shall we try that again? From the top—we're looking for a Mrs. Agnes Barker."

"I don't know," he said truculently. "I rent. I'll give you the number."

"Thank you."

The girl who answered the phone at the rental agency and who sounded about twelve years old readily admitted that they were handling the rental for Mrs. Barker's solicitor without Louise even explaining who she was. "They have a power of attorney for her," she said, which Louise translated as meaning that the aunt was gaga.

"Mrs. Barker is incapacitated?"

"She's in Fernlea. It's a nursing home."

"So she *does* exist," Marcus said.

Louise's phone rang as Marcus was reprogramming the Sat Nav. Abbie Nash was saying, "Boss? Got something on the car rental, or rather got nothing. We've phoned round every car-hire place in Edinburgh. None of them rented a vehicle to a Joanna Hunter."

"Perhaps she never changed the name on her driving license when she married."

"Mason?" Abbie said. "Yep, tried that. Zilch on that too. But while we were on the phone, I thought I might as well run Decker's name, just in case, you know, and—bingo. Decker hired a Renault Espace this morning. And this is interesting—he was with his daughter."

"He doesn't have a daughter."

"That's why it's interesting."

"The plot thickens," Marcus said happily when Louise relayed this information to him.

Fernlea was everything Louise feared for herself. The high-backed chairs gathered in the lounge around the television, the smell of institutional cooking layered over a faint but prevalent scent of Izal. It didn't matter that there was a notice board displaying activities for the residents *(Carpet bowls)* and outings *(Harlow Carr Gardens, Harrogate, including lunch at Bettys!),* it remained a place to send people whom nobody wanted. A place to die. Archie would send her somewhere like this when she was toothless and bald, wetting herself, forgetting her own son's name. She wouldn't blame him. Patrick wouldn't look after her, he was a man, so statistically he was likely to be dead, despite his golf and his red wine and his swimming.

She wasn't coming here. She would step out of her life, she would walk out into a cold, cold night *("I may be some time"),* lie down beneath a hedge, and go to sleep rather than come to a place like this. Or slit her wrists and wait, as composed as a Roman. Or get a gun—easy enough—and put it in her mouth as if it were a licorice stick and blow her brains out of the other side of her head. Part of her was almost looking forward to it. There was something to be said for dying before you ended up in incontinence pads, watching an endless loop of reruns of *Friends.* Gabrielle Mason, Patrick's Samantha, Alison Needler's sister, Debbie. Preserved in the amber of memory, forever young. Forever dead.

In the reception area, Louise showed her warrant card and her politest smile and said, "Just need to have a word with Mrs. Barker," to a heavy girl in a pink-and-white-gingham-check uniform that was too tight, revealing rippling rolls of fat trying to escape. Sausage in a skin. "Hayley," her plastic name badge said. Hayley's thin fair hair was scraped back into a scrunchie, leaving her moon face mercilessly exposed. She made cow eyes at Marcus, who politely ignored her.

The girl struggled to liberate a bar of chocolate from a pocket in her uniform. She unwrapped it and offered a piece to Louise. The chocolate was flattened and slightly melted and Louise waved it away even though she wanted it. Marcus took a piece and the girl blushed. She reminded Louise of a sugar pig. She used to like sugar pigs. "Do you think she'll be up to having a chat?" she said.

"I doubt it," the girl said.

"Because she's not lucid?"

"Because she's dead."

Yeah, Louise thought. Death did have a way of shutting you up. *An Elderly Aunt, Exit stage right.*

"Recently?" Marcus asked.

"A couple of weeks ago. Massive stroke," the girl volunteered, popping the last piece of chocolate into her mouth.

"Someone should tell her solicitor," Louise said, more to herself than the girl. Come to that, someone should tell Neil Hunter. "Did she have family?"

"I think there might have been a nephew or a niece, but they were, you know, what's it called? Like *strangled.*"

"Estranged?"

"Yeah, that's the word. Estranged."

She *doesn't* exist. The aunt is no more," Marcus said to Louise as they left Fernlea's unhallowed halls behind. "The aunt has ceased to be, she is an ex-aunt. If the plot got any thicker, it would be solid, eh, boss?"

"You drive, Scout," Louise said generously. Her headache was beginning to make her feel sick.

"So now what, boss?"

"I haven't got a scooby. Might buy some cheese. No, wait, get on the phone and tell someone to find out who visited Decker in prison in the last year. He walks away from a train crash and hires a bloody big car with a so-called daughter. Find out who the daughter really is. Someone must be helping him."

"Unless he just picked the girl up. Unless he took her against her will."

"Jesus," Louise said. "Don't go there."

"Do you think Decker might have something to do with the aunt?" Marcus puzzled.

"I don't know who has anything to do with who anymore."

There was no aunt, that was at least one incontrovertible fact. So either Joanna Hunter had lied to her husband about her destination *("Must pop down to see poor old Aunt Agnes")* or he had lied to everybody else *("She's gone to see a sick aunt")*. And who was the most likely liar—Neil Hunter or the lovely Dr. Hunter? Actually, Louise wasn't sure she knew the answer to that question. She suspected that if push came to shove, Joanna Hunter could dissemble with the best of them.

She had run and hidden once, now she was doing it again. She must have been upset by Decker's release. She was the same age as her mother when she was murdered, her baby was the same age as her brother. Might she do something stupid? To herself? To Decker? Had she nurtured revenge in her heart for thirty years and now wanted to execute justice? That was an outlandish idea, people didn't do that. Louise would have done, she would have made dice of Decker's bones, cat meat of his heart, pursued him to the end of time, but Louise wasn't like other people. Joanna Hunter wasn't like other people either, though, was she?

They parked in the center of Hawes, and Louise got out and wandered over to a bridge and gazed down at the water. She felt adrift, Louise Unbound. Joanna had walked out of her life with nothing (except the baby, which was everything) and disappeared. It was a trick that you might envy. Joanna Hunter, the great escapologist.

"Boss?" Marcus said, appearing at her side. "Okay?"

"Fine," she said, using the universal Scottish word for every state of being from "I'm dying in anguish" to "I'm experiencing euphoric joy." "Fine," she said, "I'm fine."

And then they did what you do in places like this. They went to a café and had afternoon tea.

Shall I be mother?" Marcus said, lifting a utilitarian brown teapot, all cozied up in something that looked like a bobble hat.

"I'm sure you'll be better in the role than me," Louise said.

She tossed down a couple of peracetamol and took a sip of the tan-colored tea that was strong enough to clean drains.

"Time of the month," she said when Marcus gave her an inquiring look. It wasn't, but hey.

"Of course," he said, nodding solemnly. Oh, these new boys with their respect for women, what were they like? They weren't like David Needler, they weren't like Andrew Decker, that was for sure.

Marcus had ordered a slice of fruitcake and it arrived with a large slab of Wensleydale cheese on it. (Cheese and cake, what was wrong with these people?)

"*Cheeese,* Gromit," he said. Sweet boy. Idiot boy, but nonetheless sweet.

Louise ate a toasted tea cake to cushion the painkillers. It tasted doughy and stuck in her throat. Her phone rang—Reggie Chase. She groaned and let it go to voice mail but then changed her mind and dialed Reggie's number—might as well try and calm her down. She should avoid telling her about the aunt, though, the girl would go into meltdown if Louise told her that the aunt was indeed sick, so sick that she was six feet under the soil. Reggie's phone rang five times before it was answered. By Jackson.

"Hello?" he said. "Hello?"

Go figure, Louise thought. Didn't it make sense that two of the most provoking people she could think of would somehow be together.

It's me," she said. And then realized he might not know who *me* was, although she liked to think that he would. "Louise," she added.

"That's amazing," he said, and then the line went dead. What was amazing?

"Poor reception probably, boss," Marcus said. "Too many hills."

Louise's phone rang again and she snapped it open, presuming it was Jackson. "What?"

"Whoa," Sandy Mathieson said. "Down, Shep. 'Wee jaunt' not going so well?"

"No, it's fine. Sorry. There is no aunt."

"Interesting. It's like something out of Agatha Christie."

"Well, not really."

"Anyway, I was calling to say that the North Yorkshire traffic police have been on the phone." It was true, the signal wasn't good and Sandy's voice came and went as he battled with the ether, but the triumphant tone of his message was loud and clear. "Decker's been stopped on the A1, near Scotch Corner. They're taking him to hospital in Darlington. You can be there in two shakes of a lamb's tail, boss."

"Hospital?"

"Some sort of accident."

Weird," Marcus said when she told him to step on it. "It's almost like he's after you rather than Joanna Hunter."

"That's not the really weird thing," Louise said. "You wouldn't believe the really weird thing."

"Try me, boss."

There's something else, boss," Sandy Mathieson said. "You're not going to like it."

"You could say that about a lot of things."

"Wakefield got back to us. Decker wasn't the most popular prisoner on the block. He only had three visitors in the last eighteen months. His mother, his mother's parish priest—he converted to Catholicism while he was in there, spent a lot of time with the prison chaplain and so on—easy way of dealing with guilt, if you ask me."

"It's the third visitor that's going to kill me, isn't it?" Louise said.

"Yep. None other than one Dr. Joanna Hunter."

You're joking me. She *visited* him? How many times?"

"Just the once. A month before his release. She asked for permission, he gave it."

She never said, Louise thought. She had gone to see Joanna Hunter in her lovely home and sat in her lovely living room with the Christmas box and the winter honeysuckle with their lovely scent and she had told her that Andrew Decker had been released and Joanna Hunter said, "I thought it must be anytime now." She didn't say, Yes I know, I just popped down to see him a couple of weeks ago. She didn't lie, she simply didn't tell the truth. Why?

"Victims visit prisoners, boss," Marcus said. "Looking for explanations, remorse, trying to make sense of the crime."

"They don't usually wait thirty years."

Joanna Hunter could run, she could shoot. She knew how to

save lives and she knew how to take them. "There are no rules," she had said to Louise last week in the lovely living room. "We just pretend there are." What was she up to?

Louise's phone rang again. She let it ring for a long time, she wasn't sure she wanted to know anything else.

"Boss?" Marcus took his eyes off the road for a moment and gave her a hesitant glance. "Are you going to answer that?"

"It's always bad news."

"Not always."

A crescendo of phone calls, bound to end in a big dramatic finish. She sighed and answered.

"Sorry, boss," Abbie Nash said. "Nothing dramatic. We've chased down the calls, in and out, on Wednesday for Joanna Hunter."

"Start with the ones after she got home from work, after four o'clock."

"One from her husband, two from a Sheila Hayes, and the last one at nine thirty—same number that phoned on Thursday a couple of times and again yesterday morning, a mobile, registered to a Jackson Brodie, address in London."

Well, it would be, wouldn't it?

Arma Virumque Cano

Reggie woke Jackson with a mug of tea and a plate of toast. The mug had written on it "Washed in the Blood of the Lamb," and she said to him, "Not the mug, obviously, that was washed in Fairy Liquid."

He had been baffled last night by the fact that the house she had brought him to (in an incredibly expensive taxi) was a matter of yards from where the train crash had occurred, from where he had died and lived.

"I don't actually live here," Reggie said.

"Who does live here then?"

"Ms. MacDonald, except that she doesn't because she's dead. Everyone's dead."

"I'm not," Jackson said. "You're not."

This was the deal, he was going home, to London, and he was going to meet his wife off the plane, and on the way he would make a detour to check out some aunt that Reggie kept raving on about, an aunt who was in some way connected to Reggie's missing doctor (*Kidnapped!*). When they found the aunt (whose very existence seemed to be in doubt), he would drive Reggie to the nearest train station and he would continue on home alone. Exactly how he was going to manage this he wasn't sure, perhaps in stages, like a tired old dog.

Reggie seemed to have an overheated imagination. This Dr. Hunter was probably just taking some time out from her life. Jackson wasn't one to ignore a missing woman, but there were some of them who really didn't want to be found. He had been sent to chase after a few of those in his days both in the police and as a private detective. Once, in the military, he had investigated the disappearance of a sergeant's wife, chased her trail all the way to Hamburg, where he found her in a gay bar where the women all seemed to be dressed like extras in *Cabaret*. You could see she wasn't intending to go back to married quarters in Rheindahlen anytime soon.

Still, it would be on his conscience if he wasn't sure, and he had enough women on his conscience without adding another one to the tally.

They had gone to Reggie's building society and withdrawn money. They had an agreement. Reggie gave up her life savings to him and he spent them. That's what it felt like anyway. They also bought sandwiches, juice, a phone charger for her, and a road atlas. He no longer had confidence in his ability to negotiate the Bermuda Triangle that was Wensleydale.

"You really are getting this money back," he said, as she emptied her account in a Halifax on George Street. "I'm rich," he added, something he didn't usually admit to so readily.

"Yeah, right," she said, "and I'm the Queen of Whatever."

"Sheba?"

"That too."

The only vehicle that the car-rental agency in Edinburgh had been able to provide Jackson with that he could drive one-handed—an automatic with the hand brake on the steering wheel—was a huge Renault Espace that you could have lived in if necessary. *Espace*—space. Plenty of that. "Are you needing child seats?" the middle-aged woman at the rental desk asked him. "Joy," her name badge proclaimed, like a new-age message. "It's a family car, really," she said disapprovingly, as if they had failed to fulfill her criteria for being a family. Rarely had a woman been so misnamed at birth, Jackson thought.

"We *are* a family," Reggie said. The dog wagged its tail encouragingly. Jackson experienced a twinge of something that felt a lot like loss. A family man without a family. Tessa was ambivalent about children. "If it happens, it happens," she said, although she was on the Pill, so obviously not as devil-may-care as she made out. He hadn't really broached the subject with her, it seemed too personal a thing to ask. They might be married, but they hardly knew each other.

If he had been Joy, he too would have been reluctant to hand over a set of car keys to someone who looked as if he had just been released from prison or hospital or both. "Absolutely against my advice," Harry Potter said when Jackson discharged himself. "Be it on your own head," Dr. Foster said. "You're a bloody idiot, mate," Australian Mike laughed.

The bruises and the gash in his forehead made Jackson look more criminal than victim, and the arm in a sling obviously disqualified him from driving in the eyes of any sane person, so Reggie had unstrapped his bandages and daubed the bruises on his face with her Rimmel foundation, " 'Cause you look like you're on the run or something." Generally speaking, Jackson always felt like he was on the run (or something), but he didn't bother saying so to Reggie.

With a cavalier disregard for the law he used Andrew Decker's driving license, which Reggie had produced with a flourish ("It was with your things"). Unfortunately, the fact that he had no other form of ID proved a bit of a stumbling block to Joy, who frowned with discontent at his lack of proven existence.

"You could be anyone," she said.

"Well, not *anyone*," Jackson murmured, but didn't argue the point.

He could have caught a train, of course, except that he couldn't. He had got as far as the ticket office in Waverley Station (Reggie sticking to his side like a little limpet) before a wave of adrenaline caught up with him. The climbing-back-on-the-horse-immediately theory was all very well when it was just a theory (or even when it was just a horse), but when it was the nontheoretical prospect of a brutal *iron* horse in the shape of an InterCity 125, pulling horrific memories behind it, then it was a different matter.

In the hospital, they had told him that he might never remember what had happened in the period before the train crash, but that wasn't so, he was remembering more and more all the time, a patchwork of unsewn pieces—the *High Chaparral* theme tune on a mobile, a pair of red shoes, the unexpected sight of the dead soldier's face when he had turned him in the mud. "CARNAGE!" said the newspaper headline they had showed him in hospital. It was mere luck that he was alive when others weren't, a momentary lapse in concentration from the Fates that had led to him surviving and not someone else.

The old lady with her Catherine Cookson, the woman in red, the tired suit, where were they? Jackson couldn't help but question his right to be on his feet (more or less) when fifteen other people were lying in cold storage somewhere. He had to wonder about his alter ego. Was the real Andrew Decker still lying in the hospital somewhere—had he walked away unscathed, or was his journey fatally interrupted? The name still rang a bell in Jackson's battered memory, but he had no idea why.

He supposed that this was what they meant by survivor guilt. He had survived lots of things before and not felt guilty, or at least not in a way that he was conscious of. What he *had* felt for most of his life was that he was living on in the aftermath of a disaster, in the endless postscript of time that was his life following the murder of his sister and the suicide of his brother. He had drawn those terrible feelings inside himself, nourished them in solitary confinement until they formed the hard, black nugget of coal at the heart of his soul, but now the disaster was external, the wreckage was tangible, it was outside the room he was sleeping in.

"We're all survivors, Mr. B.," Reggie said.

In Waverley Station Jackson found himself unraveling, and for the first time in his life he started to have a panic attack. He staggered to a metal bench in the station concourse, sat down heavily, and put his head between his knees. Everyone gave him a wide berth. He supposed he must look like a beat-up drunk. He felt like he was having a heart attack. Maybe he *was* having a heart attack.

"Nah," Reggie said, taking his wrist and checking his pulse. "You've just got a case of the screaming heebie-jeebies. Breathe," she advised. "It always helps."

Eventually the black spots before his eyes stopped dancing and his heart stopped jackhammering his ribs. He sipped water from a bottle Reggie bought at a coffee stall and felt himself returning to something like normal, or what passed for normal in the post–train crash world.

"Let's get one thing straight," he said to Reggie, "this isn't another saving-my-life situation. Understand?"

"Totally."

"Post-traumatic stress or something," he muttered.

"Nothing to be ashamed of," Reggie said. "It's like"—she said the phrase with a flourish—"a badge of courage. You pulled that soldier out of the wreckage, didn't you? Just a shame he was dead."

"Thanks."

"You're a hero."

"No, I'm not," Jackson said. I used to be a policeman, he thought. I used to be a man. Now I can't step on a train.

"Anyway," Reggie said, "the trains are all diverted, we'd have to get off, get on a coach, get back on again. A car would be much simpler."

Nothing?" Joy bulldozed on. "No passport? Bank statement? Gas bill? Nothing?"

"Nothing," Jackson confirmed. "I've lost my wallet. I was in the Musselburgh train crash."

"There aren't any exceptions to the rule."

Having no ID was less of a problem to Joy than having no credit card. "Cash?" she said incredulously at the sight of the money. "We have to have a credit card, Mr. Decker. And if your wallet was stolen, then how come you have money?" Good question, Jackson thought.

Jackson bared his lone wolf teeth in an attempt at friendly and said, "Please. I'm just a guy trying to get home."

"A credit card and ID. Those are the rules." *No paserán.*

"Dad's mum died," Reggie said, slipping her small hand unexpectedly into Jackson's. "We need to get home. Please."

Phew," Reggie said as they headed for the Espace. Jackson pointed the gray wafer of an electronic key at the car and it gave a welcoming beep.

Begging pathetically had got them nowhere with Joy. The fact that she had, that very morning, been made redundant ("Surplus to requirements," she sneered, "like every other woman of my age.") was much more effective. "You can drive off into the sunset with the bloody thing as far as I'm concerned," she said, but only after having given herself the satisfaction of arguing them ragged.

He used the gray plastic wafer to start the car and explained to Reggie how to put the Espace from "park" into "drive." Reluctantly he admitted to himself that he needed her, he wasn't sure that it was a journey he could make on his own, and not just because she knew how to strap his arm back up again and put the car into drive mode.

Jackson eased himself into the driving seat of the Espace. It felt good, it felt like home. Driving with one hand didn't unnerve him as much as driving with Reggie Chase in the passenger seat. Half child, half unstoppable force of nature.

"Okay, let's roll," Jackson said. The dog was already asleep on the backseat.

In a triumph of idiocy over adversity, they made it as far as Scotch Corner, stopping only twice at service stations so that Jackson could "take a few minutes." His body craved rest, it wanted to be supine in a darkened room, not driving on the A1 with one hand. He was surfing a wave of strong painkillers given to him by Australian Mike. He was sure that if he looked closely at the label, it would have some warning about driving with them in his system, but from somewhere he had dredged up his army self, the one that kept pushing through beyond the bounds of reason. When the going gets tough, the tough take drugs.

Reggie was making a meal of navigating. She had the disturbing habit, shared with his daughter, his real daughter, of gleefully verbalizing (and occasionally singing) every road sign— *"hidden dip, sharp bend, Berwick-on-Tweed twenty-four miles, roadworks for half a mile."* He had never had a front-seat passenger apart from Marlee who could get so much enjoyment from the A1.

"I don't get out much," she said cheerfully.

She had an address for the dubious aunt. It was in a Filofax that belonged to Joanna Hunter. Reggie also had her own bulky backpack, Joanna Hunter's large handbag, which she was concerned with to the point of obsession *("Why would she leave it behind? Why?")*, a plastic carrier bag containing dog food, plus the dog itself, of course. She didn't travel light. Jackson had, literally, the clothes he stood up in. It was a kind of freedom, he supposed.

"Here, here, we have to go right here," Reggie said urgently as they approached the big junction at Scotch Corner.

Tomorrow he would see his wife. His wife, shiny and brand-new. And have a lot of new-wife kind of sex, although, to be honest, sex was the last thing he felt capable of at the moment. A warm bed and a large whisky sounded much more appealing. He would go home and carry on with his life. His journey had been broken (but not fatally), he had been broken (but not fatally), although he had a small, nagging doubt that he might not have been put back together in quite the same way as before.

"Right at Scotch Corner," Reggie said, "and that takes us into Wensleydale. Where the cheese comes from."

He had been here on Wednesday (in the pre–train crash world. A different country.). He had bought his OS map in Hawes, a newspaper, a cheese-and-pickle roll. They would pass within a cat's whisker of where his son, Nathan, lived. They could visit, stop off at the village green, they could park outside Julia's house. He was back where he had started. Again.

At Scotch Corner he had been obediently following Reggie's slightly hysterical instructions to go right, when some kind of slippage occurred, in the car, in him, he wasn't sure. He wondered if he'd been asleep with his eyes open. This was what happened when you drove in the aftermath of a concussion, you didn't turn the wheel far enough and then you tried to compensate by turning it too far and then you made the mistake of slamming on the brakes too violently, mainly because of a small frantic Scottish voice yelling in your ear and disturbing the gyroscope in your brain, so that you skidded in a scream of rubber and clipped a four-door Smart Car, sending it spinning like a top across the road, and you were yourself clipped by an army jeep coming from Catterick Camp. The Espace gave as good as it got, but they still ended up facing the wrong way, slewed on the verge, with their teeth rattling in their heads. The dog had fallen onto the floor when they (Jackson sharing the blame equally with the car) lost control but picked itself up now with a certain aplomb.

"Phew," Reggie said when they finally came to a stop.

"Fuck," Jackson said.

Take a deep breath, sir," the traffic cop said, "and then breathe out into this monitor." He held a digital breathalyzer the size of a mobile phone towards Jackson, who sighed and said, "I haven't been drinking," but he supposed he looked in such poor shape that any sensible officer of the law would be suspicious of him.

No one was injured, which was a relief. One disastrous crash was enough for anyone's week. "It's me," Reggie said gloomily, "I attract these things." They had helped out the dazed passengers from the Smart Car and sat them down at the side of the road. The army guys had put hazard lights out and phoned the police.

"Fuckwit," one of them muttered at Jackson. Jackson tended to agree with him.

Despite the fact that the breath test was negative, the traffic cop wasn't happy. "Mr. Decker, sir?" he said, scrutinizing his driving license. "Is this your vehicle?"

"It's a rental."

"And what relation is this young lady to you?"

"I'm his daughter," Reggie piped up. The traffic cop looked her up and down, took in her bruises, the large dog glued to her side, the variety of bags she was toting. He frowned. "How old are you?"

"Sixteen." He raised an eyebrow at her.

"Sweartogod."

An ambulance arrived, surplus to requirements, like Joy. Another unnecessary one followed on behind, siren wailing. By now it looked like a major accident scene, traffic cones, lane closures, emergency vehicles, a lot of noise on the police radios, God knows how many attending officers, including a large incident van. Considering that no one was injured, not even walking wounded, the tension and excitement in the air seemed out of proportion to the circumstances. Perhaps it was a slow day on the A1.

"I used to be a policeman," he said to the officer who had breathalyzed him.

He hadn't had much of a positive response to this statement lately, but he wasn't expecting to be suddenly brought down by two officers who seemed to come out of nowhere and who flattened him to the tarmac before he could say anything helpful, like "Mind my arm because you're ripping my stitches out." Luckily, Reggie had a good pair of lungs for someone so small and jumped up and down a lot, asking them if they couldn't *see* his arm was in a sling and that he was an injured man—which didn't go down well with the army boys, who wanted to know why he was driving at all, then, but Reggie was more than a match for a bunch of squaddies. It was like watching a Jack Russell fending off a pack of Dobermans.

A police radio crackled, and he heard a voice say, "Yeah, we've got the nominal here," and Jackson wondered who the wanted man was that they'd collared. He sat on the road while Reggie inspected his arm. At least he wasn't pumping out blood like spilled petrol all over the road, just a couple of stitches out, although he still felt squeamish when he looked at the wound in his arm. Reggie was coaxed away by one of the paramedics, and then, without warning, a police officer cuffed his good arm and, speaking into the radio on his shoulder, said, "We're taking the nominal to hospital," so it turned out that Jackson was the wanted man. He couldn't think why, but somehow it didn't surprise him.

Sitting in the A and E waiting room in hospital in Darlington, bookended by two police officers as silent as funeral mutes, Jackson pondered why they were treating him like a criminal. Driving on someone else's license? Kidnapping and beating up a minor *("I'm sixteen!")*? What had happened to his unshakable little Scottish shadow? He hoped she was giving his details to reception and not locked up in custody somewhere. (The dog was in the back of a police car, awaiting a verdict on its immediate future.) Not that Reggie knew his details. He had a wife and a child (two children) and a name. That was all anyone needed to know, really.

Another couple of uniforms put in an appearance, and one of them cautioned him and passed on the interesting information that there was a warrant out for his arrest.

"Are you going to tell me why?"

"Failure to comply with the conditions imposed on you when you were released from prison."

"You see, I'm not actually Andrew Decker," Jackson said.

"That's what they all say, sir."

He had a feeling it was going to take more than Reggie jumping up and down shouting to get them out of whatever trouble they were in. Where was a friendly policeman when you needed one? Detective Inspector Louise Monroe, for example, she would do nicely at this moment.

A phone rang, a mobile. The police officers both looked at Jackson and he shrugged. "Don't have a phone," he said. "Don't have anything."

Indicating the pile of bags that Reggie had left at his feet, one of the officers said, "Well, it's in *that* bag," in a tone of voice that for a brief, bizarre moment reminded Jackson of his first wife. With some difficulty — stitches ripped, good arm handcuffed to a police officer, et cetera, he extricated the phone from the front pocket of Reggie's backpack and answered it. "Hello, hello?"

"It's me."

Me? Who was me, he wondered.

"Louise."

"That's amazing—" He got no further *(I was just thinking about you)* because the police officer who was handcuffed to him leaned over and pressed his finger on a button on the phone and ended the call. "Mobiles aren't allowed in hospitals, Mr. Decker," he said with a look of satisfaction on his face. "Of course, you might not know that, having been away for so long."

"Away? Where've I been?"

Half an hour later, when he was still waiting for a doctor to look at his arm, she appeared in person, marching through the automatic doors of the A and E as if she were going to break them down if they didn't open fast enough. Jeans and a sweater and a leather jacket. Just right. He had forgotten how much he fancied her.

"The cavalry's arrived," he murmured to his yellow-jacketed bookends.

"You've finally gone insane, then?" she said testily to Jackson.

"We have to stop meeting like this," he said. She was joined by a youthful sidekick who looked as if he would jump off a cliff if she told him to. He would do well, Louise liked obedience.

She flashed her warrant card at the bookends and said, "I've come for the one-armed bandit. Uncuff him."

One of the bookends dug his heels in and said, "We're wait-ing for the Doncaster police to come and get him. With respect, ma'am, he's out of your jurisdiction."

"Trust me," Louise said. "This one is mine."

Reggie appeared and said, "Hello, Chief Inspector M."

"You know her?" Jackson said to Reggie.

"You know *him?*" the sidekick said to Louise.

"We *all* know each other?" Reggie said. "How's that for a coincidence?"

"A coincidence is just an explanation waiting to happen," Jackson said, and Louise said, "Shut it, sunshine," as if she were auditioning for *The Sweeney.* He put one, uncuffed hand in the air and said, "It's a fair cop, guv," and she replied with a curse so black (and blue) that even the bookends blanched.

"Not to be a nuisance or anything," Jackson said to her, "but I need stitching up. If I haven't been already."

"Enough of the comedy," she said.

Now what?" Jackson said when they finally made their escape.

"Fish and chips?" Reggie said hopefully. "I'm starving."

"No one eats in my car."

Road Trip

I got four fish suppers, boss," Marcus said, climbing back in the car. "I didn't know what to do about the dog but he can have some of my fish, although it'll be a wee bit hot for him just now."

"A dog person, are you?" Louise said, but he failed to catch her sarcasm and said, "Love 'em. They're everything people should be."

He was in the front passenger seat, Jackson and Reggie in the back, the dog sitting awkwardly between them. Louise had suggested putting the dog in the boot, an idea that was received with a chorus of horror from Reggie and Marcus. "Just kidding," she said, although they clearly didn't believe her.

"Still a hard-hearted woman, I see," Jackson said. "You know that I'm not actually going in the same direction that you are."

"How true. In so many ways."

"If you could just drop me somewhere—a train station, a bus station, the side of the road, anywhere, really. I'm on my way home, to London."

"Tough," Louise said. "You've committed a crime, several crimes, actually. Obviously you're taking the stupid pills again—driving on a license that isn't yours, driving when you're not *fit* to drive, what were you thinking? Let me guess, you weren't thinking at all. You've got mince for brains."

"You haven't arrested me," he said.

"Not yet."

The Espace had been towed away, Louise had confiscated his driving license—Andrew Decker's driving license. It was obvious that neither Jackson nor Reggie had a clue who Andrew Decker was.

"So this," Marcus said, turning and looking at Jackson, "this is the guy in the hospital bed, the guy who was mistaken for Decker. Who keeps on being mistaken for Decker." He blew on a chip to cool it down. "And you know him, boss?"

"Unfortunately."

"You never said. Shouldn't you have let the North Yorkshire police charge him?"

("Ma'am," one of the bookending officers had ventured, "are you taking the prisoner back into custody?"

"He's not a prisoner," Louise said. "Just an idiot.")

"Yes, I should. Anyone got any more questions to plague me with, or can I just drive?"

When they set off she claimed the driving seat before Marcus had a chance to offer to drive. Everyone in this car, as far as Louise was concerned, needed to know who was in charge.

"You look terrible," she said, studying Jackson in the rearview mirror. "Even worse than you did earlier."

"Earlier? When was there an earlier?"

"In your dreams," she said.

"Congratulations," Jackson said.

"On what?"

"Your promotion. And your marriage, of course." She glanced round at him, and he nodded at her wedding ring. She looked at her hand on the steering wheel, she could feel how tight the ring was on her finger. The diamond was back in the safe, but she had kept her wedding ring on even though it was squeezing her flesh. A penance, like wearing a hair shirt. A hair shirt reminded you of your faith, a wedding ring that strangled your finger reminded you of your lack of it. *Strangled, estranged*—fat Hayley had been right, the words were very similar.

"You're married as well, apparently," she said to him in the mirror. "Sorry I didn't send a card or anything, that would be because—oh yes, you forgot to tell me." She could feel Marcus cringing in the passenger seat next to her. Yeah, the grown-ups are fighting. Never pretty.

"It didn't take you long to get over Julia," she carried on. "Oh no, wait a minute, she *cuckolded* you, didn't she? Carrying another man's baby and all that. That must have made being dumped easier." Jackson, rather admirably in Louise's unvoiced opinion, didn't rise to this remark. "So don't even think about commenting on my relationships."

"Your small talk hasn't improved," he said, and then, unexpectedly, "I missed you."

"Not enough to stop you getting married."

"You got married first."

"I never had a full set of parents," a small voice in the back interjected. "I often wondered what it would be like."

"Probably not like this," Marcus said.

The aunt, the aunt," Reggie had chanted when she first saw Louise. "The aunt lives in Hawes, it's not far away. We have to go and see if Dr. Hunter's there. She's been kidnapped."

"Well, not by the aunt, I can assure you of that," Louise said.

Reggie's little face lit up. "You're down here to see the aunt! You've spoken to Dr. Hunter? You've seen the baby?"

"No."

The little face fell. "No?"

"The aunt's dead."

"She must have been very sick, then," Reggie said solemnly. "Poor Dr. Hunter."

"She's been dead awhile," Louise admitted reluctantly. "Two weeks, to be precise."

"Two weeks? I don't understand," Reggie said.

"Neither do I," Louise said. "Neither do I."

Reggie inventoried the entire contents of Joanna Hunter's handbag again, announcing each item loudly from the back—"a packet of Polos, a small pack of Kleenex, a hairbrush, her Filofax, her *inhaler*, her *spectacles*, her *purse*. These aren't things you leave behind."

Not unless you were in a hurry, Louise thought.

"Not unless you were in a hurry," Jackson said.

"Don't start thinking," Louise warned him.

"Look at the facts," he said, ignoring her advice. "The woman has definitely gone AWOL, but whether voluntarily or against her will, that's the question."

"No shit, Sherlock," Louise muttered.

"Something bad has happened to Dr. Hunter," Reggie said stoutly. "I know it has. *I keep telling you* the man in Mr. Hunter's house was threatening him, he said something would happen to 'you and yours.' He wasn't joking."

"I'm just kicking the wheels on this," Jackson said, "but maybe the husband's covering for her?"

"Why?" Louise said.

"Dunno. He's her husband, that's what spouses do."

"Do they?" Louise said. "What's she called?"

"Who? What's who called?"

"Your *spouse*."

"Tessa. She's called Tessa. You would like her," he added. "You would like my wife."

"No I wouldn't."

"Yes you would," Jackson said.

"Oh, just shut up."

"Make me," Jackson said.

"Stop it," the small voice of reason in the backseat said.

She left everything," Reggie said. "Her phone, her purse, her spectacles, her inhaler, her spare inhaler, her dog, the baby's blanket. Plus she didn't get changed, the first thing she does is get changed, and the men who were threatening Mr. Hunter said he would never hear from her again if he didn't come up with the goods. And the aunt doesn't exist! *WHAT MORE EVIDENCE DO YOU NEED?*"

"Get her to breathe into a paper bag or something, will you?" Louise said to Jackson.

But," Marcus said, "does it have anything to do with Decker or not? Is it just a coincidence that he appears at the exact moment that she disappears? And what? He just walked away from the train crash?"

"He hasn't actually appeared anywhere," Louise pointed out. "He's the invisible man."

"Decker," Jackson murmured, gazing thoughtfully out of the car window. "Decker? Why do I know that name?"

The absence of Decker, the presence of Jackson. As if they had changed places in some mysterious way. Jackson had lost his Black-Berry in the train crash and mysteriously acquired Decker's driving license at the same time. Had he unknowingly swapped with Decker? Was Decker the man who rang Joanna Hunter's phone when Louise was in the house yesterday morning? He had been looking for "Jo," not Joanna, not Dr. Hunter. Is that what she had said to him when she visited him in prison—*Call me Jo?* What else did she say to him?

"What else did you lose?" Louise asked Jackson.

"Credit cards, driving license, keys," Jackson said. "There's an address book in the BlackBerry."

"So your whole identity, basically. What if Decker's using it? You get the driving license of a Category A prisoner with a warrant out against him, and he gets you—upstanding citizen (so-called)—credit cards, money, keys, a phone. The last person who phoned Joanna Hunter on Wednesday called on your phone, your BlackBerry, so perhaps it was Decker. He phones Joanna Hunter and then she disappears. Neil Hunter says she left at seven but we only have his word for it. Maybe she left later, after the phone call. And if she did drive away—somehow or other, not in her car, not in a rental—and she wasn't driving down to see the aunt, then where was she going? To meet someone else? Decker? Did he catch the train to Edinburgh because they had arranged a meeting? He gets derailed, literally, he phones her afterwards, and she goes off to meet him."

"And then what?" Marcus said.

"That's the bit that worries me. What about CCTV, there must be cameras up where she lives, lots of rich people live on that street, and—"

"Back up a minute," Jackson said. "Why are you so interested in this guy Decker? I don't understand."

"Yes," Reggie said. "Who *is* Andrew Decker? And what's he got to do with Dr. Hunter?"

Sorry, kid, Louise thought. She hadn't wanted to be the one to tell Reggie about Joanna Hunter's past. As she expected, this information made Reggie even more vocal. ("*Murdered?* Her *whole* family?") The girl was a terrier, you had to hand it to her. She wasn't even related to Joanna Hunter and yet she seemed to care about her more than anyone else. Louise couldn't imagine Archie feeling like this about her.

"Jesus," Jackson said. "Of course—Andrew Decker. How could I have forgotten that name? We were on maneuvers on Dartmoor. We were called in to search for the missing girl, the one that got away."

"Joanna Mason," Louise said. "Now Joanna Hunter."

"And now you have to look for her again," Reggie said to Jackson.

"Just because something bad happened to her once doesn't mean it's happened again," Louise said to Reggie.

"No," Reggie said. "You're wrong. Just because something bad happened to her once doesn't mean it *won't* happen again. Believe me, bad things happen to me all the time."

"Me too," Jackson said.

You're worried that this Decker's going after Joanna Hunter?" Jackson asked Louise. "It seems unlikely, I've never heard of anyone doing that."

"To tell you the truth, I'm beginning to worry that Joanna Hunter is going after Andrew Decker."

On the other hand," Louise said.

They were parked on the forecourt of a service station. Marcus and Reggie were in the shop, buying snacks, and Jackson had slipped into the front passenger seat. He was giving off heat. Louise wondered if he had a fever or if she was imagining it because of her own overheated state. She wanted him to hold her, she wanted to let her bones melt, even if for a moment. She never felt like this with Patrick, never wanted to stop being Louise, but sitting here on the brightly lit forecourt, she wanted to give in, leave the battlefield. Was there a way of keeping him this time, locking him up in a prison, a box, a safe, so he couldn't get away again?

"On the other hand what?" he prompted.

"Neil Hunter, Joanna's husband, is hardly above suspicion. For all we know, he's done away with her himself. And the baby. Maybe she was leaving him and he lost it."

"It happens."

"On the *other* hand . . . he also knows some quite interesting people."

"Interesting?"

"What we in the trade call 'criminals.' Some guys from Glasgow we've been hearing rumors about for a while. A guy called Anderson. He's trying to get into town, muscle in on some legit businesses. Private-car hire being a particular favorite apparently."

"Minicabs?"

"Yeah. And amusement arcades. Health clubs. Ropy beauty parlors. Guess who owns all of those?"

"Neil Hunter?"

"Bingo. One of his amusement arcades burned down last week and there's been some other stuff."

"Stuff?"

"Technical term. We were looking at Hunter for willful fire-raising, but now I'm seriously beginning to wonder. What if Anderson's threatening Hunter's family? *Kidnapped,* Reggie keeps saying, and she's been right about everything else so far. Bizarrely."

" 'You and yours. Think about it. Sweet little wife, pretty little baby. Do you want to see them again? Because it's your call.' That's what Reggie said."

"You've got a good memory for an old man."

"Lot of rote learning at school. And I'm forty-nine. Younger than your *spouse,* I believe. *'Do you want to see them again?'* Do you think they're being held somewhere?"

"And the aunt was just a red herring. A wild goose. A way of throwing anyone off who was worried about Joanna Hunter's sudden disappearance," Louise said. "The ironic thing is that her husband needn't have bothered, Decker leaving prison gave Joanna Hunter a really good reason not to be around. Neil Hunter should never have gone down the aunt route."

"Good theories," Jackson said. "How are we going to prove or disprove them?"

"*We're* doing nothing. Just me. I'm the real police, you're just a waster. Basically."

"Thanks." He reached his hand out and took hers and said, "I really did miss you, you know." Her mouth went dry and her heart slipped into overdrive as if she had some kind of virus, and she thought about starting the engine and driving him away to the nearest hotel, barn, or lay-by, but Marcus and Reggie were already barreling out of the shop and she only just had time to reclaim her hand before they bundled back into the car, bringing in a draft of cold night air and ripping open crisp packets.

"Do you want your seat back?" Jackson said to Marcus, and he said, "No, you're all right, I'm happy back here with the dog," but Louise said to him, "Actually, you can drive, I'm feeling tired, I'll sit in the back," because she couldn't bear to be so close to Jackson and not be able to touch him again.

"No probs," Marcus said. "All change. Men in the front, women in the back, just how it should be. Joking, obviously," he added swiftly, catching sight of Louise's face in the rearview mirror.

It was dark long before they recrossed the border. The miles after Berwick dragged. They dropped Reggie and Jackson in Musselburgh. "You're sure you want him staying with you?" Louise said doubtfully to Reggie.

"He hasn't got anywhere else to go,"

"Well, I do have a home to go to, actually," Jackson pointed out. "It's just that the world and his wife seems intent on stopping me reaching it."

"You have to help find Dr. Hunter," Reggie said.

"Finding Dr. Hunter is my job, not his, Reggie," Louise said. "I don't want any amateur interference." She turned to Jackson and said, "We can do this without your help, thank you."

"Go home to your kids, Herb, kind of thing?"

"Exactly."

"Nice wheels," he said, patting the roof of the BMW affectionately as if it were an old friend.

"Bugger off."

"I'll see you tomorrow," he said.

"Will you?"

"Yes, of course."

Her heart lifted, she would see him again tomorrow. This was how teenage girls felt, how Louise had never felt when she was a teenage girl. Patrick was right, she'd never had an adolescence. *Making up for it now.*

"I wouldn't go home without saying good-bye," he said.

Bastard. She wasn't enough to keep him, couldn't compete with the pull of his new wife. Tessa. Bitch.

She wanted to say, Come home with me—well, not home, she could hardly take him home, introduce him to her husband, to Bridget and Tim. "This is Jackson Brodie, the man I should have married." Not married. Marriage was for fools. The man she should have run away with. Over the hills and far away. "Take a leap of faith with me"—that's what she wanted to say to him. But of course she didn't.

"Who's Herb?" Marcus puzzled.

★   ★   ★

Shit. I should have taken that handbag off Reggie." What was happening to her? She wasn't usually forgetful. Now she was beginning to feel as if her brain were fraying.

"I'll organize a uniform in the morning, boss."

"You're a wee treasure, so you are."

Marcus said, "Just drop me somewhere," and she said, "Don't be silly, I'll take you home." He lived in South Queensferry, miles out of her way.

"I'm miles out of your way, boss."

"Not a problem, really. I've got my second wind." He still lived with his mother. Archie wouldn't still be living with her when he was twenty-six.

· "Girlfriend?" She'd never thought to ask before, Marcus had never seemed like a boy who had a girl.

"Ellie."

"But not living with her?"

"Next step, boss. We went to view a house last night as a matter of fact. Malbet Wynd."

Yes, of course, he was a boy who did things properly, in steps and stages. A girl called Ellie, a house in Malbet Wynd. He prepared for things.

After he'd climbed out of the car Louise slid back into the driving seat and rolled the window down. "First thing in the morning we need to find out if Jackson Brodie's credit cards have been used and where. And see if we can put some kind of trace on that phone."

"Right, boss."

" 'Night, Scout."

" 'Night, boss."

She waited until he'd unlocked the front door and turned and waved good-bye before he disappeared into the house. A curtain twitched in a downstairs room, his aspirational mother, she supposed.

She sat for a while longer, wondering if there was somewhere she could go that wasn't home. Fife and all points north was just across the water. How far could she get before anyone noticed she was gone?

Tribulation

With hindsight, Reggie could see now that perhaps she should have mentioned her criminal relations to Jackson Brodie. If she'd warned him about her brother, for example, before inviting him to stay with her tonight, then he might not have walked into Ms. MacDonald's living room ahead of her (while she locked the front door so they would be safe—irony, ha, et cetera) and found himself with a nasty-looking penknife nicking the skin covering his carotid artery at almost the exact spot where she had desperately felt for a pulse on the night of the train crash. Billy was on the other end of the knife.

"Surprise!" Billy said flatly. "Who is this joker?" He pressed the knife deeper into Jackson's neck. "What's he doing here?"

"Let him go," Reggie said. There was no point in appealing to Billy's better nature because he didn't have one, but a person had to try. "He's nobody to you."

To her surprise, and Jackson's too, Billy did let go of him, shoving him to the floor, where he landed heavily as he only had one good arm to break his fall. Reggie was caught off guard by Billy grabbing her instead, putting his arm round her neck, almost crushing her windpipe. He used to do the same thing when they were little. Mum would say, *"Give your little sister a kiss to say sorry,"* because he was always having to apologize for some misdemeanor—snatching her doll, kicking over her Lego, biting (he was a terrible biter)—and he would sing out, *"Soreee, Reggie,"* and under cover of kissing her would half strangle her, and Mum would say, *"Bad boy, Billy."* He looked wild-eyed, like the horses in the field did when Sadie got too close to them.

Jackson struggled onto all fours and then got slowly to his feet. Billy stopped trying to choke Reggie and instead pressed the point of the knife against her neck and said to Jackson, "Don't even think about doing anything." She could feel the blade, cold and sharp on her skin. It was such a small knife, yet it could do so much damage to her.

There were books all over the place. Jackson stood in the middle of the floor amongst the wreckage of Ms. MacDonald's library, tensed and on his toes like a fighter ready to go into battle. She could see him thinking, weighing up possibilities, and she thought, Oh no, don't.

"I'm your sister, Billy," she whispered to her brother. "Your own flesh and blood." Better nature, appealing, no point, et cetera, but still you had to try.

"He's your *brother?*" Jackson said. "You little fucker," he said to Billy. "It's your job to *look after* your sister."

"Says you and whose Bible?" Billy said, but Reggie did feel his hold on her lessen a fraction.

"Your friends have been looking for you," she said to him.

"What friends?" Billy said. "I don't have any friends." The sad thing was that he said it like he was proud of the fact.

"You told them you were called Reggie, didn't you?" Reggie said. "Told them you lived in Gorgie. They came and threatened *me,* they set fire to my *home.*"

"Yeah, it's a funny old world, as dear old Mum would have said."

"Don't speak about Mum like that." If she could just keep him talking, he would get bored, he had the lowest boredom threshold of any human being ever, and then he would leave and then Jackson wouldn't do whatever it was he was about to do—go for Billy with his bare hands, by the look of it.

And then she heard it. It was the primeval sound of a huge wolf roused from its ancient lair. The creature was standing in the doorway, its hackles raised, its fangs bared, a great growling, snarling noise in its savage chest.

Reggie had forgotten about Sadie. The dog had raced up the stairs when they first came in the house, still in pursuit of Banjo's ghostly trail.

The dog rose on its haunches and with one leap was on Billy, grabbing on to his forearm and sinking its teeth in, so that Billy dropped the knife and started screaming at Reggie to get the dog off him. Reggie tried yelling, "Down, Sadie," but it had no effect. Then Jackson did something you wouldn't expect him to do: he punched the dog hard on the side of the head and its jaws slackened and it dropped to the floor like a sandbag. That was when things went a bit blurred for Reggie. Within a second, Jackson had Billy on the ground, kneeling on his kidneys while he shoved his good hand on the back of his neck.

Billy's arm was bleeding from the dog bite but not in a life-threatening way, not in a way that made Reggie want to rush to his help. Like any good first-aider, she treated the most injured party first, cradling Sadie's big head in her lap and murmuring soothing words to her. Jackson got to his feet and said to Billy, "Don't move. Not so much as a twitch." Then he turned to Reggie and said, "Your brother, your call. Want me to phone the police?"

They let Billy go. Gave him a second chance. Not really a second, more like a hundredth. "Blood is blood," Reggie said. "After all."

Considering he used to be a policeman, Jackson didn't seem to care one way or the other. Anyone could see, he said, "anyone except his sister, perhaps," that "Billy boy" was hurtling at breakneck speed towards a bad end without any intervention from anyone. No, she assured him, his sister could see that too.

"What was he after, anyway?" he asked and Reggie shrugged and said, "Oh, something and nothing. This and that. You need to go to bed," she added. "It's been a long day."

"Bit of an understatement," he laughed.

High Noon

Y ou need to go to bed," Reggie said to him. "It's been a long day."

"Bit of an understatement," he said.

He couldn't sleep. The thin, damp pillow and even thinner, even damper sheets didn't help. (Who was this Ms. MacDonald to have lived in such a bleak house?) He lay awake for a long time, listening to Reggie moving about in the living room. He couldn't work out what she was doing but when he came down to investigate, he found her putting all the books back on the shelves, like a busy little nocturnal librarian. "Tidying up," she said. "I'm not keeping you awake, am I?"

He went back to bed and looked for something to read, but the only thing he could find in the bedroom was an ancient copy of Latin unseen translations. He hadn't gone to the kind of school where they did Latin. After tossing and turning some more he went back down to look for some livelier reading matter and found Reggie fast asleep on the sofa with all the lights on. The dog was lying on the floor next to her, and when it heard Jackson, it woke up and stared intently at him. He lifted his hands in a no-threat gesture, a mime which did little to mollify the dog, who tracked Jackson with its eyes all the way round the room. You could hardly blame it for distrusting him, he'd given it a real whack to the head, but it seemed none the worse for the blow. Nonetheless, Jackson felt bad about hitting it, the dog was only doing what he would have done himself, after all.

He couldn't find a readable book in the whole place. Then he forgot about reading because he caught sight of Joanna Hunter's handbag, sitting on what was probably a coffee table, but it was covered in so much crap that it could have been a Second World War tank and you wouldn't have been able to tell.

He was surprised that Louise hadn't taken the bag into her custody. If it had been his case, he would have found it very interesting that a woman who for all intents and purposes had disappeared off the planet had left a bag full of information behind. He carefully opened the bag, watched all the time by the dog, lifted out the bulging Filofax, and leafed through it until he found what he was looking for. Joanna Hunter's address.

She had been found once, she would be found again. She wasn't Joanna Hunter anymore. She wasn't a GP or a wife, she wasn't Reggie's employer ("and friend"), she wasn't the woman that Louise was concerned about. She was a little girl out in the dark, dirty and stained with her mother's blood. She was a little girl who was fast asleep in the middle of a field of wheat as men and dogs streamed unknowingly towards her, lighting their way with torches and moonlight.

Later, when he was a policeman himself, he never went on a search that carried on after nightfall, and he realized that on that warm summer night in Devon, all of them—squaddies, policemen, members of the public—must have entered into some unspoken communal agreement to carry on looking for Joanna Mason even when it was impossible, so great was their sense of desperation.

He covered Reggie with the tatty crocheted blanket that was on the back of the sofa. He was surprised at how paternal he felt towards her, he had thought he would only ever feel that way towards his own. He made a kind of farewell gesture to the dog and turned the lights out before tiptoeing down the hall to the front door.

He had his hand on the latch when a voice said, "I hope you're not thinking of going anywhere without me." A little, insistent voice.

"As if," Jackson said.

There was a Nissan Pathfinder parked in the drive of the Hunters' house, behind Neil Hunter's Range Rover.

"I've seen it before," Reggie said. "The guys who threatened Mr. Hunter were driving it."

"And here they are again."

"We should follow them," Reggie said. "When they leave. If they leave."

"On foot?" Jackson said. "I don't think that will work." They had taken a taxi from Musselburgh and it had dropped them off at the end of the Hunters' street. The place was deserted, not a light on, not a cat out.

"Well," Reggie said, "we can take Dr. Hunter's car. It's in the garage."

Jackson wondered if it was possible to hot-wire a Prius. Modern car technology was killing the handy criminal methods of car starting.

"The spare key is in the garage," Reggie said. "On a shelf, behind an old paint pot. Clouded Pearl."

"What?"

"Clouded Pearl, it's the name of the color. Dr. Hunter said no one would ever look there. I'll get it."

He held back. It was a while since he'd tailed anyone in a car. First it had been criminals, then it was adulterous spouses. Now it was big men in bad cars. Or vice versa. They had crept across the lawn and into the garage only seconds before two guys came noisily out of the house and climbed into the Nissan. Jackson had come with the intention of interrogating Hunter, but he reckoned there might be a chance that the Nissan would lead them, if not to Dr. Hunter, then at least to something or somewhere interesting. Louise had proposed three theories on the garage forecourt — revenge, murder, and kidnap. He was going with kidnap. He should have kissed her. He had held back because they were both married, but maybe he was using that as an excuse, maybe he was just a coward. Anyway, she would probably have hit him if he'd tried.

To drive, he removed his arm from the sling. Adrenaline was keeping the pain away; in fact, he felt remarkably energetic, thanks to a fresh dose from Australian Mike's pharmaceutical cornucopia.

"Don't crash this car," Reggie said.

The dog in the backseat gave a soft whine. "She's happy to be back in Dr. Hunter's car and at the same time sad that Dr. Hunter isn't in it."

"You speak Dog, do you?"

"Yes."

Reggie had insisted they bring the dog. Jackson could feel its eyes boring into the back of his head and he wondered if it was planning on getting its own back on him.

Reggie was reading road signs again. "Loanhead, Roslin, Auchendinny, Penicuik," she said.

"Okay," Jackson said, "I can read."

"Just like old times," she said.

"You mean yesterday, which, since neither of us has slept, still counts as today?" He was getting really good at this time thing now.

The road out of Edinburgh was quiet but not deserted, it was five o'clock on a winter morning but there were already people on the move, making their grudging way through the early-morning dark. A few supermarket lorries thundered along and a speeding motorcyclist hurtled past, eager to donate an organ in time for someone's Christmas, but nothing happened to stop Jackson from keeping the Nissan in his sights.

It became more difficult when it turned off the main drag. Jackson held back as much as he could, but he didn't know these roads and he was worried the Nissan would take an unexpected turning and be gone before he could spot it. For a while he did think he'd lost it but then he saw taillights ahead, sitting high on the road, and guessed it was his target. They turned off onto what looked like a farm road, taillights bouncing along now. Jackson drove past the turning and then reversed back, turned off his lights, and followed from afar. There had been no sign at the turning to indicate where it led to, but it didn't seem like the kind of road that went many places.

After a couple of hundred yards, he parked the car at the entrance to a field. It wasn't entirely hidden from view, but it wasn't completely in the open either.

"Right," he said to Reggie. "You—and the dog—both stay here. I mean it, okay? I know that you are *exactly* the kind of person who will get out of this car the minute I'm out of sight, but I'm asking you to solemnly promise to *stay here*. Promise?"

"Promise," she said meekly.

He had found a hefty Maglite in Joanna Hunter's glove box. In an emergency it was an excellent weapon and he could have done with it himself, but he gave it to Reggie and said, "If anyone comes near you, hit them with this."

He got out of the Prius and listened. He heard the Nissan's engine up ahead and then the engine stopped. He set off on foot.

The Nissan was parked in front of a house, next to a nondescript Toyota, and the guys were climbing out, stiffly, as if they'd had a long night. Jackson watched as one of them knocked on the front door of the house before both of them went inside without waiting for an answer. After a few seconds he heard them yelling excitedly at each other as if they'd found something that they hadn't been expecting—or hadn't found something that they *had* been expecting (or indeed both)—and then they came racing out of the house and back into the Nissan, one of them on the phone to someone as he ran, and Jackson had only just enough time to throw himself into a dry ditch at the side of the road before they were haring back up the track towards the road. To his relief they drove straight past the Prius.

He set off in the direction of the house, wondering what it was that had alarmed them so much. Not death, he hoped. There'd been enough of that for one week.

A movement in the overgrown bushes that surrounded the house startled him. He thought it might be a fox or a badger, but a person, not an animal, stepped onto the path. There were enough lights on in the house to make out that it was a woman, and then she was suddenly illuminated, held like a moth in the beam of the Maglite in the unsteady hand of (a typically disobedient) Reggie, and Jackson could see that it was not just a woman but a woman with a child in her arms. She was veiled in blood from top to toe and had a knife clutched in her hand. Not so much a Madonna as a great, dangerous avenging angel.

The dog barked with joy and ran towards her.

"Dr. Hunter?" Jackson said, approaching cautiously.

"Can you help me?" she said to him. More of a command than a request, as if a goddess had unexpectedly found herself on earth and was in sudden need of an acolyte. And Jackson had never been one to say no, either to goddesses or to requests for help.

La Règle du Jeu

Margaret, are you grieving Over Goldengrove unleaving, sumer is i-cumin in, loude sing cuckoo, there was an old lady who swallowed a fly, Adam lay ybounden bounden in a bond and miles to go before I sleep, five little bluebirds hopping by the door. Run, run Joanna run. But she couldn't run because she was tethered by the rope, like an animal. She thought of animals gnawing off a leg to escape from a trap and she had tried tearing at the rope with her teeth, but it was made from polypropylene and she couldn't make any inroad on it.

She knew that this was the dark place she had always been destined to find again. Just because a terrible thing happened to you once didn't mean it couldn't happen again.

The men spoke to her only when it was necessary but they didn't seem bothered that she could see their faces. There was something military about them and she wondered if they were special forces. Mercenaries. She thought it best to talk to them even if they didn't talk back. One was slightly shorter than the other and she called him Peter *(I'm sorry I don't know your name, do you mind if I call you Peter?).* The slightly taller one she called John *(How about John—that's a good name?).* She said, "Thank you, John," when they gave her water or, "That's very kind of you, Peter," when they took away the pot to empty it.

She guessed they were going to kill her eventually, when she'd served her purpose, whatever that was, but she was going to make it difficult for them because they would have to remember that she had been friendly to them, she had called them by their names, even if they weren't their real ones, she had made them see that she was a person. And that they were people too.

As well as water they gave her food, microwaved ready-meals that she would never have considered eating normally but that she looked forward to because she was very hungry. They gave her jars of baby food and cow's milk in a cup, which she didn't give to the baby but drank herself and breast-fed the baby instead. They gave her a pack of disposable nappies as well, the wrong size, and a bin-bag to put the soiled ones in, although they never emptied the bin-bag.

The baby was very subdued, and she supposed it was because they'd given him a sedative. They'd given her an injection of something that made her head feel like wool for the first day, some kind of liquid benzodiazepine or maybe intravenous Valium. She had prepared the vein for them herself after they put a knife to the baby's throat.

They brought in some toys—a ball and a plastic box with different-shaped holes in the side. Lights came on and a bell rang if you posted the correct shapes in the holes. They were both secondhand and still had little handwritten price stickers on, as if they'd come from a charity shop. They were both soon bored with the toys. Mostly she played pat-a-cake with the baby and peekaboo and she sang and recited rhymes and jiggled the baby around to keep him amused, to keep him warm as well because there was no heating in the house. Hypothermia was a more immediate problem than boredom. They had given her a couple of blankets, old things, but it wasn't enough. She wished she had her inhaler with her (she had to work hard to stay calm), she wished she had the baby's comforter and that they were both wearing warmer clothes.

They had walked into the bedroom as she was getting changed. She had heard Sadie barking dementedly downstairs and a banging noise that she didn't understand until she realized the dog was trying to break down a door to get to her. She had gathered up the baby and rushed out onto the upstairs landing, and that was when she saw them.

The rope was too short to reach the window, but she could stand on the bed and from there she could see out. Fields, nothing but brown fields, winter barren, lit by a bright, cold moon. No sign of another house.

On the second day, Peter gave her a pad of paper and a pen and told her to write a note to "your husband." What should she say? That they would die if he didn't do as he was told, Peter said. She wondered what Neil had done to bring this about and what he was doing to end it.

She became a doctor because she wanted to help people. It was a terrible cliché but it was true (but not true of all doctors). She wanted to help all the people who were sick and in pain, from measles to cancer, from heartsickness to depression. If she couldn't heal herself, then she could at least heal someone else. That was why she had been attracted to Neil—he hadn't needed healing, he was whole in himself, he didn't suffer the pain and sadness of the world, he just got on with his life. She was a bowl, holding everything inside, he was Mars throwing his spear into the world. She didn't have to tend to him, didn't have to worry about him. Necessarily, that meant there were drawbacks to living with him, but who was perfect? Only the baby.

She had spent the thirty years since the murders creating a life. It wasn't a real life, it was the simulacrum of one, but it worked. Her real life had been left behind in that other, golden field. And then she had the baby and her love for him breathed life into the simulacrum and it became genuine. Her love for the baby was immense, bigger than the entire universe. Fierce.

The guy we're working for," Peter said, "wants your husband to sign over his business. You're the price. He's got all the papers ready for him to sign, nice and legal."

She thought that was absurd and said, "But that's coercion, it would never stand up in court," and he laughed and said, "You're not in your world now, Doctor." She'd hoped that this was the beginning of more conversation between them, but he lost interest and nodded at the pen and paper and said, "So make it good." She wondered if Neil had known what the people he was dealing with were like and decided he probably had.

"And if he doesn't?" she said. "If he doesn't sign everything over to your boss, what happens to us?" But he just stared at her as if she weren't there.

So she wrote, "They are going to kill us if you don't do as they say."

Sometime in the early hours on Saturday, John woke her up and gave her the paper and pen again and told her to write something—"Anything. Time's running out for you"—and then he left the room. She wrote with the Biro, "Please help us. We don't want to die." Despite what they said about doctors, she'd always had a neat hand. She crossed the *t*'s and dotted the *i* and underlined the *Please,* and when John came back for the note, she jammed the pen into his eyeball as hard as she could. It surprised her how far it went in.

She took his pulse. Nothing. The baby slept on. She started to panic, it wouldn't be long before Peter came back. She had to be ready. She searched all over John's body for a weapon, but there was nothing. Peter had a knife in an ankle sheath, she'd seen it when he bent down to put food on the floor.

The door opened and Peter said, "What the fuck?" when he saw her sitting on the floor, cradling John in her lap like a pietà. She couldn't get the pen out of his eye in time so she had turned his head towards her and half-covered the pen with her hands. "Something's happened to him," she said, looking at Peter, "I don't know what, I thought maybe he'd just fainted, but I'm not sure . . ." She tried to sound professional, like a doctor.

Peter squatted on his haunches and turned John's head towards him, and as he did so, she rose up, rolling John off her lap and onto the floor, and then slammed the heel of her hand upwards into Peter's windpipe as hard as she could. He fell over backwards, holding his throat, his eyes bulging, and she leapt forward and grabbed the knife from his ankle and sawed through the rope around her own.

She crouched down by his side and watched him. He was having a lot of trouble breathing but he wasn't finished. She could feel her own breathing compromised, the airways constricting and whistling. She was drenched in sweat even though it was so cold in the room.

She didn't let him see the knife, but nonetheless he was squirming and wriggling, trying to get away from her. "Shh," she said, laying a hand on his arm and then quietly, so he couldn't see it coming, she stuck the knife into his common carotid artery, the left one. And then for good measure she stuck it in his right one as well, and the blood gushed as if she'd struck oil.

The baby woke up and laughed when he saw her and she said, "Little Tommy Tittlemouse lived in a little house, he caught fishes in other men's ditches."

A Clean, Well-Lighted Place

The Prius was no longer in the garage. Lights spilled out from the back of the house. It was six o'clock in the morning on a Saturday, perhaps Neil Hunter was up early, but it seemed more likely he hadn't been to bed. Through the glass of the French windows, she could see him slumped on the living-room sofa, his eyes closed. Louise tapped on the glass, the ghost of Miss Jessel, and Neil Hunter jerked awake, a look of terror on his face, which subsided when he recognized her. He got to his feet unsteadily and unlocked the door. "Don't tell me — you again," he said. He looked completely burned-out.

"Do you want to tell us who your friends are?" she said, walking into the room, and he laughed grimly and said, "Friends? What friends? It turns out that I don't have any friends." The guy looked dead on his feet.

"And your wife? What's happened to her, Mr. Hunter? I think we've been messed around enough, don't you? She never rented a car to go down to Yorkshire, there was no phone call from the aunt, in fact — and this is a bit of a clincher — her aunt died two weeks ago. So what's going on exactly?"

Neil Hunter sank into a chair and put his head in his hands.

Louise squatted down beside him and said gently, "Just tell me, has she been kidnapped, yes or no?" He drew breath noisily and said nothing.

Louise stood up and in her best official voice said, "Neil Hunter, I am going to ask you some questions. You are not obliged to say anything in response to the questions, but if you do say anything, it will be taken down in writing and may be used in evidence."

He burst into tears.

Louise stood on the Hunters' front doorstep, breathing in the chilly early-morning air. It was at times like this she wished she smoked, because then she wouldn't be so badly tempted to raid Neil Hunter's Laphroaig.

It was the middle of the morning and the street was alive with police. Horses, bolts, and stable doors came to mind.

Neil Hunter had been taken in for questioning but he wasn't making much sense, and the Strathclyde police had knocked up Anderson from his luxury penthouse but he was all lawyered-up. No one had any idea where to start looking for Joanna Hunter. They'd picked up the Nissan on the M8 with the registration that Reggie had given them, but the guys in it weren't talking either.

Joanna Hunter was dead, Louise was sure. The baby too. Lying in a ditch somewhere or being fed to pigs. Hunter said she was gone when he got home on Wednesday evening and that an hour later he'd received a phone call telling him that if he went to the police he'd never see her again. "Find the money to pay Anderson or sign over everything," he said to Louise before they took him down to the station.

"And that was Wednesday?" Louise said. "And today's Saturday and you didn't simply sign everything over straightaway?"

"I was trying to find the money."

"You didn't sign everything over straightaway?"

"Don't make out I don't care about my family."

"You. Didn't. Sign. Everything. Over. Straight. Away."

"You don't understand."

"I do understand—you didn't sign everything over straightaway. The documentation would have been laughed out of court. You would have still kept everything and you would have had a chance of getting your wife and baby back."

"And he would have come after me some other way. Anderson's a maniac, his henchmen are maniacs. Once he gets his teeth into something, he doesn't let go. If I took him to court, he'd come after us, kill us for sure."

A uniform came out of the house and said, "Boss?" He had *important news* written all over his face and she thought, that's it, Joanna Hunter's dead, but then the uniform broke into a big grin.

"You're not going to believe it, boss. She's back. She's in the house."

"Who? Dr. *Hunter?*"

"Dr. Hunter, and the baby. And a girl."

"A girl?"

What kind of a magic trick was that? Joanna Hunter was sitting on the sofa in the once-lovely living room. She was wearing clean jeans and a soft pale blue sweater that looked like cashmere. It had little pearl buttons on the cuffs. It was the details that seemed so at odds with everything. She looked scrubbed clean. Her hair was damp, as though she'd just had a shower. "The baby's asleep in his cot," she said before Louise asked.

Reggie was sitting on the sofa next to her with a bright, bland expression on her face as if she was determined to say absolutely nothing about anything. Joanna Hunter, on the other hand, was completely relaxed. "Sorry if I've given you any trouble," she said as if she were apologizing for being late for a dental appointment.

"I went away for a couple of days. It's all a bit of a blank, I'm afraid. I think I had some kind of temporary amnesia. *Disassociative fugue state* is the medical term, I seem to remember. Trauma brought on by the memory of a previous trauma. Andrew Decker, I suppose. And so on."

"And so on?" Louise echoed.

She was trying to think of a way into an interview with two consummate liars—she wasn't sure how to find the truth, let alone follow it—but she was saved from the problem for now by a knock at the door. Karen Warner lumbered into the room.

"Sorry to interrupt, boss." She was breathing heavily, as if she'd been running. She didn't even give the miraculous reappearance of Joanna Hunter a second look. She had the kind of grim expression on her face that could only mean something bad had happened.

"Oh God," Louise said, holding on to her heart. "It's Needler, isn't it? He's back," and Karen said, "Yes. He is."

"Someone's dead," Louise said. "I can tell from the look on your face. Who? Alison? One of the kids? All of them?"

"None of them, boss. It's Marcus."

Touch and go. It was a funny phrase if you thought about it. Marcus was in the operating theater. Louise and Karen were sitting in the deserted "sanctuary" in the RIE. There was some kind of non-denominational greenery to indicate Christmas.

"What happened?" Louise asked.

"I don't know, there seems to be a lot of confusion. He heard the call and responded, I think he was on the ring road coming into work. Local uniforms were there already, I think it was all a bit casual, you know, the woman who cried wolf too many times."

"Casual. Jesus."

Needler had kept his family at gunpoint all night. One of the kids had managed to get hold of the panic button, and the local police had responded, the "first officer on the scene" had rung the doorbell, and Needler had opened the door and shot him in the chest. That "first officer" was Marcus. "He wasn't wearing a vest," Karen said. "He should have waited for the IRV. Idiot."

"Fools rush in," Louise said. "He was trying to help."

By the time Karen and Louise arrived, it was all over bar the weeping.

Needler had walked out of the house, giving an IRV officer a clear shot, but before they could take it he had turned his gun on himself.

"The bastard," Louise said. She had wanted to be in there at the kill, she wanted to have torn him apart with her bare hands, like a crazed maenad.

Marcus had been taken to St. John's Hospital in Livingston and then transferred to the Royal Infirmary in Edinburgh, where he had been operated on.

When the surgeon came out of the operating theater, he recognized Louise and raised his eyebrow a fraction, a minimal gesture missed by Marcus's mother but caught by Louise.

"Oh God," she moaned.

"Don't think He's going to help," Karen said.

★   ★   ★

Louise stood at the foot of the bed. Marcus's mother was sitting by the side of the bed, clutching her son's hand. He was on life support in the intensive care unit.

"He's an only child," his mother said. Her name was Judith, but it was impossible to think of her as anything other than "Marcus's mother."

"His father's dead," she said. "I've always worried that something would happen to me and he would be left alone." A motherless child. Now she was going to be a childless mother. Louise was losing him too, her sweet boy.

A girl appeared, led to the bed by a nurse, and sat across from his mother. "This is Ellie," Marcus's mother said to Louise. Ellie didn't acknowledge either of them; if she could have brought Marcus back with the power of her thoughts, then he would be up walking about. His mother reached across his body and took the girl's hand. With her free hand she stroked her son's close-shaven curls. "He's such a good boy," she said. "He looks as if he's sleeping."

Louise said, "Yes, he does." He didn't. He didn't look as if he were asleep, nobody looked like that when they were asleep, but hey.

He had already left, he was just waiting for them to say goodbye. To infinity and beyond.

Sweet Little Wife, Pretty Little Baby

Lassie came home. She didn't need anyone's help in the end. She got back all on her own.

It wasn't light yet, so it was difficult to make out who it was. Just a shape, a shape moving closer. But the dog knew who it was.

Reggie nearly fainted. She felt sick with the rush of chemicals in her body. A great cascade of adrenaline flowing through her, making her heart feel like a tight, hard knot in her chest. So many emotions flooded Reggie that she could hardly untangle them into their different threads. Relief and disbelief. Happiness. And horror. Lots of horror.

Dr. Hunter was walking towards them, the baby in her arms. She was barefoot and she was still wearing her suit and the baby was still in his little matelot outfit. She was covered in blood. It matted her hair, it stained the skin on her face, her legs. The baby had streaks and splashes of red on him too.

Not their blood. The baby was laughing at the sight of Sadie, and Dr. Hunter was walking straight and strong, like a heroine, a warrior queen.

The dog cantered ahead and was the first to greet Dr. Hunter, as playful as a puppy. When the baby was almost close enough, he held out his fat little arms towards Reggie and did his starfish jump. She caught him and held him tight and said, "Hello, sunshine. I missed you."

Jackson went in the house and came back out, looking sick, then siphoned petrol out of the Toyota that was parked outside and used it to set fire to the house.

You would think it was exactly the kind of situation in which a person would call the police — kidnap, murder, self-defense, et cetera — but no, apparently not. "I don't want this in the baby's life forever," Dr. Hunter said to Jackson, "do you understand? The way I've had it in mine?" and Reggie supposed he must have done because he got rid of a whole crime scene — *poof!* — just like that.

Then they left, walked back down the track to the car, the flames rising behind them into the dark morning sky. They must have looked as if they were walking out of hell.

Dr. Hunter said, "Just let us out here," as if he'd given them a lift back from a supermarket, and Jackson dropped them in the small car park at the side of a field. "I can see my house from here," Dr. Hunter said. "We'll be fine. Thank you." The baby reached out his fat little hand and Jackson shook it and said, "How d'you do," and the baby laughed.

"Good-bye, Mr. B.," Reggie said and kissed him on the cheek, as lightly as a sparrow.

There had been a lot of policemen at the house, but they had walked in from the field, through the gap in the hedge in the back garden, and into the kitchen, and the only sign of life was finger-print dust all over the kitchen surfaces, so Dr. Hunter and Reggie went straight up the back stairs and into the bathroom as if they were invisible or charmed. Dr. Hunter ran a bath and gave the baby to Reggie and said, "Will you give him a bath, Reggie, while I take a shower?" and when they were both clean and warm and wrapped in towels, Dr. Hunter said, "It's surprising just how much you miss soap and hot water." And then she said to Reggie, as if it were a normal thing, "Do you think you could take our clothes and put them in your bag and dispose of them somewhere?" And Reggie, who was pretty good at dealing with bloodstained clothes by now, stuffed the baby's matelot outfit and Dr. Hunter's suit, T-shirt, and pretty underwear—all ruined by the blood—into her backpack. The blood wasn't quite dry, which was a thought she didn't dwell on.

Then she got clean clothes from Dr. Hunter's bedroom and the baby's room—more fingerprint dust—and they looked as good as new. Not Reggie, Reggie was old, she had lived a lifetime in a day.

When they came downstairs again, all the police in the house looked completely stunned at the sight of them. One of the forensic officers said, "Who are you?" and Dr. Hunter said, "Joanna Hunter," and the forensic officer said, "What are you doing, this is a crime scene, you're compromising it," and Dr. Hunter said, "What crime scene?" and the policeman said, "A kidnapping," and then looked as if he felt pretty stupid because the kidnap victim was sitting right in front of him saying to Reggie, "Do you want to put the kettle on?" and Reggie said, "And we'll all have tea."

And then everyone wanted to ask her questions, of course, and

Dr. Hunter just kept on saying, as polite as pie, "I'm really sorry, I don't remember." When they'd had tea, Reggie said, "Well, better be off, Dr. H. Things to do, people to see." And then she said to all the police officers, "Bye, folks," and hoisted her bag on her back as if it contained books or messages or anything really rather than two sets of bloodstained clothes.

Great Expectations

Jackson was waiting outside the hospital, collar hunched up against the cold. She ignored him and walked past, but he reached out and grabbed onto her hand. Her skin was dry and cold. She snatched her hand back and carried on walking. He caught up with her.

"I'm sorry about your boy Marcus."

They sat in her car and he held her while she cried. When she finished crying, she shook him off as if he were a nuisance and blew her nose.

"You know we found her?" Louise said. "Don't you?"

"Dr. Hunter? Yeah, I heard that. Reggie told me."

"How?"

"She phoned me."

"You don't have a phone."

"Yeah, that's true."

"Aren't you even going to *try* to lie?" she said. "I know you've been up to something, it's written all over you. You're a terrible liar."

What was he going to tell her? That he pulled the pen out of the guy's eye, that he had put the knife into a household bin on the street minutes before it was collected by the refuse men. That he had set fire to a house and destroyed a crime scene and had been complicit in covering up a double murder? She was police and he used to be. There was a chasm between them now that could never be bridged because he could never tell her the truth. She was always going to be in his past, never in his future.

"You should go home, Louise."

"So should you."

He caught a coach. He hadn't thought of that before. It was surprisingly comfortable, an overnight express that handily deposited him at Heathrow before first light. His odyssey was, finally, over. He went and had a coffee and waited for his wife to reach earth.

According to the arrivals board in Terminal 3, Flight VS 022 had landed at Heathrow twenty minutes ago. It took a while to decant a huge bird like an A-340 Airbus, and then, of course, there was the further ordeal of baggage reclaim to be undergone by the passengers, so Jackson had shifted into waiting gear, an unreflective Zenlike state he had learned to be comfortable in when he worked as a private detective, tutored by endless hours of sitting in a car waiting for missing husbands and unfaithful wives to cross his radar.

The arrivals gate was crowded with people ready to welcome passengers off the flight. Jackson had never seen such an assortment of nationalities in one place, certainly not in such benign good humor, especially considering the early hour. A line of considerably less enthusiastic drivers and chauffeurs held the outer perimeter, corporate signs and handwritten names aloft. Technically speaking, Jackson belonged in the first group, but it was the latter band of brothers that he identified with.

There had been a lull for several minutes and an edge of anticipation was growing in the crowd, anticipation that turned suddenly to excitement as the automatic doors opened with a hiss and the advance guard of passengers strode through—first-class men in suits with cabin baggage, heroically indifferent to the waiting crowds.

"Have you come off the Washington flight?" Jackson checked with a harassed-looking man who mumbled an affirmative as if he couldn't believe a complete stranger would address him at this time of the morning.

A few minutes later and a steady flux of people began to disgorge from the plane and be absorbed into the arrivals concourse. After a while the flow slowed down until it was only exhausted-looking families with children and babies straggling through. Finally, the wheelchairs brought up the rear.

There was no sign whatsoever of his wife.

There were several explanations of course. Her luggage might have been lost and she was still filling out forms in the baggage hall. Or she had been stopped by Customs or Immigration or Passport Control, a check or a mistake. Jackson had once been held up for hours because the laminate on his battered passport had begun to lift. He waited another twenty minutes to see if Tessa would appear, no Buddhist-like patience this time for him, just sheepdog agitation.

She must have missed the flight, he said to himself. She would have phoned or texted him. Perhaps Andrew Decker had read a cheery message from her on Jackson's BlackBerry (*Had to change my flight* or *Been bumped! Rebooked on next flight*).

Maybe he was wrong about what flight she was on, his brain

had been scrambled by the train crash, *"mince for brains,"* Louise had said.

He tried ringing Tessa's mobile from a pay phone, but he had no credit card and soon ran out of change. Reggie's money had been almost used up on the coach fare.

Eventually he went looking for an airline official, and a woman ("Lesley") who was dressed in a uniform that would have allowed her to drown in a vat of Heinz tomato soup without anyone noticing informed him that no one by the name of Tessa Webb was on the passenger manifest.

"She missed the flight, then," Jackson said.

"She was never booked on the flight," "Lesley" said, scrutinizing her computer screen. "Or on any flight. In fact, there's no one by that name in our entire database."

Perhaps she'd got the carrier wrong, he had never seen her ticket, perhaps she'd been booked with British Airways, not Virgin. The BA woman didn't seem keen to talk to him—could have been the bruises, he supposed, or the sling, or his general air of desperation, there were a lot of reasons for not engaging with him—but she did say that the next BA flight from Dulles was due to land in an hour. So he waited for that one as well. No Tessa. In fact, he waited all morning before giving up and catching the Heathrow Express to Paddington, from where he walked all the way to Covent Garden. After all, he didn't have anything else to do.

He used the last of Reggie's money to buy a bag of croissants. He was looking forward to a cup of good coffee made in his industrial machine. He hadn't had a good cup of coffee since he set off early on Wednesday morning.

What he hadn't considered, what now seemed entirely logical, was that Tessa had arrived already, on an earlier flight, or even yesterday, and would be completely baffled by his absence from their flat. He quite talked himself into this view of affairs and was whistling with optimism by the time he climbed the stairs to their little eyrie ("love nest," he had called it once and she burst out laughing, at his sentimentality or the cliché, he didn't know).

He rapped loudly on the door. He didn't have any keys, of course, but his wife was at home, what did he need keys for? She was sleeping off her jet lag. Sleeping soundly. Or she had popped out to buy a bag of croissants. Fresh coffee for her beloved, to bring back to their nest of love. The beams of their house were cedar and their rafters were of fir.

Where the fuck was she?

Unbeknownst to their downstairs neighbor, Jackson kept a spare key to their flat above the lintel of the neighbor's front door. A thief might look there for a key, but he was unlikely to realize it was for a different door. Thieves, generally speaking, were opportunistic and stupid. He thought of the Prius's keys behind the tin of Clouded Pearl. It would have been a good name, in another life, for Joanna Hunter. An inscrutable Chinese life. She said she killed the two guys who were holding her in the house because they were intending to kill her and the baby, but he didn't know that for sure. She would have got off on self-defense, he was pretty sure, but the house was a bloodbath, she would never have escaped the notoriety. For the rest of her life she would have been the woman who killed her kidnappers, and the baby would have been the son of that woman. He could see her point. She'd spent thirty years running from one nightmare only to crash headlong into another.

It was with a sense of relief that he slipped the key into the lock. It turned and he was home. Finally.

No sign of Tessa. No bag of fresh coffee on the counter. No croissants. *Whither is thy beloved gone?*

★   ★   ★

He could smell it before he could see it. Not coffee, that was for sure. It had been there at least a day by the abattoir smell of it. Not an *it,* a guy. A gun fallen to the floor at his feet, a Russian number — Makarov, Tokarev, he couldn't remember — there'd been a lot around in the Gulf, quite a few of the lads brought them home as trophies. Perhaps the guy was ex-army, took a clean way out and blew the top of his head off. No, not clean, the opposite of clean. Blood everywhere, brains, other stuff, he didn't look too closely, didn't want to contaminate the scene. He had destroyed one crime scene in the last twenty-four hours, he thought he should probably preserve this one.

Given that most of his head was blown off, it was difficult for Jackson to tell whether or not he knew the guy. The suit looked familiar, looked a lot like the tired suit who had sat next to him on the train, just an average Joe. Stranger or not, why would someone choose to break in and kill themselves here? Jackson was fairly inured to the sight of dead bodies, he'd seen a fair few in his time. What he wasn't accustomed to was finding them in his own home. Not broken in actually, no sign of doors or windows being forced.

Gingerly, trying not to step in any blood, Jackson inched nearer the body and using his thumb and forefinger tweezered out a wallet from the dead guy's inside pocket. Inside the wallet there were two familiar photographs and a driving license. He contemplated the photograph on it. He had never liked that picture, he didn't take a good photo at the best of times but on his driving license he looked like a refugee from a war. He was tempted to probe further in the guy's pockets but resisted. A driving license said it all — the guy's name was Jackson Brodie.

He thought about phoning Louise and telling her that Andrew Decker had finally stopped running, but in the end he just dialed 999.

★ ★ ★

While he waited for new credit cards to be sent, he asked Josie to transfer money into his account online *("Now what have you done, Jackson?")*. If he could have accessed his passport, he could have gone to the bank and withdrawn cash, but his passport was in the flat, and everything in the flat was off-limits to him until the police gave him the all clear. "Potential crime scene," one of the investigating officers said. "We can't be sure it was a suicide, sir." "Yeah," Jackson said. "I used to be a policeman."

Before contacting Josie he had phoned Julia, but she wasn't interested in his predicament. Her sister, Amelia, had died in the operating theater on Wednesday. ("Complications," she sobbed. "Trust Amelia.")

The money was enough to get him by for a few days. He'd checked into a cheap hotel in King's Cross while the Covent Garden flat remained a crime scene, not that he was thinking of moving back. He couldn't imagine putting his feet up on the sofa and popping a can of beer in the same room where someone had, literally, blown their brains out.

The hotel was a dive. This time last year he was staying in Le Meurice with Marlee, Christmas shopping in Paris, wandering out in the evenings to gaze in the Christmas windows of Galeries Lafayette. Now he was staying in a fleapit in King's Cross. How are the mighty fallen.

On Tuesday morning he went to the British Museum.

No one there had ever heard of anyone called Tessa Webb. "She's a curator here," he insisted. "Assyrian." No Tessa Webb, no Tessa Brodie. No conference in Washington that anyone knew anything about.

He called in a favor from a guy called Nick who until recently had worked for Bernie, an ex-coms tech guy from the Met. Bernie himself was away somewhere.

Nick reported back that no Tessa Webb had ever been to St. Paul's Girls' School, nor to Keble College, Oxford. There was no National Insurance record for her, no driving license. He wondered what kind of a reception he would get if he went into a police station and reported his prodigal wife as a missing person. And how did you report someone as missing when they seemed never to have existed in the first place?

The DI in charge of the case said, "They've held the autopsy, pathologist says he's one hundred percent sure that Decker killed himself."

"In my flat?"

"I guess he had to do it somewhere. He had your keys, your address. Maybe he'd started to identify with you in some way. We've no idea where he got the gun, but he's been mixing with cons for the last thirty years, so it probably wasn't that difficult."

On Wednesday he was allowed back into the Covent Garden flat. He retrieved his passport and went to the bank to draw money out and discovered that he didn't have any. The same with his investments.

"Boy, she's one clever cookie, this so-called wife of yours," Nick said admiringly. "She moved everything out of your accounts into untraceable ones. Slick, really slick."

Tessa gone, the money gone, Bernie gone. It had all been one big setup, right from that initial "chance" encounter on Regent Street. Between them they had designed her to appeal to him—the way she looked, the way she behaved, the things she said—and he had fallen like the biggest fool ever. It had been a perfect con and he had been the perfect mark.

He was too tired even to rage. And after all, he had never earned the money in the first place, so now it had simply moved on to someone else who had never earned it.

VI
Christmas

A Puppy Is Just for Christmas

"A Faithful Friend." What did that mean? Did it refer to the contents of the basket—wicker, with a lid like a hamper, tied with a large red satin bow—or did it refer to the person who had left the basket on their doorstep? The words were written on a Christmas gift tag, one of those expensive glittery ones that were reproductions of Victorian Christmas scraps. The whole thing looked old-fashioned, you expected to lift the lid of the basket and find a feast inside—plum pudding and an enormous glazed pork pie, bottles of port and Madeira.

Louise hadn't expected a dog. A puppy, a tiny thing. Black and white. "Border collie," Patrick said knowledgeably. "I had one as a boy. A sheepdog."

It was Patrick who had found the basket on the doorstep. It was Christmas Eve and they had been sitting quietly, listening to the radio, a peaceful, timeless scene of domesticity that belied their feelings. Louise was set aside from it even while she was part of it. Patrick was doing the *Scotsman* crossword while Louise converted the Christmas cards she hadn't got round to sending into New Year greetings, *Sorry this is late, been laid up with flu*. It wasn't true, but hey. Upstairs, Archie was shut in his room, on his computer, talking to his friends, unseasonal music seeping through the floor. Someone rang the bell and Patrick got up and went to the door.

Did you see who it was?" she asked.

"No," Patrick said.

"Nothing? What about a car? A car engine? You must have noticed something. It didn't just drop out of nowhere, someone rang the bell."

"Take it easy, Louise. I'm not a suspect here. Perhaps the dog was meant for Archie."

"A dog? Archie?" How unlikely was that?

It was him, she knew it was. "A faithful friend," he had a streak of sticky sentimentality a mile wide. The whole thing, the basket, the message, the ribbon. It was him.

She ran out into the street, holding the puppy in her arms. She could feel the fast heartbeat against her own. Its roly-poly little body was solid in her hands at the same time as it weighed a feather. She stood in the middle of the road and willed Jackson to come back. But he didn't.

"Louise, come on in, it's freezing."

She drove to Livingston on Christmas Day. Alison Needler had the Trinity house on the market and was looking for somewhere else to buy. "I expect it will go for a knockdown price," she said. "Not many people want to live in a house where three people were murdered."

"Oh, I don't know," Louise said. "The Edinburgh property market's pretty ruthless."

She had taken round a tree the week before because you could see that Alison wasn't up to that kind of thing. She had taken presents as well, toys for the kids, anything that was plastic, noisy, and garish—nothing remotely tasteful or educational, she had been a kid herself once, she knew what they liked.

Today she had brought with her the things people were supposed to have at Christmas—nuts, satsumas, dates—the kind of stuff nobody really ate. A bottle of malt, one of vodka. "Vodka," Alison said. "My tipple of choice." Now and then you saw a glimpse of another Alison, the one that predated her marriage to David Needler. She retrieved two glasses from the kitchen and said, "You're a whisky drinker, aren't you?" Louise put her hand over the glass and said, "No, you're all right, I'll just have an orange juice or something," and Alison raised an inquiring eyebrow and said, "Because you're pregnant?" and Louise hooted with laughter and said, "God, what are you, a witch? *No*, because I'm *driving*. What? What are you giving me that look for? Honest to God, hand on my heart, on the grave of my mother, I am not pregnant." But hey.

The door in her heart had been wedged open and she couldn't shut it, no matter how hard she pushed against it. And she had tried as hard as she could, even got as far as an appointment at a clinic, but sometimes, once something has been opened, it can never be closed again. Not all boxes stay locked.

She was going to leave Patrick at Hogmanay, then they could start the new year with a clean slate. New broom, fresh start. Roll out the clichés, Louise. Not at Christmas, it would be a cruel thing to do to him, his last wife had left, albeit involuntarily, at Christmas. Every future Christmas would be marred by the memory of another wife abandoning him. He'd get a new one. He was good at marriage ("Lots of practice," she could imagine him laughing to the next one.). He was a good man, shame she was such a bad woman.

Love is the important thing. That was Joanna Hunter's parting message to her on the third and last time she interviewed her. Tried to interview her. The woman was as intransigent as marble. "You were just wandering around for three nights? You claim you don't remember *anything?* Not where you slept or how you ate? You had no car, no money. I don't understand, Dr. Hunter."

"Neither do I, Chief Inspector. Call me Jo."

Louise supposed she could have pushed it, found some forensic evidence somewhere. The clothes she left the house in, for example—the black suit, where was it? Or the Prius, parked in the street and freshly valeted of all trace evidence. To every question, Joanna Hunter just shrugged and said she couldn't remember. You couldn't break her. Not Neil Hunter either. He'd recanted his whole story about Anderson and extortion.

Maybe you could have broken her if you had really wanted to. Maybe if you had pushed her on the two bodies found in a burned-out house in Penicuik, guys whose identities were still in question almost two weeks later. They'd finally got one of them, the marine, through his dental records, left the service ten years ago and no one really knew what he'd been doing since. The other guy remained a mystery. No sign of the knife that had finished off the guy with the crushed windpipe, no sign of whatever had been rammed through the other guy's eye into his brain. The fire destroyed any fingerprint evidence. "Looks professional," the lead DI on the case said when they talked about it at a Task and Coordinating Group meeting.

There was no mention of a possibility that it might be linked to Joanna Hunter in any way. She disappeared, she reappeared. End of story. Anderson came up smelling like roses, Mr. Hunter, on the other hand, was being prosecuted for willful fire-raising for the purposes of a false insurance claim.

Marcus's death was big news for several days. "Hero Policeman" and so on. His mother turned off his life support after a week, so his funeral was just before Christmas. "Makes no difference to me," she said. "There'll be no more Christmas now." The day after the funeral she jumped off the North Bridge at three in the morning. Give her a medal too.

And as for Decker, Louise couldn't get her head round that at all.

"You visited him in prison," she said to Joanna Hunter. "Why? What did you say to him?"

"Oh, nothing much," she said. "This and that, you know how it is."

"No, I don't," Louise said.

Joanna Hunter was decorating her Christmas tree, hanging cheap glass baubles as if they were precious jewels. "He was very remorseful for what he'd done. He'd become religious in prison," she said, contemplating the white, top-of-the-tree angel that she was holding in her hand.

"He converted to Catholicism," Louise said. "And then killed himself. He must have known that means eternal damnation to a Catholic."

"Well, perhaps he thought that would be the right punishment for him," Joanna Hunter said, climbing on a stepladder to reach the top of the tree.

"You know how to shoot a gun," Louise said, holding the stepladder steady.

"I do. But I didn't pull the trigger." And Louise thought, No, but somehow or other you persuaded him to do it.

"I went to see him because I wanted him to understand what he had done," Joanna Hunter said as she reached to fix the angel on the top of the tree. "To know that he had robbed people of their lives for no reason. Maybe seeing me, grown up, and with the baby, brought it home to him, made him think how Jessica and Joseph would have been." Good explanation, Louise thought. Very rational. Worthy of a doctor. But who was to say what else she had murmured to him across the visitors' table.

She had taken the baby. The good and the evil in her life in the same room, and the evil had been vanquished. If she was ever in a perilous situation, if she was at the end of a dark street on a dark night with nowhere to run, Louise would opt for Joanna Hunter to be fighting on her side. She'd certainly rather fight with her than against her.

And had it satisfied her when Decker blew his brains out? It hadn't satisfied Louise when David Needler shot himself. It was the easy way out—Shipman, West, Thomas Hamilton, still in control even of their own deaths. She would rather have seen Needler in front of a firing squad, facing the moment when he knew that he too had been vanquished.

Joanna Hunter climbed back down the stepladder and switched on the Christmas tree lights. "There," she said. "Doesn't that look lovely, Chief Inspector?"

"Call me Louise."

Cheers," Louise said, raising her glass of orange juice, and Alison said, "Cheers."

I got a puppy for Christmas," she told the Needler children. "When he's a bit bigger I'll bring him round to see you."

"What are you going to call him?" Cameron asked.

"Jackson," Louise said.

"That's a funny name for a dog," Simone said.

"Yeah," Louise said. "I know."

The Rising of the Sun,
the Running of the Deer

M erry Christmas," Dr. Hunter said, raising her mug. They toasted Christmas morning with coffee and mince pies and brandy butter for breakfast. ("Oh, for heaven's sake, why not?" Dr. Hunter said.) The baby had porridge and a boiled egg. Then they opened presents around the tree. The baby had a push-along dog that looked a bit like a Labrador, although he was more interested in the wrapping paper. Sadie, a real dog, was given a handsome collar and a new ball that bounced as high as the ceiling. Dr. Hunter made Reggie cry because she gave her a PowerBook, brand-new, that no one was going to take away, when all Reggie had given Dr. Hunter was a velvet scarf. It was a nice one, though, from Jenners, that she'd scraped her remaining money together to buy.

Jackson Brodie had insisted on giving her a check for a lot more than the amount he had borrowed from her, even though she said, "No, no, you don't have to do that," but when she went to the bank to try and pay it into her account, the bank said they would "have to refer it," which Mr. Hussain said meant that it had bounced and that Jackson Brodie had no money, despite what he had said about being rich. Which just went to show that you thought you knew a person and they turned out to be someone else. He still belonged to her, but she wasn't sure she wanted him anymore.

Reggie was staying here now, "Until you find somewhere else," Dr. Hunter said, "but of course you might prefer to stay here for good. That would be nice, wouldn't it?"

They didn't really talk about what had happened. Some things were best left alone. They never talked, for example, about whose blood it was that Dr. Hunter and the baby were covered in. Jackson wouldn't let Reggie go inside the house *("Don't you dare!")*, so she didn't know exactly who was inside or what had happened to them. Something bad, obviously. Something irreversible.

Of course, Reggie read in the *Evening News* later about how two unidentified men had been found in a burned-out house and how it was all a mystery, and it struck her that a person who was going to do anything to protect their baby might be someone the police would want to consider for the murders, but they didn't. And no matter how many times Dr. Hunter was questioned by the police about what had happened to her, she always told them that she had gone out for a walk and suffered some kind of amnesia, which was crazy, but they didn't have much choice other than to believe her.

"What do you think happened, Reggie?" Chief Inspector Monroe asked her, and Reggie said, "I honestly don't know," which was the truth, the whole truth, and nothing but the truth.

Dr. Hunter wore the scarf all Christmas Day, she said it was the prettiest scarf she had ever had. They drank champagne and ate roast goose and Christmas pudding, and the baby had pink ice cream and fell asleep on Reggie's knee while they watched *The Muppet Christmas Carol* and, all in all, it was the best Christmas Reggie had ever had, and if Mum had been there it would have been perfect.

Ms. MacDonald was buried just before Christmas. Sergeant Wiseman and the Asian policeman came to the funeral, which Reggie thought was beyond the call of duty. She had a regular Christian kind of service because her weird religion didn't really run to funerals. Most of the members (five out of the eight) of her church stood up and said something about rapture and tribulation and so on, and Reggie stood up and said, "Ms. MacDonald was always good to me," and some other stuff that was a bit more complimentary than Ms. MacDonald really deserved, because a person shouldn't speak ill of the dead unless he was Hitler or the man who killed Dr. Hunter's family. No one mentioned that Ms. MacDonald had caused the Musselburgh train crash. Death absolved a lot of things, it seemed.

Reggie had organized the funeral with the Co-op because they'd done Mum's funeral as well. She chose the same hymn, too, "Abide with Me." She went to see Ms. MacDonald lying in her coffin. It was lined with white polyester satin, so she kept her preference for synthetics right to the end. The Co-op undertaker said, "Shall I leave you alone?" and Reggie nodded sadly and said, "Yes," and then when he left the room she tucked all the little plastic bags of heroin that she'd found in the Loebs' secret hearts into the coffin with Ms. MacDonald. Ms. MacDonald was one person that you could guarantee wasn't going to come to harm from drugs. After she took them out of the Loebs, she had kept them on the shelf in Dr. Hunter's garage behind the paint tins, because, as Dr. Hunter said, no one ever looked there.

It hadn't been all the Loebs, but quite a few. She had weighed the plastic bags on Ms. MacDonald's ancient scales and they came to almost a kilo, which represented a lot of money. She supposed Billy must have been taking something off the top from what he was dealing and hiding it, but she didn't ask him because she hadn't seen him, and now all the little plastic bags had gone up in flames along with Ms. MacDonald, and Ginger and Blondie were never going to get their drugs back. They had known that Billy was keeping the drugs in the Loebs, but they had never suspected there was a whole library of them in Ms. MacDonald's front room.

Ms. MacDonald left a will in which she said her house had to be sold and the proceeds shared between the church and Reggie, so now Reggie had her college fund, just like that.

What's your brother doing for Christmas?" Dr. Hunter asked.

"I don't know. Spending it with his friends." One truth, one lie, you couldn't spend time with your friends if you didn't have any friends. She had no idea where he was. He would turn up again, the bad penny, the rotten apple.

The thing was. How did Dr. Hunter know about Billy? Reggie knew for a fact that she had never mentioned her brother to her. One more puzzling thing to add to the pile of puzzling things that surrounded Dr. Hunter, enough to fill the junk repository to overflowing.

Mr. Hunter wasn't there on Christmas Day. Dr. Hunter said he could come on Boxing Day and say Happy Christmas to the baby. He had been charged with burning down one of his arcades and was on bail, staying in a ropy-looking B and B in Polwarth while Dr. Hunter "made up her mind" about whether she wanted him back in her life, but you could tell that she'd already made it up. It looked like he was going to be declared bankrupt, so it was lucky that the house was in Dr. Hunter's name.

"He did try, I suppose," Reggie said, surprised to hear herself standing up for Mr. Hunter, who'd never done her any favors, after all, but Dr. Hunter said, "But not hard enough." She said that if Mr. Hunter had been in her place, she would have done anything to get him back, "And I mean anything," she said with such a fierce look on her face that Reggie knew that Dr. Hunter would walk to the ends of the earth for someone she loved and that she, Little Reggie Chase, orphan of the parish, savior of Jackson Brodie, help of Dr. Hunter, daughter of Jackie, came within that warm circle. And now, for better or worse, the world was all before her. *Vivat Regina!*

God Bless Us, Every One

Billy sloped past all the lit-up windows in the street. A huge inflatable plastic Santa was hanging off a balcony on the neighboring block of flats, pretending to climb up. The Inch was crap at Christmas. Edinburgh was crap at Christmas. Scotland, the Earth, the universe. All crap on Christmas Day. He'd got fags from the Paki shop, at least they were open. He was going to kill his sister, he nearly had killed his sister.

He might have to move town, to somewhere where no one knew him. Start again. Dundee, maybe. "You're such an enterprising boy," the old holy cow used to say to him when he came and fixed her lights or unblocked her drains or whatever. Take a book from the shelf, put his stash in it, put it back. Reggie was banned from those books and the old holy cow couldn't see to read anymore so he thought it was safe.

At least he had the money that Reggie's precious doctor gave him for the Makarov. He couldn't imagine what she wanted it for. Funny old world.

An old drunk staggered past him and said, "Merry Christmas, son," and Billy said, "Away to fuck, you old cunt," and they both laughed.

Safely Gathered In

Westminster Bridge, at dawn. There was a poem and he was relieved to find that he couldn't remember any of it. It was freezing cold. The city was almost deserted in a way that you never saw it normally. This wasn't how he had expected to spend Christmas Day. On his own, on his uppers, in the Great Wen. They had planned to book something last minute to somewhere hot and relatively un-Christmassy. "I don't like Christmas too much," Tessa said to him. "Do you?"

"Hadn't really given it too much thought," Jackson said.

"North Africa," she had suggested, running her finger down his spine so that he quivered like a cat. "A flight into Egypt. I can probably educate you. Antiquities and so forth."

"You probably can," he said. "Antiquities and so forth."

A pair of young guys, still drunk from the excesses of Christmas Eve, passed by and gave him a peculiar look, perhaps because he was contemplating the Thames with an intensity that suggested he was thinking of joining himself with the icy waters. He wasn't. His brother had done that to him, he wouldn't do it to his daughter. The two young guys probably thought he was some poor schmuck with no home to go to, no family bosom to be warmly welcomed into at the festive season. They were right.

He held it in his hand. *"I found it in the pocket of your jacket,"* she said. The plastic bag with Nathan's hair. Reggie had returned a postcard to him as well, the one Marlee had sent to him from Bruges. *Missing you! Love you!* The postcard looked as if it had been through a war.

It was funny because he was actually missing Reggie more than he was missing Marlee. Marlee had plenty of people who cared about her, but they were thin on the ground for Reggie. *"We're all on our own, Mr. B., that's why we have to care for each other."* The Christmas spirit had got to her, he supposed. He hadn't saved her life ("Not yet," she said), hadn't repaid the debt that had been written in his blood.

He wondered, too, about the strolling woman. Was she waking up in a bed in a house to the sound of carols on the radio and the smell of a turkey in the oven, or was she still walking the empty roads on the high tops in the snow and the wind and the rain.

Everywhere you looked, there was unfinished business and unanswered questions. He had always imagined that when you died, there was a last moment when everything was cleared up for you — the business finished, the questions answered, the lost things found — and you thought, "Oh, *right,* I understand," and then you were free to go into the darkness, or the light. But it had never happened when he died (*"Briefly,"* he heard Dr. Foster say), so perhaps it never would. Everything would remain a mystery. Which meant, if you thought about it, that you should try and clear everything up as much as you could while you were still alive. Find the answers, solve the mysteries, be a good detective. Be a crusader.

He had planned, originally, to take Nathan's hair for DNA analysis. Nathan who would be waking up this morning to spend Christmas in the country with Julia and Mr. Arty-Farty. Jackson fingered the filthy plastic bag. He supposed the noble thing to do would be to cast it into the river, to let it go, to let Nathan go. But he wasn't feeling very noble on this cold, gray English Christmas Day. He'd lost everything. His new wife, his old wife, his money, his home. He put the bag back in his pocket.

Tessa didn't get everything. The sale of his French house was delayed and the money came into his account just before Christmas. It wasn't the kind of sum you turned your nose up at, so "yet again you fall on your feet," Josie said.

Time to move on, begin again. It felt late to be making a fresh start. Jackson wondered if he was just too old a dog to learn new tricks.

He was feeling about as bad as a man can feel when he thought about finding Joanna, which was a warm sunbeam kind of thought that could cheer a man even on the darkest of days.

Not the second, bloody, time, but the first time, on that balmy night in the Devon countryside. He remembered moving his torch in a wide arc across the wheat and spotting her just in time before he stumbled over her small, still body. He thought she was dead. Within the course of one year of his life when he was twelve, he had watched his mother die in hospital, he had seen his sister's body dredged unceremoniously out of a canal, he had found his brother hanging. He was only nineteen and he knew that he couldn't bear it if the girl was dead, that it would snap what was left of his heart from its moorings and he would cease to be Lance Corporal Brodie of the Prince of Wales's Own Regiment of Yorkshire and become himself a small child alone forever in the dark.

But then she stirred in her sleep and for a moment he was so choked he could hardly speak. Then he found his voice and stuck his hand in the air and shouted louder than he'd ever shouted in his life, or would ever shout again, "Over here, I've found her, she's over here!"

And he lifted her up and held her as if she might break, as if she were the most precious, miraculous, astonishing child ever to walk the earth, and to the first person who reached them, a police constable, he said, "Look at that, not a scratch on her."

And Scout

was the name of their dog. "I couldn't remember for the longest time," she said. She put both hands over her heart, like bird wings, as if she were trying to keep something inside her chest. "Scout," she said to Reggie. "He was *such* a good dog."

"Totally, Dr. H.," Reggie said. "Totally."

"Bow-wow-wow, whose dog art thou?" she said to Sadie, and to the baby she said, "A carrion crow sat on an oak, sing heigh ho, the carrion crow, fol de riddle, lol de riddle, hi ding ho," and to Reggie she said,

> "A little cock sparrow
> Sat on a tree,
> Looking as happy
> As happy could be,
> Till a boy came by
> With his bow and arrow,
> Says he, 'I will shoot
> The little cock sparrow.
> His body will make me
> A nice little stew,

And his giblets will make me
A little pie too.' "

And Reggie said,

"Says the little cock sparrow,
'I'll be shot if I stay,'
So he clapped his wings
And then flew away."

And they both clapped their hands and the baby laughed and clapped his hands too.

Acknowledgments

Thanks are due to the following for their assistance and information (I'm sorry if any of it came out wrong once I got my hands on it):

Martin Auld, Malcolm Dickson (Assistant Inspector of Constabulary for Scotland), Russell Equi, Detective Superintendent Malcolm Graham (Lothian and Borders Police Service), my cousin Major Michael Keech, Dr. Doug Lyle, Detective Superintendent Craig Naylor (Lothian and Borders Police Service), Bradley Rose, Detective Superintendent Eddie Thompson (Metropolitan Police Service), Dr. Anthony Toft, and, last but not least, my cousin Timothy Edwards for the title.

I have played a little fast and loose with the geography of Wensleydale and also that of Southwest Edinburgh. Apologies — artistic license and so on. I have never seen a horse in Midmar field, but that doesn't mean that there will never be one.

Reading Group Guide

WHEN WILL THERE BE GOOD NEWS?

A novel by

KATE ATKINSON

A conversation with
Kate Atkinson

Nancy Pearl talks with the author on the occasion
of the U.S. publication of *One Good Turn*.

*I have to say first of all that I am a huge fan of your books. I think I began
with your first novel,* Behind the Scenes at the Museum, *with that
wonderful, wonderful opening line.*

"I am conceived."

*"I am conceived"—right. It's just been so gratifying to me as a reader to
follow your career and see how you've gone in many different directions.*

Thank you.

One Good Turn *is a sequel to* Case Histories, *and it seems to me that
in some ways in both books you've taken literary fiction and given it a little
mystery twist. Is that accurate?*

I never set out do anything, I should say first. The question of genre
has been much more prominent in America, I've noticed. I set out to
write a book in the same way I always set out to write a book. I didn't
think, I'm going to write a book that's a mystery or a crime novel.

Originally the characters in *Case Histories* were going on a boat.
But they had such huge backstories that I realized they would
never embark. So I went back to the backstories, and because they
involved old cold crime cases, they needed someone to investigate
them in order for those cases to be solved. That's really how the
detective figure came about. And once you put a detective into a
book it becomes a crime novel. There doesn't seem to be any way
around that. Not that I wouldn't want to write a crime novel but,

you know, that's it, it's become one. I still don't think I write crime novels. But everyone else now does.

We do pay so much attention to that here in the States, partly because in libraries and bookstores we insist on shelving those separately. I can argue against our practice of doing that because then I think you sometimes lose out on other works by the author or you're so narrowly categorizing yourself and your reading.

In Britain, and on the continent as well, because I have a big established readership, they haven't changed anything, it's still a Kate Atkinson novel. They just sort of say, "Well, it's got crime in it," or "It's a crime novel"—but they don't really classify.

Whereas here, because I've had a new publisher for the past three or four years, and they have relaunched me, I've been "reborn." I get a lot of people in America saying to me, "I really liked your first book," and they mean *Case Histories.* I never say, "Well, actually, there's another four you could read." It's like I'm a new Kate Atkinson. That worries me a little, because . . . I'm not being called a crime writer so much as the books are being called crime novels. It worries me that now when I don't write a crime novel there's going to be this huge disappointment.

You kind of have to remain true to how you feel about your writing. Otherwise you get very confused because you'd be trying to please readers. And how could you possibly please readers? You can't. The only person you can please is yourself.

Do you think it's true that you write the novel that you want to read?

Yes, I think I do. Although really I'd prefer if someone else wrote it, because it would be much easier!

I am my best reader. I am the reader who understands the book completely, and I write to amuse myself. I mean I never feel that I'm writing for other people. I am conscious of how the book will be read by other people, because that definitely modifies certain things, but they're to do with comprehension. You know: Will someone understand this? Does this dialogue make clear the tone that it's being said in? And things like that. So you are aware of a kind of universal — not so much a universal reader, but just how it reads.

I was so pleased when you just said you write to amuse yourself because one of the things that struck me especially about One Good Turn *is how much fun you must have had writing it, because it's so clever — not clever in a show-offy way, but it's so intricate. It's a book that in some way keeps turning on itself.*

I think the actual amusement or the pleasure that I get from that is in achieving it, because it's very nerve-racking. When you suddenly realize a hundred or so pages into the book you're writing that it's quite complicated, and it's going to get more complicated, then you begin to worry that you can't actually do it. That you can't get everybody into the right place, doing the right things, whatever it's going to be. Because I don't know what the characters are going to do, it's also a case of: What *are* they going to do? Why are they here? What am I doing with it? And that becomes not amusing at all, actually, more like a strain. So in a sense the amusement is in the characters — well, I suppose *amusement* is the wrong word. I am entertaining myself. I am pleasing myself, I suppose. And it's in the characters, that's where the pleasure is. The characters are easier to be inside than the plot is to control, in some ways, I think.

Is Jackson Brodie, who is the main character, the detective, in Case Histories *and* One Good Turn . . . *do you have strong feelings for him? Are you in love with Jackson Brodie?*

Absolutely not. I would really dislike having to live with Jackson, I have to say. I think he's a bit of a pain. In this book I think he's more depressive than he has been previously.

He's really a woman, I've decided. It's difficult to create a male character, I think, for a woman, because you're not sure, you're never very sure about it. And I think I just made him a woman with very manly attributes. You know, lots of women really like him and I'm sure that's the reason. Inside he's soft, and he likes women, and he wants to protect women. The fact that he wants to protect women is the reason women like him. He definitely has that type of sheepdog herding instinct which I think women really value.

In my own family I have a son-in-law who's a herder, he's a sheepdog, and we always say — as a family we're all girls — if we got stuck on this hillside and we couldn't get back because we'd all broken our legs and nobody knew where we were in the whole world, *he* would find us. I think that's the kind of paradigm of a guy — the guy who will find you. That for me is Jackson's great attribute. But, actually, as a man — I don't know — I think he'd get on my nerves.

Do you then feel that it's easier for you to create your women characters? Because your other books were about mothers and daughters, for example, and those kinds of female relationships.

I think it's much easier for me to get into the head of a woman, yes, because there are so many things I don't have to think about, which I have to be conscious of with male characters. So in this book the two women, Gloria and Louise — I never had to think twice about how they would feel about their families, their partners, their lives. It just came naturally. Whereas with the men I had to think, Well, how would a man feel about this? The other man in the book is a wimp, he's a nerdy kind, not a manly man at all, and in a way that's easier. It's when you come to the more heterosexual males that you have to think.

One of the reasons I now realize that I didn't approach men as characters is that I had no brothers, and I've had no sons, so I've never seen how little boys develop. I've never seen boys grow into men. I don't know what forms the male psyche, because I've never witnessed it at close hand. Now I have a grandson, and my attitude is quite different because I observe him. I'm kind of terrible, really, because I watch him and I go to my daughter, "Why is he doing that?" And she's going, "I don't know." There's a sense that they're so different.

But your characters are not in any way based—or are they?—on real people.

No, not at all. A lot of people always think we writers base our characters on real people or we use real people as inspiration. There are moments when you look at people—usually when you don't know them, and you observe in airports or in restaurants or something—and you think: That would be a good character. I can see what he's like, I can see what she's like—that'll be a character. You either forget, of course . . . that's the other thing I do, I'm not one of those writers who carries notebooks around. But when it comes to the book, the necessities of plot and structure are such that they will always dictate what has to be done with the characters. So that you may start with this idea for a character, but it will be changed almost immediately, because you can't use real people like that. Characters are always either entirely imaginary or they have bits of people or things you've observed.

Sort of mosaics . . .

But, really, they're mostly imaginary.

Do you start then with your characters?

I don't know how I start.

I start with a feeling. Not my feeling, but how I want the book to feel. I have this sense, and I don't know what it is and I can never describe it, but it's like an ambience. You know, you kind of know how it would feel if you were reading it. And in a way that is voice. You know, that mysterious thing that people always talk about— "Find your voice"—and you think, what does that mean? But in a way each book has its own voice and it's finding what that voice feels like that's important. Once you've got that, you're OK. Sometimes it takes a long time to get the feeling of a novel. But characters come with it.

In *Case Histories* I had these characters before they had a book. With this book a couple of the characters actually started off in another book, so they came quite fully formed. Characters in a way occupy their own little microcosm, and sometimes they can be just slotted into the book, which is very handy.

How much do you have on hand, say, about a character—I mean, you talk about the backstory. So how much of that do you actually write before you begin? Or is that mostly in your head?

Oh, nothing. I never do all those character notes. They just come. It is an act of creation. You know, one minute nothing, the next minute character. I find it fascinating. I find creating characters a really interesting puzzle. People don't really talk about that much. I'm sure there are people who sit down and think, Well, she's going to be in her fifties and have green eyes and . . . but that's not how characters are. I never really know how they look.

Really?

And I never really describe much how they look. Just occasionally a character gets a little bit more of a description than another, but generally speaking, to me they're pretty amorphous. It's their interior lives that are interesting. And once I've got the feeling— again—of what they're like inside, then that's it. I can slip into them, and I know them, and that makes them very easy to write.

Are there any characters in your books who have surprised you, who have demanded in their own way to do something that you didn't expect?

There's a character in *Human Croquet,* to go way back, called Vinny, who is an old woman, a sort of dried-up stick of an old woman, who I always meant to be nasty and vicious. But I grew very fond of her and she got infinitely more mellow and likable. So she surprised me. I thought the book would dictate that she would have to have this certain character and she didn't. Also, in the same book, I killed off my favorite character, and I didn't think I would do that. That was Eliza, the mother, and I was quite surprised that I killed off a character I liked so much and indeed gave her so little room in the book and so little time on the page.

There are always things that characters do that I don't know they're going to do, and that again is part of my entertaining myself in a book. In this book, without giving any of the plot away, I never knew the ending. I could have gone a different way. And that was a very large part of a particular character. So there are always things I hold in reserve for myself. Not because I wanted to surprise myself, but I'm never really sure how the book will go and how things need to be done. Sometimes characters have to do surprising things because the book needs them to do surprising things. Which is always quite interesting.

Did you have a feeling when you were writing Case Histories *that you would bring back Jackson and Julia?*

I felt I would revisit Jackson at some point, but I didn't think it would be straight away. But when I finished *Case Histories,* I thought, I'll carry on, because it had written very easily, and I thought, Well, I've still got, you know, the feeling of that book.

But then I thought, No, don't do that, you don't want to write a sequel. And I stopped for a year and then came back to it and I approached it in a very different way. So although it's got two of the same characters in it, it's got a very different feel. *Case Histories* is very sad and melancholy with a very emotional heart, whereas this book has a much more playful heart, I think—even though the body count is quite high.

After having messed about a bit for a year, thinking, What am I going to do next? I am now kind of drawn back to thinking, Well, it would be more balanced to have a trilogy here, just to do another one and then say, OK, I'm leaving that for a while because I've done enough of that. I find the rule of three quite powerful. So I think that's probably what I will do. Because I will leave the character in a bettered state. You know, I don't actually like the way I've left Jackson at the end of this book entirely.

Oh. See, I thought the ending in a way opened the door for . . .

It opens the door, certainly. But it doesn't quite leave me happy with Jackson as a character. And I feel that he has a journey to go on that he may as well go on now as opposed to waiting a couple of years, so I think I will send him on that journey.

That's so interesting.

This is a very complicated plot, and it's told from different points of view. To me it's a sign of an enjoyable read—I'm really getting into the book—that when I came to the end of one person's section I wanted to go on with that person. And then there was this new person and I wondered, Oh, what's going to happen? I kept thinking about what it must have been like juggling a lot of balls.

Because it's in a very tight time frame—it's four days, mostly three days, in fact, which is what I had wanted to do—and because there are four main characters, and you don't often stray beyond those four main characters, I found that as long as I knew where they were I was all right with them. I would think, It's morning, they're all going to wake up, basically, they're all going to have early morning, so where is Martin when he wakes up? And then I would sort of do his morning and then I would think, Where was Jackson when Martin was doing all that? So I always sort of had them level pegging, and I write sequentially nearly always, so I just would move from one character to the next and think, OK, it's lunchtime now and he's over at Northbridge, so where is she going to be at lunch? And that way I kept track of them and it was actually easier than I thought it was going to be.

Do you enjoy writing more in the first person, or do you think each book just says, "This is how I need to be written"?

Well, my first three books are in the first person, I think, aren't they? Gosh, I can't even remember. I'm pretty sure they are first-person narratives. I really wanted to move away from that, because I thought, Enough's enough.

That's really one of the reasons I wrote a volume of stories at that point, because I wanted to get out of the "I" narrative and also because I wanted to discover a kind of more spontaneous joy in writing. In the course of those stories I discovered the interior monologue, which I never really explored before. It kind of looks as if I did in those first three books because I'm writing in the first person. But it's not true. I think that was a great liberation—to be able to explore inside a character and not really have any strictures on you. You know, the parameters are quite wide once you move inside a character's head.

So I'm no longer in the first person, but I'm not really in the third person either. I was just thinking that today. You know, when you're on a plane—I've just flown in here—you think a lot about what it is you're writing back home that you're not getting the chance to actually write. And I was thinking: I find it very hard to move into a straight third-person, omniscient kind of narrator, and I think it would be a nice challenge for me perhaps in another book to really do that. But then I think I'd become an overly omniscient narrator, perhaps.

Interior monologue is absolutely my favorite form at the moment, because I find it so easy. Once you're inside that character's head you just somehow know. You know what they would do, how they would behave, what they would think. It involves much less *authorial* thinking.

Do you look for that in other books — not that you've written, but books that you've read and enjoyed?

I don't look for anything in another novel. No, really. I'm just always amazed that anyone can write. I just think writing is . . . what astonishes me is that there are so many books. There are so many people who can write, I just find that amazing. I'm delighted by books even when I dislike them.

Do you think you write comedies of manners?

I think that's a lovely phrase, *comedies of manners.* In fact, I should start saying that, because whenever you're in a cab the cabdriver says, "What do you do?" and you say, "I'm a writer," and they go, "What do you write?" and I always kind of go, "Books." So I shall start saying, "Comedies of manners."

I think that's great, because that's how I would describe your books.

And that is how I shall describe them in the future.

Good. If somebody was going to ask you to describe your books, what adjective would you use to describe your fiction?

Funny. Well, *humorous* perhaps would be a better word. *Dark.* What else? *Entertaining.*

See, I would say—

What would you say? Now three words from you.

Three words from me. I would say intelligent . . .

Oh, that's not—I can't say that. That would be hubris, you see.

I think they're extremely intelligent in the sense that the plots are complex. I can't imagine, as a reader, how you manage to bring it all around to a satisfactory ending. I think that that complexity is something I always appreciate as a reader. So I think intelligent, *I think* complex plots, *and I think* humorous. *And not* funny, *because I don't think these are laugh-aloud, but they are comedies in that kind of social comedy sense.*

But I'm thinking, when you said darkish, I'm thinking about Hilary Mantel, who I think is very dark indeed. And I don't know that I would say you're quite as dark.

Well, I suppose because I do dark and light. I'm a dualist at heart. I have tried to write seriously, without any humor, and it doesn't work because the humor, such as it is, always comes out naturally. So I cannot write an entirely serious piece. It just doesn't work. I can't do it. Physically I can't do it. Nor can I write a completely comic piece. When I write, it's just . . . they seem to roll over each other naturally.

And don't you think that that's like a definition of a comedy of manners in a sense? Because the humor in your books arises from the human condition.

It arises from behavior, yes.

Which is intrinsically human behavior.

And it's dark and light as well.

Exactly. One last question: If someone said, "I've never read a Kate Atkinson book. What should I read?" which one would you say?

I would say the stories, *Not the End of the World,* because, to me, that's my best writing. Also because I enjoyed writing them, so my attitude to them is one of great friendliness.

Well, I guess I have one more quick question, too. What about reviews?

I don't like reviews.

Good or bad, you don't like them.

Good or bad, I don't like them. Some of my best friends are reviewers, but I never review, because I just couldn't write about someone else's writing. But that's from a writer's point of view, obviously. I don't like reviews because I don't like being out there, being—generally speaking, always, at some point—misunderstood. And you have no comeback. It's not a discussion, it's not a dialogue, it's one person saying what they think about you, and you never get to say what you think about them, which is very irritating.

Adapted from the interview with Kate Atkinson that originally aired on Book Lust with Nancy Pearl *on the Seattle Channel on December 4, 2006. To view the entire interview, visit www.seattlechannel.org/videos/watchVideos.asp?program=booklust. Reprinted with permission.*

Questions and topics for discussion

1. Many of the characters in *When Will There Be Good News?*
have lost family members: Joanna loses her mother, sister, and
baby brother in the novel's opening pages; Reggie's mother
has recently drowned; and Jackson lost his mother, brother,
and sister in the course of a year when he was twelve. In view
of these tragedies, compare Joanna's, Reggie's, and Jackson's
respective outlooks on life with those of the other characters
in the novel.

2. The question of Nathan's paternity haunts Jackson Brodie.
Why? How might Jackson's life change if he discovered he was
Nathan's father? Is Jackson a good father to Marlee?

3. With *When Will There Be Good News?* — and previously also in
Case Histories and *One Good Turn* — Kate Atkinson introduced
elements of the traditional crime novel into her fiction. Other
than the "crime," what elements make up a crime novel? What
crime-fiction conventions can you discern in this book?

4. *When Will There Be Good News?* has three central female
characters: Joanna, Louise, and Reggie. Discuss the ways in
which these three central characters are similar. Which of the
three would you most like to encounter again in a subsequent
novel by Kate Atkinson?

5. Of Jackson Brodie, Atkinson writes, "How ironic that both
Julia and Louise, the two women he'd felt closest to in his
recent past, had both unexpectedly got married, and neither
of them to him" (page 90). What are the chances that Jackson
will ever have a successful romantic relationship? Why do you

think he has been unlucky so far, even though he is such an appealing character?

6. Discuss the idea of "good" characters and "evil" characters in *When Will There Be Good News?* Do you think the novel's central characters are either essentially "good" or essentially "evil," or are they a combination of both? How do Louise, Reggie, and Jackson — each of whom breaks the law to achieve the "right" result — figure into your viewpoint? What is the moral code at work in the novel?

7. Death, violence, and hardship seem to stalk Reggie, yet she remains remarkably resilient. What do you think sustains her?

8. Discuss the institution of marriage as it is portrayed in the novel. Consider Louise's marriage, Joanna's marriage, Jackson's marriage, and Julia's marriage. Are there any characters in the novel who are happily married?

9. Jackson Brodie believes that "a coincidence is just an explanation waiting to happen" (page 319). Discuss some of the coincidences in *When Will There Be Good News?* Do they make the story seem more real? Or less real?

10. Despite the novel's title and the early statement that "everything was bad. There was no question about it" (page 10), there are many instances of humor in the story. Do you think *When Will There Be Good News?* is essentially a humorous novel with tragic events or a tragic novel with moments of levity?